The
VICTORS

AN AMERICAN FAMILY PORTRAIT

Book One:
THE PURITANS

Book Two:
THE COLONISTS

Book Three:
THE PATRIOTS

Book Four:
THE ADVERSARIES

Book Five:
THE PIONEERS

Book Six:
THE ALLIES

Book Seven:
THE VICTORS

Book Eight:
THE PEACEMAKERS

JACK CAVANAUGH

The VICTORS

RIVEROAK®
Good News in Fiction

COOK COMMUNICATIONS MINISTRIES
Colorado Springs, Colorado • Paris, Ontario
KINGSWAY COMMUNICATIONS LTD
Eastbourne, England

RiverOak® is an imprint of
Cook Communications Ministries, Colorado Springs, CO 80918
Cook Communications, Paris, Ontario
Kingsway Communications, Eastbourne, England

THE VICTORS
© 2006 by Jack Cavanaugh, second edition,
previous ISBN: 1-56476-589-X

First edition published by Victor Books in © 1998.

Printed in the United States of America

1 2 3 4 5 6 7 8 9   Printing/Year   10 09 08 07 06

Cover Design: Jeffrey P. Barnes
Cover Illustrator: Ron Adair

Scripture quotations are taken from the King James Version of the Bible and Geneva
Bible of 1560, both of which are Public Domain. Author has modernized some terms
for easier understanding. Italics in Scripture quotations are added by the author for
emphasis.

ISBN-13: 978-1-58919-071-9
ISBN-10: 1-58919-071-8

LCCN: 2006925516

This book is dedicated to the following men
who served their country faithfully in World War II:

Private First Class William J. Cavanaugh
Fireman First Class James D. Cavanaugh
T/5 Walter S. Brand
Second Lieutenant Charles Scharr

ACKNOWLEDGMENTS

Special thanks go to Bernd Breuer, German translator and friend, for steering me toward the novels of Heinrich Böll whose works opened my eyes to the plight of the average German who was never sympathetic to Hitler's Nazi agenda.

To my father, William Cavanaugh, who answered a hundred and one questions about life in the army during World War II. I learned from him things I could never have learned from research.

Thanks go to the staff of the San Diego Historical Society for their assistance in securing original documents and maps relating to San Diego during the war years.

And to my wife and family for their constant support.

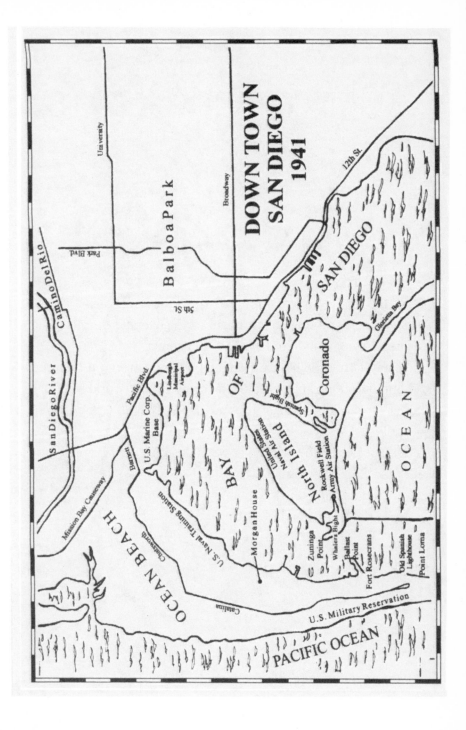

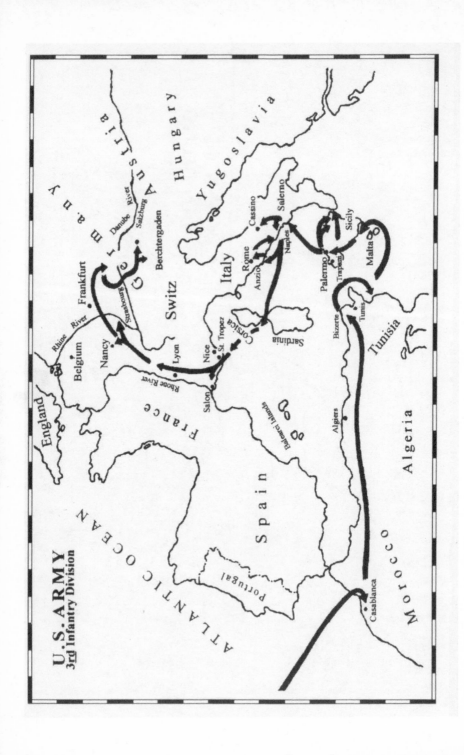

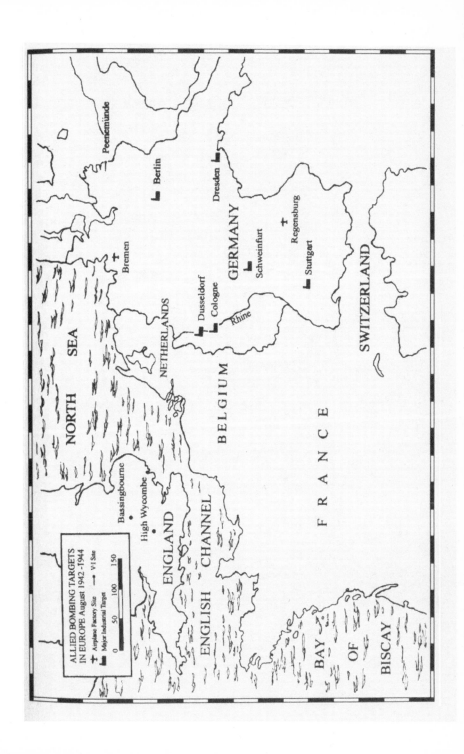

ALLIED BOMBING TARGETS
IN EUROPE August 1942 -1944

✝ Airplane Factory Site   → V-1 Site
■ Major Industrial Target

0   50   100   150

NORTH SEA

Peenemünde

Berlin ■

Dresden ■

GERMANY

Regensburg ✝

Schweinfurt ■

Stuttgart ■

Bremen ✝

NETHERLANDS

Dusseldorf
Cologne ■

Rhine

BELGIUM

SWITZERLAND

Bassingbourne ●

High Wycombe ●

ENGLAND

ENGLISH CHANNEL

FRANCE

BAY
OF
BISCAY

1

On the day the bombs fell at Pearl Harbor two battles were begun; one with the world's aggressors and the other within Laura Morgan.

Sitting next to the center aisle in the fourth pew from the front she sensed something was amiss the moment she caught sight of the church usher. His eyes and mouth were distorted with alarm as he filed unsteadily past the stained-glass window that bore the likeness of Jesus carrying a little white lamb in his arms.

Charlie Haddox, a short, good-natured Canadian and usher at San Diego's Fifth Avenue Church, approached the pulpit in the middle of the sermon, his tear-glazed eyes fixed steadily on his destination. With jaw clenched tightly, he looked as though the news he bore would escape from his mouth with any less guarded expression.

Noticing the usher's unorthodox movement, the preacher became distracted. He stumbled in his delivery.

Laura watched the impending encounter. It was bad news all right. Something catastrophic. Her breathing became shallow and rapid in anticipation of what was to come.

Everyone's attention was now on the usher as he passed the

front pew and crossed the carpeted breach that separated the preacher from the congregation. The preacher halted his delivery midsentence. And as the usher cupped his hand and leaned forward to whisper in the preacher's ear, the assembled worshippers collectively held their breath in the dubious belief that by eliminating their breathing sounds they might be able to hear the news as it passed between the men.

Even the children ceased their fidgeting. Like frightened forest creatures catching a scent, they froze and stared wide-eyed at their parents.

Time slowed. An unnatural hush fell over the congregation like a ponderous, black funereal pall.

Laura read the preacher's eyes as he received the usher's message. It was a skill she picked up during the Great War. The British nursing staff had taught her to measure a man's physical condition by monitoring his pulse and other vital signs. Battlefield experience taught her that the pulse of a man's soul could be measured by staring into his eyes.

What she saw in her pastor's eyes chilled and frightened her. It was a look with which she was all too familiar.

England, 1915. It was the same expression worn by London residents as they watched incendiary bombs rain from the sky, leveling their homes and businesses, laying to waste structures that for centuries had been familiar landmarks.

It was the desperate and helpless expression of a Camden mother cradling her infant daughter as the child choked to death on smoke from the inferno.

France, 1918. It was the expression worn by British nurses as they sifted through the tall grass, retrieving body parts of young men who had been ordered over the top.

It was the expression of half-conscious soldiers as they lay in stinking hospital wards. Glassy-eyed. Scared. Dying. Peering beyond life's precipice into eternity. Hungry eyes that yearned to see a sweetheart, a homeland, or a mother one last time before they closed forever.

Charlie the usher pulled away from the preacher's ear. He had fulfilled his duty. The message had been delivered.

Laura shuddered. The incongruity of her memories and her present circumstances frightened her. Mentally, she tried to push the images back into the past where they belonged—thousands of miles and several decades away.

Her tactic didn't seem to be working.

Angrily, she reminded herself that this was Southern California, not France. The things that happened in England and France could never happen here. She was being silly. She was jumping to ridiculous, unfounded conclusions.

Try as she might, she could not reason her anxiety away. On silent cat's paws, fear crept into her heart.

On the dais the preacher, a middle-aged man, thick of waist and thin of hair, stared blankly over the heads of his congregation. He tried to speak. His lips and tongue moved thickly as though swollen by a bee sting. No sound was forthcoming.

Laura glanced down the length of her pew. At the opposite end sat her husband, Johnny, in a gray three-piece suit. He balanced the famous Morgan family Bible on his lap. Leaning slightly forward he was keenly awaiting the preacher's announcement. Seated beside him were his parents, Jesse and Emily Morgan, visiting from Denver. Next to them was Johnny's older sister, Katy, a missionary to South Africa, home on furlough.

The four Morgan children, all grown or nearly grown, sat between Katy and Laura. There were the boys: Nat, who slouched in his herringbone twill suit; and Walt, smartly dressed in his army uniform. Next to Walt was Alexandra, the oldest. She pulled uncomfortably at her dark-blue skirt and jacket. Finally, there was Lily, the youngest, who sat complacently next to her mother, wearing a colorful floral shirtwaist dress.

The entire family in a single pew. Laura had looked forward to this date for more than a year. Now it was about to be ruined.

From behind the pulpit the preacher lowered his head and muttered, "God help us." His words were a sincere plea, not framed for public hearing. Nevertheless, they were picked up by the microphone and amplified. Startled by the sound of his own words, he said weakly, "Please give me a moment to compose myself."

Charlie, his mission accomplished, yet apparently uncertain as to whether he should leave his pastor alone, shifted uncomfortably from one foot to the other. Then, with a self-conscious effort, he patted the preacher on the shoulder and descended the platform steps, making his way back up the center aisle. As he passed Laura, he glanced sadly down the Morgan pew. For some reason, he was taken aback by Walt's uniform.

Then, with a grimace, he mumbled, quoting Job 1:21: "The LORD gave, and the LORD hath taken away; blessed be the name of the LORD."

Laura's brow wrinkled. *What on earth would prompt Charlie to say something like that?* Before she could fend his words off, they impacted her.

As the moon pulls on the ocean's shores and raises the tide, so did the usher's comment raise Laura's anxiety to a higher level.

The preacher cleared his throat. Emotion choked back the first word. With a grating sound, he cleared a fresh passageway for them and tried again. "I'm afraid it's bad news."

A sympathetic sob caught in Laura's throat as she watched her pastor struggle. She glanced again at her boys. Then back to the man behind the pulpit.

With a trembling voice, the preacher said, "According to news reports, the Japanese have attacked Pearl Harbor. Folks, it looks like the war has finally caught up with us."

The congregation sat motionless. Stunned. Like a snake swallowing an egg, the ingestion of news this enormous would take a while.

Feeling the need to fill the silence, the pastor said, "I'm sorry, but that's all I know at the moment … I don't have any further details." He paused for a moment, then added, "I suggest we pray and then … um, go home … I guess … unless there's something we should be doing to prepare … I've never been at war before."

A sailor in uniform jumped up. Grabbing his girlfriend by the hand he rushed out the back doors. His action broke the ice. Soon the room was abuzz with gasps and commentary and expressions of disbelief. Several more families left.

Behind Laura, a man cursed the Japanese as he bolted from the pew. Laura winced. Such words, though common on a battle-field, seemed grossly out of place here where stained-glass representations of Jesus gazed lovingly down upon the shocked worshippers.

She glanced anxiously down the pew at her husband. Johnny held his head in his hands. Was he praying? Beside him, Jesse and Emily were huddled together. Katy sat erect, her eyes closed, her face expressionless. Walt and Alexandra were animated by the news. Nat and Lily showed signs of distress, each in his or her own way.

In all the commotion, Laura's eye caught sight of Charlie Haddox. He was staring at her boys. Tears tracked down his cheeks.

The LORD gave and the LORD hath taken away; blessed be the name of the LORD.

Her boys! Charlie was afraid for her boys!

Of course! Charlie had been an infantryman in France. At

more than one church fellowship he and Johnny had swapped stories. He knew all too well what lay ahead for Walt and Nat and other young men their age. One of four brothers, Charlie was the only one to return home alive.

Suddenly, the images that had come to mind earlier were not incongruous at all. The nation was at war. And as in all wars, young men die.

Nat and Walt were young men.

O Lord, please no!

With the congregation breaking up, the preacher stood immobile behind the massive wooden pulpit. It seemed all he could do was grip the sides. His eyes were fixed on the second row where his wife sat. As they stared at each other, they both wept.

Their reaction was understandable. Three weeks earlier the church had held a farewell fellowship for their twin sons. Both boys had joined the navy and were preparing to ship out to their duty station—the USS *California* based at Pearl Harbor.

※

"Have you been stocking up on sugar?" Katy asked.

Laura didn't answer right away. She kept her gloved hands firmly on the steering wheel and her eyes on the road as they approached the intersection. A spectacular view of San Diego Bay lay before them as the car eased down Laurel Street, an avenue comprised of a series of steep grades that ended at bay's edge. The view is normally reserved for passengers; drivers are too busy braking to enjoy it.

A wave of moist ocean air rose up to meet them as they made the descent. The morning clouds were dissipating. An emerging sun flashed against the white sails in the harbor as they mingled with several hulking gray light cruisers moored in the bay.

Preceding them down Laurel Street, Johnny drove the larger

family car. His parents rode with him. The blue Buick passed through the intersection and nosed down the next grade, momentarily disappearing from sight.

Laura glanced in her rearview mirror. In the vibrating mirror she saw Alexandra seated comfortably behind the wheel of her ragtop Ford. Her sister and two brothers were with her. The top was down.

On a typical Sunday one car was sufficient to carry the Morgans to church. But this was not a typical Sunday. It hadn't been planned that way, and now the news from Pearl Harbor ensured that it would be a day not soon forgotten.

"Sugar … that was the first thing to be rationed, wasn't it?" Laura said in response to Katy's question. "I'm sure meat and gasoline will soon follow. Looks like hard times ahead. Come spring, we'll have to double the size of our vegetable garden."

She glanced at her passenger who was distracted momentarily by the glittering of the sun on the bay's cupped surface. While Laura had padded her figure over the years with a few extra pounds, Katy remained thin, almost gaunt. The hard African sun had dulled the older woman's hair and dried her skin. But the hardships of missionary life had been unable to extract the fiery spark from Katy's eyes or the spirited smirk that appeared frequently at the corners of her mouth.

"Such a lovely harbor," Katy said. "You're fortunate to live in such a beautiful city. I know it was always a treat for Fred and me whenever we got to spend a few days on the coast. The bay at Cape Town is truly lovely."

"Will you be going back?" Laura asked.

The question surprised Katy. "To Africa? Of course. Why wouldn't I?"

"Is it safe on the mission field … a woman alone? Does the London Missionary Society allow that?"

Katy gave a half smile. "I work in a compound with six other people. Besides, where else would I go?"

"You could stay here with us—Johnny and me."

Katy reached across the seat and patted Laura on the arm. "It's sweet of you to offer," she said. "But Africa is my home now."

Katy's eyes glazed over momentarily in thought. She chuckled.

"It's funny," she said. "My first impressions of Africa were not favorable, to put it mildly. Truth is, I loathed the place. I remember approaching the compound in an old wagon, that to this day, I believe did permanent damage to my backside."

Laura laughed.

"We saw some children sitting in the dirt. They were playing. As we drew closer, I was horrified when I saw their toys. They were nothing more than dung figures held together by sticks. Then, an entourage of Khoi men appeared, each one wearing animal entrails around his neck! You could still see the undigested grass in the entrails! And when we reached our hut, there was a Khoi woman polishing the floor with blood and dung! I cried the first two days we were there."

Laura grimaced. "What was Fred's reaction?"

"Fred was fascinated with the land and the animals." As Katy's memories stirred, her face glowed at the recollection. "Oh, Laura, the sunsets in Africa take one's breath away. And the waterfalls ... and the way the stark desert gives way to mountains and meadows that are carpeted with flowers of every imaginable color! And the animals! It's almost a religious experience to watch a herd of eland flow effortlessly across a vast savanna. The country is nothing if not captivating."

Laura's attention was momentarily diverted as the Chevrolet eased through another intersection, the last one before bayside.

"And while Fred fell in love with the land," Katy continued, "I eventually fell in love with the people ... that is, as soon as I grew accustomed to their way of doing things, most of which are, by the way, quite practical. For instance, polishing the floor with animal blood? It keeps fleas away. If you don't do it, they'll eat you alive."

"I guess I'll have to try a little blood and dung on my kitchen floor," Laura quipped.

Katy laughed, taking no offense at the gibe.

They rode in silence for a time. Laura steered the car to the right, following Harbor Drive as it skirted the edge of the bay. People strolled casually along the boardwalk, stopping occasionally to point at a sailboat or ship or playful seals as they crowded atop the buoys. Had it not been for a pair of sailors who were racing down the boardwalk, announcing the news of the Japanese attack to everyone they met, it would have appeared to be just another weekend in California.

Katy pointed at the sailors. "They remind me of Paris. Do you remember the day we heard that America had entered the war?"

Laura nodded, glancing in her rearview mirror. "How are you holding up?" she asked, steering the subject back to Africa.

"Some days are harder than others."

"Your letter said Fred died of fever. Do you know what caused it?"

"An insect bite. Tsetse fly." Katy smiled weakly. "Even when he knew he was dying Fred managed to keep his sense of humor. He told me, 'I always knew that I'd be done in by something that flew in the air. However, I thought it'd be something a little larger … like a German Fokker.'"

Laura grinned as she remembered how Katy and Fred met. It was in a London hospital. Fred was a patient, the result of one of several aeroplane accidents.

She looked in the rearview mirror. In the back seat of Alexandra's car the boys were shielding their eyes and staring into the skies over Point Loma, the peninsula bordering the westernmost edge of the bay. Alexandra glanced furtively that direction, alternately keeping an eye on the road in front of her. Lily was chewing gum, fiddling with the car radio.

Laura glanced toward Point Loma. The sky was clear.

"Just like old times," Katy said. "You and me riding together like this. Except I did most of the driving in the ambulance."

"And we're not dodging bombs," Laura said. She almost added "yet" to the end of the sentence, but thought better of it. Nevertheless, an image of Japanese planes swarming over the bay came to mind.

It isn't fair. Isn't one war enough for a lifetime?

She checked her rearview mirror again.

Katy said, "I'm doing my best to keep from assuring you that everything will be all right."

"Huh? I don't follow you."

"Laura, that's the third time you've checked on your children, at least that I've noticed."

Laura's cheeks colored. "Am I that obvious?"

"You have every right. You're a mother. And we're entering dangerous times."

Laura looked in her rearview mirror and said, "If we really are at war … it frightens me to think what lies ahead for my boys. I mean, we made it through the war. You. Me. Johnny. Fred. But that's no guarantee…. How many young men did we see who didn't make it?"

"Sometimes it was the best and kindest who were killed."

"Percy."

"Exactly."

The two women spent several moments of silence in memory of Percy Hill, Johnny's best friend, who was courting Laura when his aeroplane was shot out of the sky over France.

Laura was the first to speak. Emotion clouded her voice. "Katy, I fear this war is going to be harder for me than anything we faced in France. For the first time in my life I'm beginning to understand what my mother went through. Do you remember how worried she was when you and I joined the ambulance service? I scoffed at her concern at the time. But look at me now! My boys haven't even left home and already I'm at my wit's end worrying about them."

She started to say more, then stopped, thinking she was rambling. But the flow of words, once started, could not be held back.

"I keep thinking about how some general who I'll never meet can order my boys over the top, knowing full well they don't have a chance of surviving." A single tear made its way down her cheek. "Katy, I fear it will drive me bonkers! How am I going to make it through each day? Every time a car pulls up the hill beside our house I'll think it's someone delivering a telegram … *Dear Mr. and Mrs. Morgan, I regret to inform you....*" She paused to brush aside the tear with an angry swipe. "A half sheet of paper with a standard military phrase telling me one of my boys has been shot or blown up or died of some disease in a foreign hospital. I don't think I could survive it!"

Laura's attention was momentarily redirected to the road as she made the left turn that routed them toward Point Loma. The diversion was sufficient to dam up the verbal flow.

Katy waited a moment. Then, when it was clear Laura would not continue, she said, "Having no children of my own, I'm not going to pretend to know how you feel. I can only imagine."

Laura smiled through her grief. "Thank you, dear. Your being here today is a comfort in itself."

But Katy wasn't finished. "I wasn't exaggerating when I told you how beautiful South Africa is, but it is also quite deadly. There are any number of ways a person can be killed in South

Africa. It used to tear me apart inside every time Fred would go into the wilderness with the Khoi or the San or the Zulu. Every time he left I knew there was a good chance I'd never see him again. I found myself wasting the entire day scanning the horizon, waiting for him to return. Of course, I never let on to him that I felt this way. But with each new trip I started making up things in feeble attempts to keep him home."

"How awful it must have been for you," Laura said.

"It was awful! It was awful because I was making myself miserable over something I couldn't control. Worse yet, it was awful because I was playing the hypocrite."

Laura's brow pulled together creating furrows.

Katy explained. "One day it dawned on me that on Sundays I was teaching the Khoi women to trust God while they could clearly see that I wasn't trusting him the rest of the week."

"So you're telling me you simply trusted God and stopped worrying?"

Katy chuckled. "There was nothing simple about it. But from that moment on, every time I started to worry, I'd stop what I was doing, close my eyes, and pray, '*Lord, Fred and I placed ourselves in your hands years ago, and I'll not be taking us out of them now.*'"

A noncommittal smile formed on Laura's face.

"It took a while," Katy said, "but I gradually learned to let go and trust God."

Laura didn't comment. She pretended to concentrate on her driving as she followed Johnny's car up the road to the house. Alexandra and the others were close behind. Behind the caravan of cars, the bay and city skyline appeared, peacefully drenched in the early December sun.

As they approached the house, Katy said with a grin, "Has Dad driven every car you own yet?"

"He's driven this one and Alexandra's car."

"Not the Buick? Does Johnny not like people driving his car?"

"No, I don't think Johnny would object to Dad driving his car. Dad probably hasn't asked yet."

"Johnny's waiting for Dad to ask?" Katy said laughingly. "That rascal! He knows full well that a car not yet driven is an itch to Dad; he won't be happy until he's scratched it."

The three cars pulled to a stop in front of a spacious house with red Spanish tile roofing. Johnny helped his parents out of the Buick while Laura set the parking brake. She watched as Jesse Morgan cast an appraising eye at the front fender of the Buick. It was apparent that Johnny, too, noticed his father's admiring gaze, but he said nothing.

"Maybe Johnny's toying with his father," Laura said.

Katy grinned. "Now that sounds more like my brother."

Behind them, Alexandra's Ford clattered to a stop. The four young adults piled out of the car noisily.

Emerging from the car, Laura and Katy stood to one side as a progression of youth passed them.

"I've got to call my squadron!" Walt cried, rushing past them. Alexandra was close behind him, her heels clicking briskly on the walkway. "I'm going to carry the radio onto the veranda; is that all right?" She didn't wait for an answer.

Nat sauntered casually behind his brother and sister. The smile he directed at his aunt and mother was more chagrin than smile. With a shrug of his shoulders, he thrust his hands into his pockets and went inside.

"Hi, Aunt Katy! Mom!" Lily wiggled her fingers cheerfully in a little wave as she passed.

While Johnny ushered his parents into the house, Laura and Katy followed in their wake.

Katy leaned toward the younger woman. "I must say, Laura,

you have four wonderful children. You and Johnny should be proud."

Laura accepted the compliment with a smile. "God has indeed been good to us."

Her reply was more than polite response. Laura truly believed herself to be blessed to have such a good family, a fact for which she happily and faithfully credited God.

So then why, in the very next instant, did Charlie Haddox's words wash over the good feeling with brackish waters?

The LORD gave and the LORD hath taken away; blessed be the name of the LORD.

Once again, Laura found herself fighting back a rising tide of panic.

Why did these words sound so much like a threat?

2

Isn't it enough that the war ruined the church service? Must it now ruin our family reunion as well?

"Honey, is something wrong?"

Johnny stood in the kitchen doorway. Laura turned away from him and busied herself mashing a pot of potatoes. She was being foolish and she knew it. But she couldn't help it. And that made her angrier still. "Nothing is wrong," she said.

Footfalls on the tile floor signaled his approach. She felt warm hands rest on her shoulders. "If nothing's wrong," he whispered close to her ear, "then why are you pulverizing those potatoes?"

Laura lifted the masher from the pot. Lump-free gobs of white potato dripped from it.

"What's wrong?" he repeated.

Before she could answer, Walt appeared in the doorway, his shoulders nearly filling the frame. Laura was struck by how manly her son looked. When he'd gone away to flight school he'd been just a boy. Now, a matter of months later, he was nearly a mirror image of his father—solid, tanned, strong jawed.

Johnny turned toward their son. "Did you make contact with your squadron?"

Walt brushed a hand through wavy brown hair in a relieved manner. Blue eyes sparkled with self-confidence. A boyish grin, absent at the moment, was the only telltale sign that remained of his youth.

"The phone lines are really jammed," he said. "Everybody in America must be on the phone today."

"Considering the news …" Johnny said. "Did you reach the squadron?"

Walt's cheeks puffed with an exhausted sigh. He nodded. "It took me over twenty attempts, but I finally managed to reach my captain."

With the pot of potatoes still steadied with one hand and the masher poised midair in the other, Laura held her breath in anticipation of her son's news.

"Captain Stafford said that when he heard the news about Pearl he went straight to the office knowing we would be calling in. He said nearly everyone in the squadron has already called. The only two that haven't called yet are …"

"Did he cut short your leave?" Laura interrupted.

Turning to include his mother in the conversation, Walt said, "Captain Stafford asked me when I was scheduled to return. I told him Tuesday, but that if I was needed …"

"Will you just answer the question?" There was a sharpness in Laura's tone, sharper than she'd intended. "Did he cut short your leave or not?"

An astonished father and son stared at her. Then Walt said, "No, Mother. He didn't cut short my leave."

"At least we have something to thank God for," Laura mumbled. She set the pot on the kitchen counter and reached into the cupboard for a serving bowl.

For a moment the only sound in the kitchen was the creak of the cupboard door and the rattle of porcelain bowls. Then Walt continued: "Captain Stafford said there was no need for us to return ahead of schedule. He said there was no way we could ship out before Tuesday. But he did take our phone numbers in case something else happens between now and then."

"Unless the army's changed since I was in it," Johnny said, "there will be plenty of time before you ship out. Then, once things get rolling, they'll rush you around like the world's coming to an end, only to leave you sitting around doing nothing again for weeks at a time."

Walt chuckled. "Where are the others?" he asked.

"On the veranda listening for news from Pearl. Alex looks like a bird-watcher. She has those huge binoculars and is training them on anything that moves."

Laura cringed. *Her name is Alexandra!* she said only to herself. She was the only person who called her daughter Alexandra. And though she had resigned herself to the fact that everyone else, including Alexandra, used the nickname, there were times when it grated on her nerves. Like now.

Walt's voice was low and serious when he said, "Dad, do you really think the Japanese will attack San Diego?"

Johnny shrugged. "That's the rumor. And it makes sense. Knock out Pearl, San Diego, San Francisco, and you have control of the Pacific. And what better time than right now? San Diego is less equipped to withstand an attack than Pearl. From what I've heard about our level of preparedness, the Japanese could waltz into the middle of San Diego Bay any time they had a notion."

"Johnny Morgan! What a horrible thing to say!" Laura said. She flung mashed potatoes from the spoon to the bowl so hard they splattered on her and the counter.

With a concerned tilt of his head, Johnny grabbed a dish towel and went after the splatters. With a measured tone, he said, "Dear, hoping an enemy won't attack isn't enough to prevent it from happening. Of all people, you should know that. You know what it's like to be at war."

Laura's response was to turn away from him and toss the empty potato pot into the sink. It clanged noisily.

Walt gave a wary glance his father's direction. "I think I'll join the others on the veranda," he said.

When they were alone Johnny said to his wife, "Do you mind telling me what's bothering you?"

Laura didn't answer him. She turned to the gravy simmering on the stove.

"You've been this way ever since we got home. Are you upset about church today?"

Her answer was the sound of a spoon scraping the bottom of a skillet.

"Honey, there will be plenty of other Sundays to tell the story of the Morgan family Bible. Granted, today would have been ideal with the family here, but it just wasn't meant to be. It's not as though the Japanese chose today to start a war just to ruin our personal plans!"

Swinging around, Laura leveled a dripping gravy spoon at her husband. "Do you really think that …"

Katy breezed through the kitchen door. "If one of you will point me toward the dishes and silverware, I'll set the dining room table." When she saw Laura's posture and the dripping spoon, she hastily added, "Excuse me, I didn't mean to …"

Alexandra was close behind her aunt. "Dad, can we eat out on the veranda? The radio's set up out there and …"

"Of course not!" Laura snapped. "Don't be ridiculous! It's December for heaven's sake!"

"Actually it's really quite nice on the veranda," Katy said with a nod toward her niece. "And it's not often that I get a chance to dine bayside."

Alexandra smiled appreciatively at her aunt.

"Katy's right," Johnny said. "How many people get a chance to dine alfresco this close to Christmas? It'll be fun. I'll have the boys help me move the table out there." With a swipe he took care of the gravy drippings on the floor, then tossed the dish towel onto the counter, hurrying off to get the boys.

Katy and Alexandra silently mustered the plates and flatware and took them out to the veranda. Laura was left standing alone in the kitchen. Motionless, she stared vacantly at the floor. Then, biting her lower lip, she returned to the simmering gravy. Pouring it from the skillet to the boat, a speckled brown stream slopped over the side and dribbled its way down the cabinet door. An enlarging puddle formed on the floor.

It was such a little thing, inconsequential really, but it was enough to collapse the weakening dam that had been holding back her emotions. A steady stream of tears spilled next to the gravy puddle. Her shoulders shook so hard she had to brace herself against the kitchen counter.

Laura Morgan, get hold of yourself! This is disgraceful! Why are you acting like this? No one else is falling apart over this stupid ...

"Laura dear, are you crying?"

Emily swept quickly across the room, moving to Laura's side. A comforting arm held still the shaking shoulders.

One year shy of her seventh decade, Emily Morgan was still tough and spirited—an embodiment of the females that had attracted Morgan men for centuries. Laura despised herself for acting like this in the presence of such a strong woman.

"Tell me, dear, what's wrong?" Emily asked.

"Nothing ... it's really nothing, Mother." Laura raised her head. She sniffed and wiped moistened cheeks with the edge of her apron.

Emily squeezed her daughter-in-law's shoulders even more tightly. "No tear ever was born without good cause, my dear."

The phone jangled noisily in the living room. Johnny burst into the kitchen through one door and out the other to answer it, taking no notice of his mother and wife.

"You're worried about your children, aren't you?" Emily asked, ignoring the rush-by interruption.

Laura looked at the older woman with amazement. "How did you know?"

"You forget," Emily said soothingly. "I was a mother during the last war. I know what it's like to have a son and a daughter on the front lines." She paused, chuckled, then confessed, "Besides, Katy told me what you said in the car coming home."

Laura grinned. The smile gave her strength to fight back the tears.

"I despise war," she said. "Everything about it. It's been more than two decades and still I have so many bad memories. I just don't want my boys to have to go through what we went through. And my girls … all this talk of an invasion …" She began to weep again. In a whisper, she said, "What will happen to them if the Japanese invade? I can't even bear to think about …"

"Mom! Where's Dad?"

Nat appeared suddenly in the doorway. Even though he was clearly in a rush, he slumped against the doorframe as he waited for an answer. Nat was always leaning against something.

"Your father's on the phone," Laura said, trying to hide her feelings from her son with a clear voice. Apparently, she was successful. Nat didn't seem to notice anything wrong.

"Thanks," Nat said, turning away. He stopped himself and swung back around. "Um, when he comes back in here, can you tell him there's going to be a news update about Pearl on the radio!" He hurried back to the veranda in a stumbling half run.

"Do you see how unnatural war is?" Laura said, forcing a smile. "It has Nat running!"

Emily shared her smile.

"That was Reuben Fleet." Johnny burst into the kitchen. "He just shot off a telegram to President Roosevelt advising him that we at Consolidated Aircraft are on the job and at his command." With uplifted eyebrows, he added, "Vintage Reuben!"

"To send a telegram to the president?" his mother asked.

Johnny nodded. "That, and telling everyone he sent a letter to the president. Fact is, Reuben has been advising the president for some time regarding the aircraft industry. He always seems to work it into the conversation ..." Deepening his voice, Johnny imitated his boss, "Just got off the phone to FDR."

"Dad!" It was Walt's voice coming from the veranda. "Come quick! You'll want to hear this!"

"Excuse me," Johnny said, hurrying off.

Laura gazed after her husband forlornly.

"There's nothing you can do about it, dear," Emily said.

"The war or my children?" Laura asked.

"Do you remember when you and Katy joined the ambulance corps and left for France? I cried for nearly three days straight."

"I never knew that!" Laura said. "It just doesn't sound like you."

"Enough water came out of these eyes to fill a small lake."

Emily released Laura. Reaching for the dish towel that Johnny had thrown on the counter, she knelt down and mopped up the puddle of gravy.

"Let me ask you this," she said, getting the last of it. "Are you afraid for them or for yourself?"

Laura's brow furrowed in puzzlement. "I don't know. I've never really thought about it that way."

"It's a question I asked myself many times." Emily stood and ran the dish towel under running water. "Here's another one I used to ask myself: Am I afraid that God will allow something bad to happen to my children?"

"Now that I've asked myself," Laura said softly, "why is it that my faith in God falters when it comes to my children?"

"You don't want to see them get hurt."

"And God does?"

Emily dried her hands. Her face sobered. "It's in our pain that we discover the extent of our faith in God."

Laura's eyes glassed over with tears. "I just don't know how I'd handle it if something bad should happen to them."

"Of course you don't, dear. None of us knows how we'll respond. All we can do is lay a foundation for our faith and pray it will stand in the day of testing."

"My concern exactly!" Laura said. "I just don't know if my children have the spiritual resources to withstand the evils of war. All Alex and Walt care about is flying. Nat has his photography and Lily her music. They have no idea what lies ahead of them."

"But you do."

Laura's eyes lowered sadly. Fingers worried the edge of her apron. "Some nights ... in my dreams ... I still see the empty eyes of all those soldiers staring up at me."

Emily cradled her daughter-in-law's face in her hands. "What can I do to help, dear?"

3

The veranda resembled a war room. While Nat huddled over a large atlas of the Pacific with his grandfather, Johnny and Walt sat with their ears glued to the Philco radio console at the end of the out-of-place dining room table. Leaning against the pillared railing Katy peered through binoculars as Alex directed her aunt's attention to one building after another on the San Diego skyline.

Laura set the platter of roast in the middle of the table, which had yet to be clothed. The cups and plates remained in stacks. The flatware lay in a heap.

"Dinner's ready, if anyone's interested," Laura said flatly.

Emily emerged from the kitchen carrying the bowl of mashed potatoes. She scowled.

"Jesse! Get that book off the table!" she scolded. "It's dinnertime. Katy, I thought you and Alex were going to set the table."

Katy glanced at Alex beside her and gave a sheepish shrug. "Yes, Mother," the grown woman said with an amused grin.

"And Johnny," Emily said, still using her motherly tone, "turn that radio off and get it off the table. Didn't you hear Laura? It's time for dinner."

Alex objected, "But, Grandma, we need to keep the radio on! What if …?"

Emily didn't let her finish. "Alex dear," she said, "take it from one who survived numerous air attacks on England. If the Japanese choose to attack today, we will know it long before the radio station!"

"Dad?" Alex appealed.

Johnny turned the radio knob, cutting the announcer off mid-sentence. "We can always turn it back on if we need to."

"Now," Emily said, maintaining control, "we need napkins, tea, and a couple more chairs. Let's move! If there's anything I despise it's cold potatoes and gravy. Walt, help your mother carry in the rest of the food. Jesse, I want to talk with you."

The veranda came alive with pre-dinner activity.

When Laura next returned to the veranda carrying a basket of biscuits in one hand and a butter dish in the other, she found Emily whispering in Katy's ear. No sooner was she done with Katy than she moved to Johnny, who also received private instructions.

In short order, the table was set and everyone was in place. Roast beef, potatoes, gravy, corn, biscuits, butter, and a variety of jellies lay before them.

"Johnny," Emily said, "you are the head of this household. You should be the one to lead us in a blessing."

All eyes turned to Johnny at the head of the table. His usual practice was to appoint someone to say the prayer. Nine out of ten times he appointed Laura or one of the children. Whenever his parents visited, he delighted in asking his father to do the honors. From the surprised look on his face, that had apparently been his plan for this occasion. His mother had other plans.

He cleared his throat. "Yes, well …" He looked around as though he'd lost something on the table, slapped the arms of his chair, then scooted it back and stood. "Well, umm, as you all know, I'm not …" he cleared his throat, "not comfortable, speaking in public … or leading prayers like this, but … umm … this is a special … and umm, memorable occasion." He glanced at the glistening bay beyond the veranda. "Hopefully, not too memorable." He chuckled at his attempt at humor. "Well, anyway, umm, here goes."

Heads bowed for the prayer.

"Our gracious heavenly Father, umm, we come to you today … on this momentous day … to thank you for watching over our family and for bringing all of us together again. As we, umm … how should I say it … prepare for another war, we pray … that you will keep our family safe … and our nation too. Be with those families who have men stationed at Pearl Harbor today. And protect our men there. And bless this food to our bodies. Amen."

A chorus of soft-spoken amens followed.

"Well, everyone," Laura beamed from the opposite end of the table, "help yourself."

After a moment of initial free-for-all serving, the table fell into a concert of platters and bowls being passed from hand to hand.

"According to the radio, initial reports from Pearl are encouraging," Johnny said, ladling gravy into a well of mashed potatoes.

Emily glanced at Laura, then shot her son a disapproving look. He didn't see it. His attention was focused on filling the well.

"Casualties could have been a lot worse," he said without looking up.

"Laura, these potatoes are so creamy," Emily said. "You must whip yours longer than I do. Jesse always complains of lumps in mine." She gave a knowing look to Katy who sat across from her.

Johnny suppressed a smirk as he ladled his last and passed the gravy to Walt.

"Very creamy," Katy echoed. "Everything looks wonderful. And so American. It's been years since I've had a traditional Sunday meal like this."

"I hadn't thought about it until the news commentator brought it up," Walt mused. "But it will be interesting to see what Hitler will do now that the Japanese have attacked. We all know that Churchill wants us in Europe. But does Hitler?"

"Makes a big difference, fighting a two-front war," Johnny replied. "The Germans are already fully aware of that. As for us, it would be best if we could concentrate on Japan, then if we're still needed in Europe we can go over there."

There was a moment of silence as the two men chewed. They alone seemed oblivious to Emily's clear displeasure at the topic of conversation.

"But then this is exactly what Hitler might be hoping for. By forcing us into a two-front war ..."

Emily cut in. "I certainly think Mrs. Hitler would agree with me that these kinds of political conversations should be held at times other than Sunday afternoon dinner."

Walt grinned boyishly. "Grandma, there is no Mrs. Hitler. Although I have read that ..."

A grandmother's stern gaze cut his comment short.

"Sorry," he said.

"It's hard to avoid the subject," Johnny said diplomatically. "We've just been attacked. We're at war."

Jesse cleared his throat. It was his way of sticking his foot in the door of conversation. "Son, you will indeed have a war on your hands," he said, "unless you heed your mother's warning. Believe me, I know."

Nat grinned in amusement at his father being disciplined by his parents. The grin faded the instant his father spotted it.

Johnny chose not to reply. He reached for his tea glass.

Lily spoke up. "Well, I don't know what the fuss is all about anyway. Everybody knew this was going to happen! So why spoil a perfectly good Sunday afternoon worrying about it?"

In the other room the phone rang.

"I'll get it," Nat said.

Laura stopped him. "Let it ring."

"But it might be ..."

"Let it ring," she repeated.

Emily nodded approvingly at Laura.

No one said a word while the phone rang. Six, seven, eight times. Then it stopped.

Katy said brightly, "Somebody catch me up on the family news. What has everyone been doing this past year?" She looked around the table waiting for someone to start.

Johnny took her cue. "Of course, you know Walt has been in flight training. He's learning to fly the B-17, a monster of a bomber. And Alex gets some flying time in with me at Consolidated. Reuben Fleet calls them Lindy and Amelia."

A puzzled look crossed Katy's face. "Lindy is Charles Lindbergh, and Amelia is ..."

"Amelia Earhart." Alex smiled, pleased with the association.

"You have been away a long time, Aunt Katy," Lily said.

Katy smiled. "Oh yes. And you're completing your senior year in high school?"

Lily nodded.

"What do you want to do when you graduate?"

"Sing."

"Professionally?"

"I'd like to sing with a big band. You know, Benny Goodman, Artie Shaw, Glen Miller, Harry James ..."

Katy chuckled. "Even in the bush we've heard of the big bands." Turning to Nat, she said, "And you?"

Lily answered for him. "Nat's a moron."

"Lily Morgan!" her mother scolded. "That's not a very nice thing to say!"

"It's all right, Mom," Nat said, laughingly defending his younger sister. "I am a moron."

Laura was not mollified.

"Nat was inducted into the Royal Order of Morons last night," Lily explained. She seemed pleased and excited about the dubious honor.

Nat, Alex, and Walt grinned at the older Morgans' befuddlement.

"At the ice-cream shop last night!" Lily explained. "Any person moron enough to finish a Moron's Ecstasy is eligible for membership in the Royal Order of Morons!"

"It's a quart of ice cream," Nat added, "eight different flavors with eight fruit and nut toppings. It only costs a dollar."

"A quart?" Emily exclaimed. "It's a wonder you didn't freeze your insides!"

"It wasn't that bad." Nat shrugged.

"What flavors?" Katy asked, enjoying the youthful spirit.

"Let's see …" Nat rolled his eyes upward in an effort to remember them all. "Vanilla, of course, chocolate, strawberry, tutti-frutti, pistachio, fudge ripple …"

"Lime sherbet," Lily added. "I remember the green from pistachio and lime mixing in with the chocolate. It was disgusting."

"And french vanilla," Alex added.

"That's right! There were two different scoops of vanilla," Nat said.

"And all this mess had toppings too?" Katy asked, wrinkling her nose.

Nat nodded. "Bananas. Two peach halves. Raspberry. Pineapple …"

"Mixed nuts," Walt said.

"Right," Nat acknowledged his brother's contribution. "Mixed nuts, whipped cream, and a maraschino cherry."

"Lord o' mercy," Emily cried.

"And you ate all that?" Katy laughed.

"Like I said, he's a moron!" Lily declared happily.

"Bit of ice cream sounds good about now," Jesse said.

Emily nudged him. "Family business first."

Following the meal Emily orchestrated the clearing of the table with orders snapped so crisply one would have thought she'd graduated from West Point. In the midst of it all, the doorbell sounded. A couple of boys from the church had dropped by to see Lily. Emily intercepted the youngest of the Morgans and informed Lily's guests that she would be indisposed for the remainder of the afternoon.

With a prearranged nod of her head, each of the elder Morgans struck up a conversation with one of the Morgan children. Johnny took Walt aside. Katy spoke with Lily. Jesse corralled Nat. And Emily grabbed Alex.

Laura busied herself with the last of the cleanup, wiping off the table and chairs, and gathering up the napkin holder and salt and pepper shakers. She looked lovingly at Emily who sat opposite Alex listening as the oldest Morgan child used a flat hand to simulate an airplane just as her father had done hundreds of times before.

Catching Emily's eyes, Laura mouthed the words: "Thank you! You're wonderful!"

The corners of Emily's mouth turned upward slightly in response. Laura continued the cleanup, listening in on each of the conversations as opportunity afforded.

"There will be lots of boys!" Katy said laughingly as she reached over and touched Lily on the arm. "They don't all go to war at once. Besides, San Diego is a navy town. There will be sailors from all over the country in and out of here all the time."

"My parents don't let me date sailors," Lily said.

"And that's a good rule for now," Katy affirmed. "But you

won't be eighteen years old all of your life. Besides, there's more to life than boys."

"There is?" Lily asked, blonde hair flashed with a toss of her head as bright-blue eyes opened wide and innocent. Fluttering eyelids completed the effect.

Katy laughed appreciatively. "I'm sorry," she apologized. "You're more grown up than I'm giving you credit for."

But Lily wasn't offended. From the way the two women addressed each other, it was evident they shared a common bond of admiration. It warmed Laura's heart to see how Lily could carry her end of a conversation with a woman older than her mother.

"Other than church and the school glee club, there aren't too many places for me to sing," Lily explained to her aunt. "Most of the popular places serve alcohol, so that rules them out for me."

"The right opportunity will come along," Katy said reassuringly. "And music is important during wartime."

Lily wrinkled her nose and straightened her floral dress as though she was brushing aside the suggestion. "'Over There' is not exactly my style of song," she said.

"No, no, no!" Katy said. "I'm not talking about war songs. I'm talking about …"

She searched the room. Spying Laura she said, "Over in France. At the hospital. What was the name of that woman who promoted music concerts?"

Dish towel in hand, Laura walked over to the two women. With pursed lips she tried to remember.

"Fred introduced her to me," Katy prompted.

"Ashwell …"

"Miss Lena Ashwell!" Katy said. "Thank you, Laura." Addressing Lily again, she continued, "This lady organized concerts all over France behind the lines for the soldiers to enjoy when they came off the front. She could make a stage out of just about anyplace—the woods, a barn, hangars, or when I saw her, a hospital courtyard. And the music was fabulous! Some classical. Some popular. There were violinists, a cellist, a clarinetist, a trumpeter, and a pianist." Looking to Laura she asked, "Did I miss anyone?"

"The singers."

"Of course!" To Lily, "Singing like you wouldn't believe! A soprano, a contralto, a tenor, and a bass. They were marvelous!"

From the preoccupied look in Lily's eyes, Laura could tell she was picturing the scene in her head.

"Listening to that music after weeks of nothing but artillery fire and rifles and explosions … well, suffice it to say, it was heaven! But the best part …" Katy touched Lily's arm to bring her back to the present and reestablish eye contact. "The best part— and you have to remember, I'm a nurse—was the therapeutic effect it had on the men. We could count on at least three days of improved attitudes and working conditions following one of Miss Lena Ashwell's concerts."

"And the men appreciated the music so much," Laura added.

Lily nodded. "Using music to make a difference in people's lives. More than just entertainment. I like that," she said.

"You could sing at hospitals right here in San Diego. You have a naval hospital here, don't you?"

Both Laura and Lily nodded.

"You could start there!" Katy said.

Lily's gaze deepened as she pondered the possibilities. "I'd never thought of singing at a hospital before."

※

Nat lounged in a chair next to his grandfather. "Just my luck," he said. "I've been trying since high school to land a job at Ogden Wells Portrait Studio. And now that I have, it looks like war is going to break out and I'll be drafted."

"How old are you now?" Jesse asked. "Nineteen?"

"Twenty."

A faraway look crossed Jesse's eyes. "Don't know if I can even recall what I was doing at age twenty," he said. "Running away from home, if I remember correctly. Headin' west."

Nat nodded politely, but it was evident he didn't much care what his grandfather did when he was twenty. He had more immediate concerns.

"Don't suppose there's much use for portrait photographers in a war," Jesse said, rubbing his wrinkled chin with a forefinger. "That is, unless you stumble into a gaggle of generals. They love havin' their pictures taken."

Jesse was more amused at his joke than was Nat.

"Do you have any other skills?" he asked.

Nat let his head flop against the back of the chair. "Not really," he said. "I'm not athletic …"

His appearance confirmed his self-assessment. Gangly legs draped over each other as he slouched in his chair. An open collar looked relieved that it was no longer pinned down by tie and coat. His hair was brown and full like his brother's, but his features were sharper—thin nose, thin cheeks, and a thin mouth with just a hint of lips.

"You know," Jesse Morgan said, his aged eyes taking on the light of an idea, "I just might have something that will give us a clue." With a groan, he slowly pushed himself out of his chair and disappeared into the house. When he returned he was carrying two sheets of thick paper. He held them out to Nat.

"Take a look at these," he said.

Laura maneuvered herself so that she could see over Nat's shoulder.

"One of my uncles drew them, during the War between the States."

The first picture had a grotesquely low angle to it, as though it were drawn from a hole or a ditch looking up. A house rose in the foreground at sharp angles, portrayed with bold, angry strokes. Beside the house was a man sitting in a chair under a tree, his feet and legs largely prominent due to the perspective.

"Willy Morgan drew those. That's his house and father, Jeremiah Morgan."

Nat's eyes squinted in artistic concentration. After a time he moved the second picture to the front and studied it.

"That one there is from Andersonville Prison," Jesse said. "Willy was a prisoner there for a time. This picture and others were used as evidence against the South in the criminal trials that followed the war."

The picture was of a man in rags lying facedown on the ground. His cheek rested in a pool of blood. His own. He lay across a string stretched between two poles and continuing on, paralleling a spiked wooden fence. Other ragged prisoners gaped at the dead man in horror while two Confederate soldiers looked down from a tower. One held a rifle in his hands, the other was shouting exuberantly, his arms raised in joy.

"That line there was called the Dead Line. Anyone crossing it for any reason—even by mistake—was fair game to the guards. The way I heard it, the guards had a point system which kept record of their number of kills."

Nat stared at the picture, then looked again at the first one. He nodded appreciatively.

"He had talent," Nat said of Willy Morgan's abilities.

"That he did," Jesse said, taking the pictures and looking at them again himself. "Some of his pictures were published in newspapers and magazines too."

Nat resettled himself in his chair, unsure why he had been shown the pictures.

"You could do the same thing," Jesse said.

Nat shrugged. "I'm not very good at drawing. I have an eye for composition, that sort of thing, but my best work is done with a camera."

"So why don't you use your camera to do in this war what Willy did in his war?"

Nat's eyes narrowed to a slit as he considered his grandfather's words.

"There was another man," Jesse held up an index finger and shook it slowly as he tried to remember the man's name. "Riis, I believe it was. Jacob Riis. That's it … Jacob Riis. He came to New York and took hundreds of pictures of the tenements where I grew up. Showed the world the squalor and filth. Stirred up so much interest that some of those New York politicians felt uncomfortable enough to do something about it."

Nat nodded. He was catching a vision. "Show the world the atrocities of war, maybe document the life of the everyday foot soldier."

"Now you got it!" Jesse proclaimed.

Alexandra pulled at her skirt. It was painful for Laura to see her daughter wear female clothing, not that she didn't look good in them, she did; the pain came from watching her feel so uncomfortable in them. Alexandra was more at home in slacks or a flying jumpsuit.

"Alex, dear," Emily was saying, "believe me, adventure will find you. You don't have to go out looking for it. If you need proof, look at today. The war has been delivered right to our very doorstep."

"When you were young, did adventure come to you, Grandma?"

"No, dear, it didn't have a chance. I had a knack for finding it before it even knew it was looking for me. But times are different now. With the boys going off to the war, you're needed here more than ever."

"I can second that!" Johnny's voice came from across the room. "We're going to need you at Consolidated. All the men are going to be heading out and, if the last war is any indication, the women are going to be coming to work in droves. We're going to need you to help manage them!"

Alex smiled at him noncommittally.

Turning his attention back to Walt, Johnny closed the front cover of the Morgan family Bible. "As you can see, this Bible has seen a lot of history. Much of it during war. The Revolution. Civil War. The Great War. And now this present conflict. The Morgans have a strong military heritage. One that you will continue."

Walt's shoulders sagged a bit as he assumed the responsibility of the entire Morgan line. But they sagged only briefly. He quickly straightened them, accepting the responsibility given him.

"I'll do my best," he said.

"I know you will, son. Your mother and I are proud of you." Johnny handed the Bible to his son. "I want you to take this with you."

Walt recoiled slightly. "Dad, I don't know ..."

"I want you to have it now," Johnny said. "It will see you through the war. Bring it back to me when all of this is over and we'll add your name to the list, right under mine."

Walt took the Bible. From the way he handled it, it was heavier than he'd remembered it being.

As the afternoon faded into twilight the personal discussions blended with one another until the entire family was engaged in a single interaction around the table.

"Hermann Göring! The commander of the German air force?" Walt looked with questioning surprise from grandfather to father.

"Dad, is Grandpa pulling my leg? You shot down Hermann Göring?"

Johnny grinned an ambiguous grin.

Walt looked at Alex. "Grandpa's pulling our leg," he concluded. But a table full of grins from the older Morgans set him to wondering again.

"Help me out here, son," Jesse said to Johnny. "My reputation as a grandfather is on the line."

For a significant time Johnny said nothing. Finally, he pushed his chair back and disappeared into the house.

"Where is he going?" Lily asked.

"Probably to get Hermann on the phone to verify the story," Nat quipped.

When Johnny returned he handed Walt a folded yellow scrap of paper. Eyeing his father suspiciously, Walt took it. Unfolding the paper, he read silently. His eyebrows shot up.

"What does it say?" Lily asked.

Walt stared at his father. "Really?" he said.

Without commenting Johnny lowered himself back into his chair.

"Walt! What does it say?" Lily asked again.

Reading aloud, Walt said, "Captain Eastman, Let it be known that on this day, Mr. Johnny Morgan disabled my two escort aeroplanes and shot down my plane." Lowering the note he said, "It's signed, Hermann Göring."

Slumped in his chair, Nat chuckled and shook his head, refusing to believe the note's authenticity.

"Let me see that!" Alex said. Taking the paper from her brother she read it for herself. "Well, I'll be. Look at the old-school penmanship."

"Göring's penmanship was fine, but his English was terrible," Johnny commented. "I had to dictate the thing to him and help him spell a few of the words."

Nat demanded to see the paper. His lips silently formed the words as he read. When he finished, he shook his head, still not believing. "This is some kind of practical joke that Dad played on his buddies. Who ever heard of a pilot writing a you-shot-me-down note?"

All faces turned to Johnny for a response. He folded his hands casually behind his head. "Believe whatever you want to believe about the note."

"It's genuine," Katy insisted on behalf of her brother. "Fred told me about it. He said it was the talk of the pilots for weeks."

"I'm still not buying it," Nat insisted. "Why would Göring write this note?"

"Because I had my guns trained on him, that's why." Johnny's tone had an edge to it. "It was quite simple, really. I needed corroboration. There were no witnesses so I needed something to prove to my captain that I had downed a German plane, otherwise he never would have given me credit for the kill. I'd already lost out on one kill for lack of a witness, I wasn't about to miss out on another."

Nat stared at the note again. A wrinkled brow indicated he was still not convinced.

Jesse changed the subject. He directed his question at Lily specifically and the other Morgan children indirectly. "Did you know that your aunt and grandmother were aboard the *Lusitania* when it was sunk by a German U-boat?"

"We've heard that story," Lily said.

"About a hundred times," Nat added.

"How about Edith Cavell? Have you heard about her?" Katy asked.

Response was hesitant.

"A little," Alex said as a bunched-up face tried to squeeze the facts from her memory.

"What do you remember about her?" Katy asked.

"Ummmm … that she was a British nurse who remained in Belgium even after the Germans occupied it. Wasn't she the one who was executed for smuggling British pilots back to England?"

Katy nodded. "She was also the one who inspired your mother and me to join the volunteer ambulance corps. And where did you hear about her?"

"From Mother."

"Not in school?"

Alex looked to her sister and brothers. They all shook their heads. Their response did not please Katy.

"Well, the children at our mission school in South Africa have certainly heard about her," Katy said. "But then, I'm the teacher. They hear about your mother too."

"You tell your children about Mother? Why?" Lily asked.

"What could you possibly tell those children about me?" Laura asked, feeling her face redden.

"I tell them about you whenever I teach the Bible lesson about loving your enemy and doing good to those who hate you. I tell them the story of how Laura Kelton treated the wounds of a German sniper who only moments earlier had been trying to kill her."

"Mom, you never told us about a German sniper!" Alex protested.

"It's not a topic that comes up frequently," Laura said.

"Weren't you scared?" Lily asked.

"Terrified beyond words."

"Your mother shielded that German boy with her own body when one of our soldiers wanted to finish him off," Katy said.

"All right, Mom!" Walt cried.

"He was just a boy. And he was as frightened as any of us," Laura said.

"Did he ever thank you for saving his life?" Nat asked.

"He didn't survive," Laura said softly. Sadly.

Jesse cleared his throat. Everyone recognized the signal and waited for him to speak. "What about Bruno? Did you tell them about Bruno?"

"Sounds like the name of a dog," Nat said.

"A Great Dane," Lily added, laughing.

"A young lady," Jesse corrected them. "And a rather remarkable young lady at that."

"Young lady?" Walt asked.

"She was just a girl at the time," Katy said. "For years after the war I kept in touch with her. Then, about the time Hitler began rampaging across Europe, my letters were returned as undeliverable."

"I didn't know you'd kept in touch with her," Laura said, pleasantly surprised.

"The woman's name is really Bruno?" Lily asked.

Katy deferred the question to her father who deflected it right back to her. "Go ahead," he said, "I'm anxious to hear what has become of the young woman myself."

To Lily, Katy said, "Her name isn't really Bruno. It's Allegra. Bruno was the code name for an underground espionage network that comprised her entire town. But she was the key to the operation. At the time she was only eight years old. She's blind and a savant."

"Savant?"

"A person with an exceptional skill. In Allegra's case it is her memory. Everything she hears, she remembers and can quote back to you on demand."

"We didn't even know she was blind when we first met her," Laura added. "She moved around so freely."

"She had the place memorized," Nat suggested, obviously intrigued by the girl.

"Exactly!" Katy said. "She counted steps. Knew the entire town by heart."

"So what happened to her after the war?" Laura asked eagerly. "I had no idea you were still in contact with her." To her children, she added: "Allegra took a liking to your Aunt Katy the moment they first met. Already knew everything about her. It really shook up your aunt."

"Anybody would react like I did!" Katy defended herself. "Imagine coming face-to-face with a little girl you've never met before who can rattle off everything you've ever done in your life—the names of your parents, things about your family, where you live and work, everything!"

"How did she know all that about you?" Nat asked.

"Your grandfather, who was infiltrating German espionage in the States at the time, had been in contact with Bruno. Part of their security was to investigate his family and background. All the information was fed to Allegra."

"She really was fascinated with the Morgans," Laura said, "and Katy in particular. Knew everything about the family all the way back to Drew Morgan."

Johnny said, "Maybe we should have her come here when it's time for the family ceremony to pass the Morgan family Bible. I'd be more than happy for her to tell the family history in my stead."

"To answer your question, Laura," Katy said, "a few years after the war Iva died." To the children, she explained, "Iva Bettencourt was Allegra's guardian. She, too, was a remarkable woman. Taught me an invaluable lesson in Christian humility."

"And none too soon," Johnny quipped.

Katy ignored her brother. "Allegra was taken in by a family in

Agneaux who finished raising her. The girl is a bottomless pit when it comes to learning. She can't get enough. There weren't enough people in all of Agneaux to read to her. And she loved being read to, especially the Bible. For our correspondence, she would dictate her letters to Katherine, one of the girls she lived with and whom she considered a sister. The last I heard from Allegra, she was moving to Paris to study French literature at the Sorbonne."

"She reminds me of Helen Keller," Alex said.

"I hadn't thought of it before," Katy replied, "but you're right. It's a good comparison. Both of them are exceptional women."

Jesse stretched his arms high in the air and groaned loudly. His gesture served as a signal that it was getting late.

The veranda was no longer dappled with sunlight and shade. A cool grayness had engulfed it. The panorama of the city saw the sun's rays ricocheting off the skyline with flashing orange and yellow hues.

"Can we turn the radio on now?" Alex asked.

The question was directed at Emily, which caused Laura to chuckle.

"Don't ask me, child," came Grandma's incredulous reply. "This isn't my house."

"Dad?" Alex asked.

Johnny looked to Laura. When he saw no objection, he nodded.

After a moment of static, the news announcer's voice sliced across the veranda. It still grated on Laura's ears, but not nearly as badly as before. The events of the afternoon had appeased her somewhat. For at least a few hours she had managed to hold back the war.

The sweetness of her victory spoiled quickly.

※

Darkness covered the city. A darker darkness than Laura had ever seen in San Diego. What few lights reflected in the bay were quickly extinguished, so that the buildings comprising the skyline resembled tombstones in a graveyard at midnight.

A blackout had been ordered. With the darkness came nervousness, tension, and fear.

Rumors of a Japanese attack whizzed all around them like shrapnel at the front. Radio. Phone calls. Neighbors.

Heavy blankets were draped across windows. Everyone spoke in hushed tones. Everyone had advice. Concerns. The latest news.

There was no consensus. Other than the certainty that the Japanese were on their way.

Laura folded her arms and shivered as she gazed across the bay. The sound of pounding came from inside the house as the last of the windows was covered. Like a black specter Johnny emerged from the darkened doorway.

Standing behind her, he encircled her in his arms, resting his chin on the top of her head. Together they stared at a patch of renegade lights just beyond the airport.

It was Consolidated Aircraft.

"Got hold of the foreman," Johnny said. "He refuses to turn off the lights. Says he's too busy building airplanes and that he hasn't got time to play games."

"What does Reuben have to say about that?"

"Doesn't matter," he replied. "The marines have already given them an ultimatum. If the foreman doesn't turn out the lights, they'll cut the power."

"So what will he do?"

In answer to her question, the lights at Consolidated Aircraft winked out. It was darker than ever.

MONDAY. Johnny was already up when Laura awoke at 5:30 a.m. It was still dark.

He wasn't in the bathroom. Nor did she find him in the living room or kitchen.

Voices came from outside. She walked onto the veranda. The voices came from across the street. Johnny was talking to a group of green-clad soldiers standing at the base of a monstrous artillery gun that had appeared overnight in the adjacent vacant lot.

He offered them something to eat. They accepted only coffee, saying their breakfast was due to arrive soon. By night the gun was gone; moved on to a more strategic location.

Laura was glad. The last thing she wanted was to have an artillery gun next to her house for the duration of the war.

At noon the entire family sat grim-faced around the Philco console on the dining table on the veranda. President Roosevelt's voice crackled sharply through the radio's speaker.

> Yesterday, December 7, 1941—a date which will live in infamy—the United States of America was suddenly and deliberately attacked by naval and air forces of the Empire of Japan.
>
> The United States was at peace with that nation and, at the solicitation of Japan, was still in conversation with its Government and its Emperor looking toward the maintenance of peace in the Pacific....
>
> The attack yesterday on the Hawaiian Islands has caused severe damage to American naval and military forces. Very many American lives have been lost. In addition American ships have been reported torpedoed on the high seas between San Francisco and Honolulu.
>
> Yesterday the Japanese Government also launched an attack against Malaya.
>
> Last night Japanese forces attacked Hong Kong.
>
> Last night Japanese forces attacked Guam.
>
> Last night Japanese forces attacked the Philippine Islands.
>
> Last night Japanese forces attacked Wake Island.
>
> This morning the Japanese attacked Midway Island.
>
> Japan has, therefore, undertaken a surprise offensive extending throughout the Pacific area. The facts of yesterday speak for themselves. The people of the United States have already formed their opinions

and well understand the implications to the very life and safety of
our nation....

Hostilities exist. There is no blinking at the fact that our people,
our territory and our interests are in grave danger.

With confidence in our armed forces—with the unbounded determination of our people—we will gain the inevitable triumph—so help
us God.

I ask that the Congress declare that since the unprovoked and
dastardly attack by Japan on Sunday, December seventh, a state of
war has existed between the United States and the Japanese Empire.

Part of Laura's mind had held out hope that somehow war
might be avoided, that the Japanese would come to their
senses and back away from their announced intentions of
Pacific conquest.

She looked at her children. She had always hoped they would
never know war.

But they would. It was official.

"God be with us," she said in a whisper.

TUESDAY. Early in the morning Walt climbed aboard a train
bound for Los Angeles. From there he would fly to Lockbourne
Army Air Base near Columbus, Ohio, where he would rejoin his
squadron. Laura stood under the station arches and wept. A steady
stream of tears accompanied her all the way home. She had cried
when he first went away to flight school, but nothing like this. It
was different this time. Her youngest boy was going to war.

Later that same afternoon Katy boarded another train with
Jesse and Emily. She would accompany them to Denver, where
she would stay a couple of weeks before returning to South Africa
and the mission field. Again Laura wept.

For months this had been the plan. Still, she couldn't help
feeling that Katy and Emily were abandoning her. She hated
herself for feeling this way. She knew in her heart it wasn't so.

But that didn't stop the pain she felt, nor the loneliness as their train pulled out.

THURSDAY. Germany and Italy declared war on the United States. Nat came home from the photography studio and announced he was joining the army. "It's just a matter of time before Congress extends conscription to everyone my age," he said. "Might as well join up before they come and get me. Maybe I'll get a better pick of duty stations."

FRIDAY. Nat packed his bags and departed for the army induction center. Just like that. One day he was there, the next he was gone. Laura knew this day would come. She hadn't counted on it coming so soon.

He chose the army over the navy for a couple of reasons. First, he figured there would be more opportunities to document the horrors of war in Europe than on the Pacific. Second, and more important, every time he'd ever been out on a boat beyond the bay he'd gotten seasick, and the thought of being nauseous through an entire war just didn't appeal to him.

Laura did her best to keep from crying until after he walked out the door. No sooner had the sound of the car faded down the street than she dissolved in tears. Less than a week had passed and already both of her boys were gone. She didn't know if she'd ever see them again.

The house seemed so empty with Christmas less than two weeks away. It would be a bleak holiday at best.

SATURDAY. More complete reports reached the mainland from Pearl Harbor. Of the eight battleships stationed there, three were sunk: the *Arizona*, the *West Virginia*, and the *California*. With national tragedy came personal loss. Both of the pastor's sons perished aboard the *California*. They were the first blood spilled from among the members of Fifth Avenue Church.

She'd heard an interview on the radio which haunted her now. One of the survivors-turned-rescuers was talking:

We could hear tapping all over the ship, SOS taps, no voices, just those eerie taps from all over. There was nothing we could do to help them. Nothing we could do....

The images of the preacher's boys came to mind. Redheaded. Heavily freckled. She could still see them sitting in her third-grade Sunday school class. She could see them running in and out of the waves at the youth beach party. She could see them—no matter how hard she tried to block it from her mind—tapping endlessly on a gray bulkhead. Tapping ... tapping ... until the sea rose up around them.

That night Johnny and Laura visited the pastor and his wife at their home, offering their condolences.

SUNDAY. The day dawned gray and overcast. The mood was equally somber as the members of Fifth Avenue Church gathered to worship. Although no one would have faulted the preacher for not preaching on this Sunday, he insisted. His text was taken from the eighteenth Psalm:

For thou hast girded me with strength unto the battle: thou hast subdued under me those that rose up against me.

Throughout the sermon Laura kept her head lowered, knowing that if she looked at the pastor, or his wife seated in the second pew, she'd cry.

It helped that Charlie Haddox didn't make it to church that Sunday. His wife said he was ill. Though Laura wished the sweet man no ill will, considering the man's prophecy the previous Sunday and the events of the week, it was just one more thing with which she didn't have to cope.

She made it through the service by looking frequently at her daughters and husband in the pew next to her, refusing to let her eyes wander any farther down the pew that had been filled with family members a week ago.

It was a minor victory for her to make it through the service without falling apart.

That night, in bed, Laura thanked God for helping her get through a difficult day. Taking her cue from a familiar hymn, she counted her blessings, naming them one by one. She knew difficult days lay ahead, but instead of worrying about them, she determined to give her attention to Alex and Lily and Johnny who were still within her immediate care, while handing over to God those distant.

She slept peacefully for the first night in a week.

MONDAY. Laura found a note on the kitchen table. When she read it, she had to sit down. She had no choice; the strength left her legs.

It read:

Mom and Dad,

Have left for Texas. I know I should be telling you this personally, but I couldn't bring myself to do it. I've seen how hard Walt and Nat's leaving has been on you. I know you want me to stay in San Diego, but an opportunity has arisen that I simply cannot pass up.

Two weeks ago I received a letter from a woman who is looking for female pilots to fly military planes. We have corresponded by phone and letter and she has invited me to join her team.

I'm sorry to disappoint you like this. I hope someday you'll understand. I just can't see myself working on an assembly line at Consolidated. I have to fly. And if I get into this program in Texas, it will give me a chance to fly every day. I just can't pass up this chance.

Mom, please forgive me.

Alex

P.S. I'll send a forwarding address as soon as I'm settled.

4

The woman seated behind the metal desk was a person Alex knew she could respect. There was a toughness about her that was softened by large brown eyes, striking blonde hair, and a touch of Southern drawl. The woman's image fit her reputation.

Jacqueline Cochran had been a successful beautician in the fashionable Antoine's Salon at Saks Fifth Avenue in New York. On a credenza behind her was an impressive display of her former career—a variety of lipsticks, pressed powders, bottles of lotion, and perfume in blue packages bearing the distinctive silver scroll-work of Cochran's "Wings to Beauty" cosmetics line.

Yet this former beautician was outfitted in khaki flight over-alls, and her office was a shed at one end of an airfield hangar. This, too, was Jacqueline Cochran, the winner of the 1938 Bendix Race in which she flew 2,042 miles from Los Angeles to Cleveland nonstop in eight hours, ten minutes, and thirty-one seconds.

"Tell me about your flying experience," Cochran said. "How many hours do you have in the air?"

Alex felt Cochran's hard, businesslike gaze as it traveled from her toes to her head. She shifted uncomfortably, exchanging her folder of documents from one perspiring hand to the other. Having been on the road for three days in her Ford convertible, her face and blouse and pants were generously dusted with West Texas dirt. Upon her arrival at Houston Municipal Airport, she had excitedly inquired about the Women's Flying Training Detachment. She hadn't expected to be led to Jacqueline Cochran's office and interviewed before having a chance to shower and change clothes.

"Umm … about twelve hundred hours."

"Twelve hundred hours?" Cochran said. "Twelve hundred? Where could a young lady like you have possibly logged so many hours?"

"In San Diego … that's where I come from."

"In what type of aircraft?"

"I learned in a single-engine Cessna Piper Cub when I was ten years old. But I've also flown a PT-1 double-engine trainer, a Catalina PBY, a PB-2a fighter.…"

Cochran was leaning forward, her forearms on the desk. Her eyes bunched with skepticism. "Those are military aircraft," she said.

Alex nodded.

"You're telling me you've flown military aircraft?"

"I flew them before they became military aircraft. My father is a test pilot for Consolidated Aircraft."

"And your father is?"

"Johnny Morgan."

Cochran flopped back in her chair. Her eyebrows rose appreciatively. She was impressed. "You're Johnny Morgan's daughter? The flying ace from the last war?"

Alex nodded.

The favorable expression remained for but a moment. The look that replaced it told Alex that she could expect no partiality from her father's notoriety. She'd have to create her own reputation.

"Do you have a completed Form 64?"

Alex fumbled through her folder until she found the multipage physical exam report. She handed the document to Cochran.

"Did you have trouble taking the physical?"

"The flight surgeon said it was the first time he'd ever performed the examination on a woman."

Cochran chuckled as she scanned the report. "I don't doubt it."

"He wasn't very happy about it."

Cochran looked up.

"They had to close off an entire ward temporarily so that I could go from lab to lab," Alex explained. "I was wearing one of those short, open-back hospital gowns."

With an understanding nod, Cochran returned her attention to the form.

Alex waited as Cochran read. Her mind wandered back to the day she took the physical exam. She winced at the remembrance, not from the exam itself but from the circumstances surrounding it.

She hadn't left San Diego on the day the farewell note to her parents implied. The day was spent being pricked and prodded and interrogated by an array of army hospital staff. Then, when they were finished with her, instead of returning home she'd checked into a hotel. Her memory of standing in the hotel room at dusk and looking across the bay at the darkening Point Loma peninsula brought a fresh pang of guilt.

"The reason I require the Form 64 physical examine," Cochran said, "is because I want to assure the Army Air Corps that my women trainees can compare favorably to their highly selective combat flying squadrons."

Alex was given no indication a response was expected, so she didn't give one.

"Let's see what else you have," Cochran said, extending an open palm toward Alex's folder.

The folder exchanged hands.

Cochran leafed past Alex's pilot's license and various certification papers. She pulled out the Women's Flying Training Detachment application form and studied it.

"Your given name is Alexandra?"

"I prefer Alex."

"Let me hazard a guess here. Your father named you?"

Alex felt a slight grin crease her face. "Shortly before I was born he read a book about Alexander the Great. My father was hoping for a boy."

"Did he ever get one?"

"Two, eventually. After giving birth to me my mother miscarried twice. They were told they'd not be able to have any more children. Then, a couple of years after that, my brother Nat was born. A year later Walt was born, and a year after that Lily. Walt was the one Dad was waiting for."

Cochran raised her head to look at Alex. "He's your father's favorite?"

Alex gave an unconcerned shrug and nodded. "Nat and Lily are the artistic ones. Both Walt and I are more like Dad. But Walt's the boy."

"Is he a pilot too?"

Alex nodded. "He's stationed at Lockbourne."

Cochran looked intrigued. "Have you been competing with him all your life?"

Again Alex shrugged. "Walt's pretty good about it. He knows he's Dad's favorite. We all do. We laugh about it sometimes. Walt isn't one to take advantage."

Squint-eyed, Cochran studied her. "Doesn't the inequity make you angry?"

"It just makes me try harder."

Leaning back in her chair Cochran signaled a more casual bent to the interview. "You're single."

"Yes."

"Engaged?"

"No."

"Boyfriends?"

Alex grinned. "That's my sister Lily. She collects boyfriends like so many bracelet charms. I prefer flying. There's no room in my life for a boyfriend."

"There certainly won't be if you're accepted into this program," Cochran said. "Have you heard about the Women's Auxiliary Ferry Squadron in New Castle, Delaware?"

"Yes, I have."

"Why aren't you applying for that program? You're certainly qualified."

"They didn't send me a letter inviting me to join them. You did."

"You realize, don't you, that my letter was sent to every woman in the United States I thought might qualify for the program?"

"Still, it was an invitation. And it was from you."

Cochran's eyes searched for any trace of patronization on Alex's face. Alex was relieved when she found none, because none was intended.

Closing the folder, Cochran rose. "Let's see what the famous Johnny Morgan has passed on to his daughter," she said.

"We're going up right now?"

"Unless you have another pressing commitment."

"Well, no," Alex stammered. "Do you have a flight suit that will fit me?"

"Of course not," Cochran laughed. "None of the flight suits fit, they're all too big."

Within a matter of minutes Alex was high over Houston, Texas, in a two-seater PT-19 trainer with Jacqueline Cochran. Because it was an open cockpit, which limited communication in the air to hand signals, Cochran gave her instructions before they took off.

"Just show me what you've got," she said.

After a conservative takeoff and one expertly flown circle of the field, Alex executed a couple of stalls, spins, chandelles, and lazy eights.

Cochran said nothing after they landed. She said nothing as they walked through the hangar to her office. Not until she was once again seated behind her desk did she speak.

"What we are doing here is part of an experiment," she said with all seriousness. "If this program succeeds, it will do more to advance the cause of equality for women than anything that has been done so far."

When Cochran paused, Alex stood by silently.

"This is no boarding school," Cochran continued. "I want to start my own training school for women pilots. They won't let me unless I can prove women can fly army airplanes. It won't be easy. There are plenty of men out there who believe very strongly that women do not belong in the air. And there are others who will be threatened by our accomplishments.

"When I was with the Air Transport Auxiliary, the chief pilot admitted I was qualified to fly for the ATA but recommended against it, stating that women were at a physical disadvantage and were unable to handle the brakes in an emergency. Eventually, the ATA overruled his objections. Then, when I was assigned to fly a Lockheed Hudson from Montreal to Prestwick, Scotland, my copilot/navigator and radio operator filed a joint protest. They called a mass meeting and threatened to strike. They argued that if a woman flew a bomber across the Atlantic, it would belittle their jobs. A compromise was reached. I was permitted to fly the bomber, but the male copilot/navigator would take off and land.

"On the day of the flight, as I performed a preflight check of the airplane, I discovered that the window of the pilot's cabin had been smashed, a life raft was missing, and a wrench used to activate the oxygen system had been removed. While the window was being repaired, I bought a wrench from a passing mechanic.

"I tell this to all the applicants because I want to make sure everyone knows exactly what they can expect. But then, I believe you already know, don't you? What has most impressed me about you, Miss Morgan, is not your number of flight hours, which are considerable, nor your ability to handle an airplane, which is commendable, but the fact that you have been battling for equal recognition all of your life.

"Flying experience is not enough. We're going to have to prove to the world that we can fly the army's airplanes as good if not better than any man. Our success or failure will depend on you. Are you interested?"

With her oversized flight suit unzipped and hanging loosely on her shoulders, her hair dirty and windblown, a pair of goggles dangling from her fingers, Alex said, "I wouldn't have come this far had I not already committed everything I am to the success of this program."

By the third ring Alex had an incredible urge to hang up the telephone.

"Hello?"

The voice was her father's.

"Daddy?"

"Alex?"

"Yeah, it's me."

"Where are you?"

"Houston."

"Texas?"

"Yeah, that's the one."

Alex shifted the receiver nervously from one ear to the other. *You're twenty-three years old! Stop feeling like you're a little child!*

"Is someone with you?" her father asked.

"What do you mean?"

"I mean, is someone with you? Or did you drive halfway across the United States by yourself?"

"I came alone. I was careful. Took frequent rest stops, that sort of thing."

Alex noticed something her father didn't say. He didn't tell her that it wasn't safe for a young woman to be traveling alone, especially after the fact. Besides, this was the father who had taught a ten-year-old girl to fly.

"And the car ran all right? What kind of mileage did you get?"

What is it about fathers and cars and mileage on trips? "The car ran fine. I haven't calculated the mileage yet. Dad, I just wanted to call and let you know where I am and that I'm all right."

"So, what's the big attraction in Houston?" her father asked.

"There's a flying program here called Women's Flying Training Detachment. Jacqueline Cochran is the person who started it. Do you remember who she is? She's the woman I told you about, the one who won the Bendix Race a few years ago. I showed you the magazine article about her."

"I remember."

"Well, this program trains women to fly army airplanes. We'll be ferrying them from their point of origin to various military bases."

"You already know how to fly army airplanes."

"Some models, and those unofficially. This program will certify me to fly a number of different models, possibly even the B-17."

"The B-17? That's too much airplane for you."

It wasn't like her father to put limitations on her like that. His words stung. She didn't know what to say, so she didn't say anything at all. The phone line crackled.

After a time, her father said, "So what will they have you flying first?"

"They have an assortment of airplanes to get us started—Taylorcraft and Piper Cubs, Aeronca trainers and other small planes."

"You could fly any of those when you were twelve years old!" her father said.

Alex agreed. "But we all have to start together," she said. "They want to make sure we all know how to fly the army way."

"Sounds like the army. Are they paying you for this?"

"One hundred and fifty dollars a month."

"And will they reimburse you for your expenses to Houston?"

"No. Everyone had to get here on her own." She decided not to add that if she were to wash out of the program, she'd have to pay her own way home as well.

"I understand your wanting to do this sort of thing," her father said, "but I can't say that I approve of the way you went about it. You hurt your mother leaving the way you did."

It was one of those parental jabs. It hurt. But then, she deserved it. Like a rapidly swelling tide, tears surged within her. She swallowed hard to keep them in check. "I know," she said in a voice that was barely audible.

"Well … it's water under the bridge now," her father said. "Here's your mother. She wants to talk with you."

While the phone was being exchanged in California, in Texas Alex mustered all of her strength to hold back the tears that were already wetting her eyes.

"Alexandra?"

The sound of her name. That was all it took. The determined dam was breached, the flood loosed. No one called her Alexandra. Only her mother.

"Honey? Are you all right?"

Alex wiped her nose and sniffed. "Yes, Mother. I'm all right."

"Where are you? All I got from your father was that you were in Houston, Texas."

"I'm in a hotel not far from the Houston Municipal Airport. It's right next to Ellington Field Air Base."

"Why a hotel?"

"The training program is just getting started. We don't have permanent facilities yet. They can't secure them too soon for me. The water bugs here are atrocious!"

"I think you'll find that's true for that entire Gulf Coast region," her mother said.

An awkward pause passed between them.

"Well, dear, this phone call is costing you a fortune...."

"Mother? Before you hang up?"

"Yes, dear?"

"I'm ... I'm sorry I hurt you. It was just that ..." The tide within her rose again, choking off her voice. She tried to speak through it. "... after hearing you talk about how much you needed Lily and me to stay ... I couldn't bring myself to tell you I was leaving. I wish now I had."

"I know, Alexandra." Tears could be heard on the other end of the line. "It was selfish of me to put you in that position. I only hope that you will be happy doing what you're doing."

"I'm doing what I want to do most. Are you sure you're all right with this, Mom?"

"When will you be able to come home for a visit?"

"I have no idea what my schedule is going to be like. As soon as I know I'll write."

"Then we'll just leave everything in God's hands, won't we? At least there is one consolation. You're not in a war zone."

Alex dried her eyes.

"Are you still there, dear?"

"Yes, Mom."

"We love you, Alexandra."

"I love you, too, Mom."

5

Instruments served as Walt Morgan's eyes. He was flying blind.

The low-pitched, high-volume throb of four enormous engines vibrated every square inch of the B-17 aircraft, an intense vibration that rattled the muscles and nerves of every crewmember. Walt's eyes bounced from instrument to instrument with concentrated attention. Air-speed indicator. Directional gyro compass. Altimeter. His life and the lives of everyone in the aircraft depended upon his training. Months of reading and study and simulation and practice were reduced to this moment.

He felt a sudden loss of power.

"Engine number four has cut out," said the copilot.

Walt reacted quickly, instinctively, calling upon his 130 hours of training practice in B-17s. Stomping on the rudder pedal to correct the imbalance of thrust, he adjusted the three other throttles to compensate for the dead engine.

The bomber responded. It was sluggish, but it responded. He checked his instruments again. They were still on course.

Again, there was a loss of power.

"We just lost engine three," said the copilot.

No time to panic. The aircraft was capable of flying on two engines. Walt pushed harder on the rudder. His leg began shaking from the steady exertion needed to keep the plane trim. He adjusted the throttles on the two remaining engines.

Another check of the instruments. Still on course.

Out of the corner of his eye Walt caught a glimpse of the co-pilot scribbling on a clipboard of loose papers. Then, a hand appeared and unsnapped the black canopy enclosing the pilot's seat.

Like magic, the city of Columbus suddenly appeared below Walt. To his right propellers three and four windmilled lifelessly in the airstream. The switches for those two engines were in the Off position.

"Do you think you can land this crate?"

The copilot asking the question was Squadron Commander Major Eugene Shaw.

"Yes, sir."

"Then do it."

"Should I restart three and four?"

"Just land the plane, Morgan."

"Yes, sir."

Sitting in a jump seat immediately behind the pilot and copilot's seats, Captain George McCarver, the director of flying, said, "You want him to land with only two engines?"

Major Shaw scribbled busily on the clipboard. Either he didn't hear the question, or he chose not to answer it. Fearing the latter, Captain McCarver sat back in his seat and gave Walt a look that said, "You're on your own!"

Walt banked the bomber to the right until the Lockbourne Army Air Base runway came into view.

Shaw began reading from the landing checklist. For each item, Walt made the appropriate check and responded.

"Altimeter."

"Set."

"Crew position."

Walt glanced at McCarver behind them, the only other crewmember onboard. "OK."

"Autopilot."

"Off."

"Booster-pumps."

"On."

"Mixture controls."

"Auto-rich."

"Intercooler."

"Set."

"Carburetor filters."

"Open."

"Landing gear."

Walt toggled the landing gear switch. He heard the whir of the wheel mechanism moving the gear into place. The three-man crew made a visual check.

The B-17 was ready to land.

A lot was riding on this check flight. Walt's qualification to fly B-17s hung in the balance, and more than a few bets were riding on his success.

That morning only three points had separated him from second-place Randall Katz, a former insurance salesman from Dayton, Ohio. Popular sentiment was with Walt Morgan. Katz was an obnoxious, foul-mouthed braggart who had been suspected of sabotaging the efforts of several promising flyers in the squadron. Some of these had washed out of the program as a result.

It wasn't so much that Walt wanted to win top honors; all he really cared about was being certified so that he could get into the war. He just couldn't bear the thought of Randall Katz being honored as the outstanding pilot of the squadron, the example for other pilots to follow. The image of Katz earning the squadron's top award settled with him about as well as a greasy hamburger would settle in the stomach of a flight-sick civilian. So when it became clear that it was either him or Katz, Walt Morgan fixed his sights on the top spot.

From the start he and Katz had been battling back and forth. First one would take the lead, then the other. Neither of them seemed able to hold onto the top spot for long. Soon it became clear that the squadron's premier pilot would not be determined until the final check flights were concluded on the final day.

When Walt swung his legs up into the belly of his B-17, Katz had already completed his final check flight. He'd aced it. The pressure was on. Walt would have to fly a near perfect flight in order to maintain his narrow lead over Katz. A single mistake and Katz would win.

Walt's odds of winning dipped appreciatively when it was announced that he would be evaluated by Squadron Commander Major Eugene Shaw while Katz had been paired with the more genial director of flying, Captain George McCarver.

It was Major Shaw who had predicted failure for many of the trainees the first day they arrived at Lockbourne. In a short but volatile speech he voiced his displeasure over the inferior caliber of recent trainees who had been sent to him, and he vowed to weed out all the unsuitable candidates. For those who remained the major promised them that their meager skills would be honed— and here he employed a proverb—as iron sharpens iron. He left little doubt as to who would play the role of the grinding abrasive.

Walt Morgan clenched his teeth. It was all he could do to maintain enough pressure on the rudder pedal to keep the hulking aircraft from slipping off course. His cheeks shook from the physical strain; streams of perspiration raced down them and dripped from the ridge of his jaw.

The camouflaged wings passed over the edge of the runway.

Black streaks where other planes had touched down raced with increasing speed beneath them. Walt grimaced. His leg was cramping. Hold on, just a little farther.

There was a soft thud as the main wheels touched the ground. At this speed, by design, the plane instinctively wanted to take wing again. Walt asserted his control over the machine. He coaxed the plane until the nose wheel touched down. That done, it resigned itself to being earth-bound again. Walt throttled back.

The freely swiveling tail wheel had no steering capabilities. The aircraft's direction on the ground was determined by manipulating the throttle controls. And because engines three and four were dead, the aircraft began drifting to the right.

"Taxi over there and line up beside that B-17." Pointing with his pencil, Major Shaw identified the spot. It was to the left.

"Yes, sir!" Walt replied. Throttling forward, he guided the airplane in a large looping circle to the right.

A gaggle of mechanics and pilot trainees had gathered near the hangars, drawn into the open by the aircraft that was landing with only two engines. Now, they watched in amusement as the craft left the runway, cut a circle through the grass, crossed over the runway again, and came to a rest.

It was precisely where the eraser tip of Major Shaw's pencil had indicated. Walt cut the engines.

An inverted grin hung heavy on Major Shaw's jowls as he scribbled casually on the clipboard.

"The results will be posted on the bulletin board," he said, lifting himself from the copilot's seat. Captain McCarver made way for him as he climbed out of the plane.

Captain McCarver moved into the cockpit beside Walt. Together they watched the major as he headed toward the hangars.

"Walt, you handled this bird like a veteran," McCarver said.

"So you think Shaw will certify me?"

McCarver's answer was slow in coming. "To be frank, I don't know. For months he's been bellyachin' for more funds for training. The army won't give it to him. So he's been looking for a way to prove to them that our pilots are undertrained and ill-prepared to enter a war zone. He needs a scapegoat; someone, real or imagined, he can point to as an example of inadequate training."

"Why me?"

"You're the top of the class. If he can prove that the very best is inadequately trained, in effect he disqualifies the entire program. What better way to convince the powers-that-be that he needs more money?"

Walt grabbed the post-landing checklist.

McCarver took it from him and moved into the copilot's seat preparing himself to run through the list with Walt. He said, "If you ever tell anyone I said this, I'll deny it to your face."

Walt looked at the director of flying.

"I was hoping Shaw would find his scapegoat in Katz."

※

A week before the Women's Flying Training program had its official start, Jacqueline Cochran acquired an additional PT-19 trainer plane. There was a condition attached to the acquisition. Someone would have to pick it up and fly it to Houston.

Alex was selected for the task.

Taking a train to Camp Gordon, Georgia, she signed for the trainer and filed a flight plan for Houston. A storm front threatened from the Gulf so she took to the air immediately, hoping to stay ahead of it.

She was in the air only a couple of hours when ominous black clouds threatened to overtake her. In the open cockpit the air against her cheeks turned heavy with moisture. Winds buffeted the plane.

She had no choice. She'd have to land.

Checking her charts Alex located the nearest army base, Camp Ellis. As the sky closed above her in anger, she nosed the trainer downward to a precariously low altitude. She had to stay beneath the clouds, otherwise she'd never find the base.

The wind picked up. Alex gripped the controls until her knuckles ached. It was the worst weather she'd flown in. One minute it was sucking her up into the clouds, the next it was trying to dash her against the earth. Raindrops slammed against her goggles and stung her face.

It was the first time since she was twelve years old that she didn't feel in control of an aircraft. It rose and plunged and slipped and, at times, nearly tumbled and there was nothing she could do about it. She *had* to land.

Just then, she spied the airfield.

The PT-19 was not equipped with a radio, so she would be arriving unannounced, which didn't seem to be a problem. Considering the weather, there wasn't exactly a traffic jam over the airfield. In fact, the sky was completely devoid of other aircraft. And she was eager to reduce that number by one more plane.

The landing was bumpy. A crosswind nearly swept her off the runway. But Alex refused to let the wind beat her, and soon she was taxiing toward the base's only hangar.

Never before had she been as grateful to be on the ground as she was at this moment. She climbed out of the cockpit and looked around. There was no one in sight. Everything was closed up or tied down in preparation for the storm.

Though it was only midday, the low black ceiling made it dark as night. Alex lifted her goggles. Better, but visibility was still restricted. She wandered toward a large shed with lighted windows. Pulling the door, she scooted through a sliver of an opening. The door slammed shut behind her.

A youthful lieutenant stood behind a counter leafing through a sheaf of papers. His lips formed silent numerals.

"Excuse me," Alex said. "I'm the pilot of the plane that just landed. I'd like to request a RON due to the severe flying conditions."

Without looking up, the lieutenant halted his count momentarily, his lips having just finished forming the number twenty-four. He showed her his palm as an indication that she'd have to wait, then he continued his count with a silent twenty-five.

At fifty-four the lieutenant came to the end of his stack. He wrote down the number on a sheet of paper that was set off to one side, then lifted the stack and banged it against the counter until the edges were uniform.

"A RON?" he asked with a bored tone.

"A Remain Over Night request."

An exasperated line spread thin his lips. "I know what a RON is," he said.

Alex had pulled off her flying cap. Dark brown hair fell nearly to her shoulders. The sight of her hair wiped the exasperated look from the lieutenant's face and replaced it with a dumbfounded expression with, in Alex's opinion, an emphasis on dumb.

"Since you know what a RON is," she said, "you shouldn't have any trouble finding one for me then, should you?"

"Major!" Without taking his eyes off Alex, the lieutenant called over his shoulder in the direction of an office door. "Major!" he called again.

The door rattled before it opened, as though someone missed the knob and ran into the door that was supposed to have opened, but didn't. The rattling was accompanied by cursing. The door swung open and out stepped a large man in a major's uniform.

His mouth, which clenched a cigar, looked as though it had not known a smile in over a decade. The man's waist was as round as the top of his head was bald. The buttons on his shirt strained to hold back the burgeoning flesh behind it.

"What is it, Davis?" the major bellowed.

"Sir, it's a girl." The lieutenant pointed at Alex.

The major's eyes squinted hard at Alex while his teeth clamped down on the chewed end of the cigar. "How did you get on base?" he yelled.

"I flew in," Alex said. Men like the major didn't intimidate her. She'd witnessed bullying tactics and experienced them firsthand before. "It's not safe to fly. All I'm asking for is a RON. God willing, the weather will clear and I'll be on my way in the morning."

"A RON," the major repeated.

"Yes, sir," Alex replied.

The major squinted and chewed. "How did you get past my guards?"

"I told you, I flew in." She moved to a window and pointed. "That PT-19. The one beside the hangar."

The major looked askance at Lieutenant Davis. "She's more brazen than most, isn't she?"

Lieutenant Davis nodded.

"I'm not buying it, lady," the major said. "There's only one reason why a woman would be on an army base...."

Alex's face reddened as quick as a photographer's flash. "Major ..." she looked at his nameplate, "Wyndham, I will overlook your filthy-minded innuendo. Just give me a bunk and I'll be out of your hair."

The cliché was out before she could stop herself. If the balding Wyndham was offended, he didn't show it.

"Get off my base," he said.

"Major Wyndham, I will not leave my plane unattended."

"Get off my base!"

"You don't believe I flew a plane in here, do you?"

Wyndham gave her a sarcastic look. "No, I don't."

"That plane is property of the Women's Flying Training Detachment in Houston, Texas." Pointing to a phone, she said, "Jacqueline Cochran can vouch for me."

"There is no such thing as a women's training whatever," said Wyndham.

"Call!" Alex insisted. "You'll find I'm telling the truth."

After staring at Alex for nearly a minute, Wyndham glanced at Lieutenant Davis and nodded. Alex gave him the number of the municipal airport.

Davis made the connection and requested to be transferred to Jacqueline Cochran. He held his hand over the receiver and said, "They never heard of her."

"At the Women's Flying Training Detachment!" Alex explained.

Davis repeated her instruction. Covering the phone again, he said, "This guy never heard of it either."

"Give me the phone!" Alex shouted. Leaning over the counter, she snatched it off the lieutenant's ear. "Who is this? Mr. Edwards, how long have you worked there? Three years. Good. At the end of the runway there is a five-room shed and hangar that used to belong to Aviation Enterprises, Ltd. Are you familiar with that hangar? Yes, I know they moved out. Do you know who moved in? Yes, that's it. The Women's Flying Training Detachment."

She handed the phone back to Davis who nodded, then said to the major, "He claims it's there now. He's connecting me."

The three of them looked at one another while Lieutenant Davis waited for the connection to be completed.

After a time, Davis began counting. "Five rings … six … seven … eight …" He hung up. "No answer," he said.

Wyndham looked at him. "Call the MPs," he said.

Two broad-shouldered, armed, unsmiling soldiers came for Alex. They loaded her in a jeep and drove her off base.

"Where's the nearest town?" Alex asked them, standing on civilian ground.

"Five miles down the road," one of the MPs said, pointing the direction.

As Alex began walking toward the town, the skies unburdened themselves. Within a half mile, she was drenched. By the time she reached town, she was soaked to the bone and shivering.

She found a motel for the night. The next morning dawned sunny with a spattering of leftover clouds. Alex walked back to the base, walked the perimeter until she found an isolated section of fence, climbed over, sneaked to her airplane, and was in the sky before anyone could stop her.

She vowed never again to set foot in Camp Ellis.

"It's up! The results of the check flight!"

Walt took a deep breath and relaxed in his chair. There was no use going to the bulletin board. A stampede preceded him. Those who had placed bets on who would get the squadron's top award were anxious to see if they'd won or lost.

"It's Morgan! It's Morgan!" one of the winners shouted.

Drawn by the commotion, Randall Katz wandered into the room. When the news registered with him, he shot a look of pure hatred at Walt Morgan.

6

Alice stepped through a looking glass. Dorothy Gale of Kansas swung wide her farmhouse door and stepped into the land of Oz. Nat Morgan's crossing of a threshold was no less strange or startling. He stepped into the world of the United States Army.

His first impression of the induction center was that his experience was the opposite of that of the Kansas farm girl as portrayed in the MGM cinematic production. While the film cleverly spliced black-and-white farm footage to contrast with the Technicolor of Oz, Nat left behind a world of color for a world of drab olive green.

One aspect of the crossing, however, he found identical to Dorothy Gale's experience. He was in odd and unfamiliar territory. He would undoubtedly be called upon to make some personal adjustments. No problem. He'd always considered himself flexible, easygoing, able to adjust.

Just inside the door he came face-to-face with a short-haired, olive-green-clad man with a crooked nose and a single fold of skin for a neck. The man was seated behind a small wooden table. One hand held a sheaf of papers, the other a pencil.

"Name?"

"Nat Morgan."

Sarcastic eyes squinted at him in exasperation. Nat had been in this new world only a few seconds and already he was made to feel stupid.

"Last name first, first name, middle initial."

"Oh! Sorry. Ummm … Morgan, Nat … well, legally it's Nathaniel, Dean … I mean D. You only wanted the initial, didn't you?"

Squinty eyes stared disdainfully at him.

Reading the upside-down print, Nat spotted his name on the list. He pointed to it, repeating it as printed. "Morgan, Nathaniel D. Right there."

A heavy check was placed next to Nat's name. Behind him, the door swung open and a wide-eyed recruit with a boyish face poked his head in. He looked like a frightened rabbit checking a forest clearing for predators.

Looking past Nat at the boy, a wolfish grin turned up the corners of the soldier's mouth. With his eyes fixed on the boy, the soldier gave Nat his first army order.

"Line to the right."

Nat glanced right. Young men of various dress and size formed a scraggly line leading into a room. Without exception they had positioned themselves so they could see the activity inside. From Nat's vantage point, he was unable to discern what was attracting them.

"Excuse me," Nat said, returning his attention to the man behind the desk. "I'm a photographer. Who do I talk to about being assigned …?"

"Line to the right," the man with the crooked nose repeated.

"That's the line for assignments?"

Taking his eyes off the boyish recruit who, still rabbitlike, had inched his way inside the door, the soldier fixed them on Nat. The man's eyes were as hard and gray as musket balls.

"Line ... to ... the ... right!" he growled.

Nat noticed the two chevrons on the man's sleeve. He didn't know yet what rank they signified, but he knew enough to know they didn't mean much. "I'm simply asking for a little information," he said. "When I enlisted, the recruiter told me that I could probably ..."

Scraping wooden chair legs interrupted him as Crooked Nose rose ominously behind the desk. The man's hands, balled into fists, pressed against the sheaf of papers as he leaned forward to within an inch of Nat's face. The man's forehead and cheeks were scarlet, accentuating his colorless crooked nose, which bunched up like accordion bellows. When he spoke, the man's breath reeked of onions and knockwurst.

"Look, soldier," he bellowed, "I don't know nothin'! Got it? Alls I know is, 'Line to the right!' Now get into the line to the right!"

No longer was the row of scraggly recruits peering through the doorway. They had found a new diversion in Nat and Crooked Nose.

Nat had always taken pride in his ability to get along with people. It was essential in his line of work as a portrait photographer. The moment someone walked through the studio door it was his job to build a relationship that would result in a relaxed, serene portrait of his client.

Naturally, he'd met all kinds of people. Most of them entered the studio doors exhibiting some degree of tension. Either they had rushed to make the appointment, or they were uncomfortable with the formal clothes normally worn for portraits, or they hated the way photographs made them look. But whatever their anxiety, Nat would put them at ease. He liked to borrow Will Rogers' famous line and say that he'd never met a man he didn't like.

Crooked Nose was an exception.

Nevertheless, not wanting to draw unfavorable attention to himself on his first day in the army, Nat walked over and took his place at the end of the scraggly line.

As the line snaked its way forward and Nat crossed another threshold, he received his second army order.

"Keep it moving, soldier!"

A long-faced barber barked at him, with one hand motioning for Nat to sit in a recently vacated barber's chair, while his other hand held high a buzzing set of hair clippers. A pile of black, blond, red, and brown hair engulfed the barber's boots.

Nat's backside no sooner hit the chair than clumps of his hair tumbled past his shoulders, falling on top of the growing mountain on the floor. In a matter of moments it was over. There was no talk of the weather or the war or the Padres minor league baseball team.

Nat felt like a sheep who had been sheared.

"Next!" Horse Face yelled from behind him. "Come on, soldier, move it! Move it!"

Wading through the rising tide of hair, Nat followed those who preceded him through the room's only other doorway.

"Strip!"

Another soldier in drab green greeted everyone who emerged from the doorway with the same one-word greeting. If you could call it a greeting. He stood against the adjacent hallway wall, his hands resting belt-level behind him. He gave the command without expression, without making eye contact, and without explanation. A scratched record could have done his job just as well.

"Strip! Strip! Strip! Strip! Strip!"

All around Nat men began taking off their clothes.

"Everything?" Nat asked.

The hallway soldier turned his head toward Nat, his eyes hardened. "Strip!" he shouted.

Nat began removing his clothes.

Moments later, another unsmiling soldier in drab green appeared at the end of the hallway. He ordered everyone to gather up his clothing and led them past a window where they were ordered to hand everything to still another soldier.

As Nat's clothing was whisked away, he felt a sudden unexplainable sense of loss. The feeling wasn't based on the value of the clothing, sentimental or otherwise. It was as though he had just surrendered the last vestige of his identity without knowing if he'd ever get it back.

Along with a host of other pink bodies, Nat was herded up a flight of stairs to another doorway where another line had formed. The coolness of a bare head together with the chill of the green tile floor beneath his bare feet caused him to shiver. He could feel chill bumps growing on his legs and arms.

He wasn't the only one. The back of the man immediately preceding him in line had a generous display of bumps stretching from wing-bone to wing-bone.

Suddenly, an embarrassed panic swept over Nat when he realized he was staring at another man's bare flesh. He averted his eyes just as the man turned around.

"Physical," the man said. With a nod of his head, he motioned for Nat to follow his gaze through the open door ahead of them where a green uniformed man was seen holding an inductee's tongue down with a depressor while he shined a light in the man's mouth.

Nat nodded, self-consciously aware of their lack of clothing.

There was a time when Nat found it difficult to meet new people. The business of portrait photography had helped him overcome his shyness. At the moment, however, the awkward shyness had returned. He attributed its reappearance to the fact that he was accustomed to meeting people clothed.

His mind flashed to dreams he'd had where he'd been in this very predicament. On occasion he had dreamed of finding himself in stages of undress in a school classroom or at church. Once he dreamed he was feeding pigeons at the Horton Plaza fountain in the middle of downtown San Diego. With the dream came shame and embarrassment.

So why was he surprised at the appearance of these twin emotions now? Maybe it was the fact that in his dream he was the only one naked. In his present reality, he was one of many.

Having stumbled upon that difference, he'd hoped it would help. It didn't. He wondered if everyone else in line was experiencing the same discomfort.

"You a navy washout too?" the man ahead of him asked. He stood casually with his arms folded across a chest carpeted heavily with black hair as though they were meeting at Fourth and Broadway.

The man's eyebrows were incredibly bushy, probably more so now that his head was bald. When he spoke they looked like two twitching caterpillars.

"Washed out?" Nat asked, making an effort to keep from staring at the caterpillars.

"Yeah. I tried to get into the navy. Was washed out 'cause of my eyes. Navy has somethin' against guys who wear glasses."

A puzzled frown formed on Nat's face as the comment prompted him to look for glasses he knew weren't there.

"Don't have to wear 'em all the time," the man explained. "That's why I thought the navy might let me in."

"The army was my first choice," Nat said.

"What? You crazy or somethin'?"

"No, I'm a photographer. Didn't want to spend my time in the service developing pictures of gray bulkheads."

"A photographer? Really?"

"Yeah."

"And you want to take pictures for the army?"

"That's the plan."

The caterpillars on the man's brow nearly kissed as they met at the bridge of his nose to form a sarcastic frown. "Don't bet on it," he said dryly.

"Why not?"

"If you really want to be a photographer, you'd be better off tellin' 'em you're a shoe salesman or an electrician or somethin'. The army don't like givin' guys jobs they already know. I had two buddies in high school. One of 'em was a crack mechanic, could rebuild an engine and have it purrin' in two days. You know what the army made him? A cook. The other guy was a baker. Went into his father's bread business after graduation. You know what he's doin' now?"

Nat shook his head.

"Heavy weapons. Water-cooled machine guns and them big mortars."

"But it only makes sense that the army would want to utilize a person's talent and experience."

"See? That's where you got it all wrong! The army don't make no sense! Never has, never will! If they needs tank drivers, they'll make you a tank driver. They don't care nothin' about your civilian training. Trust me. I know about these things. You see, my dad and grandpa and uncle was all in the army, the whole family, for generations."

"So then why did you try to join the navy?"

"I hate my old man. Simple as that. By the way, my name's Kotter." He extended his hand.

There was something Nat found oddly repulsive about shaking the hand of an unclothed man, a gesture he wouldn't have thought twice about had the man been clothed. Nat overcame his revulsion and gave the man's hand a quick single shake.

"My name's Morgan," he said.

Nat Morgan followed Kotter through what seemed an entire regiment of inoculation needles. Not only was he punctured repeatedly, but every inch of him was scrutinized, inside and out—eyes, ears, throat, teeth, heart, lungs, and liver.

Following the physical they were corralled through yet another line where they were loaded down with underclothes and pants and shirts and jackets and hats and blankets and bedding and papers and manuals and a pillow.

Nat, being one of the taller inductees, could barely see over the stack in his arms, which he eventually managed to hold in place with his chin. Other shorter men weren't so lucky. Towers of clothing and papers and books toppled every which way.

They were led to a barracks that featured long rows of bunk beds lining the walls. The rest of their day was spent making beds, reading manuals, and being called out to assembly after assembly for a myriad of announcements.

Their first trip to the mess hall was followed by a lecture from a brigadier general whose leathery brown face reminded Nat of a basset hound. The general spoke of the proud tradition of the Third Infantry Division of which they were now a part. His lecture was laced with generous praise for the American fighting tradition and more than a few contemptuous remarks for the Japanese Empire, German aggression, and Adolf Hitler personally. After predicting that America would once again make the world safe for democracy, he dismissed them.

The raw recruits were then marched back to their barracks. Lights-out followed quickly thereafter.

Sleep was elusive for Nat. He couldn't lie on his side because the shoulder he normally slept on throbbed from the repeated violations it had suffered. In addition, his stubbled head scratched unnaturally against the pillow. And the breathing sounds and snores and moans and grunts of dozens of men who shared his sleeping quarters combined with the squeaks of springs and the groans of metal beds to create a symphony of disturbances. Nat doubted he would ever adjust to these conditions.

He felt like he was in the state penitentiary. He could not come and go as he pleased. He was told what to do and when to do it. He was constantly standing in one line or another. They all looked the same, dressed the same, ate the same thing, did the same things, worked together, showered together, and now slept together.

He'd been in the army's world for less than twenty-four hours and already he was sharing intimacies with strangers he'd never shared with family.

Nat lay on his back staring up at the springs and mattress of the top bunk that swayed in the middle from Kotter's weight. He wanted to turn over onto the shoulder that didn't throb, but movement set the springs to squeaking and he didn't want to disturb anybody.

His mind meandered from incident to incident in his brief but already unforgettable army pilgrimage. Kotter's words came back to him.

The army don't like givin' guys jobs they already know.

Maybe not as a rule, but Nat Morgan was going to be the exception. He needed something familiar; something in which he could excel. Besides, there were times when photographers acted alone. Not even the army would send five hundred photographers out on a mission together. Then there was darkroom time. Developing negatives. Making enlargements. These things were done individually. As a photographer he could at least have a semblance of private life.

Besides, he was a photographer. He didn't want to do anything else.

In the inky black darkness of his company's barracks, Nat Morgan determined that he would become an army photographer. No matter what forces arrayed against him, he would overcome them.

His sanity depended upon it.

※

The army. Another day, another line.

Having endured hour after hour of basic orientation, marching drills, and aptitude tests, Nat stood in line. This was the day for which he had prepared himself. This was the line in which duty assignments were made.

One by one, the men approached a small table outside their barracks. The table was manned by two soldiers. One found each soldier's name on a sheet of paper and gave him the corresponding assignment.

The majority of the men were pulling infantry duty. This was evident by the way the second man who stood next to the table reached into one of several stacked wooden crates and produced a rifle, which he handed to recruit after recruit.

"I hear they're lookin' for medics."

Nat recognized the voice behind him. It was Kotter.

"I don't want to be a medic," Nat said.

"Neither do I, but it sure beats bein' a foot soldier. Medics wear them big red crosses on their helmets, the ones that say to the Jerries, 'Don't shoot at me, I'm only a medic!'"

"So what are you going to do to convince them to make you a medic?"

Kotter grinned a foxy grin. "I'm tellin' 'em I come from a long line of army foot soldiers and that I joined this man's army for one reason and one reason only, and that's to be a foot soldier."

"And that'll make you a medic?"

"Or a cook, or a truck driver, who cares? As long as they don't hand me one of them guns."

Nat shook his head doubtfully. "I don't know …"

"That's the army way, Sherlock! They can't give you what you want, so's you ask for what you don't want so's you won't get it."

"I'm holding out for a photographer's assignment," Nat said.

"Welcome to the infantry!" Kotter said. "But don't say I didn't warn you."

It was Nat's turn to approach the table. With a deep breath he filled his lungs with air and his heart with resolve. He was determined not to leave that table until they promised him a camera.

Then he got a look at the two chevrons on the sleeve of the man seated behind the table and his steely resolve liquefied and melted into his boots.

Corporal Crooked Nose.

"Name!" the corporal barked without looking up. Beside him a private was already reaching into the wooden box for another rifle.

"Morgan, Nathaniel D."

The corporal's head remained lowered as he flipped a page and scanned down the list of names.

Had he forgotten already? Nat could only hope.

As a beefy finger ran over the MAs and MCs and MEs and MIs and approached the MOs, it slowed. Corporal Crooked Nose looked up. A snide grin creased his ugly face.

"The photographer?" he asked.

Nat mustered as much of the melted resolve from his boots as he could and said, "Corporal, I strongly request …"

Corporal Crooked Nose wasn't listening. With a flick of his finger and a smile of evil delight he said to the private, "Hand this man a rifle."

Nat stared at the rifle in the private's outstretched hands as though it were a rattlesnake. Somehow he knew that if he touched it, he would die. Not immediately. Eventually. In some French or German field. And some photographer would see him and take a picture of him with his vacant eyes staring up at the sky with flies crawling in and out of his open mouth—the kind of pictures Matthew Brady took of the Civil War dead.

Suddenly, it was crystal clear to him. He knew this would happen to him if he touched the rifle. He wasn't cut out to be an infantryman. He had no business handling a rifle.

What happened in the next few moments would determine his destiny. It all came down to this moment. Somehow he had to convince Corporal Crooked Nose.

Keeping his hands defiantly at his side, Nat ignored the private's outstretched arms.

"Corporal," he said, "I urge you to reconsider."

Corporal Crooked Nose had anticipated an objection. Skipping several steps from their first encounter, he jumped to his feet. His chair flew backward. His gray, musket-ball eyes quivered with such intensity that it drew all attention away from the man's broken nose.

"Take the rifle!" he ordered.

"I'm a photographer, not an infantryman."

Calling down a string of curses upon Nat Morgan's head, the corporal bellowed, "I SAID, 'Take the rifle!'"

The private holding the rifle jumped back at the corporal's thundering rage. Nat's instincts told him to take a step back too. He resisted them. But it was all he could do to hold his ground.

He said, "Corporal, I insist that I speak to your superior off …"

"TAKE THE RIFLE!" With one swipe, the wooden table went flying, papers fluttered to the dirt, leaving nothing between Crooked Nose and Nat. The corporal's face was beet-red, arteries bulged in his neck, his fists shook with rage.

"I hear you're looking for medics," Kotter offered in a soothing voice from behind Nat.

"Corporal, what's the trouble here?" A youthful first lieutenant appeared. He couldn't have been a year, maybe two, older
than Nat.

Everything about him portrayed a poster-boy image. Not the
rugged army type, more like a sporting-goods model. His sandy-
colored hair was neatly trimmed. His skin was smooth and
tanned. There were sharp creases in his shirt and pants. There
was even a sun sparkle on the corner of his aviator-style sunglasses.

Corporal Crooked Nose snapped to attention. After saluting,
he pointed an accusing finger at Nat. "This man won't take his
rifle," he said.

Removing his sunglasses, the lieutenant took a step toward
Nat. Amusement lurked in the man's eyes. "Is that right, Private?
You're refusing to take the rifle?"

"Sir," Nat said, "I'm a photographer, not an infantryman." He
hesitated, then added, "Giving a rifle to me would be like handing
command of the entire Third Infantry to Gracie Allen."

The quip popped out without forethought. At the sound of the
radio entertainer's name, the lieutenant visibly started, the corporal scrunched his nose up even more, and the private stared on
dumbfoundedly.

No sooner had Nat said it, than he wished he hadn't. He knew
that humor was lost on army-types. He never should have said it.
It had just slipped out. But the mistake was made. He could
already feel the rifle in his hands.

Slowly, a grin formed on the lieutenant's face, one that
stretched from ear to ear. Dazzling white teeth appeared in a perfect smile. "Gracie Allen," he laughed. "Very good! I like that!"

Nat risked a smile. Crooked Nose glared unhappily.

"Or, how about this one," the lieutenant offered playfully. "Giving you a rifle would be like putting Fibber McGee in charge of supplies!"

Nat laughed at the reference to the radio comedian's running joke of opening his hall closet door only to have its contents come crashing down around him. Quoting McGee's standard line, he said, "Gotta straighten out that closet one of these days!"

The lieutenant pointed a finger at him and guffawed, pleased that Nat had made the connection. "'Tain't funny, McGee!" he said laughing, using another of the comedian's well-known lines. Then he said, "What did you do before the army, soldier? Besides listening to radio programs, that is."

"I'm a photographer, sir."

"A photographer?"

"Yessir. I specialize in portraits, but I'm experienced in other kinds of photography as well. Before getting hired at Odgen Wells Studios, I was a stringer for the San ..."

"Odgen Wells?" the lieutenant repeated. "Impressive ..." He thought a moment. Then, donning his sunglasses, he said, "Soldier, come with me."

"But, sir!" Corporal Crooked Nose objected. He searched the ground frantically for the appropriate paper. Finding it, he pointed to Nat's name. "Sir, my orders are that this man is to be assigned to the infantry."

The printing on the paper did nothing to deter the lieutenant. "Orders can be changed," he said. "Carry on."

"But, sir!"

"Carry on, Corporal!"

The paper bearing Nat's name crumpled in the corporal's hand. With the other hand, he saluted. "Yes, sir."

The lieutenant turned and walked away. Nat followed after him. He had no idea where they were going or what he would be doing, but at the moment it didn't matter. He was walking away from the rifle and Corporal Crooked Nose.

Behind him he could hear the corporal ordering the private to right the table. A moment later, the corporal's distant voice could be heard again.

"Name!"

"Kotter, William P."

There was a moment of silence, then Kotter's voice could be heard again.

"Corporal, I come from a long line of infantrymen. It's a proud tradition in our family. My only request is that I be allowed to continue this tradition."

Nat couldn't help himself. He had to turn around to see if Kotter's ploy would work. Walking backward, he watched as the corporal motioned to the private to hand Kotter a rifle. The private offered the piece that had been meant for him to Kotter.

Kotter stared at it dumbly. "But ..."

"Take the rifle, soldier!" the corporal said.

"I hear you need medics," Kotter stammered.

Corporal Crooked Nose slammed his fist on the table, cursed, and shouted, "Take the rifle!"

7

"Hey, kid, aren't you the canary whose parents won't let her sing at a nightclub?"

Lily paused in the application of her lipstick. The smudged mirror reflection of the woman squeezing next to her revealed a woman who was attempting to stave off an attack of wrinkles with generous applications of makeup. Heavy cosmetic layers gave testimony to the woman's desperate but futile battle.

With a flourish that reminded Lily of one of the Three Musketeers drawing his sword, the blonde unsheathed her lipstick, puckered at her own reflection and began to paint her lips passionate red. Lily scooted to one side to give the woman room, which she quickly occupied.

Returning her attention to her own lips, Lily said, "My parents don't like the idea that I'm singing in a place that serves liquor."

The woman wrinkled her nose in disdain. "Holy Rollers, huh?"

"If you mean by that that they're God-fearing people, then yes, I guess they are."

Passionate red lips turned upward at the corners. "But you're singin' tonight anyway? Good for you, kid!"

"It's my last night," Lily said, sheathing her own lipstick in its tube. "My original agreement with Mr. Maxy was only for two nights. I'm simply fulfilling my agreement." She stepped back to take a look at herself. Full blonde hair with natural curls fell to her shoulders. A fashionable red lily added a splash of color to it. Sparkling blue eyes were set above a delicate nose. A single bare lightbulb cast dark shadows against extremely fair skin. The elderly ladies in church called it alabaster; the kids on the playground when she was growing up called her Snow White.

"Let me get this straight," the woman said. "You're gonna quit this gig just because your parents don't like liquor?"

Lily's hesitation indicated that the decision had not been an easy one for her. Adjusting long white sleeves that were slightly askew, she said, "I'll have other chances to sing."

Turning around, the woman leaned against the dressing room table. "How old are you, honey?"

"Nineteen."

"Nineteen? You're old enough to do whatever you want!"

"They're still my parents."

The woman shook her head sadly. "You're gonna have to cut the cord someday, honey. Have they ever heard you sing?"

"Lots of times. In church … glee club …"

"I mean at a place like this. Honey, I've worked here for nearly twenty years. I've seen 'em come and go, and I'm here to tell you, you've got it!"

Lily's face warmed. "Thank you."

"I'm serious, kid! You've got a set of pipes that won't quit. You could be a recording star."

"They heard me last night … my parents. They came because Maxy offered me a permanent job."

"And you're not taking it?" the woman asked. "Honey, you've got a lot of growing up to do."

The dressing room door swung open. A short man with a black horseshoe ring for hair and a cigar clenched in his teeth said, "Five minutes, Lil."

Muted horns playing "Moonlight Serenade" wafted through the opening.

"Harriet! What are you doin' in here?" the short man yelled.

"I'm takin' my break, Maxy!" She pulled out a pack of Chesterfields and lit one. "What does it look like I'm doin'?"

"So what are you up to now? Three breaks an hour?"

Harriet replied by blowing smoke at her boss who disappeared before it reached him.

Lily checked the flower in her hair, her dress, and her makeup one last time.

Removing a couple of bottles of cleanser from the room's only chair, Harriet plopped next to the mop and pail in a corner and watched her.

"You get nervous before you perform, kid?"

"A little."

Taking a long drag on the cigarette, Harriet let loose a long string of smoke that was beginning to cloud the room. "I heard you last night. Nothing to be nervous about," she said. "Not with the pipes you got. And if I were you, I'd tell my parents to take a leap. This isn't exactly the Cotton Club, but more than a couple big names got their start with Maxy."

Satisfied with what she saw in the mirror, Lily turned toward the door. "Nice to meet you, Harriet."

"Break a leg, kid."

Lily stood in the wings waiting to be introduced. She tingled inside. It was a good feeling—enough of a tingle to dispel her natural shyness, not enough to cause stage fright.

Closing her eyes, she relished the feeling. Nothing else in the world made her feel more alive than when she was onstage and singing.

She'd seen other people—people with gifted voices—tremble to the point of incapacity the moment they stepped on a stage. It was not something with which she could identify. She could not recall a time when she was afraid to be in front of a crowd. Just the opposite. The lights. The microphone. The music. The audience. The feel of her own voice. These things energized her.

Personal conversations. Small talk. Meeting new people. Carrying on a conversation with someone you don't know—like Harriet in the dressing room—these were the things that made her nervous, self-conscious.

Give her a stage any day.

It sure beat school and volunteering at the filter center. Having recently graduated from high school, San Diego State College and an elementary education degree loomed ahead. It would be the practical thing to do. But practical didn't give her the feeling she got while singing.

The filter center was her contribution to the war effort. Responding to a civil defense ad posted on the church bulletin board, Lily applied and was tested for a position. Located on the southwest corner of Third and Broadway, the filter center received calls from spotters all over San Diego County who phoned in to report airplane sightings. The courses of the planes were plotted on a large center board. Any plane that could not be identified was reported to the military, which would send an aircraft to intercept it. From 4:00 p.m. to 8:00 p.m. three nights a week Lily had manned one of the phones. A week ago, her cool-headedness during a crisis had caught the attention of her supervisor who promoted her to spotter.

It was interesting and necessary work. But it wasn't singing.

Maxy strode self-importantly to center stage to a chorus of good-natured razzing from the audience. The razzing increased a notch when he had to lower the microphone.

"All right, you longhairs," he began.

"Better than being a no-hair!" a heckler shouted.

The place erupted with laughter and clapping as Maxy rubbed the top of his head and laughed with them.

When the laughter died down a bit, he said, "You bums don't deserve what's comin' next, but I've already paid her so I have no choice but to bring her out."

Lily performed one final check. Flower. Hair. One final hand brush of her dress.

"Ladies and gentlemen … Maxy's is proud to introduce one of the finest canaries it's been my pleasure to introduce—and that ain't no joke, I mean it—ladies and gentlemen, I give you Liltin' Lil Morgan!"

Maxy gestured toward Lily. Her cue. As she stepped into the spotlights, he joined in the applause. With two spotlights on her, Lily could see the stage and nothing else. Sounds of an audience came from a black void.

The instant she appeared, the band played the introduction to her first number, "Swing Low, Sweet Chariot."

Maxy adjusted the microphone for her and then backed off-stage, still clapping. From the mainly male audience, there were several catcalls, invitations, and wolfish howls.

There was a time when Lily would have been distracted by such things. Uncomfortable with her beauty, she was self-conscious with the way people looked at her. She wished they would stop staring at her long enough to listen to her voice.

Once, when she confided her frustration to her mother, her mother told her, "Dear, whenever that happens, sing in such a way that they forget all about your looks."

As Lily stepped up to the microphone, she reminded herself of her mother's advice. She began to sing.

From the first note, she was in command. By the end of the first verse, the audience was under her spell. They were so quiet, it was as though she were singing to an empty warehouse. Even when the last word and the last note had died away, there was silence.

A long silent beat.

Then applause. Enthusiastic, thunderous applause erupted from the darkness.

And no wolf sounds.

"Thank you. Thank you very much."

She stepped back from the microphone. The applause continued. She bowed slightly. Still there was applause.

Approaching the microphone, she said, "Thank you. Thank you very much. According to American legend …"

She had to wait for the applause to abate.

"According to American legend, that song was inspired by an incident that occurred in the Old South. A slave woman in Tennessee, who had been sold and was about to be separated from her daughter, was just about ready to throw herself and her child into the Cumberland River when an old woman halted her. The old woman said, 'Don't do it, missy. Don't do it. Let me reads the Lord's scroll to you and let the chariot of the Lord swing low for you.' Well, according to the legend, the old woman's reading saved the woman and child that day.

"I've loved that song since I was a little girl. So you can imagine my delight when Tommy Dorsey came out with this arrangement."

Applause for the nationally known big band leader allowed Lily the time to nod to Maxy's bandleader who launched into the next song.

"Here's another of my favorites," Lily said. "'I Cried for You.'"

Generous applause indicated it was a favorite with many in the audience as well.

This was Lily's showcase song. It contained everything she needed to display her talent—emotion, phrasing, and range ... a high D-flat. And perfect pitch. You could tune a horn to Lily's voice. She was always on key and if you weren't with her, you were wrong.

Tonight she had the audience hanging on every note and she knew it. It was fantastic. No feeling in the world was quite like it ... a symbiosis of music and voice and audience. Only the second song of the set and already she and the band and the audience were knocked out, as the musicians called it—so totally engrossed with the song and the music that nothing else mattered. No, it was deeper than that. Nothing else even existed.

She hit the D-flat. Clear. Resonating. Powerful.

The note flowed through her, sustained by a taut diaphragm, formed into a thing of beauty by relaxed vocal cords, oscillating within her head, projected in such a way that it made people's hearts pulse with emotion.

The bandleader beamed with delight. He felt it too.

The audience cheered, not waiting for the song to end.

Lily glowed with pleasure. This was why she was born. She was a canary, and God made canaries for one purpose and one purpose only—to sing.

As the song concluded, the ovation rocked the room.

Then, as it began to die down, a single voice came out of the blackness.

"Schmaltz! Nothing but schmaltz!"

Lily's joy was tempered by the heckler's shout.

First one voice countered that of the heckler in defense of Lily, then another and another until there was a chorus of defense.

The heckler stood his ground. The occasional slur in his speech suggested that his behavior was bolstered by a few drinks.

"No, no, no, no … don't get me wrong! The little girl's got talent … she's good … but the songs she's singing … they're schmaltzy!"

Maxy appeared from the wings of the stage. Shielding his eyes with an uplifted hand, he peered intently in the vicinity of the heckler. His other hand directed security to that location. He ordered the houselights to be turned on.

The heckler persisted. "What is this? A church or a nightclub? The canary can sing schmaltz, but what I want to know is can she swing?"

As the houselights came up, Lily could see a man standing. Impeccably dressed in a navy pinstripe suit. Dark wavy hair was combed back stylishly. A gorgeous blonde sat on his right, an equally stunning brunette on his left. No one at his table seemed put off by his disruptive behavior. In fact, they seemed entertained by it.

"Can she, Maxy? Can she swing?"

"Jerry? Is that you?" Maxy shouted.

The heckler opened his arms wide and matched it with a toothy white grin.

"Ladies and gentlemen!" Maxy shouted. "Jerry Jupiter!"

The audience needed no further introduction. They burst into enthusiastic applause, which Jupiter drank in. Every hand clap.

Maxy motioned to him with his arms. "Come up here! Come up here, Jerry!"

Jupiter waved him off halfheartedly. He wanted a little more coaxing.

"Ladies and gentlemen," Maxy motioned to the crowd now, "help me get him up here!"

The audience responded. Applause. Shouts. Enthusiastic

pleas. The women on each side of him looked bored. They'd seen this act before.

Lily clapped with them. For the first time in as long as she could remember she was nervous standing on a stage as this nationally known big bandleader made his way to the platform.

For a moment he disappeared through a backstage door. When he reappeared on stage the applause rose to a crescendo.

While Lily took a step backward, the spotlights hit Jerry Jupiter. Maxy was at the microphone. "For any longhairs in the audience, Jerry Jupiter was just named by *Downbeat* magazine as the most exciting new big band leader on the scene today!"

Applause.

"And this bum got his start right here at Maxy's!"

Maxy offered his hand enthusiastically to Jupiter, who took it and placed his arm around the shoulders of the smaller man. The response in the room was deafening.

Skillfully, Jupiter maneuvered his way in front of the microphone. He didn't speak until the last of the clapping died out.

"You never answered my question," he said.

Maxy's reply was a puzzled expression.

Still gripping Maxy's hand, with his arm still around Maxy's shoulder, the big band leader turned and stared at Lily.

He took his time about it.

Lily could feel the blush rising up her neck and into her cheeks.

"She's gorgeous, I'll give you that," Jupiter said. He stopped staring at her only long enough to direct his remarks into the microphone.

At his comment the wolf calls returned.

"I mean REALLY gorgeous!" he shouted into the microphone.

Wolf calls bounced off the walls.

"And she can sing," he said. "Schmaltzy, but she can sing. What I want to know is …"

He paused for dramatic effect. Then, turning squarely into the microphone he shouted, "BUT CAN SHE SWING?"

The audience was on their feet. Clapping. Shouting.

Maxy took the microphone.

"Can she swing?" he asked. "Can she *swing*?" Directing his next comment to Jupiter, he said, "You just plant yourself behind that mothbox of a piano and she may teach you a thing or two about swing!"

Playing to the audience, Jupiter made a face that said, "*Can she now?*" Then, adopting an I'll-be-the-judge-of-that attitude, he took a seat at the piano, which had been vacated for him. It took him several attempts to adjust the bench and limber his fingers, not that anyone in the club was going anywhere.

When he was finally set, he looked at Lily. "Do you know this one?" He plunked out a few notes.

Lily smiled sweetly and nodded.

From behind the piano Jerry Jupiter took control of the band. Lily approached the mike and sang.

"It don't mean a thing if it ain't got that swing …"

She started in a little tentatively. Jupiter's style was different from the arrangement Maxy's band used. But it didn't take but a moment for her to adjust.

There was a Jupiter improvisation thrown into the middle of the song, and when it ended it ended with a flourish.

The audience went wild.

For the rest of the evening Jupiter led the band from one song to another.

"A String of Pearls."

"Don't Sit Under the Apple Tree."

"Chattanooga Choo Choo."

People danced with abandon. The band never sounded better. Neither did Lily. It was as though she and Jupiter had rehearsed for weeks. He joined her on the piano mike for the duets.

The entire club was in the groove.

From the instant Jerry Jupiter took control of the band, the energy and level of playing rose to a higher plane.

Jupiter joined Lily beside the microphone.

"Cut the apple!" he shouted.

With a cheer the dancers formed circles numbering eight to ten people.

"Come on, come on! Swing! SWING!"

The dancers broke into a more violent version of the Charleston, which had been made popular a couple of decades earlier. Forward on the left foot, kick up the right foot, step back on the right, and kick the left to the rear.

The circles became a flurry of feet with arms and elbows flying in counter motion.

"Truck to the right!" Jupiter called.

Everyone faced right. Raising an index finger, they shook it while stepping forward and pivoting, first on one heel, then on another.

"Truck to the left!"

The circles reversed themselves as the band stepped up the tempo. The entire room was alive with heart-pounding sound and motion.

"Peck to the east!"

Dancers turned their heads left and made chicken-pecking motions.

"Peck to the west! And you peck and you peck and you peck your best!"

Lily glanced over at Jupiter as she followed the calls on stage. Perspiration glistened on his forehead and temples, streaming down the sides of his face. Perfect white teeth flashed in joyful celebration to the music and the beat and the spontaneous response of the crowd.

"Suzy-Q!" he shouted.

Each dancer clasped his hands together and swung his arms to the right while pivoting his feet to the left. The entire dance floor looked like Olympic hammer throwers warming up.

Jupiter cranked the band up even faster. Dancers danced to a frenzy. Lily's heart pounded excitedly, happily within her.

When the music reached a fever pitch, Jerry Jupiter threw his hands in the air, his face lifted high.

Lily too raised her hands and shouted. In the groove. Sent. Knocked out. The words had not yet been invented to describe the exultation she was feeling. This was what swing jazz was all about. This was the world in which she felt most alive.

Lily didn't want to leave. Except for those with mops in their hands and rags with which they wiped tables, there was no one else in the room.

To her it was a magical place. A room of music and dancing. How could she walk away from it? She didn't understand her parents' objections. What was so bad about singing in a place that served alcohol anyway? It wasn't as though she was drinking it herself.

She looked with dread at the doors leading outside. What lay beyond them? Boring college classrooms and slow hours at a dark filter center.

God had gifted her with song! Life wasn't worth living if she couldn't sing!

Just as she was about to walk out the doors, on the far side of the club Jerry Jupiter and Maxy appeared from backstage. Grinning, with uplifted hand, Jupiter hailed her. He excused himself and made his way through the labyrinth of tables and chairs.

Taking her hand in his he said loudly, "I just wanted to tell you how wonderful you were tonight!" Then, leaning close to her, he whispered, "Have you signed a contract with Maxy?"

Lily looked past Jupiter at Maxy who was occupied giving instructions to the cleanup crew. In response to Jupiter's question she shook her head.

He pressed a card into her hand. "Don't," he said. "I'll be in touch."

The next thing Lily knew Jupiter was off again with Maxy, bantering back and forth like they had done all night long.

8

Like a dream, Lily's farewell performance at Maxy's faded from her mind until it was as colorless as the rest of her routine existence.

For the first week, she held on to Jerry Jupiter's card and looked at it every morning, wondering if this would be the day he would call her. She imagined taking the call a hundred times a day.

Her mother would answer the phone and call her name. She would wonder who this Jerry Jupiter was on the other end of the line, and Lily would just smile as she took the receiver. She would speak sweetly into the phone and he would tell her ...

This is where the daydream varied. Sometimes he would ask her to join him in a gig. At other times he would ask her to be a permanent member of his band—with variations here ranging from his opening a new club in New York to taking a world tour. And then there was the dream in which he informed her that a Hollywood producer wanted him to star in a new movie and he wanted her to be his leading lady.

Of course she told none of these things to her parents. Why borrow tomorrow's trouble today?

After eight weeks she was glad for another reason she hadn't told them anything. Jupiter still had not called and her hope was evaporating from the heat of her anger.

Her one chance. Gone.

After the tenth week she threw away his card.

Classes had started at San Diego State. She was a singer no longer; she was a coed. The tempo of her life had slowed from that of a swing band to the plodding and monotonous beat of early American history and freshman English.

After school she gave her time at the filter center where she pushed markers around with a stick, each one signifying an enemy that never came.

Her life had been reduced to an early-morning alarm, college classes, work at the filter center, homework, and sleep. The weekends, of course, were different. There was nothing. Church on Sundays, but nothing before or after.

Boys came by. Most of them were younger, still in high school. Those her age were at war. Lily wasn't interested in the things that interested the younger boys. They listened to music, but only while working on their cars or talking about football or baseball. She doubted they had ever been in the groove, let alone knocked out.

Even the joy she used to have playing her 78s had turned against her. Each song only served to remind her of what might have been, but never would be. The music merely taunted her. She felt like a starving child with her nose pressed against a nobleman's house staring at a sumptuous meal. Better to walk away than to torture yourself with all the things you cannot have.

She resigned herself to the fact that she would get her degree, secure an elementary teaching position, and use her vocal talents teaching first-graders how to sing about an itsy-bitsy spider.

Laura looked up from her mending. Johnny sat in the easy chair next to the living room Philco. The evening newspaper folded on his lap, he fiddled with the radio dial. A pole lamp bathed him and the radio and the newspaper in a soft yellow light.

"Signal's not very strong tonight," he said.

With nothing but static coming from the speaker, he let out a frustrated sigh, sat back in his chair, and opened the paper.

"We're just not going to get CBS tonight," he said. "Maybe if we got a bigger antenna."

"What's on CBS?" Laura asked.

"Major Bowes' Amateur Hour."

"That's right, it's Thursday."

Johnny read aloud: "Our options are: *Good News* on NBC-Red ..."

"Who's the guest?"

"Let's see ... it says here ... Fanny Brice."

Laura smiled. "Fanny always makes me laugh."

"The Toronto Promenade Concert is on NBC-Blue ... and ... *The Harmonaires* are on MBS."

Laura crinkled her nose. "I don't care, dear. You choose."

Leaning over the arm of the chair, Johnny slowly turned the dial back and forth trying to coax the *Amateur Hour* out of the radio.

"Have you noticed anything different about Lily recently?" Laura asked.

His ear against the speaker, Johnny said, "Huh?"

"She seems downhearted. Ever since college began. Do you suppose she's having difficulty with her classes? When I ask her about them, she insists she's doing fine."

"Uh-huh."

"Does she seem different to you?"

A weak and scratchy CBS signal crackled from the speaker. "That's the best we're gonna get," Johnny said. He fell back in his chair, dissatisfied with the sound coming from the radio. "Hardly ever see her anymore," he said of Lily. "Other than that, haven't noticed anything."

"She seems different to me."

"It's the war. All her male school chums are away. Many of the women, too. Her brothers and sister are gone. She works in a place where they're constantly on guard against possible invasion. These things change a person. Not only her ... us."

Laura's needle paused just as it was about to make a pass at the hole that remained in one of Johnny's black socks.

"You think we're different? How so?"

Before Johnny could answer there was a knock at the front door. Johnny looked at his watch. "Nine o'clock. Late for callers."

Laura dropped the mending in her lap. Her heart began pounding with rapid, heavy thuds. Her first thought was that it was a telegram. Bad news. Neither Walt nor Nat had gone overseas yet, but there were always training accidents when men played with airplanes and guns.

She stood on unsteady feet and accompanied Johnny to the door. As he placed his hand on the latch, she didn't want him to open it. Some things were better not knowing, if the knowing was ...

Johnny swung open the door. Standing in the porch light was a good-looking man with dark, wavy hair. Definitely not a telegram delivery boy.

"Mr. Morgan?" the man said.

"Yes?"

The man extended his hand. "My name's Jerry Jupiter."

Johnny shook it, but not eagerly. "It's a little late to be selling Fuller brushes, don't you think?" he quipped.

The man laughed heartily, just shy of a patronizing laugh. "Mrs. Morgan, I presume?"

Laura nodded at him.

"I stopped by to see Lily," he said. "Is she home?"

He's a little old for Lily, Laura thought. *Must be in his early-to midthirties.*

"May I inquire what this is about?" Johnny asked.

Good question, Johnny!

"Oh, of course," Jupiter said, though the expression on his face led Laura to believe he didn't think it was their business. "Lily and I performed together one night at Maxy's," he said.

"You're a singer?" Laura asked.

"A bandleader, ma'am."

Laura nodded. "I'll get Lily," she said.

Lily was lying on her bed reading about the early Puritan settlements in colonial America when Laura opened her bedroom door.

"You have a guest."

"This late?"

"An older man."

"Older? How old?"

"Thirties."

Lily shook her head as she got up. "Did you get his name?"

"He says he's Jerry Jupiter."

Laura wasn't sure she liked the way her daughter's face lit up at the sound of an older man's name. But light up, it did. Like a Christmas tree.

"Jerry's here? In the house? He's not on the phone?"

"He's standing in the living room talking to your father."

Lily let out a little squeal. She ran to her dresser mirror and quickly brushed her hair. "He's a bandleader, Mom! A very famous man!"

"I've never heard of him before," Laura said.

Lily was out the door and down the hall. Stopping shy of the living room, she made a nonchalant entrance.

After a moment or two of small talk, Jerry asked to speak to Lily outside. The front door closed behind them.

"Do you think we should trust him?" Johnny asked.

"He's a famous bandleader," Laura replied.

"Really? I never heard of him."

Realizing that the conversation outside was going to take longer than just a few minutes, Johnny gravitated back to his radio dial and Laura returned to her mending, but her attention was on the closed front door.

The door burst open. Lily bounded into the living room. She was out of breath.

"Mom, Dad, please say yes. I've dreamed all my life of this moment."

Laura was on her feet. Johnny too.

"It might be easier for us to say yes if we knew what you were talking about," Laura said.

Jerry Jupiter appeared in the doorway with his arms folded. He smiled warmly, but stayed at a distance.

"Mr. Jupiter has asked me to join his band! To be their lead singer! Isn't that wonderful?"

"So far … yes, it is wonderful," Johnny said cautiously, taking a look at the man who made the offer. "But we'll have to know more. For example, where will you be singing?"

From the doorway, Jupiter answered. "We'll be traveling all across the United States," he said. "I just landed a gig … a contract, with the army. We'll be entertaining troops at army bases."

"So there won't be any alcohol!" Lily said.

"Army bases?" Johnny echoed.

"Yes, sir."

"And how many days will you be gone?" Laura asked. "What about your college classes?"

"I'll have to drop out of college," Lily said. "It's a full-time gig … job."

"I see."

"Do you, Mom?" Lily pleaded. "Do you really? Haven't you seen how miserable I've been lately? I hate college. I don't want to be a teacher. I want to sing. But until now I haven't had the opportunity."

"You sang at Maxy's," Laura said. It was a weak play made from a losing hand. She knew it. But it was beginning to dawn on her that she was in the process of losing her last child to the war effort and she couldn't help herself.

"Maxy's served liquor, remember," Lily said.

"And Lily was good enough to respect our wishes by not singing there," Johnny added.

Laura gave him a hurtful glance. He was siding with Lily.

"When … when do you leave?" Laura asked.

Lily turned to Jupiter.

"Actually … right now," he said. "The bus is loaded outside and we have to hit the road tonight."

"Tonight!" Laura cried.

"Mother, this is a dream come true for me! And I can do something really useful for the war effort. Remember what Aunt Katy said about how the music helped the wounded soldiers at the hospital in France?"

Laura was losing her daughter. She knew it and there was nothing she could do.

"But what about your things? You have to pack."

"She can pack for just a few nights, Mrs. Morgan. I'll give you an address where you can ship her things."

"Will there be other people with you? Other women?"

"Six or seven," Lily said, "and all the band members. Please, Mother? It would make me so happy!"

An hour after the knock first sounded on the door, Lily was gone. The last and youngest of the Morgan children.

Laura tried to mend, but her eyes kept watering, and her mind kept wandering. Thoughts of war. Her children. Off on their own. It was so quiet, painfully quiet.

Johnny sat glumly in his chair. The radio played in a fashion—half music, half static—but he wasn't listening.

There was no other sound in the house.

9

Alex searched the cloud cover below for an opening. For as far as the eye could see there was nothing but a cottony layer of clouds.

Not good, Alex. Not good at all.

She swung the small Piper aircraft around for another pass. The Houston Municipal Airport was below her somewhere. She checked her fuel gauge. It was low.

"You are so exasperating!" she shouted at the Gulf fog. "A small opening, is that too much to ask for?"

The shimmering white blanket ruffled serenely beneath her, unconcerned with her plight. Overhead the sky was so blue it hurt her eyes to look at it. The sun sparkled like an enormous gem.

The fleecy boundary over which she flew never ceased to amaze her. On this side of the separator, the day was bright and clear; on the other side, the day was dark and gloomy. As a rule, she preferred the sunny side. However, the engine that made the crossing possible required a steady supply of juice to keep her there. Should it run out, she would be pulled rather rudely back across the boundary to the gloomy side. It was the kind of crossing that could ruin a person's day.

"Come on, give me an opening!"

The fog had rolled in off the Gulf without warning. Alex had taken the civilian craft up to practice some solo maneuvers. She had flown in fog cover before in San Diego, but nothing this thick. And without a radio to check ground conditions, she had no way of knowing how thick the fog was on the ground.

She needed a break in the fog and she needed it soon.

Alex circled back around again, craning her neck from side to side looking for a portal to earth.

Ah!

A small gap appeared in the fog. She could see black earth and buildings. The sunlight that streamed through the hole shined on them like a spotlight. She recognized them. Airplane hangars.

Alex pushed the plane into a dive and plummeted through the hole. The airport runway came into sight. She lined up her approach and descended. Above her, the hole closed in on itself and as it did, the day turned dark and foreboding.

Once again she had successfully crossed the boundary that separated the two worlds.

After landing, she taxied toward the hangar. A man holding a set of earphones came running toward her from the tower. She recognized him as the tower operator. The wind whipped his hair and tie furiously.

The tower operator was shouting something at her. From the redness of his face and the fervency of his finger-shaking gestures, she guessed he was cursing, though she could hear nothing over the sound of the engine.

Alex cut the engine and climbed out of the cockpit.

"I could yank your license for that stunt!" he shouted.

"What stunt?"

"Do you see that?" he turned and pointed toward the tower. "That's a beacon. We turn it on when we want to tell the pilots something. Can you guess what we want to tell the pilots today?"

His patronizing tone was working its way under her skin. It

was a tone with which the female pilots were familiar, but that didn't make it any easier to endure. They were under strict orders not to reply in kind, nor to resort to rudeness.

"We are going to show the world we're professionals in every sense of that word," Jacqueline Cochran had warned them. "And if that means occasionally swallowing our pride, then that's a small price to pay."

Alex agreed with every word. Except the part about the small price. For some, she thought, the price was rather high.

She calmly looked the tower operator in the eyes and said evenly, "That's the 'Field Closed' beacon."

"Yes! And it means that the field is closed. No planes taking off. No planes landing! Is that so hard to understand?"

"No, sir."

"Then why …"

"What's going on here, Larry?" Jacqueline Cochran appeared in a flight suit.

"One of your trainees doesn't think our airport's rules apply to her!"

Cochran looked to Alex for a reply whereupon Alex described the circumstances that led to her landing.

"What did you expect her to do, Larry?" Cochran demanded.

"All I'm saying is that nobody lands on my runway when the 'Field Closed' beacon is on. I won't accept excuses. It had been on a good fifteen minutes before she landed!"

"And how was she to see it?" Cochran asked.

"That's not my problem. The airport is my concern. A pilot's plane is his concern. I'm afraid I'm going to have to file a report on this."

"You do that, Larry," Cochran said. "It'll give you something to do while the field is closed."

The tower operator let out a *humph!* and stomped back to his tower, but not before first writing down Alex's name and the registration number of the aircraft.

"Don't let him get under your skin," Cochran said when he was gone.

"Too late," Alex replied.

Cochran laughed.

"Thank you for interceding."

"I can get away with some things that would be out of line for a trainee. It looked like the situation needed my special touch. Besides, you won't have to put up with him for much longer."

"Oh?"

"Tell the girls to start packing," Cochran said. "We're moving."

"Moving?"

"To Sweetwater, Texas. I got us an entire air base of our own."

It was the first cross-country trip for many of the women pilots as they ferried twenty-six BT-13 basic trainers to Sweetwater, 375 miles northwest of Houston. The new air base was called Avenger Field.

They flew in two roaring-square formations. Because Alex was one of the most experienced of the pilots, she was chosen to be a flight leader.

The formations landed for lunch at an air base in San Angelo, Texas. Wearing rumpled, oversized flying suits and hairnets, the women sat off to themselves in a corner of the base cafeteria. They whistled at every attractive GI who walked through the door.

From the cockpit of her BT-13, Alex peered down at two crisscrossing gravel runways. They had reached Avenger Field and their new home.

Narrow taxiways connected the runways with one another and with the hangars and flight line. Eight buildings, running parallel to each other like railroad ties, were the barracks. A larger building situated near one of the runways held class-rooms and a "ready room" where the trainees would await their turn to fly. A control tower and a large hangar were under construction.

Forty miles west of Abilene, Avenger Field sat at 1,350 feet above sea level. The terrain was typical for West Texas—mesquite trees, buffalo grass, and a few greasewood shrubs. The women were informed that a northerly wind blew at a constant twenty-five miles an hour. On occasion it could whip up a dust storm from the parched red dirt. In early summer, temperatures climbed to 100 degrees and didn't leave for five months.

Using hand signals, Alex instructed her formation to begin landing.

"OK, I guess I'll start. My name is Peggy Rayburn. I was born and raised in Pueblo, Colorado. My father is a florist. And I first knew I wanted to fly when an Electrolux salesman introduced me to a good-looking pilot."

The bay echoed with feminine laughter.

Having received their barracks assignments, the women had wandered the hallways until they found their designated bunks. Each of the six-woman bunk units were called bays.

Alex reclined on her bunk, her hands behind her head, listening as each of her bay mates introduced themselves. While they were somewhat acquainted with each other from Houston, the six women thought it a good idea, since they would be sharing quarters, to begin afresh in their new location.

Peggy, a blazing redhead, her shoulders spangled with freckles, self-consciously adjusted the straps on her summer blouse. "So this pilot took me up in his single-engine Taylorcraft. One flight and I was addicted."

With a shrug to signal the end of her self-introduction, Peggy sat on her bunk.

"Wait a minute!" one of the women asked. "What about the pilot?"

Peggy blushed slightly. "It didn't work out."

"How about the Electrolux salesman?"

"Well, you've heard of bug-eyed Betty? He was the male equivalent."

The women laughed. Alex chuckled. Talk among the female pilots centered mainly around two things: flying and men. That meant her interests were limited to half of most every conversation.

A tall leggy blonde stood up next. "My name is Loretta May and before becoming a pilot I was a model in Hollywood ..."

On the bed next to her, the woman slapped the top of her cot. "I knew I'd seen you somewhere before!" she enthused. "Ipana toothpaste! *Good Housekeeping* magazine!"

Loretta smiled a toothpaste-ad smile. "Ipana for the smile of beauty!" she said in sing-song fashion, mocking the producers of her ad.

All around the bay the women looked at Loretta with the kind of expression reserved for celebrities. Their staring didn't seem to bother the tall blonde.

"And just like Peggy, my first time in the air was at the invitation of a male friend. It was the intense concentration and mechanics of flying that fascinated me, everything from plotting a flight plan to knowledge of engines and aerodynamics. You know, the mental challenge."

Loretta sat down.

"You weren't raised in Hollywood, were you?" Peggy asked.

"Los Angeles," Loretta answered.

"What about the guy?" It was the same woman who'd asked Peggy about the Electrolux salesman.

Peggy smiled. "He was a stand-in for Clark Gable. But he was also a real drip."

"I think I could put up with a drip if he looked like Clark Gable!" the woman said.

It was her turn to introduce herself. Still reacting to the Clark Gable look-alike, she fanned her face with a hand, prompting more laughter.

She began, "My name's Virginia Giles and I'm still waiting for my chance to soar among the clouds with some man!"

"All of our trainers are men," Alex said soberly.

Placing a hand on her hip, Virginia replied, "Honey, the trainers we've had ain't men. Believe me, I've checked. I don't know what they are, but they ain't men!"

Alex merely smiled as the other women enthusiastically voiced their agreement with Virginia.

"Anyway," Virginia continued, "before I came here I was a physical education teacher …"

She looked like one. Broad shoulders. Thick calves. Short-cropped, light-brown hair. Tanned complexion.

" … and I knew I wanted to fly the day I read Amelia Earhart's article in *Cosmopolitan* magazine."

A chorus of responses resounded.

"Me too!"

"I read that article!"

"Was that the article, 'Try Flying Yourself'? It was great!"

"I've always worshipped Amelia!"

An instant bond was felt in the bay. They had all been touched by the infectious passion of the legendary Earhart.

"So when I got the letter from Cochran," Virginia continued, "I knew this program was for me. I want you to know, it wasn't easy for me to get here. When I told my father what I wanted to do, he pitched a fit. I mean, it was a real lollapalooza! He said if

I wanted to do something worthwhile I should join the lady marines."

"How did you convince him?" Peggy asked.

"I didn't. I left without telling my family where I was going."

"They don't know where you are?" Loretta asked.

Virginia sat on the edge of her bunk. "They don't know, and as far as I know, they don't care."

The mood in the bay had sobered as a brown-haired, bookish woman stood.

"Dorothea Hughes," the woman said, introducing herself. "From Fort Wayne, Indiana. I guess I'm the only one here who is married …"

She looked to Alex and the only other woman who had yet to introduce themselves. Both of them shook their heads.

"… so anyway, my husband is a high school science teacher. He was always talking about the marvel of flight, and I always imagined what it must feel like to fly. I started taking lessons, and, well, here I am."

"Your husband let you come?" Virginia asked.

"He didn't object when I asked him."

"Do you have any children?" Peggy asked.

Dorothea shook her head sadly. "We can't."

"Where did you meet him?" Loretta asked.

"At Indiana State. I was getting my master's degree in Personnel Administration. My father is on faculty there. He teaches theater, and he's a playwright. He once studied under Eugene O'Neill."

"My name is Evelyn Post," said the next girl.

"Emily Post?" Virginia asked. "The manners lady?"

"Evelyn," Evelyn repeated with a smile. "But I get that all the time." She smoothed her black hair with a delicate hand.

Alex could understand how the connection could be made.

Other than the Hollywood model, Evelyn was the woman in the bay you would least suspect of being a pilot. She was small, dainty, and soft-spoken.

"I was a stenographer for the Cessna aircraft company. And all the talk about airplanes and flying, well, I found myself daydreaming about it and finally thought, why not give it a try? So I took lessons. And when I got Miss Cochran's letter, I took the physical."

Virginia sized her up rather obviously. Evelyn took notice.

"I didn't pass it the first time," Evelyn admitted. "I had a sinus condition that needed correcting."

"Correcting?" Peggy said.

"Two operations."

"You had two operations just to get into this program?"

"It was the only way I could pass the physical," Evelyn said matter-of-factly.

As Evelyn sat down and eyes turned to Alex, she wished she'd gone earlier in the rotation.

"We all know why Alex is here," Virginia said. "With a famous ace for a father like Johnny Morgan, where else would she be?"

Alex slipped over the side of her bunk and stood rather half-heartedly under the scrutiny of five pairs of eyes.

"I guess you already know my name … Alex Morgan. Yes, my father was a pilot in the last war, and yes, he taught me to fly. I guess you could say flying is in my blood. So … well, anyway … I guess that's why I'm here."

She sat down.

"Any boyfriends?" Peggy asked.

There was no guile on the young woman's face, so Alex didn't interpret the question as a malicious barb. However, she wished Peggy had chosen a different question.

"No, and quite frankly, not interested," she replied.

"Not interested?" Virginia cried.

"I'm here to fly," Alex said. "Men are a distraction."

"Let me be distracted by that kind of distraction any day of the week!" Evelyn said.

She was instantly surrounded by shocked faces.

"Evelyn!" Peggy squealed. To the others, she said, "It's always the quiet ones!"

The bay filled with female laughter.

10

When word got out about Cochran's Convent, as the all-female air base was soon dubbed, it wasn't long before a rash of mechanical failures started to appear in the skies over Sweetwater. The failures occurred predominantly in the aircraft of male pilots from nearby cadet training schools. "Forced landings" became frequent at Avenger Field. After landing and upon examination of the aircraft, the mechanical failures invariably disappeared as mysteriously as they had appeared in the first place. Many of the Texas boys, coming from predominantly Baptist homes, credited God for the miracle.

The frequent disruptions prompted Jacqueline Cochran to close the field to all outside air traffic except in an emergency—a legitimate, verifiable emergency.

Some of the women objected, finding the landings an entertaining break in what was otherwise a rigorous schedule. Alex welcomed the air base's closure.

It wasn't long before Avenger Field was in full operation. Two and three open-cockpit trainers were taking off at a time. Fifty planes in the air was not uncommon. Daily, the traffic pattern over the small air base was stacked up four or five levels high.

The instructors, for the most part, were civilian employees of the War Training Service, an attachment of the Army Air Corps. Many of them were not sympathetic to a women's flight training program. Some of them took their resentment out on the trainees, yelling at them for even the slightest mistake.

"I hear you're the best," the flight instructor said, strapping on his helmet and earphones. Small, pale-brown eyes peered at Alex. A bristly salt-and-pepper gray mustache stretched over a smirk on the man's sun-weathered face. From the posted list, Alex knew the check pilot's name was Harvey Stamler.

"The best?" Alex asked.

"The best pilot in this cat house."

"I beg your pardon?" Alex demanded.

"Just climb in the airplane, honey."

The instructor began climbing into the back cockpit of the two-seater. Alex stood with her hands on her hips. Her instructor stared down at her.

"What's the matter, honey?"

"I would appreciate a little professionalism," Alex said.

"Don't worry about me, darlin'," he said, swinging a leg into the cockpit. "You're not exactly my type." With one leg in and one leg out, he paused. "I like 'em bigger … much bigger." He was staring at her chest.

Alex removed her helmet. "I demand another trainer," she said.

From inside the rear cockpit, the trainer leaned casually over the side. "Suits me, darlin'," he said. "Except that I'll be forced to report that you failed your first check flight in this aircraft. Chances are, you'll be washed out of the program before you get another chance." He winked at her. "The army doesn't take kindly to trainees who insist they know more than their instructors."

He was right and Alex knew it. The army's attitude toward personal differences between trainees and their instructors was "that's tough." The trainee had to put up with an instructor or he (in this case, she) was washed out.

In a more conciliatory tone, Stamler said, "Come on, darlin', show me what you got." Realizing the unintended innuendo, he added with a wink, "I'm referring to your flight skills, naturally."

Alex jammed the helmet atop her head so hard it hurt. She climbed into the front cockpit, fully aware that Stamler was watching her backside as she climbed in. It only made her angrier.

It was late afternoon and Alex would be the last trainee to be checked out for the day. They would have the sky virtually to themselves.

Once in the air she could do nothing to please him. All she could hear in the open cockpit was him yelling at her through the speakers in her helmet.

He instructed her to do some coordinated turns.

"Too much rudder!" he screamed.

On the next turn, she adjusted.

Stamler cursed. "Too little rudder! Too little rudder!"

He ordered a power-on stall, followed by a power-off stall.

"Keep the nose up! Up! Up! You're losing too much altitude! I've never met a dumber woman in my life!"

It was then that Alex realized she was fighting the control stick which was jointly operated from the front and back seat. Releasing her grip slightly, it jumped from her hand and banged hard against her knee.

"Let go of the stick!" Alex shouted back.

It was a reflex action on her part, totally useless since her helmet had speakers only, no microphone. The communication between trainer and trainee was one-way-only by design.

Stamler's curses rang in her ears so loudly she could barely hear her own thoughts. Alex ripped off her helmet.

"What are you doing?" Stamler asked.

Even above the noise of the engine she could hear his voice coming through the helmet speakers now in her lap.

"Just when I thought you couldn't get any dumber! Put your helmet back on! That's a direct order!"

Alex unlatched her safety belts.

"Failure to obey a trainer's order is cause for immediate dismissal!" he shouted.

Alex throttled back to quiet the engine. Rising up in her seat, she turned around and stuck her head back out the side of the cockpit. "Stop shouting, you wrinkled old man! There is nothing wrong with my flying! Now let go of that stick and let me fly!"

A startled Stamler released the stick.

Alex took her seat, buckled up, put on her helmet, eased out the throttle, and grabbed the stick. It moved freely.

"Just land this thing! Land it! Land it!" Stamler's voice said through the speakers.

"With pleasure," Alex said, knowing he could not hear her. "When flying without radio contact with the tower, a pilot must first inspect the runway before making his approach to ensure that the runway is clear."

With a hard right, Alex nosed the plane over into a power descent.

"We're losing altitude too fast!" Stamler screamed. It was a genuine scream, not a shout; a genuine scream born out of genuine fear.

The West Texas landscape rushed toward them. Alex pulled the nose up and leveled off barely a hundred feet above it. They had yet to reach the end of the runway, but it too was racing toward them.

"Too fast! Too fast! You're going too fast!" Stamler screamed.

When she crossed the runway's edge, Alex flipped the plane over and flew inverted the length of the gravel strip.

Stamler was wailing in her ears. It was a sweet sound.

"Inspecting the runway ..." she said, "... looks clear to me."

Righting the plane, she leveled off, circled the field, and touched down so smoothly it was as though they glided in on a cushion.

By this time the flight line was teeming with women as Alex taxied toward the hangars. Standing prominently among them was Jacqueline Cochran.

She was not smiling.

※

"This review board will examine the unsatisfactory rating given to one Miss Alexandra Morgan and the resulting recommendation that she be discharged from the Women's Flying Training Detachment."

Three people sitting behind a mahogany desk comprised the review board: Major Pettijohn who was the commanding officer, the WFTD staff executive, and a WFTD staff assistant who had formerly washed out of the program but who had been hired as an administrative assistant. Major Pettijohn held the discharge recommendation in his hands.

He was a round-faced, solidly built man with thinning white hair. When at rest, gentle folds around his eyes and fleshy laugh lines around his mouth projected an amiable personality; these facial lines, however, also suggested that they were capable of hardening into a stern army countenance when called upon. Alex hoped they would not be called upon during her hearing.

Sitting at the defendant's table beside her, Jacqueline Cochran rose to address the board. "Major Pettijohn," she said. "This is clearly a case of personality conflict between Miss Morgan and her instructor. Miss Morgan is without doubt one of my best pilots who has experience in aircraft far more sophisticated than the trainer in which she was being evaluated."

Major Pettijohn momentarily weighed what she said, then leafed through the papers. "Who was Miss Morgan's check pilot? Ah! Here it is. Mr. Harvey Stamler." He looked up. "Mr. Stamler, are you present?"

Stamler stood. He was seated in the third row of a small cluster of chairs. A half-dozen WFTD pilots occupied some of the other seats. A generous amount of empty seats separated them.

"Mr. Stamler, do you agree with Miss Cochran? Would you characterize this as a personality conflict?"

Sticking his chest out (Alex assumed he did this to establish authority, like a bull moose posturing for a fight) he said, "No, sir, I do not. Miss Morgan refused a direct command. According to regulations, that offense alone is sufficient to give her an unsatisfactory rating and request her dismissal."

The folds around Major Pettijohn's eyes gathered with concern as he turned his gaze on Alex. "Miss Morgan," he said, "would the command you were ordered to execute have placed you or the aircraft in danger?"

"Possibly," she answered. "He ordered me to replace my helmet."

"Had it fallen off?"

"I took it off."

"Took it off? For what reason?"

"Mr. Stamler's shouting was affecting my ability to concentrate on flying, sir."

"Mr. Stamler, were you shouting at Miss Morgan?"

"Yes, sir. I was."

"For what purpose?"

"For inept flying, sir."

"She was unable to control the aircraft?"

"Yes, sir."

"I see … is it possible you might be mistaken in your judgment?"

"No, sir."

"I see," said the major again. He studied the recommendation in front of him, after which he conferred with the other two members of the review board.

Alex could hear a soft buzz of conversation behind her coming from the other trainees. Then a voice, clearly Virginia's, said, "You can sit down now, Captain Maytag."

Both she and Cochran glanced over their shoulders to see Stamler shift his feet hesitantly, then sit down.

"Captain Maytag?" Cochran asked Alex.

"Like the washing machine, because he has washed out so many trainees. Another version is because he needs to wash out his mouth."

Cochran was amused. Then she stood. "Major Pettijohn?"

The major held up an index finger signaling he'd be with her shortly. He finished his discussion with the other members of the board, then said, "Yes, Miss Cochran?"

"It's possible that this board is examining the wrong person."

There were confused looks on all three members of the board. Alex felt a similar expression form on her own face.

"Miss Cochran, are you saying that Mr. Stamler has filed a report against the wrong pilot?"

"No, sir, I believe that Mr. Stamler himself is the one who should be examined by this committee for prejudice against female pilots in general and Miss Morgan in particular."

"You are accusing Mr. Stamler of purposely failing Miss Morgan based solely on the fact she's a woman?"

Alex didn't think the major was surprised that such a thing *could* happen; his question was more for clarification than anything else.

"Not only her, but others as well," Cochran said. "If I may present some facts...." She paused to flip open a file folder and look at the top page in a stack of papers. "First of all, his percentage of washouts is significantly higher than any of the other check pilots."

Alex placed a hand over her mouth to hide a smile. Cochran was giving the impression she was referring to relevant statistics. In reality, the top page in the folder was Alex's application to the program. It was Alex's guess that Cochran's statement was prompted by Virginia's Captain Maytag remark. Either Cochran was bluffing, or she was confident the true statistics, if researched, would confirm her accusation.

"Second," Cochran continued, "I selected Miss Morgan for this program because of her extraordinary number of flight hours. And I would be willing to bet that she has more time in the air than the man who was performing the check on her."

The major was intrigued. He asked both Stamler and Alex how many flying hours they had logged. Alex had three times as many hours as Stamler.

"Finally," Cochran said, "I personally witnessed, as did more than a hundred others, Miss Morgan in action during the final portion of her check flight. She performed a difficult maneuver flawlessly."

"Difficult maneuver? Which one?" the major asked.

From the slight flush in Cochran's cheeks, it was evident she was hoping the major wouldn't ask that question. Nevertheless, she answered it.

"Miss Morgan flew inverted the length of the runway at an altitude of approximately one hundred feet after which she touched down with one of the smoothest landings I have ever seen."

A flurry of confirmation sounds came from the other trainees. A scowl from the major quieted them.

"Miss Morgan," the major said, "you flew inverted over the runway?"

"Yes, sir."

"For what purpose?"

"I was performing a visual inspection before landing, sir."

The folds around Major Pettijohn's mouth stretched into an amused grin, then vanished. Suddenly, his eyes were lit up by a thought. "I seem to recall hearing about similar incidents ... during the days just before our involvement in the Great War ... performed by another Morgan. Any relation of yours?"

"It was probably my father, sir."

"You're Johnny Morgan's daughter?"

"Yes, sir. But I don't expect any special treatment because ..."

"And you'll get none here, young lady," the major snapped, all amusement vanishing from his eyes at the thought.

"Yes, sir."

"Is it your father who taught you how to fly like that?" the major asked.

"My father taught me how to fly, sir. Not the aerobatic stuff, though. I learned that on my own. My father would have skinned me alive if he knew I did those things in his planes."

The amused grin on the major's face returned. Addressing Stamler he said, "Mr. Stamler, you are not the subject of review by this board." The major's inflection startled Stamler but pleased the female trainees behind him. "But after hearing Miss Cochran, would you care to revise your report?"

Stamler stood, chest out, mustache bristling. "No, sir. My report stands. Miss Morgan was completely out of control during our flight. At one point she nearly climbed out of the plane in mid-flight. I feared for her life and mine."

"It won't be the last time you fear for your life," Virginia muttered low enough that the board did not hear her.

Major Pettijohn visibly reacted when Stamler mentioned the part about Alex coming out of her seat. He looked at Alex and started to ask her something, then apparently reconsidered. Instead, he said, "This review board will consult, then render its decision."

The board members conferred for nearly fifteen minutes. Then, straightening himself in his chair, Major Pettijohn addressed the hearing.

"Given the limitations of this board and this hearing, we have concluded that it is unlikely we will ever determine exactly what occurred during the check flight in question. That there were inequities on the side of both the trainee and the check pilot is certain. Though we cannot confirm that a personality conflict between the trainee and the check pilot influenced the results of the flight check, neither can we rule it out.

"Therefore, it is the consensus of this board that Miss Alexandra Morgan be given another check flight to determine her flying abilities in the aircraft in question." Looking at Stamler, he added, "I myself will be the check pilot for the flight. It will give me an opportunity to see for myself how well Miss Cochran's training program is progressing, and to evaluate the quality of our check pilots." In a lighter tone, he concluded, "Besides, I can't resist the urge to see what flying ace Johnny Morgan passed on to his daughter."

The second check flight was held the next day. It was witnessed by all the WFTD trainees who congregated on the flight line and by Mr. Stamler whose presence was ordered by Major Pettijohn.

Once they were in the air, Alex couldn't have been more pleased. Major Pettijohn's voice coming through her helmet speakers was a welcome change to the shouting Stamler. It was sharp, crisp, and military.

After completing all the required maneuvers, the major said,

"All right, Miss Morgan. Show me what else you can do. Give me a good ride."

Alex grinned. For thirty minutes she indulged herself with aerobatics. At one point, though she could have been mistaken, she could have sworn she heard Major Pettijohn let loose with a childlike, "Wheeeeee!"

"Do you think you can land this thing?" the major asked.

Alex nodded the affirmative.

"Make certain you first make a careful visual inspection of the runway."

"Sir?" she shouted to him over her shoulder.

"You heard me, trainee," his voice came over the speakers.

"Yes, sir!" Alex shouted, amused.

To the wild acclaim of the crowded flight line, Alex made an inverted pass over the runway before landing.

"Congratulations, Miss Morgan," Major Pettijohn said in military fashion as she climbed out of the front cockpit of the trainer. "You passed."

Turning on his heel, he motioned Stamler to his side. With his arm around Stamler's shoulders, the major led the check pilot beyond the end of the runway into the desert. Alex couldn't make out the words, but the major's tone of conversation was loud and heated.

"Scratch one check pilot," Virginia said cheerfully as Alex's bay mates gathered around her.

"Ring the bell! Ring the bell!"

Beginning with her bay mates, the chant was soon taken up by the entire flight line. Alex was led in a procession to the administration building where she rang the big fire bell, the fledgling tradition for all who passed their flight checks.

11

It was one of those still, hot Texas nights when it had been so long since the mesquite bushes had rustled in the wind it seemed they'd forgotten how; when even the jackrabbits sat on earthen mounds, their twitching noses lifted high, praying for a breeze.

The bay was stifling. Exhausted from trying to induce sleep, Alex quietly slipped out of the barracks, careful not to wake any of the others who had somehow managed to drift off despite the heat, and stood between the buildings hoping that the air would stir.

Suddenly, a black figure darted around the corner of the building, startling her.

"Alex?" the figure whispered.

"Evelyn?"

"What are you doing out here?" Evelyn asked.

"Couldn't sleep. What are you doing out here?"

"I couldn't sleep either," Evelyn said.

Even in the dark Alex could tell she was hiding something. It appeared the rumors were true.

"You sneaked out to be with Frank, didn't you?"

Evelyn's eyebrows parted into a pleading slant. "You won't tell on me, will you?"

Her plea was as good as a confession. Alex felt a pang of disappointment. She had hoped the rumors were unfounded. After everything Evelyn had gone through to get into the program, she was jeopardizing it all for a man.

"He's a trainer, Evelyn! You could get kicked out!"

Evelyn hung her head. Black hair fell like a veil, covering her eyes. "I know!" she said. "Don't you think I've told myself that a thousand times? I just can't seem to help myself."

Alex felt herself heating up. This time from the inside. She hated when women acted like victims of love. That was the stuff of Hollywood and songwriters.

"We all make choices," she said. "You have to choose which is more important to you, Frank or flying."

Evelyn threw her head back. The black veil parted to reveal tears glistening in the moonlight. "Every day when I'm in class or flying, I tell myself that I have to break it off. And I really mean it, Alex! I don't want to wash out of this program!"

She brushed tears from her cheeks.

"But then, I see him again … and even though I tell myself it's wrong and I know I'm jeopardizing everything I've worked for all these years … I find myself agreeing to meet him again."

"Evelyn, it's a matter of priorities!" Alex insisted. "No man is worth what you would have to give up if you're discovered."

The tears stopped. Evelyn looked at Alex with you-don't-understand eyes. Which was true. Alex didn't understand. For her, the answer was clear, there was no choice at all. Evelyn had to break it off with Frank.

"Are you going to turn me in?"

Alex shook her head slowly. "I'm not going to be responsible for ruining your career. But, please, Evelyn … break it off with him. You're too good a pilot. Better than most. I'd hate to see you wash out over something silly like this."

Evelyn's eyes brightened. "You think I'm a good pilot?"

"I think you're the best pilot in our bay."

"After you."

"I just have more hours logged."

"You really think I'm good?"

Alex smiled and nodded.

"Thanks," Evelyn said, walking to the barracks door. She stopped. "And thanks for not saying anything."

Alex stayed outside for about another hour. She couldn't get Evelyn off her mind. Maybe she was a victim in this. A victim of the girl-crazy banter that was constantly going on between groups of men and women. A victim of women's exaggerated late-night tales of their amorous adventures with men. A victim of the entertainment industry and its standard theme of hopeless love. A victim of a society that taught women they were not complete unless they had a man.

A slight breeze stirred. Refreshed to the point of feeling she might be able to fall asleep, Alex stepped back into the barracks. The air inside was so hot and thick it engulfed her like a liquid.

Taking her bunk, she carried it outside and slept between the buildings. When she awoke in the morning, a half-dozen cots were situated around her. That night all the spaces between the barracks were lined with cots.

The army was on Alex's side. It attempted to submerge the trainees' sexuality by keeping them physically tired. Four hours on the flight line and five hours of ground school were followed by a rousing game of softball or volleyball. The trainees were slimmer and fitter and tanner than ever. And there were few males around to see them.

The sun was lowering itself into a glorious pink and blue bath. Alex stood on the flight line. She had watched Evelyn perform a few solo maneuvers and the two of them had just finished review-ing the practice. Evelyn had gone to change out of her flight suit, and Alex was headed toward the cafeteria when she heard the drone of another aircraft high above.

It attracted her attention because she was sure Evelyn had been the last of the trainees to land. Looking up, she saw a cadet military trainee aircraft. It circled for an approach and came in for a landing.

Despite the base closure to all cadets except in case of emer-gency, there was still the occasional "forced landing" by nervy, wide-eyed trainees who were often no more than boys. Some even went so far as to puncture their own fuel lines to create a legitimate repair problem, foolishly risking the chance of fire for a brief visit to the all-female air base.

Alex walked determinedly toward the taxiing craft. She was taking it upon herself to see that this cadet would have a short and extremely unpleasant visit to Cochran's Convent. If she did her job well, maybe his report to his fellow cadets would discour-age others from making the attempt.

The craft braked to a stop and the pilot cut the engine. Catching sight of Alex, a white smile spread beneath his goggles. Removing his goggles and helmet, he said, "I must say, you are without a doubt the prettiest crew chief I have ever come upon at an army air base."

Alex took up a position in front of his wing. "You can just start that thing back up and zoom out of here, flyboy. This is a closed base. There's nothing here for you."

The pilot looked at her quizzically. He scratched the top of his head vigorously, disturbing a shock of light brown hair. He looked older than most of the trainees, and larger too. Wide shoulders pressed the limiting confines of the cockpit.

"This is a closed base?" he asked.

Alex folded her arms, her hip jutting out sarcastically. "Feigning ignorance? Somehow, that suits you. I would have taken you for the type that would puncture his own fuel line."

"Puncture a fuel line? That's crazy."

"And so are you if you think you're going to get away with this. Now either fly this crate out of here, or I suggest you get used to walking, because when I get finished with you, that's all you'll be doing."

Placing large hands on the side of the cockpit, the pilot began lifting himself out. "I certainly hope you're not the regular welcome committee, ma'am."

"What do you think you're doing?" Alex asked. "You just climb right back into that cockpit."

Her words had no effect on him. He hit the ground and ambled toward her. His size nearly took her breath away. Wide shoulders were only the start. He had a massive chest, thick arms, and a neck that mushroomed out of the top of his flight suit.

"If it's all the same to you, ma'am," he said, "I think I'll stay awhile."

Alex sputtered, "Of all the arrogant …"

He lifted a hand toward her that was as big as a grizzly bear paw. "My name's Lieutenant Clayton Thomas. Now would you be so kind as to direct me to Miss Jacqueline Cochran? I do believe she's expecting me."

"You're no lieutenant!" Alex said.

The man had a boyish grin. "Find it hard to believe myself, sometimes," he said. Unzipping his flight suit, he showed her the single silver bar on his uniform beneath.

"A first lieutenant!" Alex muttered. "But I thought … you're flying a cadet trainer."

The lieutenant covered the bar like it was supposed to be kept secret. "It was the only mode of transportation they had available." Then, with a good-natured twinkle in his eye, he added, "Don't know if you've heard, but there's a war on."

For some reason, Alex's tongue chose this time to become inoperable. With effort she managed to say, "Please forgive me, Lieutenant. We've had a rash of unauthorized landings of late, and when I saw your plane I just assumed ..."

His uplifted hand stopped her. "No need to apologize, ma'am," he said. "A rash is not something to be taken lightly."

She looked at him oddly.

He chuckled. "Sorry, ma'am. It's just my warped sense of humor. It takes most people a while to get used to it."

"Ah!" Alex cried. "Rash. I get it."

The huge lieutenant laughed. Alex couldn't tell if he was still laughing at his joke or if he was laughing at her. She steered him toward the administration building.

"Are you a pilot?" he asked.

"Yes, sir."

"Have you been checked out on twin engines?"

"No, sir."

"Then it looks like we'll be spending some time together, ma'am," he said. "I'm the AT-17 trainer and check pilot."

"Ah," Alex said, because she could think of nothing else to say.

"Ma'am?"

"Yes?"

"Could you do something for me?"

Alex's forehead ridged in hesitation. "If I can."

"I'm almost certain you can do this one thing."

"Go on."

"Would you mind telling me your name so I don't have to call you ma'am?"

Alex flushed. "My name is Alex. Alex Morgan."

"Alex," he said. "That's a man's name, isn't it?"

"Short for Alexandra."

"I like that better," he said. "Do you mind if I call you Alexandra?"

"Only my mother calls me that."

"Hmmm. Alex … Alex … I guess I could get used to calling you Alex."

"You might try Miss Morgan."

He stopped suddenly, a man-mountain set against a fading pink sky. "Tell you what. I'll compromise with you. How about if I call you Miss Alex?"

⁂

"I just got religion!" Virginia said. She reclined on her cot and stared dreamily at the ceiling. "That flyboy is one hunk of heart-break!"

"He's our advanced trainer," Alex said. "You know the rules."

Virginia propped herself up on one elbow. "If Evelyn can have a trainer, why can't I?"

Alex shot a look at Evelyn. The angry glare she gave to Virginia told Alex that she was still seeing Frank.

It was a free evening. The women wandered from bay to bay socializing, crowding around mirrors fixing each other's hair, painting their nails, and doing all the things they normally had no time to do.

"Are you talking about our new trainer?" Loretta asked, picking up on the conversation as she entered the bay.

"Is anybody talking about anything else?" Virginia asked.

Dorothea looked up from a book that lay open on her cot. It had been opened to the same page for over an hour. Speaking to Loretta, she said, "The two of you would make an attractive couple."

"Do you think so?" Loretta said, running long fingers through blonde hair.

"Not so fast!" Virginia said. "I already claimed him!"

Peggy laughed. "You and about a hundred other women on base."

"He's so good looking," Loretta mused. "Now if we could just do something about his mouth."

"He swears?" Dorothea asked. "He doesn't strike me as the type."

"Just the opposite," Loretta said. "He's always talking about God stuff. 'Isn't God good?' 'God bless you, ma'am,' and 'Thank you, Lord!' That sort of stuff."

"Doesn't bother me," Virginia said. "If it takes gettin' religion to land that one, well then, honey, 'Praise the Lord and pass me the flyboy!'"

"I hear he's an excellent flyer," Alex said.

"Now that's something only Alex would notice about a good-looking man like him," Loretta said.

"No, really! Jacqueline told me about him. He's on temporary leave from the army. Some kind of family emergency in Austin. From what she told me, his family and her family are close. And when she was having a hard time finding a qualified trainer for dual engines, he volunteered to extend his leave to help her out. So he's only temporary."

Everyone in the bay was looking at her with amused expressions.

"Really!" she said. "Jacqueline says he's an excellent pilot."

"I'd like to take him flying," Virginia said.

"Good gracious, girl! Is that all you think about?" Peggy cried.

Virginia was unaffected by the admonishment. She said, "Family emergency, huh? I wonder if he needs a little tender loving care?"

Evelyn glanced at her watch. Without a word to anyone, she quietly got up off her bunk and slipped out of the bay.

Alex followed her.

"Evelyn! Evelyn!"

She caught up with the former stenographer outside the barracks.

"Evelyn, wait!"

"Just leave me alone!" Evelyn said.

"I just want to talk."

Evelyn whirled around suddenly. "This is my life!" she hissed. "I can't help myself! I appreciate your concern, now leave me alone!"

She turned and ran into the darkness.

Alex felt a great weight of disappointment settle upon her chest. Evelyn had so much talent. And she was throwing it away.

12

"Easy ... easy ... line it up ... that's right ... that's right ..."

Lieutenant Clayton Thomas's easy drawl came over the helmet speakers. It was Alex's first night flight with him.

"Goodness, I don't even know what I'm doing here," he laughed. "You're a natural at this!"

Keeping her eyes fixed on the rows of oil pots that served as runway lights, Alex grinned. The other women had been right. Flying with Lieutenant Thomas was fun.

She had assumed they were speaking through their hormones as they so often did (especially Virginia, who didn't know any other way to speak). Tonight, however, she learned for herself about Lieutenant Thomas. He made flying enjoyable again. He was a good teacher. A great pilot. Patient. Humorous. And just plain fun to be with. And, though she didn't want to admit it to herself, he was good to look at.

Loretta was right about his God-talk though. It got annoying after awhile. Alex didn't object to this kind of talk; she had been raised in church. Baptized. Read her Bible on occasion. It was just that God-talk seemed out of place in a cockpit of an army aircraft, like shouting in a library or cursing in a cathedral.

She guided the twin-engine into its final approach. The two

parallel rows of smoking pots rushed past her on both sides now; their fires streaked by so quickly it looked like they were passing between broken lines of light.

A gentle thud and the aircraft was down.

"Praise God, that was a good landing!" Lieutenant Thomas said. "Truly amazing, Miss Alex! You've done this before, haven't you? I declare, if this were your check flight, you'd be certified for this aircraft right now."

In spite of his giving God the credit for her flying, Alex felt good inside. Unlike all the other male trainers, Lieutenant Thomas made it easy for her to succeed.

He was beaming when they climbed out of the aircraft. The flickering lights of the runway cast dark shadows, which made his dimples appear deeper than they were. The flames from the pots reflected in his eyes in an interesting dance of yellow against a blue background.

"Outstanding, Miss Alex! You are a born pilot!"

Jacqueline Cochran and Loretta approached them, stepping from the shadows of the hangar.

"Miss Cochran, I have to tell you, you have a crackerjack pilot in Miss Alex!"

Neither of the women seemed to share in Lieutenant Thomas's exuberance. In fact, their faces were uncharacteristically drawn. It looked like Loretta had been crying.

"Peggy and her trainer haven't returned," Cochran said.

"But they were the first aircraft to take off tonight!" Alex said.

"Her trainer isn't a very good navigator," Loretta offered. "He was the one I had that time I got lost. And that was a day flight."

"We're hoping that's all it is," Cochran said. Speaking to Lieutenant Thomas, she said, "Clay, will you help us search for the missing plane?"

"Just let me put some fuel in this crate and tell me where to start looking," he said.

"Stop by the hangar when you're ready and I'll give you the grid coordinates."

She and Loretta returned to the hangar.

"Dear Jesus, give them wings like eagles and fly them safely home."

Lieutenant Thomas had doffed his cap and spoke the prayer softly without asking anyone to join him, which was just as well because Alex would have felt awkward praying with Jacqueline Cochran and Loretta.

"Let me go with you," Alex said. She had placed her hand on Lieutenant Thomas's arm and blurted the question before she'd given her actions any thought. She realized what she'd done when she felt the strength of his arm through the flight suit. Still, for some unexplained reason, she didn't take her hand away.

Lieutenant Thomas didn't appear to take notice of the physical contact. He shook his head and said, "I'm sorry, Miss Alex. That would be against regulations."

"But you could use a second pair of eyes. One of us could fly while the other searches."

"Believe me, I'd love to have you go with me, Miss Alex. But it's against regulations."

She stifled a further plea. Lieutenant Thomas was not the kind of man who broke regulations. And she knew Cochran wouldn't give her permission. Let one trainee go and they'll all want to go.

"You can help me in another way, though, Miss Alex. Refresh my memory. Describe Peggy to me."

"Redhead. A hint of freckles on her cheeks. About my height and build."

"Got it," he said. "Thanks."

He took off toward the hangar. Then, turning and walking backward, he said, "You can do something else for me too."

"Anything."

"Pray for me."

Alex gave him a thumbs-up sign. *Why did he always have to bring God-talk into these things?*

Throughout the night the lights in the barracks remained on. Women sat on their cots, speaking to each other in hushed tones. Waiting for news. Any news.

Time weighed heavily on them. They knew that the longer Peggy was out in the dark Texas wilderness, the lower were her chances of survival. They calculated the number of hours her plane could remain aloft.

When that time came and passed, the mood sunk even lower. One way or the other, her aircraft was down.

The mood was darkest in Peggy's bay. Her empty cot was a monument to her absence. The women tried to occupy themselves by reading, sewing, speculating. But inevitably they found themselves staring at nothing … and worrying.

Every hallway footstep that approached their bay attracted their attention to the door. Time after time it was only someone passing by.

"She had just written to her mother," Dorothea said in a hushed tone. "She told her mother about completing her first check flight and ringing the bell. She was so excited."

"Remember our first day here," Evelyn said, "when she told us about that Electrolux salesman? I wonder if she still knows him. If he knows how far she's progressed?"

Alex looked at her watch. Nearly two o'clock.

Fifteen minutes later footsteps sounded in the hallway. They

didn't pass by. Instead, they slowed and then stopped at the doorway. Jacqueline Cochran stepped inside.

"Ladies, I'm going to call all the others together in a few
moments for an update. But, since Peggy was your bay mate, I
wanted to tell you personally."

Alex searched Cochran's face for the slightest hint that she
bore good news. No such hint was to be found.

"They've found the plane. It crashed in the desert. Both Peggy
and her trainer are dead." Cochran's eyes brimmed with tears.
"I'm sorry, but these things happen in war."

She turned and left.

After an hour or so the barracks lights were extinguished.
Alex lay on her cot and felt warm tears spill out of the corners of
her eyes. Sounds of soft weeping filled the bay until sunrise.

From that night on, never again would Alex hear about an
Electrolux vacuum cleaner and not remember Peggy Rayburn.

Peggy's death served as a reminder to the women at Avenger
Field of the hazards of flying. An investigation revealed that the
engine of Peggy's plane had caught fire. She and her trainer were
killed instantly in the ensuing crash.

Three weeks later Alex's bay lost another person and the
training program lost another trainer when Evelyn Post ran away
with Frank to get married. Their secret romance had become
common knowledge, and instead of waiting for the inevitable
consequences, they resigned their positions.

Alex was furious to the point of tears. While the others paci-
fied themselves with comments such as, "What else could they
do?" and "They were in love!" and "At least she's happy now,"
Alex's "Look at all she sacrificed to get here!" and "Don't you
care that we have just lost one of our best pilots?" fell on deaf
ears.

Ultimately, Evelyn's departure deepened Alex's resolve. She concluded that a women's training program such as this one would not be complete until they had women trainers. This, then, became her goal: to become a certified flight trainer and to enlist other women to become trainers so that this tragedy did not happen again.

Evelyn Post's failure became Alex Morgan's rallying cry.

"Pray for me," Loretta said as she passed Alex on her way to the flight line.

Alex grinned. "You're beginning to sound like Lieutenant Thomas."

Loretta did not return the grin. "It's a heartfelt request."

"Your final check on the PT-19?"

Shoving long blonde hair under her helmet, Loretta nodded.

"You'll do fine! I've seen you fly. You're good."

"My check pilot is Stamler."

Alex felt her mouth drop open the way it was so often portrayed by animated film characters.

"Stamler? What's he doing back here?"

"Seems there's a shortage of qualified check pilots for the program. They brought him back."

"Have you spoken to Jacqueline?"

"She's the one who brought him back. It was either him or delay the program and risk losing our funding."

"Well, can't you request another check pilot?" Alex knew she was grasping at straws.

"You know the army's policy," Loretta said. "I'll be fine. I put cotton in my ears."

Alex smiled. "I'll wait for you at the administration office. Beside the bell."

Loretta smiled and gave Alex a thumbs-up sign.

Raising a hand to her eyes to shield the sun, Alex searched the skies. She discerned the standard levels of traffic as each plane awaited its turn to take off and land. It was not yet noon and heat waves distorted the runway lines into a wavy illusion. Overhead the sky was blue. A 25-knot wind had been reported during the morning briefing. It didn't feel like it from where she was standing.

"Don't you have any hobbies, Miss Alex?"

Lieutenant Thomas came up from behind her.

"You mean like knitting?"

"No need to draw your sword on me," Thomas chuckled. "I'm on your side, remember?"

"Sorry, that was uncalled for."

"It's just that some of the ladies read, others do things with their nails or hair, but you always seem to be doing flying stuff. What do you do when you're not around airplanes?"

Alex lowered her hand and turned toward him. She was struck afresh by his size and the strength of his tanned features. *I've seen him every day for weeks now*, she told herself, *why does he affect me this way?*

"Flying is my life," she said as matter-of-factly as she could manage. "What about you? What do you do when you're not flying?"

Thomas shifted from one foot to the other. "I like flying as much as the next pilot," he said, "but it's not my whole life. There are several things ..."

His eyes squinted at the end of the runway with surprise. He shielded his eyes to get a better look.

"Something's wrong," he said.

Alex swung around to see for herself. What appeared at first to be a white speck took on the shape of a plane coming in for a landing. From the wrong direction. It was going against the established pattern.

A BT-13 that was taking off swerved hazardously to one side to miss it. The errant plane landed. Lieutenant Thomas and Alex both ran toward it as it turned toward the flight line.

"That's Loretta's plane!" Alex cried.

The engine was cut off. Stamler jumped out of the rear cockpit.

"I lost a girl!" he shouted. "I lost a girl!"

"Loretta?"

Alex ran to the plane and looked in the front cockpit as though the only way she was going to convince herself Loretta wasn't there was by seeing it for herself.

Everything in the cockpit was as it should have been, with one major exception. The pilot was missing.

"What do you mean you lost her?" Thomas thundered.

"I told her to take us into a spin and the next thing I know the stupid g-g-girl just f-f-fell out!" Stamler lamented.

When Alex turned back toward him, she could see the cause of Stamler's stammering. Not only had he lost a trainee, but he now faced a man-mountain who was looking more like a volcano ready to erupt.

"You're responsible for her safety!" he shouted.

"I-I didn't know w-what to do!" Stamler was beginning to whimper.

"You just left her out there? You left her alone in the desert?"

Stamler began to babble incoherently.

Monster hands seized his flight suit. An instant later he was lifted to his toes. "Where? Where did you leave her?"

"D-d-due west."

"How far?"

"I-I-I'm not exactly s-sure."

"HOW FAR?"

"T-ten, no m-maybe f-f-fifteen miles."

Shoving Stamler aside, Thomas ran toward the AT-17 he used for training. Alex was right behind him.

"I'm coming with you," she said.

Lieutenant Thomas turned to her. "Miss Alex, we've already been over this …"

She shoved past him and climbed into the plane. "Are you coming or not?" she said.

Thomas's hands were trembling. From the copilot's seat Alex also noticed his eyes were glassy.

"Are you all right?" she asked.

The AT-17 reached takeoff speed. With Lieutenant Thomas at the controls it lunged upward steeply.

"I'm sorry you had to see that," he said. "I don't often lose my temper."

She could tell as much by the way it still bothered him.

"Would you like me to take the controls?"

"Not necessary."

"Are you afraid that because I'm a woman I'm probably too emotional to handle it?"

She gave him a grin when he glanced at her. It made him laugh, which seemed to calm him. It was a good sound, his laugh. She'd never heard it before. A chuckle, but not a full laugh. The word that best described it for her was *robust*.

"Why, Miss Alex, I do believe you are pulling my leg."

"It's my new hobby."

That prompted another laugh. It lasted but a short time. Soberly, he said, "I'm afraid of what I'll do to Stamler if something bad has happened to Miss Loretta."

An unexpected wave of emotion swept over Alex, dousing the spark of joy within her. It was one of those things she didn't know she had until it was suddenly gone.

What was it Dorothea had said? *The two of you would*

make an attractive couple.

Loretta and Lieutenant Thomas. Of course, that would explain the way he lit into …

"Don't take that the wrong way," Thomas said. "I don't have romantic feelings for Loretta. That would be against regulations."

As suddenly as it had been doused, the spark within Alex reignited. Only now she was aware it was there.

"It's just that I feel protective about you ladies. That's part of my job as a trainer. I'd feel the same way if you were a bunch of guys … only in a different way, of course."

"Of course."

"Stamler never should have left her, that's all. He never should have left her!"

He was gripping the controls again.

"We'll just have to pray Loretta is all right until we reach her." Alex heard the words come out of her mouth and was just as surprised as he that she'd said that. She didn't know why she'd said it. It just seemed the right thing to say.

A surprised Lieutenant Thomas stared at her. "I'm ashamed for not thinking of that myself! Shows how the devil can use anger to jam up the works, doesn't it?"

Without closing his eyes and while still flying the plane, he prayed.

"Lord Jesus, please don't let us lose another one. Throw a protective hedge around your little lamb until we can get there."

Alex didn't close her eyes during the prayer either. Her attention was fastened more on the man praying than the prayer. She'd never seen anyone pray with his eyes open before. But then it didn't seem odd for Lieutenant Thomas to do it. What's more, she didn't feel as uncomfortable this time as she previously did.

He forced her to reconsider her conclusion that women pilots should be trained solely by women trainers. Apparently there were exceptions to be made. Lieutenant Thomas was one of the exceptions.

She checked her instruments.

"We're almost there," she said.

From their respective sides they both began scouring the terrain below. Hopefully, they were looking for a billowing white parachute. Failing that, they were looking for a leggy blonde in a flight suit sprawled in the red West Texas dirt.

"Ten miles out," Alex said.

Mesquite and greasewood streaked beneath them, but no sign of Loretta.

"Fifteen miles out."

There was nothing but brush and dirt and an occasional small animal. No pilot. And worse, no parachute.

"Eighteen miles," Alex said.

"Maybe we should swing back around for another pass. Stamler said maybe fifteen miles."

Until now, Alex had been hopeful they would find Loretta alive. But a white parachute against a dark-red Texas floor seemed like it would be an easy thing to spot. The fact that they hadn't seen it yet did not bode well.

"Maybe you're right," she replied. "Swing around and make another pass."

Clay Thomas let out a troubled sigh. Alex shared the sentiment. Any wrong decision made now might cost Loretta her life. If the parachute hadn't opened, it would be a lot tougher to spot her. And she would need to be found that much sooner, if indeed she was still alive.

Banking the plane to the left, Thomas began swinging them around for a second pass.

Just as the floor of the desert left Alex's field of vision, she thought she saw a white speck. A flash of sunlight on the glass? Or was it that trick one's eyes play when we look away, getting us to look back and when we do we find there was nothing there at all?

"Lieutenant Thomas? I think I saw something."

"You sound doubtful."

"I am. But I have to be certain. Let's get back on our original course."

Lieutenant Thomas continued banking, past 180 degrees and all the way around to 360.

They flew in silence. Alex focused hard in the direction where she thought she'd seen the flash of white.

Nothing.

A minute passed. Still nothing.

"I guess I was wrong," she said.

Thirty more seconds.

"We had to make sure," Lieutenant Thomas said.

A few more seconds.

"I'll turn us around again."

The plane began to bank.

"Wait! I see it! And there's Loretta!"

Alex excitedly poked the glass.

"Is she hurt?" Lieutenant Thomas asked, bringing the plane around to the right.

"She's standing. Waving her arms."

"Thank you, Jesus!" Lieutenant Thomas shouted. "Oh thank you, Jesus!"

"Yes, thank you, Jesus," Alex said softly.

Lieutenant Thomas found a place suitable to land nearly half a mile distant. The underside of the wing and the landing gear suffered minor damage from the vegetation and uneven terrain.

When they reached Loretta, she was slowly walking toward them. The 25-knot wind had carried her nearly five miles from where she went down. Then, she was dragged along the ground for a good distance before she was able to spill the air out of the parachute. Her legs and arms and face were scratched and she'd lost her shoes. But she had no broken bones.

"I shoved the stick over, taking us into a spin, and the next thing I knew I was flying out of the cockpit!" she said, embarrassed. "My seat belt must have come unlatched!"

She was still holding onto the parachute handle.

Alex gathered up the chute and Lieutenant Thomas helped Loretta to the plane. A crowd of jumping, cheering trainees greeted her when they first caught a glimpse of her blonde hair in the backseat of the AT-17.

After Loretta's injuries were checked, Cochran ordered her immediately back into the air. She was to fly for at least a half hour so she wouldn't be spooked by the incident. This time, however, Lieutenant Thomas flew as her trainer.

That night Loretta was inducted into the Caterpillar Club comprised of those airmen who had safely bailed out of an airplane. She had the ripcord handles as proof.

Stamler sneaked off the base during the initial celebration following Loretta's return. He never came back. And as far as Alex knew, no one at Avenger Field ever heard from him again.

Zoot suits and parachutes
And wings of silver, too,
He'll ferry planes like
His mama used to do!

It was with mixed emotions that Alex Morgan stood on the flight line in front of the reviewing stand. Virginia Giles was on her left, Loretta May on her right with Dorothea Hughes next to her.

The four remaining women in their bay had all successfully completed their final check flight on the advanced trainer. Along with seventy other women they would receive their wings and be given their assignments. Some of the graduates would go from here to begin ferrying aircraft. Others, an elite few, would go on to Lockbourne Army Air Base where they would be trained to fly the colossal B-17 bomber.

One by one, the names of the graduates were called. They filed in front of the other graduates and a new incoming class to the reviewing stand where Jacqueline Cochran greeted them and pinned silver wings onto their lapels.

"Dorothea Hughes."

"Loretta May."

(Loretta was still wearing a few of her red streak "badges" on her face and arms from her now infamous induction into the Caterpillar Club.)

"Alex Morgan."

"Congratulations, Alex," Cochran said as she pinned the silver wings. "It's been my pleasure to have known you. It's women like you who will open doors for future generations of women pilots."

"Thank you," Alex said softly.

"Virginia Giles."

As Virginia's name was called, Alex stepped from the platform filled with the satisfaction of her achievement. As she returned to her place in the ranks, she locked eyes with Lieutenant Thomas. He smiled at her.

Hence the source of her mixed feelings.

The day she crossed the San Diego County line on her way to Houston, she confidently assumed she had the skills needed to succeed in this program. The silver wings on her chest gave testimony that her confidence had been well founded.

However, had the thought crossed her mind that with her success would come a personal attachment to a man, she would have laughed out loud. Yet here she was, standing on the edge of her dreams, finding that she was harboring sentimental thoughts about Lieutenant Clayton Thomas.

She didn't love him. Perish the thought. She respected him. Appreciated him. And would miss him. The surprise to her was how much she realized she would miss him.

But even if she stayed at Avenger Field, she would miss him. For he had been given a new assignment.

The microphone squealed as Jacqueline Cochran addressed the graduating class.

"Let's hear it for the first graduating class at Avenger Field in Sweetwater, Texas!"

Virginia let loose with a whistle so loud Alex couldn't hear her own whoop.

"May God go with you as you serve the army in your intended roles, thus freeing up other pilots ..."

Alex was amused that Cochran specifically refrained from saying "male" pilots.

"... to bring victory to America in Germany and Japan!"

Another rousing cheer.

"At the conclusion of this ceremony, you will go directly to the administration building where you will be handed your first assignment. But before we conclude these proceedings, it is my honor to read the names of a handful of you who have been chosen to continue your training at Lockbourne Army Air Base."

She unfolded a piece of paper from which she read.

"The following ten women have been selected for the B-17 flight training program ..."

Seven names echoed across the flight line. Then ...

"Virginia Giles."

"Loretta May."

"And Alex Morgan. Congratulations to these women! Graduates, you are dismissed."

"Congratulations, Miss Alex."

Alex had just finished hugging Dorothea when she heard Lieutenant Thomas behind her. She turned to see a warm, sincere smile.

She wondered if she should stick out her hand for him to shake it. She decided if he offered, she'd shake his hand. He didn't, so she didn't.

"Thank you, Lieutenant Thomas. We appreciate all you've done for us. We're going to miss you." She purposely kept her conversation in the plural. She didn't want him to get the wrong idea.

"No, you won't," he said.

She was expecting the usual reciprocal "I'm going to miss you too," or "the feeling is mutual," or even a simple "likewise."

He laughed at the puzzlement his statement had obviously caused in her.

He explained: "You won't miss me because I'm going to Lockbourne too. To the same program. You see, I'll be your instructor on the B-17."

Alex's heart leaped inside her so hard that it frightened her.

13

Combat will be nothing like training.

Walt paced beside his cot in the dark on what he believed would be the eve of his first combat mission. The words of his orientation instructor were repeating in his head.

Combat will be nothing like training.

Was he ready? Would they even fly tomorrow?

According to the veterans, all the indications that they would fly a mission the next day were there: increased late activity at Ops, the sight of petrol Bowsers—the mobile tankers used to fuel the planes—and bomb trolleys on the move, and the squadron commander's remark, "OK, fellows, hit the sack early tonight."

Even Axis Sally, the Germans' incredibly female-sounding minister of discouragement to the British Isles, was predicting on her radio broadcast that a big one was coming up.

She was seldom wrong.

Walt pulled back the frayed cloth curtains of the small window high over his bunk. He looked out at the Bassingbourn airfield. In the distance the runway stretched into darkness. There was a generous portion of stars overhead. He couldn't see the moon; however, it made its presence known by the shadows it cast. There was no sign of clouds for as far as he could see. If the weather held, by this time tomorrow he would have had his first taste of combat.

It was hard for him to believe he was actually in England.

Combat will be nothing like training.

He looked at his watch. Nearly midnight. He'd obeyed orders and gotten to bed early. But slumber took orders from no commander (himself included). Neither was scolding effective. How many times had he told himself he needed to be at his best if they were going to fly tomorrow?

The worst part of any mission is waiting to see if you are really going to fly.

Another tidbit from orientation that had stuck with him. Mere words at the time. Now it was experience in the making.

Switching on a light, Walt snatched up his crew list and read the names for the hundredth time.

> Lieutenant Walter Morgan, pilot
>
> Lieutenant Jay Keating, copilot
>
> Lieutenant Woodrow Upchurch, bombardier
>
> 2nd Lieutenant Paul Geller, navigator
>
> Staff Sergeant Edward Callahan, flight engineer
>
> Sergeant Leroy Dooly, radio operator
>
> Sergeant John Sabala, tail gunner
>
> Sergeant Eugene Fargo, ball turret
>
> Sergeant Albert Jankowski, waist gunner
>
> Sergeant Otis Northrop, waist gunner

His eyes focused on one name in particular. Tail gunner Sabala.

Eighteen years old and the boy was already living on borrowed time. He'd been transferred to Walt's crew as damaged goods from another plane that had crashed during training.

One of the engines had caught fire and exploded, ripping off an entire wing. The wing flew back and sliced through the back half of the fuselage, nearly severing it. As the plane spiraled downward, Sabala unstrapped from his tail position and tried to escape the burning craft through a gap between the rear glass and the fuselage.

It was narrow. Too narrow for both him and his parachute. Sabala managed to wedge himself in the gap. He became stuck.

He was plummeting toward the earth with a fuselage stuck around his waist.

It seemed the only way he could get loose would be to free himself of his parachute. But then he would free-fall to his death. Yet if he couldn't fit through the gap, he would perish with the plane.

He wiggled and squirmed and pushed as the glass cut into his back and the metal fuselage cut into his chest. Finally, he managed to free himself and his parachute. The chute opened a thousand feet above the ground. The plane slammed into the ground a hundred yards away. He was the crew's only survivor.

When new crew assignments were handed out, Squadron Commander Cunningham gave Walt the option of refusing Sabala, making no secret of the fact that the boy had not fully recovered from the incident and might have to be washed out of the program.

Walt chose to keep Sabala on the crew list over his copilot's objections. It was Keating who had labeled the boy "damaged goods." He feared the boy would fall apart in a crisis. Walt countered that if the boy was willing to go up again, he was willing to work with him.

Now he was second-guessing that decision.

Each new B-17 crew was given two months to train, the goal of which was to turn complete strangers into an efficient bomber crew. For the most part, the crew had accomplished that goal. With the exception of Sabala.

After two months, the boy remained superstitious, skittish, argumentative, and the fly in an otherwise sweet ointment.

That wasn't to say the rest of the crew was perfect. Keating had a tendency to act like royalty and treat the rest of the crew like serfs. Even with Walt, there were times when his superior attitude bordered on insubordination.

And the two waist gunners, Northrop and Jankowski, both from the same small California town of Hemet, got along so well with one another their antics were sometimes a distraction.

Navigator Geller, a perfectionist, often took too much time getting the pilot coordinates. And ball turret gunner Fargo practiced personal hygiene so infrequently, most of the crew wanted to lock him in the lower turret before takeoff and not let him out again until after they landed.

But when it came to flying, each was pulling his weight and they were beginning to work together as a crew. With the exception of Sabala.

He sat in the tail gunner position and never said a word unless addressed directly, and then his reply was curt and often rude. No one knew what he was doing back there.

Walt had tried to coax him into conversation with no success. He talked with the other members of the crew and enlisted a couple of them to help him try to draw Sabala out of his self-imposed seclusion. They had no better success than he did.

And now training was over and tomorrow they would fly a real mission.

Combat will be nothing like training.

In training you fly through blue skies; in combat you fly through clouds of black flak. In training you shake to the vibration of the aircraft; in combat you are buffeted all over the place by explosions. In training you maintain order and calm; in combat there is no sense of order. As for calm … the word doesn't exist in combat.

Walt lay the crew list aside. Ready or not, they would fly in the morning. Maybe. If the signs are correct and the weather holds.

He'd been told the first mission is the toughest. He hoped so. It was hard to imagine going through this same thing twenty-four more times. But then, the chances of that happening were against him as well. The average life of a bomber crew was fifteen missions.

Walt lay back on his cot, interlacing his fingers behind his head. He wondered if his father had found it difficult to sleep before a mission. But then he had only himself in his aeroplane. Nine other lives were dependent upon the decisions Walt made while sitting in the pilot's seat.

Nine other families depending on him to get their sons through the war safely.

Rising from the cot, he looked out the window again. A dark ridge of clouds was forming on the horizon. He checked his watch.

12:30 a.m.

He needed to get some sleep.

Pulling a bag from beneath his cot, he extracted from it writing materials. He also saw the Morgan family Bible that his father had insisted he take with him. He pulled it out and laid it on the cot.

Shoving the bag back under the cot, Walt had thought about writing a letter home. Thoughts of his father, combined with seeing the Bible, distracted him. He picked up the large Bible. It felt unusually heavy.

Just then an intriguing thought struck him. *The Bible is back home.* This very book had begun its journey with the Morgan family in London, just south of here. It was originally the possession of

Bishop William Laud who gave it to Drew Morgan for use in espionage, the Bible serving as the key to a code between the two men.

Reverently, Walt lifted the cover. Inside was a familiar list of names. The names of the Morgan men who down through the years had charge over the family Bible. He mentally reviewed what he knew of them.

Drew Morgan, 1630, Zechariah 4:6
The Morgan who started it all. Fled England during the persecution of Puritans, settling in the Massachusetts Bay Colony and starting the Morgan family line.

Christopher Morgan, 1654, Matthew 28:19
Became a missionary to the Indians. Lived and died among the Narragansetts, writing a primer and teaching them about God.

Philip Morgan, 1729, Philippians 2:3–4
Took up his father's search for the Morgan family Bible when they thought it was lost, only to find it among the Narragansetts in Christopher's capable hands.

Jared Morgan, 1741, John 15:13
Philip's younger brother. A one-time pirate who established the Morgans as one of the leading families in Boston.

Jacob Morgan, Esau's brother, 1786, 1 John 2:10
Twin brothers who fought over possession of the Bible and on opposite sides of the Revolutionary War until Esau gave his life so that Jacob could survive and carry on the family name.

Seth Morgan, 1804, 2 Timothy 2:15
Of all the Morgans, Walt knew the least about Seth, only that he was an educator of some kind.

Jeremiah Morgan, 1833, Hebrews 4:1
A preacher during the Civil War who became a spiritual adviser to President Lincoln.

Benjamin McKenna Morgan, 1865, Romans 8:28
A one-time enemy of the Morgans until it was discovered that he was Jeremiah's firstborn son whose existence had been hidden from the father by a wicked father-in-law when Jeremiah's first wife died in childbirth.

Jesse Morgan, 1892, Genesis 50:20
Walt's grandfather who ran away from home and brought the Bible west.

Johnny Morgan, 1918, Mark 10:43–45
Walt's father. A famous aeroplane ace in the first war against Germany.

And now the Bible was in Walt's hands. It had traveled from England to the colonial New World to the Ohio frontier, to turn-of-the-century New York, across the Great Plains to Denver, a quick hop to France to catch up with his father, then to San Diego, and now back to England just a few miles from where everything began.

He had heard of the Bible and seen it on special occasions since he was a child. But never before had its history impacted him like it was doing now.

Over 300 years had passed and both it and the Morgans had survived. That thought alone began to calm him. Through persecution and revolution and war the Morgans and the Bible had survived. And they would survive this conflict too. Walt could feel it.

He looked at the writing on the inside page. Family tradition held that it was written by Drew Morgan himself.

1. The candidate must give demonstrable proof of salvation and devotion to Jesus Christ as Lord and Savior;

2. The candidate must confess that the Bible is the supreme authority for life and faith;

3. The candidate must willingly accept the responsibility to teach the next generation of Morgans the fundamentals of our faith and the heritage of our family.

Walt had heard both his grandfather and father confess that they failed to live up to the Morgan family ideal as expressed in these guidelines. It had always struck Walt as odd when he heard them make this confession. Neither man was particularly outspoken about his shortcomings.

Maybe it was the thought of being in the birthplace of the Morgan family, or maybe it was the first time Walt was afraid he might not survive another day. Whatever the reason, at this moment, Walt felt a surge of family pride well up inside him. He wanted to be able to stand before his children and tell them that he had, to the best of his ability, lived up to the Morgan ideal and that he expected them to follow his example.

When the Puritans were persecuted, Drew Morgan rose to the occasion.

When the wilderness was godless, Christopher Morgan went to the Indians.

When our country was being formed, Jacob Morgan fought for freedom.

And when Hitler threatened the entire world with great evil, Walt Morgan fought to keep his country free.

He reached for the pen and paper, wanting to write a quick letter to his parents telling them of his determination. Pen poised, he stopped, laid the pen and paper down on the cot, and dropped to his knees.

First things first, he thought.

Walt Morgan prayed for God's strength to see him through the battle ahead. Then, he prayed for each of his crewmen. Name by name he prayed for them. He spent the most time praying for tail gunner John Sabala.

Then, he wrote his letter, confident that it would not be one of the many letters one reads about written shortly before a man dies in battle.

And then he slept. A peaceful, restful sleep.

14

At 2:00 a.m. Walt was awakened—the mission was on. He was informed of his morning schedule:

2:00 a.m. Breakfast
3:00 a.m. Briefing
5:00 a.m. Stations
5:25 a.m. Alert
5:35 a.m. Taxi
5:50 a.m. Takeoff

His night's sleep had been nothing more than a nap. It didn't seem to matter. The anticipation of his first mission was a powerful stimulant. He only hoped it would last through the day.

Walt got dressed. Then, just as he was about to head out the door, he had a thought. He picked up the family Bible to take with him.

Might be something to tell the kids someday that it flew the first mission over Germany with me, he thought.

Tucking it under his arm, he decided that carrying an oversized Bible looked rather pretentious. He had another thought. Pulling a leather pouch in which he carried all his important papers from beneath his cot, he dumped its contents onto the top of his cot and slid the Bible into it.

He went to breakfast.

The meal surprised him. Every cook was on duty, not just the normal handful. Fresh eggs replaced the usual wartime variety. And every effort was made to prepare a man's eggs according to his individual taste.

Walt's first thought was that of condemned prisoners. The army was feeding them their last meal. Apparently this thought was plastered on his face, for when the cook slid the eggs-over-easy onto Walt's plate, he explained, "It'll be a long time before you get to eat again. Drop one on Hitler for me."

The men went directly to briefing following breakfast.

All the back seats were taken by the time Walt made it to the briefing room. Most of the other men there were veterans. The room was filled with banter, horsing about, talk of previous missions, and talk of planes. It was man talk. Had there been no war and had the subject been changed from planes to cars, anyone traveling across America could have heard the same conversation in every town.

Walt sat on the front row, sliding the leather pouch under his seat. The map at the front of the room was covered.

Two other pilots crossed in front of Walt and sat in the seats next to him. It was their consensus that the day's mission wasn't going to be particularly tough because Major Harrison wasn't handing out cigars. From what one of them said, if Harrison was handing out cigars, they could expect to lose at least 20 percent of the planes.

Not long afterward, the briefing officer stepped to the front and pulled back the black curtain that covered the mission map, and Walt got his initial look at the target for his first mission.

By 4:45 a.m. Walt was riding in a jeep down one of the access roads. His B-17 came into view. It was the first time he'd seen it emblazoned with its new name.

California Angel.

Choosing a name for the plane had been one of the more challenging tasks in training. Since six of the ten crew members hailed from California, that part of the name gained easy simple majority. It was the second half of the name that proved to be a source of heated debate among the crew members. Several of the other suggestions included: Cookie, Cutie, Jewel, Lass, Lady, Starlet, and Baby.

Voting was further complicated when Sabala chose not to participate. Walt had already determined he would let the other men choose the name of the plane. With Sabala abstaining, the number of men voting was even. Consequently, this led to several tied ballots.

When the name *California Angel* came up for a vote and it looked like it was going to tie too, Sabala reversed himself and voted for the name, breaking a tie. When some of the men objected, Walt let the vote stand, insisting that Sabala had the right to vote or not vote.

Privately, he was grateful for the opportunity to support Sabala. Walt hoped that in some small way it might help the boy feel like part of the crew. However, in the days that followed, there was no outward evidence that the incident had any effect on Sabala at all. He was just as withdrawn as ever.

As Walt's jeep pulled up to the plane, his crew was already assembled, lounging around on the grass.

"Let's get this bird in the sky," Walt said. "We've got ourselves a genuine mission."

"Where we goin', Lieutenant Morgan?" Jankowski asked. He jumped to his feet and pushed back a shock of red hair from his heavily freckled face.

"You'll be informed once we're in the air," Walt said. He looked to his navigator and bombardier. "You've been briefed?"

Both replied in the affirmative.

To Keating, his copilot, he said, "I didn't see you in the briefing room."

Keating's pencil-thin mustache twitched in irritated fashion. "I was there, Mother … in the back, standing against the wall."

"Fine, son, I just didn't see you."

The other crew members chuckled at the way Walt parried his second-in-command's haughty attitude.

"All right, men, gather around. I want to say a few things."

Everyone drew closer except Keating, who stayed a short distance away.

Walt looked each of his crew members in the eyes. He saw youthful bravado masking uncertainty and apprehension.

Sabala cradled what looked like a paint can in his arms. He guarded it carefully. Walt started to ask him about it, then didn't.

"Fargo!" Northrop groaned, pushing the ball turret gunner away. "When was the last time you took a bath? You reek, fella!"

A chorus of disgust accompanied wrinkled noses as men gave Fargo a wide berth.

"That's enough!" Walt said sternly. "Forget about Fargo for a moment and give me your undivided attention."

It was easier said than done. The boy was unbelievably odious.

"Men," Walt said, "combat will be nothing like training. The goal in training is to learn how to handle this machine, and we succeed when everyone knows his job and does it. But the goal of combat is to make a difference, and we won't succeed until we've done our part in bringing Hitler to his knees.

"Now the Bible says that not even a sparrow falls out of the sky without God knowing. Since that is true, I think it only fitting that before we get in this bird, we place it in the hands of the Master of the sparrows."

He doffed his cap and waited for the others to follow his

example. Then he bowed his head. "Dear God, we pledge our air-craft and our very lives to this great cause. When the fighting is fiercest may we be at our best. Give us courage to do what must be done to halt this present evil here and now, so that it will never reach the shores of America. Amen."

There was a moment of silence followed by a solitary "Amen." It came from John Sabala.

"All right, men, let's show them what we can do!"

The crew of the *California Angel* scattered to the various hatches to board her.

"Hey, Sabala!" Jankowski shouted. "Whatcha got in the can?"

"Yeah!" Northrop joined in. "Show us whatcha got!"

They flanked the tail gunner. Sabala ignored them, clutching the can to his chest.

"What is it? Somethin' personal?" Jankowski asked.

"You can show *us!*" Northrop added.

Sabala quickened his step. Northrop grabbed his arm to keep him from getting away.

Sabala swung around, his eyes afire. "Leave me alone!" he shouted.

"Hey! What's going on there?" Walt asked.

Jankowski opened his hands and palms. "Nothin', Lieutenant," he said. "We was just askin' Sabala what he had in the can."

"It's nothin'!" Sabala shouted.

Walt shrugged. "Seems to be personal, gentlemen."

"But why is he carryin' a can of paint aboard the plane?" Northrop asked.

"It ain't paint," Sabala said.

"Then what is it?" Jankowski asked.

"It's none of your business, that's what it is!"

"I'm afraid he's got a point, gentlemen," Walt said. "I'm carrying a pouch onboard and you don't know what's inside it. Sabala has a can. It's none of your business. Now climb aboard."

The two waist gunners left Sabala alone and climbed into the belly of the plane.

"Sabala …" Walt said.

"Yes, sir?"

Nodding at the can he said, "Is there anything in there I should be concerned about?"

"No, sir."

"Very well. Get to your post."

Spotting the ball turret gunner just about to climb into the plane, Walt motioned for the boy to come to him.

"Yes, sir?" Fargo said.

He was the smallest of the crew, which was normally the case among all B-17 crews. Only a small man could fit into the cramped space of a ball turret.

Walt had to keep from wincing from the body stench when the boy got close. As difficult as it was for him to do, he put his arm around the boy.

"Fargo, I have a request … no, make that an order. For the sake of the entire crew, I order you to acquaint your entire body with generous amounts of water and soap before every flight. Do you understand me?"

Fargo looked hurt. "Yes, sir," he said.

"Now it's important that you understand me. Because if you don't follow my orders, then I'll have no recourse but to order the crew to give you a bath. Now, you wouldn't want that, would you?"

A smile trembled on Fargo's lips as he tried to determine if Walt was serious or not.

"So we understand each other?"

"Yes, sir."

5:25 a.m.

The four engines of *California Angel* were humming. The crew was in place. The dials on the instruments twitched nervously as they sat motionless.

They were waiting. Waiting. Always waiting.

Walt's headphones crackled with chatter. Banter was against regulations but he allowed it. The men were on edge. Chatter gave them an outlet.

He fidgeted in his seat trying to get comfortable.

Keating looked over at him oddly. "Why are you sitting on that thing? And what's in it?"

Walt lifted himself up and adjusted the leather pouch. "It's my family's Bible," he said. "I tried to stow it, but there's no room."

"You're sitting on your family Bible? Isn't that a bit irreverent?"

Walt settled in, having managed to find a comfortable arrangement. "There's no commandment against sitting on the Bible of which I'm aware," he said.

"Why don't you stow it back with Dooly at the radio?"

"I'd sort of like to keep it near me."

"Can't get much closer to it than that."

"Did I hear someone say Lieutenant Morgan was sitting on a Bible?" Jankowski's voice came over the intercom.

"I've sung 'Standing on the Promises,'" Northrop chimed in, "but I don't think I've ever sung 'Sittin' on the Promises.'"

Jankowski and Northrop launched into a duet of "Sittin' on the Promises."

"Put a cork in it, you Nimrods!" Walt said. "It's time to go to work."

The intercom hissed quietly as Walt eased the throttles forward and the monstrous metal bird taxied toward the runway.

A muffled voice could be heard over the intercom. "Hey, Otis, what's a Nimrod?"

Exhilaration tempered with the weight of the responsibility he was feeling surged through Walt as the lumbering aircraft took wing. The *California Angel* was one of 115 bombers in the air and one of the last to take off.

Walt guided the craft into the first of two combat wing formations. His formation was comprised of twenty-one aircraft, the lowest of box formation, and the most vulnerable. Because of its exposed position, this part of the formation had been dubbed "Purple Heart Corner."

After a time, everyone settled into a routine. Just like they had learned in training. There was one part of flying, however, that Walt didn't think would ever become routine for him—the cold.

It was colder than frigid at this altitude. Men had returned from missions with frostbite. It was not uncommon for the temperature to dip to forty degrees below zero inside the aircraft. Add to that the fact that you're thousands of feet in the air and that other men in planes are trying to shoot you down before you can drop explosives on their towns and you pretty much sum up the life and work of a B-17 crew.

"Our target is Bremen," he informed his men over the intercom. "We're going to take some of the sting out of the Luftwaffe by hitting the factory that produces their Focke-Wulf fighters."

A cheer came through his earphones.

"Let's keep sharp back there," he said.

England's coastline slipped beneath them. They were over the English Channel. This was the body of water Drew Morgan had sailed on as he accompanied the residents of Edenford to the New World. Walt wondered what the forerunner of the Morgans would have thought had someone told him that one day the Bible he carried would be thousands of feet overhead in a huge metal bird.

News was relayed from the squadron leader. Walt's pulse jumped to a faster beat. "Roger that," he said. Switching to intercom, he informed his crew. "We're in for some rough water ahead. We've been spotted by a reconnaissance plane. You can bet he'll tell his buddies. Let's keep a sharp lookout back there."

Affirmatives were heard from the ball turret, the waist gunners, and the flight engineer who was manning the nose guns. Missing was the tail gunner.

"Sabala," Walt said. "Did you hear that?"

Silence.

"Sabala?"

Nothing.

Just as Walt was going to have one of the waist gunners go back to check on the tail gunner, a weak voice crackled over the intercom.

"I heard."

"You all right back there?"

A pause. Then, "Yes, sir."

"We're counting on you, son."

No response.

Walt exchanged glances with Keating. The copilot shook his head ominously.

"He'll pull through," Walt said.

Keating's head continued its negative side to side. Nonverbally it said, *You should have listened to me. Sabala is a mistake.*

Walt checked his instruments, his position in the formation, then looked ahead. He saw them at the same instant the squadron leader reported them. Dead ahead. A long horizontal line of them, so tiny they looked like gnats. But these gnats carried stingers.

"We've got company!" Walt cried.

"Where? Where?" Jankowski shouted. There was panic in his voice.

"Twelve o'clock high," Walt said. "Dead ahead."

He checked his watch. Not good. They were still an hour from the German coast. It was either going to be a very long day or a very short one.

15

German Focke-Wulfs swarmed. No longer gnats. The *California Angel* was in the middle of a hornet's nest.

Overlaying shouts and whoops and warnings jammed the intercom. Walt had been told it would be impossible to maintain intercom discipline during an attack. An understatement.

The best he could do was sort out any messages directed at him.

"This is Geller. We're over the Friesian Isles."

"Roger that."

Walt glanced at his copilot who was looking down for a visual confirmation. Keating's distinctively thin mustache twitched to an allegro tempo.

Combat will be nothing like training.

Another understatement. Walt wondered how many more understatements he would discover today.

The noise alone was chaotic. Intercom shouts. Roaring engines. Whining interceptors. Bursts of gunfire. Squadron radio traffic. Crew reports.

Walt's job was to keep the aircraft in tight. Maintaining the formation was their best defense. Stragglers were easily picked off as enemy fighters converged on them for the kill.

In front of them and above a plane was hit in the wing. First one engine caught fire. Then the second. The wing buckled and the plane did a slow starboard roll as it fell out of formation, directly into the *California Angel's* flight path!

Walt hit the rudder and banked hard to avoid hitting it.

Everything played out in front of him like it does on the movie screen. A plane going down trailing black smoke. Men appearing in the hatches and jumping. Falling with the plane. Some of their chutes opened. Some didn't.

It was hard to believe it was real.

But reality returned soon enough. By evading the crippled aircraft, the *California Angel* had been pulled out of formation. There was open airspace all around them.

They were a sitting duck for the German interceptors.

"Get us back up there!" Keating shouted. His voice was a high-pitched squeal.

Above them the squadron droned in a relentless line toward the target as though nothing unusual had happened. They were on their own. No one would come to rescue them.

"Get us back! Get us back!" Keating shouted.

Three enemy interceptors swooped toward them, positioning themselves for a pass. Two approached from nine o'clock high, the other from twelve o'clock high.

They were trying to keep the *California Angel* from rejoining the pack, to force Walt to bank right and low. Instead, he gave the engines full throttle and pulled up, left.

"What are you doing?" shouted Keating. "You're taking us right into their line of fire!"

Ahead of them white flashes appeared on the wings of the Focke-Wulf. The gunner was firing.

"We're hit! We're hit!" Northrop shouted.

"We're hit!" Keating echoed.

"I heard him!" Walt shouted, straining to pull the nose up.

"The two on this side are breaking off!" Jankowski shouted.

The interceptor in front of them likewise pulled up and away to avoid a collision. Walt eased the aircraft back into position in the formation.

Whoops of congratulations and relief sounded over the intercom.

"Attaboy, Lieutenant!"

"And how!"

"Well, if that don't take the cake!"

"Swell flyin', Lieutenant."

"We're not outta this yet," Walt said. "We've still got a job to do. What's the damage back there?"

"Some hits in the rear fuselage," Jankowski said. "Nothin' major."

"Any injuries?"

None were reported.

"Sabala. Are you still with us?"

No response.

"Jankowski!" Walt shouted. "See if Sabala's hit!"

A mousy voice replied, "I'm not hit, Lieutenant."

"You answer up sooner, do you hear me, son?"

"Yes, sir."

"You had me worried."

Silence.

"I know you've had a rough time of it, son, but we're going to make it through this if we stick together. We need you. As far as I'm concerned, you're the only real veteran we have onboard."

"This is my first combat mission, sir."

"Sabala, as far as I'm concerned, anyone who's gone through what you've gone through and is still man enough to stick it out, qualifies as a veteran in my book."

A pause and then a very weak, "Thank you, sir."

"Sabala," Jankowski said. "What did you go through?"

"Dummy up, Jankowski," Walt said. "This isn't the time. You keep your mind on keeping those Focke-Wulfs off our side."

"Yes, sir." Muffled, Walt heard him say, "Otis, do you know what Sabala's done?"

⊠

A black cloud loomed directly in their path. It looked like a storm cloud. It wasn't. Walt would have welcomed a black storm cloud over this.

Flak.

A storm cloud with teeth. A half mile deep. Directly over the target.

In training Walt had learned that once the enemy fighters break off their attack, he could expect to encounter flak resistance.

The enemy fighters must have missed that briefing. As the *California Angel* entered the field of flak, the fighters followed them in.

They really don't want us doing this, Walt muttered to himself.

The turbulence increased remarkably, tossing the craft about like a cork at sea. The smoke from the flak was so thick it darkened the sun.

"How are we doing, Upchurch?" Walt shouted.

The bay doors swung open.

"Coming up on the target," the bombardier replied.

Another B-17 went down. Blasted clean out of the sky. Direct hit. One moment it was flying along, the next it was a fiery comet streaking to earth.

There was nothing the pilot could have done. So much depended upon luck, or lack of it. And Walt knew there was nothing he could do to escape a similar fate. No amount of skill or intelligence could save him. All he could do was keep his plane on course. And trust God.

They were directly over the target.

"You're on, Upchurch! Let's make this little trip count for something."

All around them bombers began releasing their payloads. It looked like each aircraft was trailing a deadly string of pearls.

Beneath them plumes of fire and smoke appeared, covering what had been a pattern of streets and buildings.

"Yeeeehaawwww!" Upchurch shouted.

"Is that your official report?" Walt asked, grinning.

"Yes, sir!" Upchurch shouted. "We got it! We nailed 'em!"

"Then let's get out of here!"

An explosion beneath them lifted the plane nearly into the formation above them. Walt felt like he'd been kicked in the backside with a huge metal boot. It lifted him out of his seat with such force that his seat belts felt like they were cutting into him.

Dazed, he increased the distance between them and the plane above.

"You all right?" Walt asked his copilot who was rolling his head about.

"That was close," Keating said woozily.

"Everyone all right?" Walt said into the intercom.

"You gotta watch out for those big bumps in the road, Lieutenant," Jankowski said. "Otis hit his head. A pretty nasty cut, but he's all right."

"Sabala?"

"Here, sir. I'm fine."

"Good boy. We're heading home. You protect our rear, understand?"

"Yes, sir."

Walt brought the plane around to the heading Geller had given him.

He was relieved when the skies cleared and they left the flak behind. But the Focke-Wulf fighters refused to leave them alone.

"Owwwwww!"

The howl that came over the intercom sounded like a wounded dog.

"Who is that? Who's hit?" Walt yelled.

"Jankowski?"

"Not us, Lieutenant."

"Fargo?"

"I'm swimming in casings, but otherwise fine, sir."

"Sabala?"

"It was me, sir!" Sabala cried. "I got one! I got myself a Boche!"

"There's one goin' down, that's for sure," Northrop said.

"Well, I'll be! Attaboy, Sabala!" Jankowski added.

"Congratulations, Sergeant," Walt said. "But we're not out of the woods yet."

"Yes, sir," Sabala said. The men could hear that he was beaming by the sound of his voice.

"And Sabala?"

"Sir?"

"Don't scare me like that again."

The green fields of England, which had become monotonous landscape during training, never looked so inviting as the formation's shadow crossed over them.

One by one, the B-17s landed at Bassingbourn, to the cheers and hat-waving of the assembled officers manning the two-story control tower.

Even the postflight checklist was a pleasure to perform. It was a procedure reserved for the survivors. Walt ran through the list with Keating, who was somewhat reserved. Keating read the list, Walt performed the check.

"Hydraulic pressure."

"OK."

"Cowl flaps."

"Open and locked."

"Turbos."

"Off."

"Booster pumps."

"Off."

"Wing flaps."

"Up."

"Tailwheel."

"Unlocked."

"Generators."

"Off."

Keating tossed the list aside.

"Well, we made it," Walt said. "There's one down at least."

With a grunt, Keating unstrapped and climbed out of the plane.

Walt unstrapped himself and urged weary limbs to support his weight. As he turned to leave, he spotted the leather pouch on his seat. Through all the action, he'd forgotten about it.

When he grabbed it, the pouch acted as though it was glued to the seat. He pulled. It wouldn't give.

What in the world?

With two hands he pulled at the pouch, this time straining. He heard a ripping sound, so he stopped. Exploring with his hands around the edges of the pouch, he discovered that whatever was holding it down was in the middle.

After a time he managed to work the pouch free. He turned it over. What he saw sent a jagged chill through his heart.

The rest of the crew was surveying the damage to the plane when Walt emerged from the hatch.

"We took a few in the fuselage," Jankowski said, pointing to the holes. "And a few in the wing."

"Lieutenant Morgan, is something wrong?"

It was Sabala who noticed that Walt seemed a bit unsteady. The boy was cradling his can again.

"Lieutenant?"

Walt managed a smile. He realized he was clutching the leather pouch with cold, trembling fingers.

Everyone gathered around him. Walt thought he must look more shaken than he felt.

"Remember the Bible I took onboard?"

"The one you was sittin' on?" Jankowski asked.

"It's in here." Walt held up the pouch. Then, he turned it over.

Eyes widened as big as saucers. Mouths gaped.

The object of their fascination was a six-inch piece of flak that had embedded itself in the Bible. Had the Bible not been where it was, the flak would have passed through Walt Morgan.

"I thought he was a holy man," Sabala said. "Now I know it for sure. God saved him with his Word."

After everyone had a chance to look at the flak-impaled Bible, Jankowski noticed again the can the tail gunner was carrying.

"You gonna tell us what's in that can?" he asked.

A boyish grin formed on Sabala's face. "I was saving it for our celebration," he said. "For when we got back from our first mission."

It was the first time Walt had seen Sabala smile. The kid had a grin that was infectious.

"I didn't realize we'd have so much to celebrate, what with God saving the lieutenant's life and all."

"And your kill!" Jankowski said.

The grin grew even wider.

"So what's in the can?" Northrop asked.

"Here, you'll need these." Digging in his pockets, Sabala pulled out spoons and handed them to each of his fellow crew members. With a sheepish shrug he looked at Walt. "I swiped them from the mess tent. But I'll return them as soon as we're done."

"Done with what?" Jankowski cried.

Sabala pried open the can lid with everyone crowding around to get a look inside.

"Ice cream?" Fargo shouted.

Sabala beamed. "I got to thinking about how rough the ride was in the tail and how cold it got. I thought that riding in the tail had to be good for something. So I put the mixin's in the can and added some strawberries. After all we've been through today, it should just about be ready."

Walt gave the boy a thumbs-up sign. "Pretty ingenious, Sabala. Pretty ingenious."

That night while the various crews rode into Cambridge to celebrate, Walt chose instead to spend a quiet evening in his room.

It wasn't that he wasn't in a celebratory mood, he just preferred being alone for a while. He especially enjoyed the quiet.

He wrote a letter to his parents about the Bible, apologizing for taking it with him in the first place. He had never really taken into consideration that the Bible could be destroyed, that if his plane had gone down, the Morgan family heritage would have gone down with it.

After finishing the letter, he carefully removed the jagged piece of metal from the back of the Bible. For a long time he looked at it. Then, laying it aside, he opened the Bible and read.

It wasn't until the early morning hours that he found what he was looking for. He underlined the passage in the Bible. Then, he took a piece of paper. He wanted to write down the passage so he could carry it with him.

Copying word for word, he wrote:

> He shall cover thee with his feathers, and under his wings shalt thou trust: his truth shall be thy shield (Psalm 91:4).

16

Laura pulled back the heavy blackout curtains that hung over her bedroom window. She caught the eye of the elderly woman standing on the backyard slope of the house beneath theirs on the hillside. Pointing at the curtain, Laura silently signaled the woman.

This one?

The diminutive elderly woman, wearing a pith helmet and cradling a clipboard, answered her with an exaggerated nod.

Laura pulled the curtain beyond the edge of the window and tacked it down securely. Working her way through the house, she stepped onto the veranda. Leaning over the railing, she spoke loudly.

"Better?" she asked.

Peering through glasses as thick as the bottom of a soda bottle, the elderly woman pointed at the window with a pencil.

"I can still see a sliver of light."

Straining to hear the woman's dry, scratchy voice, which sounded like two brittle leaves rubbing against one another, Laura thought she understood what Mrs. Drobnik said. She repeated it to make sure. "You can still see light?"

The pith helmet moved up and down.

Laura worked her way back through the house to the bedroom.

She examined the window and its covering. "There's no light coming through here," she said. There was no one in the house to hear
her. She was alone.

She adjusted the curtain again and made her way back
through the house to the veranda.

"Now?"

The pencil pointed at the window accusingly.

"The window at the far end?"

The pith helmet moved up and down.

Laura stood back, her hands on her hips. She couldn't imagine how light was escaping the room. But Mrs. Drobnik was the
block captain, and she wouldn't approve any house on the block
until she was completely satisfied.

Maybe it would help if Laura saw her window from where
Mrs. Drobnik was standing …

"Just a minute," Laura said. "I'll be right there."

To get to Mrs. Drobnik, Laura had to go inside the house, out
the front door, around to the side street, down the hill, and
through her neighbor's house into the backyard.

As she walked down the hill, the bay breeze came up the
street to meet her. The eastern side of Point Loma was already
engulfed in evening shadow; however, in the distance, the last of
the day's light was illuminating the city skyline. The El Cortez
Hotel, long the prominent landmark for sailors entering the bay,
glistened like a gem with the city as its setting.

It was a different city from what it had been a year ago. Many
residents had packed up and moved to the Midwest soon after
Pearl Harbor, fearing that San Diego would suffer a similar attack
by the Japanese Imperial Forces.

Other residents, many of them long-time loyal citizens, were
rounded up and forced to move away. These were the people of
Japanese descent. With its proximity to Mexico it was believed by

government officials that San Diego was the center of Japanese espionage activity on the West Coast.

Japanese residents were divided into three categories of danger. Leaders with strong Japanese ties were given an "A" classification; a "B" classification defined a person of Japanese descent; a "C" classification could be anyone who contributed to Japanese cultural society and who warranted watching.

On December 8, 1941, the day after the attack on Pearl Harbor, virtually every person with an "A" classification was either being transported to a North Dakota camp or was in a local jail. Those with "B" classifications—1,500 men, women, and children—were ordered to report to the Santa Fe train depot where they were met by armed military police and shipped 125 miles north to the Santa Anita Racetrack where they were confined in tar-paper-and-wood barracks.

But not all of San Diego's changes were outward bound. Being a navy town with a large naval hospital, the streets were soon overflowing with a massive influx of uniformed sailors looking for diversions and ways to spend their money. Downtown streets resembled a boom town.

As Laura approached Mrs. Drobnik from behind, the elderly woman's helmeted head hovered over the clipboard. In the dim light, she put pencil to paper and scratched hasty words. While the woman wrote, Laura studied the exterior view of her bedroom window.

She could see no light around the edges, or anywhere else for that matter.

"Mrs. Drobnik ..."

Without looking up from her writing the block captain said, "The right edge of the window. I can see light."

Laura looked again. She saw no light.

"Mrs. Drobnik ..."

"Are you calling me a liar?" The woman, who was less than five feet tall, looked up at Laura with defiant gray eyes, magnified to unnatural proportions by her thick glasses.

"No, Mrs. Drobnik. It's just that …"

"I see what I see! I've been given a job to do and I'm going to do it, no matter how unpopular it makes me with my own neighbors. I'm only doing my part for the war effort."

"Yes, Mrs. Drobnik, it's just that …"

"Do you think I'm imagining things?" Mrs. Drobnik snapped. "I see what I see, and I report what I see."

"Yes, Mrs. Drobnik. All I'm trying to say …"

"I'm doing this for your own good! Can I help it if my eyes are sharper than yours?"

The woman was no longer looking at the house.

"I think I know how to fix the problem," Laura said. "I'll go do that now."

"I think you'd better," Mrs. Drobnik said. To Laura's back she said, "Instead of wasting your time badgering a civil servant. I'm only doing my part for the war effort."

Laura trudged back up the hill past her vegetable garden, which had more than doubled in size since the war began. Growing your own vegetables was the only way of guaranteeing that you'd have vegetables to eat. She had been working in the garden when Mrs. Drobnik had come by and informed her that her house was not properly blacked out.

Inside once again, Laura went to the bedroom and pulled back the curtain. She caught Mrs. Drobnik's eye, just to be sure the woman was watching. Then she shook the curtain to make it appear she was working on it. In reality, she made no new adjustment at all.

Leaving the room, she switched off the lights and closed the door.

On the veranda, she leaned over the railing.

"There," she shouted to Mrs. Drobnik. "How's that?"

The pith helmet moved side to side. The pencil pointed at the window. "I still see some light!" she said.

"No, you don't, Mrs. Drobnik."

"Yes, I do!" The pencil waggled at the window.

"You don't see any light, Mrs. Drobnik."

Gripping the clipboard with one fist and the pencil with the other, Mrs. Drobnik thrust both hands defiantly on her hips.

"Mrs. Morgan," she said, "if you fail to cooperate, I'll have no choice but to report you to ..."

"I turned off the lights, Mrs. Drobnik."

"What?"

"I said, I turned the lights off and closed the door. You can't see any light in the window because there is no light in that room to be seen."

Mrs. Drobnik looked stunned and hurt. She mumbled something which Laura didn't hear, then scribbled on her clipboard. "That wasn't a very nice thing to do," she said with a pouting voice. "I'm only trying to do my part for the war effort."

It was too dark to do anything else in the garden, so Laura gathered up her gloves and hoe and stashed them in the garden shed. She went inside and switched on the corner light in the living room next to her chair.

Johnny had been gone a week now. It would be another week before he returned home. He had gone to the plant in Fort Worth to implement new plans to distribute the bombers that were being built there. Had the assignment materialized a week earlier he could have arranged to attend Alexandra's graduation at Avenger Field. But as was typical with war schedules, she was shipping out to Lockbourne Air Base just as he was traveling to Texas.

Laura slumped into her chair. She considered turning on the radio, but thought better of it. Radio voices were poor substitutes for human conversation. So she sat alone in the silent, empty house, so quiet she could hear the kitchen clock ticking.

She reached for her knitting she kept in a bag beside her chair. Her eyes caught sight of two letters that lay atop her Bible on the stand beside her. Both letters had arrived today. Both were from Walt.

She reached instead for them. She knew she shouldn't, not at night while she was alone; but she reached for them anyway, mindlessly, like a person with an overpowering addiction who no longer had control over her actions. Mechanically her hands extracted the first letter from its envelope and unfolded it; instinctively her eyes moved from word to word.

Dear Mother and Father,

Finding it difficult to sleep on this night before my first combat mission, my thoughts turned to you. I hope you are both well. I hope the same for Alex, Nat, and Lily wherever each of them might be now. I keep you all in my prayers.

One of the reasons that prompted this letter is that I wanted to thank you, Dad, for insisting I take the Morgan family Bible with me to England. At the time, I thought your suggestion impractical. Now I'm glad you insisted. It has been most helpful to me.

Having just reviewed the names of our ancestors listed in the front of the Bible, and having read each of the Scripture verses associated with their names, I find it difficult to express what I am feeling at this moment. Pride seems too haughty of a word, but I can think of no better one. Never before have I been more appreciative of my heritage and more proud to be a Morgan than I am right now. I take great comfort in knowing that the same God who guided them in times past now guides my way.

I just wanted you to know that. I love you both.

Your son,
Walt

What cigarettes are to a chain smoker, so these letters were to Laura. She started the second after barely finishing the first.

Dear Mother and Father,

Just returned from my first mission and had to write you. First, all went well. We accomplished our mission without loss of life or significant damage to our plane.

I have to tell you, though, I don't care much for combat. Maybe that's good. A quote from my high school history class comes to mind. I believe it was Robert E. Lee who said, "It's a good thing war is so terrible, lest we become fond of it." Well, believe me, there is no danger of me becoming fond of anything I experienced today.

In spite of the experience, the day had its highlights. Our tail gunner, a sharp young man who has already experienced a near fatal accident in training, surprised us all with ice cream at the completion of our mission. He took the mixings with him in the plane and let the shaking of the aircraft do the rest. And, yes, at 25,000 feet it gets more than cold enough to freeze ice cream.

The second highlight concerns the family Bible. It literally saved my life.

I took it with me on the flight. The bad news is that it was damaged. A piece of flak lodged into it, penetrating the cover and nearly half of the pages. The good news is that had it not been for the Bible, the flak would have gone straight through me. It seems that God was watching over me.

So, once again, I find myself thanking you, Dad, for insisting I take the Bible with me, although I do feel badly that this family treasure was damaged while in my possession.

In your next letter send word about my brother and sisters. It amazes me how much I miss them.

Please don't worry about me. (I know this letter will probably upset Mom.) I trust that my life is in God's hands. My prayer is that I live in such a way that my life will honor him and be a credit to our family.

Love,
Walt

Laura set the letters aside with trembling hands. Her breathing grew rapid and shallow. Her mind began to race uncontrollably. Wildly. Thoughts came uninvited. Unwanted. There was no stopping them.

She saw gold stars hanging in her front window, replacing the blue ones. Two gold stars representing two dead sons. The same gold stars that were beginning to appear in window after window all across town.

She saw the article in the newspaper. November 13, 1942. Five brothers from Waterloo, Iowa. All stationed aboard the cruiser *Juneau*. Guadalcanal. One Japanese submarine. Five brothers killed. Five gold stars. She even knew their names. George. Joseph. Francis. Madison. Albert. *Why would I remember their names?*

She heard Charlie Haddox's voice that day in church. *The LORD gave and the LORD hath taken away; blessed be the name of the LORD.*

She saw the family Bible impaled with a metal spike. Her son, a half a book away from death. A bloody death in a cold metal cylinder at 25,000 feet.

Laura began to weep. She pulled her legs up and hugged them.

She saw the dead and wounded mangled on French battlefields.

She saw young men with empty eyes lying on their backs in field hospitals.

She heard the screams of broken soldiers, their moans, their cries for their sweethearts and mothers. Their voices became Walt's voice straining to be heard over the roar of airplane engines, and Nat's voice mingling with the surf on an isolated European beachhead.

With her hands clamped over her ears, though nothing she tried could stop the voices, the scenes, the thoughts, Laura wept and trembled uncontrollably. Her only company was the ticking of the kitchen clock.

She knew she shouldn't have read those letters at night when she was all alone.

It was three o'clock in the morning when she opened her eyes. She had fallen asleep. The room looked the same as it had when she sat down. The single light beside her illumined the corner. The kitchen clock ticked on as though nothing had happened.

Yet there was something about the middle of the night that made the setting seem unnatural. She belonged in her room, in bed.

With her awakening came the activation of her mind. And the memories. The fears. She wished Johnny were home.

She needed to do something to break the cycle of thoughts whirling in her head. A distraction. Something with which her mind could occupy itself; something for it to chew on.

Knitting? No. A mindless activity. She often dwelled on family things as she knit. She needed something diverting.

Her eyes roamed the room. They fell on her Bible beside her. Of course.

Careful not to touch Walt's letters, she slid her Bible from beneath them. She opened to the bookmark.

Job.

She began to read:

> Now there was a day when the sons of God came to present themselves before the LORD, and Satan came also among them.
>
> And the LORD said unto Satan, Whence comest thou? Then Satan answered the LORD, and said, From going to and fro in the earth, and from walking up and down in it.
>
> And the LORD said unto Satan, Hast thou considered my servant Job, that there is none like him in the earth, a perfect and an upright man, one that feareth God, and escheweth evil?

Then Satan answered the LORD, and said, Doth Job fear God for nought?

Hast not thou made an hedge about him, and about his house, and about all that he hath on every side? thou hast blessed the work of his hands, and his substance is increased in the land.

But put forth thine hand now, and touch all that he hath, and he will curse thee to thy face.

A hedge about him ... wasn't this what she desired more than anything for her own family, that God would put a protective hedge around them? And had not God done that to this point?

Walt's letter indicated he had. And Nat being plucked from the infantry. And Lily, untouched and innocent. And had not God protected Johnny as he flew experimental aircraft, and Alex with all her hours of flight time, yet without serious incident? Given the numerous aviation accidents in this day and age, was this not evidence of God's hedge?

But put forth thine hand now, and touch all that he hath, and he will curse thee to thy face.

"Dear God, do not test me in this," Laura prayed. "I am not as strong as Job. I admit, my children are my weakness. Do not put forth thy hand."

He will curse thee to thy face.

"I don't think I would, Lord. But please, don't test me with my children ... don't test me with my children. If there must be a test, put forth thy hand against me, not against them."

"Doth Job fear God for nought?"

Doth Laura fear God for nought?

The sound of the morning edition of the *San Diego Union* hitting the front porch step startled her. She had dozed off again. Her Bible lay open in her lap.

Rising, she stretched aching joints, the curse of all those who sleep in a chair. As she opened the front door to get the newspaper, her eyes were drawn to the two blue stars in their front window.

Blue stars, thank God. Not gold.

She made herself some coffee. It was one of the few luxuries of life that was no longer rationed.

Sugar had been the first item to fall under the strict oversight of government rationing. At restaurants sugar bowls had been removed from tables. Now, there was a worker who doled out the granulated commodity from a community sugar bowl. Other items that were soon rationed after the start of the war included gasoline, shoes, canned goods, meat and cheese, and rubber.

Coffee was rationed because of excessive hoarding at the war's outset. People over fifteen were limited to one pound every five weeks. According to the government this quantity provided for a cup of coffee per day per person—with a few drops over. Most restaurants limited coffee to two meals a day. Chicory tablets were sold as coffee supplements. When added to a cup, according to advertisers, the chicory gave a weak brew a stronger taste. Laura never did care for the stuff. So when the coffee situation improved and the government lifted the rationing, Laura was glad.

This in itself surprised her. Before marrying Johnny she had never liked coffee. She only started drinking it as part of her Americanization following the Great War. She was still of the opinion that truly civilized people drank tea, real British tea, not that weak sister of a product that was paraded as tea in the States.

As she sat on the veranda and sipped her morning cup of coffee, she read the newspaper, but only the stories beneath the front-page fold. She was feeling the effects of her restless night and didn't want to read any war news just yet.

She turned to the local section. There were the usual defense plant stories. Today's headline article featured a picture of seven young women hunched over a machine that checked the tensile strength of metals. The caption read:

> Man's last stronghold at Consolidated Aircraft Corp., the test laboratory, has just been invaded by this bevy of female junior test engineers.

Other stories featured celebrities advertising war bonds. An article directed at housewives reminded those who found rationing difficult:

> We still get ten times as much beef as people in England, twenty times as much as they get in Russia, and fifty times as much a week as the lucky ones get in China.

What's this?

Laura set down her cup and leaned forward to get a better look at a small article tucked away in the corner. She smiled.

It was the first smile to grace her lips since Johnny left on his trip a week ago.

※

Dressed in her best Sunday skirt and jacket—dark navy with white trim with a matching wide-brimmed hat that dipped fashionably over her right eye—Laura set out for Balboa Park.

Everywhere she looked there were reminders of the war.

There were sailors on almost every corner.

Consolidated Aircraft was conspicuous from the ground with its camouflage. Mesh chicken wire was stretched across it. The wire was covered with chicken feathers that had been dyed to look like vegetation from the air. Johnny said that during the rainy season the water that fell through it made everything it touched smell of chickens. Some of the workers even complained of getting lice from the feathers.

Even Balboa Park was changed because of the war. Large portions formerly open to the public were fenced off and used by the naval hospital. It was renamed Camp Kidd in honor of Rear Admiral Isaac C. Kidd who died at Pearl Harbor. The wounded of Pearl Harbor had been brought directly to San Diego. Rows of bunks were placed in the Museum of Natural History, 960 in all.

Parking outside the park, Laura strolled down the Avenida de Palacios and over the bridge on foot. She passed a variety of buildings that were designed to show architectural progression from prehistoric to modern times. Planter boxes, terra-cotta jars, flowerpots, and gardens created a botanical display of plants from all over the world.

She turned at the Plaza del Pacifico, passed the Spreckels Organ pavilion and the cylindrical Ford building. She entered the Federal Building and approached an army nurse.

"I'm here to volunteer," she said, laying the morning newspaper on the desk. She pointed to the small article that had started her on this journey.

The nurse, who couldn't have been much older than Alexandra, asked, "Do you have any experience?"

"Oh, yes. I was an ambulance driver in France during the Great War."

The nurse's eyebrows raised in an impressed fashion. "My, you do have experience then, don't you?" Reaching under the desk she took a form and attached it to a clipboard, which she handed to Laura with a pencil. "Fill this out," she said.

Laura took the clipboard.

"Even though you have experience, we will need to have you complete our training course. You will be taught advanced first aid, how to handle firearms, radio transmission, and how to operate and do minor repairs to heavy vehicles. Does that sound like something you would want to do?"

Laura glanced at the top of the form that had been handed to her. It read: *Women's Ambulance Transport Corps (WATC)*.

She smiled at the nurse behind the desk. "Dear, I'm tired of being a bystander. I've been looking for some way to get into this war. This is just the ticket I need!"

17

"Didn't I tell you she was whistle bait?" Lieutenant Nolan Murphy leaned into Nat and elbowed him in the ribs. "Hubba hubba!"

Nat's response was a perplexed stare at the woman onstage.

"A rare dish if ever I saw one!" Lieutenant Murphy said with a sly grin.

He wasn't the only man who was smitten by the woman's beauty. A sea of soldiers stretched from one end of the parade ground to the other. Seated on the tarmac their eyes were focused on a stage that was beset with microphones, a big band, and a female soloist. From the number of howls one would have thought it was a convention of timber wolves.

"Honestly, Nat, have you ever seen a dish with curves so perfectly ..."

"Shut up, Murphy," Nat said.

Perplexed, Murphy shot him an intrigued glance, not offended in the least by the way this enlisted man had spoken to him.

"Is there something wrong with your eyesight, pal?" Murphy teased. "That slick chick is definitely 20/20!"

"She's my sister."

Murphy laughed, thinking Nat was kidding. When Nat didn't laugh with him, Murphy's smile died.

"You're serious! Liltin' Lil is your sister?"

Nat nodded, unable to take his eyes off Lily, but for reasons that were different from every other male on the tarmac.

"Well, cut off my leg and call me Shorty!" Murphy cried in wonderment. "Why didn't you tell me your sister is Jerry Jupiter's canary?"

"Because I didn't know," Nat said. "I didn't even know she knew Jerry Jupiter."

The two of them sat side by side with matching dumbfounded expressions as Lily's magic began to work on the crowd. The howling decreased as the toe tapping and head bobbing took over.

"Do you think you can get me a date with her?"

"Shut up, Murphy."

※

Lieutenant Nolan Murphy was not your typical army officer. In fact, he had no business being in the army. He had no military background. No tactical skills. And no idea what he was doing or what he was supposed to do with the men assigned to him.

A political science major from Yale, he was in his fourth year of study when the United States declared war on Japan. His father, Andrew Murphy, a self-made Connecticut banker with powerful political ties, saw the war as an opportunity to advance his son's political ambitions.

"People love war heroes," his father told him. "Washington, Jackson, Harrison, Grant … all elected because of their warrior image. Now Washington and Jackson did all right for themselves, but Harrison was a weak sister. His inaugural speech was one of the most platitudinous, servile addresses ever delivered. Had he not died a month afterward, he most surely would have been a congressional puppet for his entire term of office. As for Grant … well, with the possible exception of Harding, we've never had a worse president! But the people flocked to the polls to elect him! Why? Because he was a war hero! People felt good when they voted for him!

"You see, son, people don't vote for a candidate based on his qualifications for the job ... oh, no ... they vote for the candidate that makes them feel good. They want to walk out of that voting booth feeling good about what they just did. And nothing makes a voter feel better than to vote for a war hero."

With this strategy in mind, the elder Murphy pulled some political strings and secured his future candidate son a commission in the army under the protective wing of a brigadier general (an old high school buddy) who knew not to expect anything militarily of the boy. In return, the brigadier general was promised he would be rewarded once the boy came into his own politically.

So it was that Lieutenant Nolan Murphy entered the army.

Nat entered the picture when Murphy learned of his experience as a portrait photographer. He figured a photographer would be a useful person to have around for anyone who wanted to be elected to public office. After all, it was well known that Teddy Roosevelt had staged many a spontaneous picture to champion his public image. And if it was good enough for Teddy ...

After pulling Nat out of the infantry line, Murphy promoted him to corporal and made him his aide with the secret understanding that Nat's primary purpose in the army was to be Murphy's personal photographer. Nat's wartime objective would be to compile a portfolio of photographs that Murphy could use to launch a political career following the war.

For this project, a man of Nat's abilities was the logical choice. The way Lieutenant Murphy saw it, there were two possible courses of action. He could attempt to be a real war hero. This would require braving bullets and charging hills just as Teddy

Roosevelt did at San Juan Hill. But such an approach had a serious drawback. Murphy was allergic to danger.

His idea of danger was charging through a women's sorority late at night. As for significant achievements, his most memorable exploit to date was to swallow twenty goldfish as part of his fraternity house initiation. He concluded that becoming a real war hero was simply too dangerous.

Murphy's other choice was to become a paper hero; preferably, an 8 x 10 glossy paper hero. That's where Nat came in. If a good professional portrait photographer could make an average woman appear gorgeous and an ugly woman appear ... well, not so repulsive, then certainly he could make a handsome political aspirant appear to be a war hero.

Lily Morgan stood confidently at center stage. Her eyes ranged over the microphone that bore the radio call letters MBS as she made eye contact with soldier after soldier seated in the front rows of the audience. Her voice was soft yet vibrant, heavy with melancholy passion as she sang the haunting words that were rapidly becoming a favorite song among the American troops.

> Underneath the lantern by the barrack gate,
> Darling I remember the way you used to wait,
> 'Twas there that you whispered tenderly,
> That you loved me, You'd always be,
> My Lili of the lamplight, My own Lili Marlene.
>
> Time would come for roll call, Time for us to part,
> Darling I'd caress you and press you to my heart,
> And there 'neath that far off lantern light,
> I'd hold you tight, We'd kiss "good-night,"
> My Lili of the lamplight, My own Lili Marlene.
>
> Orders came for sailing somewhere over there,
> All confined to barracks was more than I could bear;

> I knew you were waiting in the street,
> I heard your feet, But could not meet,
> My Lili of the lamplight, My own Lili Marlene.
>
> Resting in a billet just behind the line,
> Even tho' we're parted your lips are close to mine;
> You wait where that lantern softly gleams,
> Your sweet face seems to haunt my dreams,
> My Lili of the lamplight, My own Lili Marlene.

She cut off the final vowel. The orchestra faded until there was nothing. The parade ground was stone silent, enraptured by Lily's poignant rendition of the song.

A heartbeat passed; then, a thunderous wave of applause and cheers.

Jerry Jupiter approached Lily from behind as she bowed appreciatively. With a "come on" motion of his left arm, he encouraged their response. The cheers grew louder.

"Miss Lily Morgan!" he shouted into the microphone.

The volume of the cheers doubled. Men stood clapping, shouting, whistling.

"Miss Lily Morgan—one of the best canaries on the swing scene today!" Jupiter said into the microphone. "What a voice!"

He let the cheers die down somewhat, and then he added: "And the package it comes in ain't so bad either!" He leveled an exaggerated stare at Lily's body. "How'd you like to take this one home to Momma? Hubba hubba!"

The whistles and wolf cries that Lily had silenced earlier returned with a vengeance. Lily did her best to smile sweetly. She turned toward the stage wings.

As she crossed the stage, the drummer, following instructions given him by Jupiter, did a drumroll that swayed in rhythm to the movement of her hips.

The soldiers went wild.

Lily tried to suppress the blush she felt rising in her cheeks. She told herself it was all part of the act. Jupiter orchestrated similar antics with the other females in the touring company. The difference, of course, was that they had been hired for such antics. Lily had been hired for her voice. Or so she thought.

$$\boxtimes$$

"Be still my heart," Murphy said, feigning an internal organ gone berserk.

Nat shot a disapproving look at his superior. "You said you'd behave yourself if I introduced you to her."

"What kind of unfeeling automaton are you?" Murphy said. "She's bewitching!"

"She's my sister."

"Unfortunate lad."

Nat turned to leave. "If you're not going to behave yourself …"

Grabbing his arm, Murphy conceded. "All right! I'll do my best. But I can't promise anything. When it comes to gorgeous women, I'm a weak man."

Lily stood a dozen feet away with her back to them. She was talking to a tall man with slicked-back black hair. He was holding a trumpet. Nat recognized him as one of the band members. The trumpet player stared suspiciously at the two men in uniform approaching them. Lily turned to see who he was looking at.

"Nat!" she cried, throwing her arms around his neck and hugging him. "What a wonderful surprise! I was afraid I'd missed you. Mom said you had already shipped out."

It was the first time he could ever remember being hugged by his sister. Growing up, he and Lily had always shared something of a loose bond not shared with their other siblings, a bond forged by their mutual artistic natures as well as by their general lack of interest in all things aeronautic. The hug, however, caught him by surprise. He filed it away as one of those unexplainable things that happen during time of war.

"Aren't you going to introduce us?" Murphy asked.

"Oh, yes. Lily, this is my commanding officer, Lieutenant Nolan Murphy. Murphy … er, Lieutenant Murphy, this is my sister Lily."

Lily nodded and smiled graciously.

Murphy wanted more. He held out his hand, palm up. Lily placed her hand in his, whereupon Lieutenant Murphy kissed it. "Such a wonderful voice!" he exclaimed. "You were magnificent. Just what the men needed."

It wasn't the first time Nat had seen Nolan Murphy oozing with charm. It was a gift. The man could gush on command. Male. Female. Officer of any rank. Murphy had a gift for putting people at ease and charming them into doing whatever it was he wanted them to do.

For this very reason Nat felt uncomfortable when the charm was directed at his younger sister. He had to give Lily credit, though. Her smile was polite, even warm, but the sparkle that twinkled in Murphy's eyes did not reflect in hers. Still, Nat wanted to move quickly past this moment.

"And who's this, Lily?" Nat asked.

Retracting her recently kissed hand, Lily used it to introduce the man holding the trumpet. "This is my friend, Albert Lohmann," Lily said. "As you can see, he's a member of the band."

Lohmann extended his hand first to Nat, then to Murphy. Nat estimated him to be at least a dozen years older than his sister. The man's handshake was firm with a single pump. Friendly brown eyes looked down a thin straight nose directly into Nat's eyes and lingered there. He guessed Lohmann was as curious about meeting Lily's brother as he was about what Lily meant by calling him her friend.

"Ah! Lieutenant Murray!" Jerry Jupiter's voice trumpeted his greetings. An overstretched smile accompanied him. "I see you've met our darling Lily! Some dish, huh?"

"It's Lieutenant Murphy," Lily said, correcting her boss. "And this is my brother, Nat."

Nat's eyes turned hard as he responded to Jupiter's outstretched hand and wooden smile. He didn't like this guy. Didn't like his type, and certainly didn't like the way he treated Lily.

Jupiter gripped Nat's hand enthusiastically and shook it side to side like a dog shaking a rag. "So you're the bomber pilot!" he boomed.

Nat didn't return the smile. "I have no wings on my chest," he said.

"Well, so you don't!" With a sly wink, Jupiter said, "Did you get grounded? I've heard about you flyboys."

"Nat's a photographer," Lily said.

Jupiter wasn't listening. He'd already turned to Murphy, putting an arm around the man's shoulders and giving him a good shaking. To Lily, he said, "You owe a lot to this guy. He's the one who put you on the radio today!"

Lily's eyebrows raised in delighted surprise.

"This guy was responsible for this whole gig. The invite. The setup. The radio feed. The works!"

Nolan Murphy lowered his gaze and kicked at the ground. Nat knew it to be just one of many weapons in the lieutenant's charisma arsenal. As usual, it was effective. It drew out from Lily the response Murphy wanted.

"Really?" she asked excitedly. "This was my first time to sing on radio!"

Murphy glanced up long enough to say, "The way you sing, it certainly won't be your last time."

"How sweet!" Lily said. She leaned into him and gave him an appreciative peck on the cheek.

"Got some of that for me?" Jupiter protested. "After all, I'm the one who accepted the invitation!"

Lily ignored the bandleader.

Lohmann stood off to one side. His face was framed with blatant displeasure for Jupiter.

"Murray …" Jupiter said, seemingly unfazed by Lily's passive rebuff and Lohmann's glare, "got a sec? There's a few details we need to work out."

The bandleader led a reluctant Murphy aside. Lohmann looked from sister to brother, gave an expression that signaled he felt like an intruder, then excused himself saying he needed to pack his things.

Lily and Nat were alone. Lily smiled like she was about to burst.

"Look at you!" she gushed. "You look so handsome in your uniform!"

"You don't look so bad yourself," Nat said. In truth, he was unsettled by his sister's obvious feminine maturity first onstage and now off. He would adjust; it would just take a little time.

They stared at one another in awkward silence.

"So …" Lily said, "Lieutenant Murphy seems like a nice guy."

Nat grinned, half in amusement that the first thing out of his sister's mouth concerned Lieutenant Murphy, and half in irony that even when Murphy wasn't around he was the topic of conversation.

"He rescued me from the infantry," Nat said.

"To take pictures?"

"How did you know?"

"You introduced yourself to Jerry as a photographer."

She's sharper than everyone gives her credit for, Nat thought. *Always has been.* "Officially, I'm his aide. Unofficially, I'm helping him prepare for a life of politics."

It was Lily's turn to grin. She looked over her shoulder in the general direction of Murphy's disappearance. He was nowhere to be seen. "With his looks and charm, he can go far," she said.

"You think he's charming?"

"Sure. He's not leading-man handsome, but he's attractive. And he seems to be able to pull off that strong dose of blarney that's in him without coming across as insincere. Unlike Jerry. He's all showman."

"I don't like the way he treats you," Nat said seriously.

"Lieutenant Murphy?"

"No, that Jupiter character."

"He's harmless," Lily said. "All talk."

"I'm not so sure."

"You sound like Albert."

"Albert?"

"The trumpet player you just met. We've had this same conversation. He doesn't care much for Jerry. Personally or professionally."

"Already I'm beginning to like Albert. Why doesn't he like Jupiter professionally?"

Lily looked both ways before speaking. In a soft voice, she said, "Most of the musicians don't respect him, and this isn't for public consumption, mind you. He's a paper man."

"Paper man?"

"A musician who plays the spots."

Nat gave his sister a quizzical look. He still didn't understand.

"The musical notes," Lily explained. "Jerry can't improvise. He can only play what's written down."

"He was improvising on stage," Nat said.

Lily shook her head. "He's a showman, nothing more. He has different players in the band compose those spontaneous improvisations. He memorizes it, then plays it like he's making it up."

Nat shook his head. "Who would have known?"

"Exactly! Jerry Jupiter may not be a great musician, but he knows what audiences want and he gives it to them. I'll always be grateful to him for giving me this break."

"He should be grateful to you. You were fabulous!"

Lily smiled warmly, obviously touched by her brother's comment.

"I hear that so often," she said, "but most of the time it's nothing more than a lonely man's opening line. Thanks. The compliment means a lot to me coming from you."

"You deserve it. You're really good, Lily."

Lily gave her brother a kiss on the cheek. When she pulled away her eyes were glassy with tears.

"When are you shipping out?" she asked.

"In a few days. First to Camp Pickett, Virginia; then to North Africa."

"Are you frightened?"

"About going to Africa?"

"About going to war. You're not exactly the soldier type."

Nat was not offended by her remark. He shared her opinion of him. "I don't expect to see much action," he said. "In case you hadn't noticed, Murphy isn't exactly a model of a fighting man either."

"He lets you call him Murphy?"

Nat nodded. "When we're alone. Unless there's a superior officer around, he's pretty slack about all this army stuff. His main objective is to come out of the war in one piece with a couple pictures of himself on some foreign battlefield."

"What about the other men? Do they respect him?"

"For the most part. He works hard at seeing that they have everything they need and in return they do whatever is needed to make him look good. Like this show. He promised them something exciting if they got high approval ratings. They came through for him, he came through for them."

"Sounds like you've found the life of Riley."

Nat grinned. "You don't know the half of it. You ought to see the equipment I'm working with. A Leica 35mm with a wide-aperture lens. A Rolleiflex twin-lens twelve exposure. Let me tell you, these aren't standard army issue. Murphy's father sent them to me."

Lily smiled and shook her head. "And here I was worried about what the army would do to my sensitive brother."

"Someone's looking after me," Nat grinned.

"Hey, Lil!"

It was Jupiter's voice. Now that Nat knew more about the man, he disliked him even more.

"Lil, guess what?" Jupiter said. He and Murphy walked toward her side by side. "Do you want to know about how great this guy is?" He placed his arm around a self-consciously grinning Lieutenant Murphy and rocked him back and forth like he'd done before. "This guy is going to recommend to the brass that they schedule us for some gigs over in Europe, behind-the-lines entertainment for the boys, that sort of thing. What do you think?"

Lily was all smiles. "I think that would be wonderful!" she agreed. "Do you really think you can do it?"

Giving his best boyish grin, Murphy replied, "I'll do my best."

"Isn't he the greatest?" Jupiter said. Moving to Lily's side, he patted her on the bottom. "But for now, doll, we'd better get packing."

Nat moved toward Jupiter and started to say something.

"You go on ahead, Jerry," Lily said, stepping between her brother and Jupiter. "I want to say good-bye to Nat."

Jupiter was too elated by the news of a possible trip overseas to notice Nat's anger. Seeing a couple of the band members haul-ing their instruments toward the waiting bus, he called out to them, anxious to tell them the news.

"He doesn't mean anything by it," Lily defended her boss.

"All I can say is that he'd better keep his hands off you!"

"I can handle him," Lily replied. "And if it gets to the point where I can't, I have Albert to protect me. Satisfied?"

Nat wasn't satisfied, but there was nothing he could do about it.

Lily gave Nat a hug. "I'm calling Dad and Mom tonight. Do you want me to tell them anything?"

"Just tell them hello for me." Nat's anger still hadn't settled. He found it hard to remove his gaze from the bandleader's back.

"Lieutenant Murphy," Lily said, "thank you for everything. And I hope to see you in the near future. In the meantime, take care of my brother for me, will you?"

"He's in capable hands," Murphy said with an easy grin.

They parted ways. Lily rejoined the band while Nat and Lieutenant Murphy made their way across the now-empty tarmac.

"Are you this way around every guy who looks at your sister, or is it just me and Jupiter?" Murphy asked.

"It just irked me the way he treated her, the way he touched her, that's all," Nat replied.

"And, let's say, if I was interested in your sister … just hypo-thetically, of course … could I expect the old sockdolager from you to lay me out cold?"

Nat stared hard at Murphy. "Are you serious?"

"As serious as I can be."

It was the first time Nat saw Murphy's face completely sober. No twinkle in the eye. No boyish grin. No mischievous smirk. Nothing. He was really serious about this.

Nat shrugged. "She could do worse, I suppose."

It took a moment for Murphy to realize he was kidding. For Nat it was a delightful moment.

"'Tain't funny, McGee," Murphy said.

The humor faded quickly for Nat as they walked back to the barracks and his thoughts returned to Jerry Jupiter's groping hands. He was more preoccupied about his sister on the tour bus with the bandleader than he was about the fact that he was being shipped out to the war front.

18

"This doesn't look right."

A chill seeped into Nat's bones, and it wasn't caused by the night ocean air. He gripped the side of the assault craft as it lumbered toward the northern coast of Africa. Leaning over the side he strained to discern the identity of the distant burning object. As he did, Murphy fumbled for his binoculars. The buck and roll of the landing craft made it next to impossible for him to keep the burning object within the binoculars' field of vision.

On Murphy's orders, the coxswain was piloting the landing craft toward a blazing pillar of fire. He had assumed that the fire was coming from the oil tanks on Cape Fedala.

"That fire's in the middle of the bay!" Nat said.

"It's a French ship," Murphy confirmed.

"French?"

"This isn't Fedala," Murphy said.

Nat stared at his superior and friend. Murphy looked ridiculous in his army helmet, like a little boy at play, not at all the commanding figure the situation demanded.

Murphy worriedly scanned the waters behind them. A score of boats was following their wake. It was evident he was trying to make a battlefield decision and it wasn't coming easily for him.

Over the last couple of months Nat had seen him juggle complex schedules and arrangements, lists, requests, orders, and a mound of other paperwork with ease. He'd observed his friend soothe irate army tempers and pull diverse personalities together into a combined effort. The man was an administrative and personnel genius.

On the water, at night, approaching an enemy-occupied foreign body of land he appeared less impressive.

"If it's not Fedala ..." Nat started.

"... it's Casablanca," Murphy finished. "We're fifteen miles west of where we should be."

As if to confirm his suspicions, another French ship, which now could be seen lurking behind the ship that was ablaze, began firing three-inch shells at them.

"I thought the French were on our side!" Nat said.

"This is the Vichy French," Murphy shouted back at him as though that would mean something to Nat.

Murphy stood to yell something to the coxswain. As he did, Nat saw rocks behind him, jutting from the surf, turning aside everything that came at them with the same thrusting motion a plow blade uses as it slices into the ground and overturns the earth. Before Nat could yell a warning, before Murphy's command to the coxswain ever left his lips, the assault craft hit the rocks and overturned.

Nat went under.

Camera bags swirled around his head. His arms and legs flayed noiselessly every which way in an attempt to right himself. But which way was up? Then, the undulating light from the ship afire caught his eye. The surface. With desperate strokes, Nat clawed his way that direction, fighting the pull of his camera bags, uniform, and heavy boots.

His head broke the surface.

A shell screamed inches away from his face. The French were still firing at the overturned assault craft. Equipment floated all around him. So did a body. The coxswain.

Another shell. The assault craft took a direct hit. An explosive, cracking thunder pounded Nat's ears as a portion of the craft disintegrated. The blow was fatal. The craft wobbled front and back, then its stern slipped beneath the surface, pulling the rest of the craft down with it.

The other trailing assault boats had broken off and were turning back. Curls of white water formed as they swerved in their attempts to dodge the three-inch shells. They were too busy escaping to attempt any sort of rescue. One didn't make it. A well-aimed shell ripped it apart. Bodies flew upward, tumbled, then splashed into the ocean.

Mercifully, now that his craft was sunk, the French stopped firing his direction. However, Nat found himself faced with a new problem. The tide and the surge of the sea were on the side of the French, lifting him up like driftwood and hurling him toward the rocks. Each wave that hit splattered into fine white spray. Nat wasn't about to wait around to find out what would happen to him should he go the way of the waves.

It was one thing, though, to sense the danger, quite another to do anything about it. Between the camera equipment and his heavy wet clothing, try as he might, he couldn't put any distance between himself and the rocks.

He had to shed some weight. Reaching for the strap of the first of two camera bags, he started to lift it over his head. Then stopped. It was the Leica. How could he just toss it aside? He reached for the other strap. The Rolleiflex. He paused.

On more than one occasion Nat had heard photographers make jokes about their attachment to their equipment. His high school photography teacher told the class, "My wife accused me last night of loving my Leica more than her. I replied, 'What's your point?'" And although Nat admitted to being possessive about his equipment, he didn't realize until now how deep this feeling ran.

Ducking his head into the water, he stripped off his boots and tossed them aside. His utility belt was next. That was better. Not only could he hold his own against the tide, but he was actually making progress.

The moist air was heavy with the acrid smell of metal and powder. Nat saw several other men working their way ashore. On the beach, civilians appeared out of the darkness. They charged into the surf to pull the first of the soldiers onto land. As they did, they glanced continuously over their shoulders as if they were expecting hostile company soon.

Leading with his back, Nat stroked the water and kicked. His foot hit something. Soft and hard. Definitely not a rock. Cautiously he felt around with an extended toe. There it was again. Soft. It moved at his touch, not on its own but buoyant in the water.

Nat reached into the water. He felt cloth. Occupied cloth. Then an ear. Then hair. Nat pulled on the hair, then reached for a collar, dragging whoever it was to the surface.

Though the man's eyes were closed and there was no breath in his body, with what little light was afforded him by the blazing French ship, Nat recognized him.

Heavy black eyebrows rested atop a face that was already turning blue. The eyebrows were so bushy they looked like two caterpillars facing each other.

"Oh, Kotter!" Nat whimpered.

His previous conversation with the dead man rang in Nat's ears.

I'm tellin' 'em I come from a long line of army foot soldiers and that I joined this man's army for one reason and one reason only, and that's to be a foot soldier.

And that'll make you a medic?

Or a cook, or a truck driver, who cares? As long as they don't hand me one of them guns. Trust me, I knows about these things. You see, my dad and grandpa and uncle was all in the army, the whole family, for generations.

Nat wondered if Kotter had any brothers, or if the generations of Kotter infantrymen had come to an end with the man he held in his arms. The really eerie thing about Kotter's death was that just beneath the surface of the water Nat could see the outline of a rifle. Kotter was still clutching it. The one Nat had refused.

He let the dead man slip from his grasp. Kotter's body slid beneath the surface then hung there, his arms extended to his sides, his legs spread, suspended between the surface and the ocean floor.

"Morgan! Morgan! Nat!"

The cry was coming from his right. It was Murphy. He was clinging to a rock. Wave after wave tried to break his grip. He was visibly shaken, but had a firm grip on the rocks, the very ones Nat had tried so desperately to keep at a distance.

"Are you hurt?" Nat asked.

Murphy shook his head no.

"Pull off your boots and swim for it!"

His superior officer stared fearfully at the waves. "I can't swim!" he shouted. There was a definite tremor in the sound of his voice.

Nat looked to shore. There was no other way to rescue him than by water. And there were no boats around. Nothing that floated other than small bits of debris.

"Hold on!" Nat shouted.

"That I can do," Murphy shouted back with half a grin.

Nat rode the swells toward the rocks, fearful of their power to dash him against them. With each rising swell he paddled the opposite way in an attempt to slow his forward motion. Murphy anxiously watched his progress.

His technique managed to slow his approach somewhat. Just as he was reaching out to the rock next to Murphy, a rogue wave sideswiped him, smashing him against a mossy green rock. His ribs took the brunt of the blow, knocking the wind out of him. He wrapped his arms around the rock. It did little good. He was slipping back into the water and couldn't stop himself.

Murphy grabbed his shirt near the shoulder to keep him from slipping just as another wave pounded against his back. He felt his cheek sliding against the algae. His mouth tasted of saltwater. With all his might, he clung to the rock, his chest heaving for air, yet with each heave came pain in his ribs.

It took him several minutes to secure his position and protect himself against each new water assault.

"I don't know if I'm strong enough to get us both to shore," he said.

"Lose the cameras," Murphy replied.

Nat glanced at the bags that hung around his neck. The Leica. The Rolleiflex. *Lose the cameras.* Easy for Murphy to say. No one but a photographer would appreciate their true value. There had to be a way to save the cameras *and* Murphy.

"What's the matter?" Murphy asked.

"I think I can make it with both you and the cameras," Nat replied.

Murphy looked at him like he was insane.

"Lose the cameras, Morgan!"

Nat made no effort to unburden himself of the two camera bags.

"That's an order, Corporal!" Murphy shouted. "Lose the cameras!"

Nat clung to the rock. He could swim to shore with the cameras and come back for Murphy.

"Nat?" Murphy called. His voice was trembling again.

Nat stared at his superior officer, his friend. Debris floated all around them. Here and there a body. A ship ablaze in the harbor. The French guns had fallen silent. The assault boats that had survived had long since disappeared into the ocean darkness.

He lifted first one camera bag strap over his head, then the other and threw the bags as far away from the rocks as he could.

Between wave assaults he worked his way over to Murphy. "Don't fight me!" Nat shouted over the sound of the crashing waves. "Just let yourself go limp. If you struggle, it only makes it harder for both of us. Understand?"

Murphy tried to hold Nat's gaze, but his eyes couldn't resist an occasional fearful glance at the water.

"Limp!" Nat shouted.

Murphy nodded hesitantly.

"Don't make me knock you out!"

A grin formed on Murphy's lips, as Nat intended. It was meant as a joke. He had never punched someone before in his life, not even as a schoolboy. He'd been in some shoving matches, but that was all. He didn't even know if he could punch someone hard enough to knock him out.

Reaching his arm under Murphy's arm and around his chest, Nat timed the ocean swells. Just as one slammed against them and it looked like the next one was far behind, he and Murphy pushed off the rocks.

They were less than ten feet away when the next swell hit them. A big one, large enough to toss them back against the rocks. With a cry of pain, Murphy took the brunt of the blow, cushioning Nat.

Nat planted his foot against the rock and pushed off again, swimming with all his might. This time they got far enough away that they rose and fell with the swell, but it failed to grab them enough to dash them against the rocks again.

With Murphy's sandy hair in his face, Nat pulled for shore with his free arm. The going was slow. Murphy squirmed on occasion when he gulped an excessive amount of water, but for the most part he remained passive.

In short order Nat's lungs burned with ever-increasing intensity from the exertion and the saltwater he swallowed. He turned his head to check his progress. About a hundred yards to go. Closing his eyes, he tried not to think of the wildfire scorching his lungs and rising up his windpipe. He focused on making meaningful strokes, though his arm felt like it would snap with each new stroke against the water's resistance.

He was tiring and they were slowly sinking. He didn't have the strength to keep their heads above the water any longer. A white haze covered his eyes, blurring his vision.

Each new stroke was a major battle. His strength gone, he was driven by instinct. Yet instinct alone could not counteract the downward pull of the sea. The water was lapping over his face. Where once his eyes and nose and mouth managed to break the surface with each stroke, now there was no break. The surface grew more distant. Half an inch. An inch. Nat could still see stars overhead, but they were blurred and rippling through a liquid lens.

Just then, his foot hit something. Bottom?

He stretched his leg but found nothing.

Another stroke. Then another.

This time his foot hit and anchored itself. The bottom of the bay! With as much strength as he could muster, Nat pushed with his leg. Now the other foot found the sandy bottom. With rubbery legs Nat pushed himself and Murphy into shallow water.

Now Murphy's legs found the bottom too. Nat's burden was relieved. They both collapsed in the surf and, while wave after wave rolled over them, they crawled out of the bay and onto the shore.

Nat crumpled onto the beach, his cheek pressed against the sand. Beside him Murphy lay in similar condition. There was no one else on the beach. The civilians he'd seen earlier were gone.

So this is North Africa, he thought woozily. Even in his exhausted state he couldn't suppress the chuckle that welled up inside of him. *If I were to review the trip over here, I'd have to say these last few yards were definitely the hardest.*

※

They had been at Camp Pickett, Virginia, a little more than a week in preparation for their departure to French Morocco. Lieutenant Murphy had taken leave over the weekend to visit his father at their home at Bridgeport.

It had been a boring week for Nat. In keeping with the understanding regarding Murphy's expected role in the army, while other soldiers practiced loading and landing operations on Solomon's Island, an exercise dubbed *Exercise Quick*, Murphy's task at Camp Pickett was to oversee the waterproofing of all the vehicles. Since this assignment afforded few picture possibilities, Nat was left alone to wander the post. To his amazement, the place was virtually new, so much so that sidewalks had not yet been laid, which made for a muddy mess every time it rained.

On one of these muddy, rainy days Nat sat on his cot cleaning his camera equipment for the second time in one day.

"Morgan! Grab your stuff! We're shipping out!"

Murphy burst through the door. He was grinning ear to ear. Nat was surprised to see him. He wasn't due back from Bridgeport for another day.

"We're not scheduled to ship out for another week," Nat said.

"Change of plans."

Murphy's mischievous grin was intriguing. "What are you up to, you sly fox?" Nat asked.

"Can't say. Just pack your stuff. We leave in an hour."

"An hour?"

But Murphy didn't hear him. He was already out the door.

An hour and fifteen minutes later they were on the road, sharing a cab with the driver of a troop transport truck, the first in a line of trucks snaking through the country roads of Virginia.

"Can you at least tell me where we're headed?" Nat asked, bouncing along beside a still-grinning Murphy.

"Newport News," Murphy replied.

"And what's in Newport News?"

"Our transport ship."

"That's the news that has you grinning like a monkey?"

Murphy's grin only grew wider.

Hours later when the transport trucks pulled to a stop on the Newport News docks, Nat understood why Murphy was so pleased with himself, though questions abounded as to how he managed to arrange it.

"This is our transport ship?" Nat asked, climbing out of the cab of the truck and staring at the ship incredulously.

"Not bad, eh?"

"We're going to Africa in *this?*"

"That's the plan."

Nat laughed, shaking his head in wonder. All along the dock men poured out of the back of the transport trucks and gaped at the ship docked at the pier.

It was a French luxury liner.

"When the war first broke out, it was in a German port," Murphy explained. "The Germans confiscated it. Then the Brits captured it from them. We're borrowing it from the Brits for troop transport. When I heard about it, I figured someone would have to be transported in it. Why not us?"

The grin that Murphy wore earlier was now on Nat's face. "Indeed," he said, "why not?"

"My father had to call in a marker to help swing the deal, but he was glad to do it."

Nat admired the sleekness of the liner. "Sure beats a Liberty ship."

Murphy grinned a self-satisfied grin. "You can say that again."

As the last of the transport trucks unloaded, the dock was packed with laughing, joking, jolly soldiers. They were all singing Lieutenant Murphy's praises.

The crossing was swift and smooth. Even for Nat, whose only pleasant sailing experiences to this point were limited to San Diego Bay. And while conditions aboard ship were cramped, no one was complaining. It was light duty for everyone except the British who actually sailed the ship.

Nat's responsibility was to see that the canteen had ice twice a day. A half-dozen buckets carried up five decks in the morning and afternoon fulfilled his responsibility. For this, he got his choice of candy bars free of charge.

While most of the men slept in hammocks shoulder to shoulder in the ballroom and dining areas, Nat slept in a single bed cabin adjoining Lieutenant Murphy's cabin. It afforded him a measure of privacy, which he treasured.

Arriving well ahead of the Liberty ships, they anchored a good distance from shore and waited for the other ships to catch up with them. No one aboard seemed to mind. They all knew that once they disembarked, the luxury ended and the war began.

When the Liberty ships did join them, nearly three-quarters of the soldiers aboard were seasick, which was understandable considering their transports were designed to carry cargo, not wealthy passengers. Fortunately for the sick, a sandstorm prevented them from landing immediately. It gave them a day to recover.

As the sun set on the night of the debarkation, Nat sipped a cup of coffee while he leaned on the bow railing and stared in awe at the brilliant red strip of sky that hovered over the distant land. It was the most beautiful sunset he'd ever seen.

An auspicious omen?

Hours later, gasping for air, soaked to the bone, and coated with flesh-chafing sand, with the bay waters lapping his socked feet, Nat concluded the sunset had been nothing more than a natural phenomenon.

※

"Morgan!"

Murphy was on all fours in the sand beside him.

"Morgan!"

"Huh?"

"Your camera bags. They've washed ashore!"

Through blurry eyes, Nat watched as Murphy scrambled to retrieve the bags from the edge of the surf.

"Let's get some pictures."

Nat pretended he didn't hear, which wasn't hard to do since he could barely lift his head.

"Come on!" Murphy pulled him up into a sitting position and plopped the camera bags into his lap.

While Nat sat dazed and unmoving, Murphy recovered an army helmet that had also washed up. He tried it on. It was too large for his head. He looked like a little boy trying on his father's helmet.

"It's better if I don't wear it anyway," he said aloud to himself. "Nat! Check your equipment. We'll need a flash."

His strength barely beginning to rally, Nat fumbled with the zipper on the camera bag. It was supposed to be waterproof, but you never knew about these things until they were tested.

The inside of both bags was dry. All the equipment appeared to be in good shape.

"Hurry!" Murphy said. He was wading into the surf.

Nat's head was pounding. It was all he could do to work his face into a puzzled expression, which Murphy read.

"We'll get a picture of me coming ashore. Wading in out of the surf with the French ship blazing behind me in the harbor."

This was ridiculous. The beach was quiet. Too quiet. There were no other signs of life. No other soldiers that Nat could see. And where had all the civilians gone? The bay was tranquil with the exception of the burning ship. With no assault boats to shoot at, the guns of the other French ships in the harbor were silent.

"Get the lead out, Morgan!" Murphy said.

His mind in a fog, Nat managed to assemble the flash device onto the twin-lens camera. He struggled to his knees, the artist in him instinctively determining to shoot at a low camera angle to make Murphy appear to be larger than life. He flipped up the metal cover atop the camera and peered down into the viewfinder. He focused.

Without looking up, he instructed Murphy, "Start walking toward me!"

Murphy, waist deep in water, trudged toward the shore, the metal helmet dangling at his side, his hair plastered to the top of his head. He focused his eyes beyond Nat as though he was assessing a battle situation. Nat waited until the figure filled the viewfinder, leaving just enough room to capture the ship burning in the background.

Dramatic image. Framed nicely. Good composition.

FLASH!

Less than two seconds after the flash, Nat was pushed from behind onto the sand. The muzzle of a rifle pressed against his neck. Men with guns came running from everywhere. They encircled Murphy. Several were shouting orders that Nat couldn't understand.

The soldiers were speaking French.

Unfamiliar sounds woke him. Nat's eyes fluttered. He winced. It felt like half the beach was in them. He raised aching arms, and with filthy hands he tried to rub the scratchiness out. It only made things worse.

His eyes weren't his only problem. Still in wet clothes, he was damp and chilled. The muscles that weren't cramped ached intolerably, particularly his back which was wedged against a cold brick wall. Socked feet slipped against a matching brick floor as he tried to adjust himself into a more comfortable position.

He couldn't find one. Leaning heavily against the wall, he worked himself into a standing position.

Nat's head pounded mercilessly. The stench of stale urine was strong in the ten-by-ten-foot enclosure. Through blurry vision, cleared partially by watering eyes, he could see Murphy curled up in a corner like a cat.

Nat shuffled around the enclosure, stretching out his muscles and attempting to reintroduce his body to the idea of blood circulation. The hammering inside his head kept him off balance. He had to support himself against the walls to keep from stumbling.

A single rectangular opening, about ten feet from the floor and not nearly large enough for even a small man to squeeze through, provided the room's only light and ventilation. A bright block of light that projected through it onto the opposite wall indicated it was morning.

Nat's empty stomach complained. The inside of his mouth tasted and smelled of rotting seaweed. He was growing light-headed. Falling with his back to the wall, he slumped into a sitting position again.

So ends the illustrious army career of Nat Morgan, he mused. *Captured by the enemy on his first day of combat, he waits for the war to end in a stinking French Moroccan jail. For how long? Two years? Four? More?*

Murphy stirred in the corner. Without getting up he tried to open his eyes. Now Nat knew what the struggle looked like from the opposite side of one's eyelids.

Nat said nothing, knowing Murphy would need time to rally his senses. Although Murphy gave no outward sign, Nat knew he was grateful for the courtesy, though he would have given almost anything to have his camera right now. A picture of a wrinkled, disheveled Nolan Murphy would be priceless.

"Do you know what I'm most grateful for right now?" Murphy asked with a scratchy voice.

"What?"

"I'm grateful they took your cameras away from you."

Nat grinned. It was amazing to him how much the two of them thought alike. Sometimes it was downright frightening. And it was times like this when Nat knew the two of them would be together for a long time. After the war Murphy would need plenty of public-relations pictures and Nat knew he would never go back to commercial portrait photography.

The revelation alone surprised him. But what surprised him even more was how much he was looking forward to being a part of Murphy's campaigns.

"If I know you," Nat said, "you'll not only talk our way out of here, but you'll have them throw in a trip to Paris."

Murphy grinned appreciatively at Nat's assessment of his abilities.

"So who exactly is holding us prisoner?" Nat asked.

Before Murphy could answer, the heavy wooden door rattled with key to lock. The sound of the metal latch clanked noisily and the door scratched an arching pattern on the floor as it was shoved open.

Two French guards appeared. Both Nat and Murphy stood, but the guards wanted only Murphy. With one guard in front and one guard behind, he followed them out the door.

"Time to go to work," he said with a half grin.

The door scraped shut with a heavy thud, the latch clanked, and the lock sounded.

Nat was alone.

By the movement of the window light on the wall, Nat guessed that two hours passed before Murphy returned. During that time Nat dozed and thought of his family … San Diego seemed so far away; even though he'd lived there all his life it took on a dreamlike quality in his mind. He envisioned his mother and father sitting on the veranda, drinking coffee and reading the morning paper. He wondered if Alex was still in Texas and how Walt was faring in England.

When the door scraped and Murphy returned, he came bearing gifts. Figs, a chunk of bread, and chalice of dirty water. His hair was combed and his face washed.

"That's the best I could do," he said, handing the food to Nat. "Eat it all. I've had some already."

The wooden door thumped loudly, shutting them off from the world that Murphy had just visited.

Murphy moved surprisingly well. He showed no signs of being abused in any way. In fact, he seemed in good spirits.

"It's official," he said, sitting against the wall. "We're prisoners of the Vichy French government."

"That's better than being prisoners of the Germans, isn't it?"

Murphy studied him a moment before answering. "You don't read the newspapers much, do you?"

"I'm a live-and-let-live kind of guy," Nat replied. "I would have been content to let Germany and France and England and Japan do whatever they wanted to do with themselves as long as they left me alone. I only got involved because Japan came knocking on my back door. It's different for you. All this international mumbo-jumbo is your chosen field of study."

Murphy grinned. "Have to admit it's more fun debating it in class than it is living it in a French Moroccan jail."

"So who are these guys anyway?"

Murphy leaned his head against the wall and stared at intangibles as he seemed to pull words out of the air that would describe their situation. "When Germany conquered France, they divided the country into two zones. One was placed under German military occupation, while the other was left to the French to govern under the auspices of a National Assembly that met at Vichy; hence, their name."

"I thought the French government fled to England."

"There is a Free French government-in-exile under the command of General Charles de Gaulle," Murphy replied.

"So in reality, we *are* prisoners of the Germans."

Murphy winced. "It's not that simple. The Vichy collaborate with the Germans but aren't completely controlled by them. That's good news for us."

"I'm all for good news."

"We should be out of here in a couple of days," Murphy said with a smile.

"You're serious?"

"Major General Mark Clark is here in Casablanca. He's working out an agreement with Admiral Jean Darlan, the head of the Vichy government here in Morocco."

"How do you know this?" Nat asked. "Is that what they told you?" He was being cautious. Although he trusted Murphy, he wasn't about to let his hopes escalate based on information whose source was the same people holding them captive.

"I just finished speaking with General Clark himself," Murphy reassured him. "Part of his negotiations is an exchange of prisoners."

Lieutenant Murphy's information proved itself accurate. Two days later they were released. Within a week they were back with their unit traveling across the desert toward Bizerte, Tunisia.

※

"Come on, Lieutenant, guess how many."

"I'm busy, Suter."

Murphy pinned down the edge of the map with his hand when it threatened to blow off the charred British tank. He stared intently at the map's features, seemingly oblivious to the thousands of flies that covered his arms and chest and swarmed around his head.

Nat stood off a short distance, attempting to compose the picture while keeping the flies away from the lens and viewfinder. It was miserably hot. Nat was drenched by his own juices. It felt like he was working inside a gigantic oven.

The wind had just arrived. Even though it was hot enough to sting the flesh it at least brushed away some of the flies. But the slight reprieve from the insects would soon exact another toll on the troops. Together with the thin strip of red that lined the horizon, it announced a coming dust storm.

Nat didn't know which he hated worse, the flies or the dust. Even though the troops captured them in droves, disposing of them in heaping piles, the flies got into everything. The constant buzz and crawling sensation on any exposed piece of skin was enough to drive a man to madness.

The dust was just as bad if not worse. Nat couldn't remember taking a bite of food that didn't crunch with the grit of sand since the day they left French Morocco. It got under one's clothing, it collected in one's shoes, it stuck to one's sweaty skin, and coated one's hair. Nearly half of every day was spent brushing the gritty irritant out of his camera equipment, which would freeze up within a day if left to itself. He wasn't alone. The sand got into carburetors and watches, everything that was mechanical. It was a daily nuisance to everyone.

"Take the picture, Morgan!" Murphy complained.

"Lieutenant, just take a guess!" Suter pleaded.

"Suter, you're in the picture!" Nat said.

"Back off, Suter," Murphy ordered.

The skinny, bespectacled private shuffled backward, but not far. Here was another man, if you could call him that, who didn't belong in the infantry. He was just a kid, still fascinated with the weird and unusual. His command of minutiae together with his motor mouth at times made him an even worse irritant than the flies.

"Nine million!" Suter said finally. "One fly gives birth to nine million babies in a year!" He topped off his information in a self-pleased manner with folded arms and a grin.

"Wonderful, Suter," Murphy said dryly. "Nat, are you going to take this picture or not?"

The photo was Murphy's idea. Together with the map and the blackened British tank he felt the image would portray a warrior's leadership as well as a commitment to an American ally.

"It says, 'Here's a man coming to the aid of his country's friends,'" he explained.

Nat checked one last time in the viewfinder. The composition had Murphy off to one side balanced by the long horizontal line of the desert stretching into infinity across the remainder of the frame.

"Ready," he said.

Shooing flies away from the lens, he tripped the shutter.

"Get one with me staring off into the distance. I'll give it a he-knows-they're-out-there-and-he's-going-after-them look of determination."

Nat advanced the film. Murphy struck his pose. The shutter tripped a second time.

"Got it," Nat said, immediately covering his equipment.

"Lieutenant …" Suter said.

Murphy stopped the private with an uplifted palm before any more came out.

"Do you know what that thin red line is, private?" he asked.

"Yes, sir. It's a dust storm."

"That's right, son. Now do you know what that means?"

The eyes of the private bunched up as he tried to read his lieutenant's face. Before he could hazard a guess, Lieutenant Murphy gave him the answer.

"It means you're going to get blown away unless you secure your tent right now."

"Yes, sir, I'll do that," Suter said. "But did you know that …"

"Now, Suter. Now."

"Yes, sir."

As the private plodded in the general direction of his tent, Murphy shook his head and grinned. "Can't bring myself to dislike the boy," he said. "I used to be just like him. Only I was seven at the time."

The wind was picking up now. All around them men scurried to cover things up and fasten things down. In the distance, the width of the red line had already doubled. Just before it hit, it would become a towering red tidal wave of sand.

When they reached their tent, Murphy spied a newspaper that someone had deposited on his cot in their absence. While Nat stowed the camera equipment, which had miraculously been returned to him as part of the prisoner exchange, Murphy picked up the newspaper.

"Hey, look at this!" he said. "It's a Boston newspaper! And look who's featured on the front page!"

He held up the paper for Nat to see. It was the picture of Murphy trudging out of the bay at Casablanca. Nat strained his eyes to read the small print at the bottom right corner of the picture, a photographer's habit. Murphy saw what he was looking at, turned the paper to read it himself, then, with a huge grin, he said, "Yep, you got rightful credit."

It wasn't that Nat didn't believe Murphy, he just had to see for himself. Sure enough, his name was listed as the photographer.

"Not bad for a rube!" Murphy chided good-naturedly. He was obviously pleased with the publicity.

A short time later the tent shuddered convulsively announcing the storm's arrival. It wasn't the first one they'd encountered in their trek across the northern edge of the African continent. From previous experience, Nat knew that visibility was reduced to zero. The entire army was hunkered down. There was nothing they could do but ride out the storm.

"Be back in a minute," Murphy said.

Nat's brow bunched with concern. "Where are you going?"

"Well, if you must know, Mother," Murphy said mockingly, "I'm going to the latrine."

Jumping to the role designated to him, Nat replied, "Didn't I tell you to go before we left?"

Murphy laughed and slipped outside. For the instant the tent flap was open, the entire interior was generously coated with sand.

Nat muttered. He brushed himself and his cot off. Then, spying the Boston newspaper that Murphy hadn't finished, he picked it up and looked again at his name under the photo on the front page.

According to the accompanying article, Lieutenant Nolan Murphy was instrumental in securing a solid treaty with the Vichy French, a treaty that saved many American lives and secured the north coast of Africa for upcoming air and ground attacks on Italy.

Nat grinned. It wasn't true, of course. Murphy was with him in the local French Moroccan jail. But it was good press coverage for Murphy. He'd get a lot of political mileage out of the article.

Just as he was replacing the newspaper on Murphy's cot, he saw something that made his heart leap into his throat. Murphy had left the tent without his compass. Apparently Murphy had pulled it out to take with him, but it had slipped beneath the newspaper and he'd gone outside without it.

In a desert sandstorm, it was a potentially fatal mistake.

Grabbing the compass, Nat threw open the flap and ducked into the sandstorm, calling out Murphy's name. The latrines were about a hundred yards southwest of their location. Shielding his face and eyes with his forearm, Nat set off that direction.

Fine sand rubbed his hands and cheeks raw. Large chunks pelted him, some of them drawing blood. He had to lean into the wind just to keep his balance. To move, he had to secure each foot and push. It was like climbing uphill. Blind.

"Murphy! Murphy!"

The wind threw the sound of his voice back in his face.

He reached the latrines. No one was there. He circled them, calling Murphy's name in every direction. The roar of the wind was his only answer.

Where now? Maybe I should get help.

Nat decided to play a hunch first. If he didn't find Murphy, he'd check their tent and if Murphy wasn't there, then he'd get help.

His hunch was that, without a compass to guide him in a straight line, Murphy might have been blown off course just enough to miss the latrines. If that was true, he undoubtedly would have gone past them, using that time-worn adage of the hopelessly lost—*I'll go just a little bit farther and if I don't find what I'm looking for, then I'll turn back.*

Nat continued on, allowing himself to drift with the wind. He called Murphy's name. Still no response.

After another hundred yards, he gave up.

The search was taking its toll on him. One side of his face was nearly raw. Trickles of blood formed jagged rivers on his hands and, from the stickiness, he imagined on his neck and forehead too. His eyelids were caked and gritty. Each blink felt like someone was rubbing sandpaper across his eyes.

Nat turned around. He checked his bearings. He allowed himself to drift even more with the wind for his return trek, but his hope of finding Murphy by himself was fading quickly.

He imagined reaching the tent only to find his friend lying atop his cot quick to chide him for thinking that a lieutenant would be so foolish as to wander off into a sandstorm without a compass, at which point he would produce a second compass Nat didn't know he owned.

If this was the case Nat would, of course, feel foolish. It was a feeling he would welcome, much better than the feeling of growing panic that was currently worming its way through his gut.

He stumbled over something buried in the sand.

Falling, the compass tumbled from his hand. It was like a dream sequence. More like a nightmare. He and the compass fell at the same rate. His fingers grabbed for it. It was beyond his reach. He strained harder to reach it, but came up short. As the compass fell, it faded from sight ever so slowly in the swirling sand. He lost it.

Nat hit the ground with a bone-jarring thud.

His one thought was on the compass. Even as he fought to get some of the air back that had been knocked from his lungs, he scrambled forward searching the ground frantically, desperately for the compass.

His fingers felt something hard. Metallic. Round.

The compass!

Clutching it tighter than he would a gold nugget, he struggled to get to his feet. His foot again hit something in the sand. The object he'd just tripped over.

It was the feel of the obstacle that caught his attention. Not like a rock or a piece of wood or metal machinery, this was solid but soft. Lowering himself to his knees, yet still careful not to lose the compass, he felt around with his free hand.

He felt it. When he did, a sickening feeling came over him. It was a hand.

He followed the arm to a body that was completely covered with sand. He managed to pull the body out and turn it over. Every inch was coated with sand.

Nat felt for signs of life. The body wasn't rigid. It was still warm. He felt the neck for a pulse. The man was still alive. Bending closer, Nat brushed sand off the man's face and cheeks and forehead.

It was Murphy!

He had been gone such a short time! Time enough to be buried alive in a North African sandstorm.

Nat managed to work the weight of Murphy's body onto his back and, taking the time to check the compass regularly, he carried his superior officer and friend back to their tent.

It was well into the night before Murphy washed enough sand out of his throat and mouth to talk. From his cot he stared gratefully up at Nat.

"And you called me a rube," Nat said. "Didn't they train you in officers school never to go to the latrine without taking all the essentials?"

A tired grin formed on Murphy's cracked and crusty lips. "'Tain't funny, McGee," he groaned.

19

A whiff of the soap Clayton Thomas shaved with distracted her. The scent caught her by surprise when he pulled the curtain around her to begin the radio beam test.

Alex chided herself. *Concentrate! You're acting like a slap-happy floozy.*

They were flying at 10,000 feet. Alex was piloting the Big Friend, the term of affection given the B-17 by the women pilots. Her vision of the outside world cut off by the black hood, she focused her attention on the instruments and what she heard in her earphones. She was listening to a navigational radio that originated from a ground transmitter.

The transmitters sent signals out on a course of due north, east, south, and west. When an aircraft was flying directly into or away from one of the beams, she heard a steady hum. The humming stopped momentarily if she was directly over the transmitter in what was referred to as the cone of silence. Three degrees on either side of the beam and the sound would fade into Morse code beeps: Da-dit if she was on the left of it; Dit-da it to the right. Keeping on course was called "bracketing the beam."

Virginia and Loretta had already passed the test. Now it was

Alex's turn. She had been instructed to take them back to Lockbourne for lunch.

During practice she'd never had any trouble staying on course. One whiff of Lieutenant Thomas's shaving soap changed all that.

Alex had locked onto one of the open range beacons eleven miles north of the airport. All she had to do was head toward it, follow that compass heading, and land on the active runway.

She had the hum in her ears and followed it south. Easy. Her mind wandered to the man on the other side of the hood. The mere thought of him set her heart pounding. It was a frightening feeling for her. Never had a man affected her like this before. Never. She'd heard other women talk of such feelings, but she always thought them silly. Nothing more than a bunch of lovesick females who thought they would only be complete once they found a man to marry.

She'd also heard these same women singing a different tune a year or so after the marriage when the romance wore off and the babies came. Secretly, she used to laugh at them. They got exactly what they deserved. Any woman who depended on a man to fulfill her life was a fool. Alex was one woman who would not make that mistake. Her life was flying. She was happiest when flying. It was an activity that a woman could do all her life. It had all the joys of men without the drawbacks.

That's why Clayton Thomas was such a surprise to her. Whenever she was around him she was bombarded with feelings she didn't know how to handle. He stirred emotions inside her she thought existed only in over-romantic songs and movies. But the feelings she was feeling were not fiction. They were real. And powerful. And distracting.

In her earphones the steady hum gave way to a confusion of Dit-das, or were they Da-dits? No, there was the hum again. Now it was gone.

Alex's eyes raced across the instruments. What had gone wrong? The noise in her ears made no sense at all.

Suddenly, the hood around her was ripped away.

"You missed the cone of silence completely!" Lieutenant Thomas said, obviously angry. "Didn't I tell you to keep the volume down? You've got it turned up so loud you passed through the cone of silence and never noticed the change. How many times have I told you, it's got to be soft so your ear will be tuned to hear nothing!"

Loretta was seated in the jump seat between them; Virginia stood behind her. Both of them looked away. This was between pilot and instructor.

Thomas threw up his hands. "Just circle around and take us back."

Alex felt humiliated and ashamed. She'd been caught like a little schoolgirl mooning over one of her classmates. Besides returning them to the airport she had a new task now, fighting back her tears. With pursed lips and a red face, she banked the lumbering aircraft, swinging it around toward Lockbourne.

With each silent minute that followed, the emotion inside the cockpit grew thicker. Alex wished someone would say something. When they did, she wished they hadn't.

"I was hoping all three of you would pass today so that we could move on. No offense, Loretta and Virginia, but when the two of you passed I thought we were finished for the day. Now I see I was wrong. I have to say, Miss Alex, I'm mighty disappointed."

The runway came into sight. With quivering chin, Alex lined up the aircraft for their approach. Tears which she could no longer hold back did not prevent her from executing a perfect landing.

She was the last to climb out of the plane. Thomas was waiting for her. After telling Virginia and Loretta to go ahead of them, he spoke to Alex. He was so much taller, and his chest was so wide, his shadow engulfed her.

"What happened up there?" he asked.

Alex didn't look up at him. She couldn't. "I lost my concentration," she said. "It won't happen again."

"You'll get it next time," Thomas said. His tone was much calmer. He began walking toward the mess hall. "Going to lunch?" he asked.

"I think I'll go to my room."

Compared to the bays at Avenger Field, the quarters at Lockbourne's Center Hall were luxurious. Each woman had her own room. They shared a living room at the end of the hall.

Alex stood before a mirror and tended red, puffy eyes with a washcloth. She took a good hard look at herself; something she rarely did. Her usual morning routine was to wash her face and brush the tangles from her hair. Clean and neat, that's all she'd ever wanted to be.

This was the first time in her life she envied Lily her good looks.

Tossing the cloth into the basin, she wandered over to her bed that she'd converted into something resembling a sofa by propping her pillows against the wall. Loretta had given her the idea.

With a heavy sigh, she relaxed. It was a mistake. Her tears took the lowering of her guard as a sign of capitulation. They rose quickly to the surface. Several managed to escape before she could fight them back again.

Why do I feel this way? she wondered. Answering her own question, she said, *Because you're a fool, that's why. You have no reason to allow yourself to be distracted like you did today. You're going to ruin everything you've worked so hard for all your life!*

Then she remembered the whiff of his shaving soap and she melted onto the bed. She wrapped her arms around a pillow. The whiff of Clayton Thomas's shaving soap was only one of several memorable moments in recent weeks.

There was the time when he was teaching her how to master the B-17's throttles:

"Like this, Miss Alex," he said, taking her right hand in his. He turned it palm up. "Gripping the throttle this way gives you greater leverage."

It wasn't something new to her. She had always gripped the throttles palm up, and she was surprised that he hadn't noticed before. Or maybe he had, and he simply saw this as an opportunity to touch her hand!

Alex smiled and hugged the pillow tight.

Then there was the time he sent her to do the routine walk-around and cockpit check. It was a cold day, and he was watching from a nearby window drinking a cup of coffee. Alex sat at the controls of the plane and started the engines. All of a sudden a flash of flame burst out the number-two engine.

Lieutenant Thomas dropped his coffee mug, raced to the plane, through the fuselage, and into the cockpit.

"What happened?" he shouted.

Alex, amused at the look of concern on his face, smiled and said, "You told us if we have an engine fire we should feather the prop, so I did."

Thomas looked out at the wing. The fire was out. Squeezing her shoulder, he said, "Good job, Alex. Good job."

He'd squeezed her shoulder! And called her Alex. Not Miss Alex. Just Alex. It was a good thing they were ready to fly, because Alex's legs were so shaky she didn't know if they had the strength to carry her.

And then there was the Christmas party:

Bing Crosby singing "White Christmas" on the radio. Everyone dressed colorfully and appropriately for the season, all of them looking so different than they did in their flight suits. Especially him.

He wore a cream-colored ski sweater with a navy blue strip of snowflakes across the chest. That massive chest of his. Blue slacks. Black shoes. His manner and conversation were casual, his glances warm. He laughed often.

To each of his students, he gave a silver dollar for luck. After giving Alex hers, he asked her to dance.

It was a moment she would remember all her life. Outside it was snowing. The tree in the corner sparkled with festive lights. The music ... *may your days be merry and bright....* Her head resting against his chest. His arms, massive tree trunks, holding her close. The easy way they moved together.

Never had there been a moment like it before, and never one since. If she were to have lived all her life for that one moment, it would have been worth it.

He asked her to accompany him to church the following Sunday. She did.

She began reading her Bible again. Virginia and Loretta noticed something between the two of them too. They were none-too-casual about their remarks. That's why they were speechless when he yelled at her today when she failed the navigational radio beam test.

Alex sat up at the thought of the test. She'd failed a test. One that she should be able to pass easily. Virginia passed. Loretta passed. But she failed it!

She buried her head in the pillow. *What's happening to me?* she inwardly groaned.

Getting up, she made her way again to the mirror. *Look at you! This is pathetic! You're acting just like Evelyn!*

Her own thought startled her.

She *was* acting just like Evelyn. Lovesick Evelyn, who claimed she had no control over her feelings for that flight instructor! The woman who had two sinus operations just so she could become a pilot. The woman who threw all of that away for a man! The woman for whom Alex lost all respect because she let her emotions take over and ruin her life!

And now you're acting just like her!

You failed a simple flight test that you should have been able to pass in your sleep!

You wallow around in your quarters daydreaming about him like a silly schoolgirl.

You spend more time thinking about him than you do about flying!

For what?

If Lieutenant Clayton Thomas were to ask you to give it all up for him, would you do it?

Would you do it?

Alex wept because she didn't know the answer to her question.

The next day when Clayton Thomas pulled the hood around her for her second attempt at the radio beam test, Alex held her breath. She turned the earphone volume low like she'd been taught. She thought only of her flying and aced the test.

Afterward, Lieutenant Thomas congratulated her. He was his usual, smiling self.

Before they could take their final check flights, the trainees needed thirty more hours of cross-country flying. Lieutenant Thomas decided to take them on a long-distance flight to Houston, Texas, 1,200 miles to the south.

On the evening of the takeoff, Alex and the others donned long underwear, leather fleece-lined pants, which were held in place with suspenders, fleece-lined boots, and bulky leather jackets. It promised to be a long, cold journey.

Because of a low cloud ceiling, the first hours would have to be flown solely with instruments. "Now I know why we practice hooded takeoffs," Loretta said as she pulled the plane into the clouds. She kept her eyes fixed on the instruments.

Sitting in the jump seat, Alex stared out at the gray mass that encased them. It seemed neither to have mass nor depth, it was just there. And it was totally disorienting. She understood why Loretta kept her head down and her eyes fixed on the instruments.

As they climbed, the temperature dropped. At 10,000 feet, they all donned oxygen masks. When they reached 24,000 feet, the thermometer read twenty degrees below zero.

Standing behind Alex, Virginia was hopping from one foot to the other in an attempt to get warm. Suddenly there was a loud crash. Virginia let loose with a high-pitched yelp that set Alex's heart to hammering.

"What was that?" Virginia asked.

From the copilot's seat, Lieutenant Thomas glanced back at them. The grin of a little boy who loved to scare girls with lizards and spiders creased his face. "It's only ice." He laughed. "On the props. When it breaks off, it hits the sides of the plane."

At 35,000 feet, they broke through the clouds. The sky was breathtaking. They sailed beneath a brilliant black canopy speckled with starlight. Beneath them a carpet of clouds shimmered with reflected moonlight.

It was Alex's turn to pilot the plane. The training plan was to rotate everyone throughout the flight so they all had opportunity to be pilot, copilot, and navigator.

It took Alex a few minutes to adjust to the feel of the controls. This high up, the atmosphere was thin and the plane responded sluggishly. It felt like they were flying through a sea of gelatin.

Alex glanced over at the lieutenant who had not yet relinquished the copilot's seat to Virginia. She wanted to assure him with a nod that she had control of the plane. When she turned to him, she found that he was staring at her. Staring and smiling.

He winked.

Alex didn't know what to do, how to respond.

What did he mean by it? Was it just a friendly glad-you're-getting-the-feel-of-the-plane wink, or was it something more? Should I wink back?

She settled on a smile response. Her heart pounded. Her mind raced. Then she remembered the radio beam incident.

Concentrate on what you're doing, she scolded. *It was a wink, not a proposal of marriage. He probably didn't mean anything by it anyway. Think about what you're doing. Concentrate! Think!*

The remainder of Alex's turn in the pilot's seat passed uneventfully. She concentrated on flying and tried to forget about the wink. Clayton had her practice a few high-altitude maneuvers in the low-pressure atmosphere—some stalls and turns. After a couple of hours it was Virginia's turn.

"What are you looking for?" Alex asked, vacating the pilot's seat.

Clayton was rummaging around the back of the pilot's seat, searching for something.

"My knapsack," he replied. "Anybody see what I did with it? I remember bringing it on board."

"You set something down in the tail gunner's area when we climbed aboard," Loretta remembered. "Did you leave it back there?"

The corners of Clayton's mouth pressed into a look of chagrin. "Really? I don't think I left it back there, but I can't remember."

"Do you need it?" Alex asked.

"It's not anything vital. Just a surprise."

"A surprise?" Loretta's eyebrows raised in anticipation.

"Not a big one. Just a couple of Thermos bottles of hot cocoa. I thought it would provide us a nice break."

"Hot cocoa!" Virginia squealed. "I thought you said it wasn't vital!"

"I'll get it," Alex offered.

Clayton looked at her skeptically. "No … it was a crazy idea anyway. We'd better wait until we're below 10,000 feet and we don't need oxygen masks anymore. It'll be easier to drink then."

"It'll be cold by then!" Loretta complained.

"And we're freezing now!" Virginia chimed in. "Forget drinking it. Let Alex go get it so you can pour it on me—anything to get warm!"

"I'll get it," Clayton said.

"It would be against regulations for you to leave the cockpit area," Alex said. "I don't mind getting it."

"If you don't let her get the cocoa, we won't give you a moment's peace for the remainder of the flight to Houston," Virginia threatened.

"And back," Loretta added.

The expression on Clayton Thomas's face indicated he still had reservations; nevertheless he fitted Alex with a mask that was attached to a walk-around bottle of oxygen. It contained enough air for three to five minutes of normal breathing.

With the mask securely in place, just before leaving the cockpit area, Alex smiled at Clayton with her eyes. She was hoping for another wink from him, but all she got was a smile, and an uncertain one at that.

Alex worked her way toward the back of the plane, through the radio area, across the beam that stretched over the bomb bays, through the midsection of the fuselage that would have been outfitted with guns on each side had the plane not been a trainer, and back to the hatch near the tail section. She searched the area but saw no knapsack.

The plane vibrated and jumped unexpectedly this way and that while the low throb of the engines filled the air that was biting cold. Alex's teeth chattered uncontrollably.

It has to be here somewhere.

She worked her way farther back. The fuselage narrowed the closer she got to the tail. Still no knapsack. In spite of the heavy gloves she was wearing, her fingers were numb from the cold. A cup of hot cocoa sounded mighty fine right about now.

The knapsack has to be here someplace!

How could she go back empty-handed? Just the thought and she could already hear the wails coming from …

Alex couldn't remember their names!

This is ridiculous! I just left them a few minutes ago. And after all we've been through together!

She concentrated on remembering.

The one with the smile … Hollywood … Loretta! Of course! And the other one, the physical education teacher … father wanted her to be a marine … left home without … that's right, Virg … Vir …

All of a sudden another memory flashed in her mind. A trip to Patterson Field in Ohio. The high-altitude chamber. Oxygen deprivation. They were given pads and pencils and told to write repeatedly: "Mary had a little lamb." After a couple of times, her writing became lazy scribbles, illegible; her hand drooped and lay helpless on the top of her legs.

Oxygen deprivation! Must get back …

Abandoning the knapsack search, she made her way through the midsection of the fuselage.

Must get ba …

The next thing she knew Lieutenant Clayton Thomas was cradling her in his arms. She was slumped on the deck. He held an oxygen mask to her face.

As her eyes fluttered open, she saw his eyes crinkle into a smile. It was a smile mixed with fear. "Let's get you back up to the cockpit," he said. "For a moment there, I thought I'd lost you."

For a moment I thought I'd lost you.

The words swam luxuriously in her head. They were the most wonderful words she'd ever heard in her life. Didn't he know that he was never going to lose her? If it was up to her, she could spend the rest of her life right here in his arms.

The way he was looking at her convinced her that she belonged there. There was more than professional concern in his eyes. There were feelings for her. She could see them. And it was something she would never forget.

Clayton gave her a new oxygen bottle and helped her to her feet. When they entered the cockpit a pair of anxious eyes greeted them.

"Lieutenant Thomas clicked a stopwatch just as you left the cockpit," Loretta explained. "When you didn't come back after five minutes, he went after you."

He came after me!

Alex was lowered into the jump seat. Everything was still a little hazy, but not enough that she couldn't see the knapsack that was wedged behind the copilot's seat.

It was Loretta's idea.

After touching down in Houston, they exited their Big Friend. At Loretta's signal the three female trainees surrounded Lieutenant Thomas. Taking him by the arms, they made him walk into the operations building with the three of them hanging all over him.

The combination of Lieutenant Thomas's blushing face and the envious, open-mouthed stares of all the operations officers made for a fitting climax to the first leg of their cross-country trip.

The final check flights were almost anticlimactic. Virginia, Loretta, and Alex passed with ease. A beaming Lieutenant Thomas received rave reviews from his superiors for the job he did with the women.

Three certificates were signed, and it was official. The young ladies from Avenger Field were now qualified to fly B-17s.

The dinner-dance graduation celebration was held at the Fort Hayes Hotel in Columbus, which was festively decorated with lights for the occasion. A twelve-piece orchestra played swing tunes. Dancers crowded the floor.

Alex didn't realize how much stamina she had built up during her training. Every bit of it was needed tonight. The dance cards of all three women were filled with the names of officers, some of them fellow students who had also completed their training.

Over the shoulder of several partners, Alex watched as Lieutenant Thomas danced first with Loretta, then with

Virginia. It still looked odd to see the three of them in clothing other than flight suits. Loretta was stunning in a strapless red dress with matching high heels. Somehow, she had even managed to procure a pair of nylons for the occasion. Virginia wore her hair up and looked equally stunning, though not as classy as Loretta, in a white suit coat trimmed in gold with a matching skirt.

Alex wore a modest blue skirt with a long-sleeved white silk blouse that tied up with a bow at the neck. It was not nearly as nice as what the other two women were wearing. Alex mused that while she could fly circles around the other two women in the air, when it came to social events like this one, she was definitely out of their league.

"I know you're probably tired, but will your strength hold out long enough for one last dance with me?"

Alex turned from her dance partner, whose name she'd already forgotten, to the voice behind her which she recognized instantly. Clayton Thomas stood tall in his sharply creased military uniform with his aviator wings flashing proudly on his chest. He stretched out his arms, inviting her to walk into his embrace.

With a slight blush, she did.

The lights dimmed as the band began to play "Dancing in the Dark." Alex prayed a silent prayer. *Thank God it's not "Sing, Sing, Sing" or something equally as fast.*

"Well, Miss Alex, I guess congratulations are in order," Clayton said.

Please don't talk right now, she thought. *Let's just enjoy this moment without ruining it with small talk.* Aloud, she said a soft "Thank you."

Whether he intuited her mood or read her thoughts, for the remainder of the dance, he said nothing. Alex rested her head against his chest. She could smell his shaving soap, the same fragrance that had scuttled her radio beam navigational test. It had the same effect on her, only this time she didn't care. She wasn't flying. Well, not in a plane anyway. She was floating in a sea of enchantment.

Her contentment in the face of this transition celebration was rooted in the news that Clayton Thomas had been offered a permanent training position at Lockbourne. That meant she would still be able to see him often.

Onstage the soloist sang:

We're waltzing in the wonder of why we're here,
Time hurries by—we're here and gone ...

Then, all too soon, the song ended. The lights came up. The romantic spell was broken. Self-consciously Alex stepped away from Clayton. On the far side of the dance floor, Virginia and Loretta stood next to their partners looking at her and their instructor. They were grinning like a couple of schoolgirls.

While the bandleader announced that the evening would conclude with one more song, Clayton took Alex by the hand. "Can I speak to you alone?" he asked.

Alex nodded shyly.

As he led her off the dance floor, they walked past the man who was waiting his turn to dance with Alex. "Do you mind?" Clayton asked him. "It's really important that I talk with her."

Before the man could respond Virginia stepped between them. She grabbed the man's hand and said, "He doesn't mind at all." Taking his arm, she led him away. "Come on, honey, you're with me." Looking over her shoulder, she winked at Alex.

With snow on the ground and a brisk northern breeze, it was too cold to go outside, so Clayton led Alex to a somewhat isolated corner of the ballroom. While the rest of the crowd finished their evening to the musical strains of "Good Night,

Ladies," Clayton nervously took Alex's hands in his own. Her hands were lost in his giant bear paws.

"I guess this is the end of the road for us," he said softly. "But before we go our separate ways, I wanted to apologize."

"Apologize? Whatever are you talking about?"

For reasons Alex couldn't fathom, he found it difficult to hold her gaze. He kept looking down at their hands.

"For a couple things, really," he said. "For getting angry with you when you didn't pass the navigational radio beam test on the first attempt. That was my fault. You're such a great pilot, I expected you to pass everything the first time. That was unreasonable of me and unfair to you. I was really angry at myself for getting angry with you. Please forgive me."

He's right about one thing. It was his fault; indirectly, at least. But not for the reason he's assuming.

She smiled. There was no way she was going to tell him the real reason she failed that test. "Don't blame yourself," she said. "I simply got distracted. And you were right to get angry. Had that been a real flight, I might have endangered the crew."

A slow shake of his head told her that he was not mollified. "And then there was the oxygen incident on the flight to Houston," he confessed. "That was completely my fault. I knew better than to let a trainee go back there alone. I never should have ..."

He stopped what he was saying when Alex pulled her hands out of his grasp. A puzzled, worried look formed in his eyes.

Her hands didn't wander far. It took both of her hands to hold one of his. She squeezed it reassuringly.

"There is nothing to apologize for," she said.

"But, Alex, I could have lost you! And if anything had happened to you up there...." His voice trailed off. Biting his lower lip, he stared at her hands holding his.

She waited. This was sounding like more than typical trainer concern and she ached to hear where this was leading. One thing she noticed. He'd called her Alex. Not the usual and formal Miss Alex, but the more intimate Alex.

The protracted silence was agonizing. She could stand it no longer. Maybe if she primed the pump. "All of that is in the past," she said. "And everything turned out fine. I don't see that there's anything to forgive."

Without looking up, he smiled. "I'm glad," he said.

He wanted to say something more. Alex could see it in his eyes. What reason could he have for holding anything back? This time, Alex determined to ride out the silence.

Finally, he said, "I was offered a permanent training position here at Lockbourne ..."

Is that all? Alex thought, somewhat relieved and somewhat disappointed. She was about to say, "I know," when he completed the sentence he'd started by saying ...

"But I turned it down. I requested a combat assignment."

The news was an unexpected blow. Alex was dazed.

"I ship out tomorrow," he said. "For England. I'll be given my own plane and crew."

"So soon?" she asked. Her heart was in a free fall, plummeting into a bottomless black pit. "Is ... is this what you really want?"

Clayton shrugged apologetically. "It's what I'm trained for."

"I see."

Alex had no choice but to limit her response to two words. If she said any more she was afraid that the tremors that were shaking her apart inside would find their way into her voice.

The band finished the song. The room lights were turned all the way up and people began milling about, putting on their coats and saying their good-byes.

"I only wish things had been different," Clayton said, distracted by the growing commotion around them.

"Different? In what way?"

"Between you and me," he said. "I wish we had more time."

"More time?" Her insides were screaming, *Out with it! Say the words I so desperately need to hear!*

Clayton was getting flustered with all the people looking at them as they passed by, some nodding, some saying good night. "For us," he said. "For you and me. I was hoping we might get together sometime now that I'm no longer your trainer. Go out. That sort of thing."

He was treading on the edge of Alex's promised land. As suddenly as her heart had plummeted, now it rose with equal speed to dizzying heights.

Clayton continued to be distracted by all the people around them. Alex prayed he would suggest that they go someplace quiet where they could continue this conversation.

"I can't ask you to wait for me," he said. "It wouldn't be fair to you. I've seen too many guys ask that of a girl and then something happens and they never return."

Alex couldn't believe what she was hearing. Her mind was a flurry of responses, each one competing to be the first on her lips.

But before she could say anything, another uniformed man with wavy, black hair stopped next to Clayton. To Alex, he said, "Excuse me, ma'am." Gripping Clayton's arm, he said to him, "Sorry, Clay, but we've got to go." He held up his wrist to show his watch. "We have an early flight tomorrow."

Clayton nodded at him. The man released his grip and stepped to one side, but he didn't leave.

"This is all my fault," Clayton apologized to Alex. "This isn't at all how I wanted to say good-bye to you."

The man with wavy hair fidgeted impatiently.

With his massive hands, Clayton grabbed Alex by the shoulders. Loving, blue eyes locked onto her eyes. "I'll write you."

Then he was gone. Alex was left standing alone on the nearly deserted ballroom floor.

The first glow of dawn glimmered on the eastern horizon. Alex pulled tight her flight jacket to ward off the brisk morning chill.

Though it was still mostly night, she stood in the shadow of a B-17 wing on the flight line thinking she surely must look an odd sight to anyone who might happen to see her. She'd been up all night and hadn't changed clothes since the graduation dinner-dance, which meant her ensemble consisted of a blue skirt, silk blouse, and leather flight jacket.

Her eyes were fixed on another B-17. It was taxiing to the end of the runway. It was the plane that was taking Lieutenant Clayton Thomas away from her.

All night she'd debated whether or not she should see him off. She'd imagined throwing herself into his arms and telling him she would wait for him no matter how long he was gone. She also imagined his response would be unbridled joy at her pronouncement. They'd kiss and he'd fly away.

Her dream never had a chance to materialize.

The entire crew emerged onto the flight line tightly bunched, all wearing their flight suits and headgear. They were boarding their plane before she could even determine with certainty that Clayton was among them.

Doubts paralyzed her resolve until it was too late. All she could do now was watch from a distance as the plane took flight.

On the runway, four Fortress engines throbbed with power. A few moments later their pitch increased and the huge airplane slowly picked up speed. The nose lifted and the plane took flight, banking sharply on a course for England.

Alex watched as the mighty profile faded to a speck and the speck disappeared. She shivered uncontrollably. Her legs and feet were frozen. Her cheeks were chapped.

Instead of returning to her quarters where it was warm, she walked the length of the runway as a variety of fighters and scouts and bombers took flight.

This was what she used to do all the time. There was something magical about the instant an aircraft breaks the earth's hold on it and takes wing. She never used to tire of it.

This morning was different. On this particular morning, Alex's thoughts were not on things aeronautical. In her mind she was back in Sweetwater, Texas, at Avenger Field. She was standing in the dark outside the dormitory watching Evelyn Post hurry into the night to rendezvous with her lover.

20

While flying in tight formation over disputed airspace during a bombing mission, there is little time for a pilot to relax. However, Walt was as close to being relaxed as was conceivably possible, considering the decision that weighed on his mind.

The mission had gone well. The weather was clear. Flak and fighter resistance over the target had been moderate, lighter than expected, in fact, which was always a blessing. And although they would have to wait for reconnaissance photos to verify their success, bombardier Upchurch's shout of *bull's-eye!* still rang in everyone's ears. That, together with a fair number of fireball explosions on the ground, was a good enough reason for the crew to be in high spirits during the trip home.

All four engines droned contentedly. Walt had just received radio reports of an extensive cloud bank over the English Channel, but such reports were hardly out of the ordinary. The intercom crackled with lighthearted banter and he saw no need to enforce regulations that discouraged such use of the plane's communications.

A request came from the tail gunner. "Hey, Lieutenant," Sabala said, "how about another one of those stories about your Morgan ancestors?"

Ever since the Morgan family Bible saved Walt's life on their first mission together, the entire crew had taken an interest in that particular Bible. In fact, it had become the crew's good-luck charm. They insisted that Walt bring it with him on every mission, though he no longer sat on it—he had an eighteen-inch square piece of armor plating for that. The crew also insisted on touching the Bible just before they boarded the plane and as they disembarked. It became something of a ritual.

While Walt was somewhat apprehensive about using the Bible as a good-luck charm, he saw the crew's interest in it as an opportunity to talk to them about subjects that wouldn't come up during a typical bombing run. And the Bible's presence seemed to help in other ways too.

For instance, the swearing that was so prevalent among men in combat had been reduced to nearly nothing. It was Fargo, the now odor-free ball turret gunner, who had made the observation that put a halt to the swearing. "Hey, fellas," he said after a particularly raunchy conversation, "do you really think it's right for us to swear like this? You know, with the lieutenant's Bible on board and everything?"

Walt expected a few choice words to be hurled at Fargo in response. To his surprise, there was general agreement that they ought not to swear with the Bible onboard. Now Walt didn't think for a moment that any permanent change had come over them. The only reason they thought it best to abstain from swearing was that they didn't want to put a hex on their good-luck charm. But it was a start, something Walt might be able to build on. Besides, there were other clear victories to celebrate.

Shortly after their first mission Sergeant John Sabala, the ice-cream-making tail gunner, had bought himself his own Bible and began carrying it onboard with him. He informed everyone he wanted to start a tradition of his own after the war when he got married, and that he wanted to be able to pass along to his sons a Bible that had flown with their father during the war.

While there were several jokes at Sabala's expense about whether there was a woman dumb enough or blind enough to marry him, no one poked fun at his decision to carry around a Bible. Walt was pleased with his tail gunner and the kind of man he was becoming.

It was Sabala who had changed the most since the first mission. He who initially had been reluctant to become part of the crew was now the crew's mother. He worked hardest to resolve conflicts as soon as they occurred and to remind the men that for the duration of the war they were more than members of the same crew, they were family.

Family had become a big theme for Sabala.

He was continually using Morgan family experiences as a relational pattern for the crew to follow. When he first asked Walt to tell some of the Morgan family stories, Walt tried to beg off, thinking that the other crew members weren't interested. A surprising chorus of pleas convinced him otherwise.

"Last time you told us about Philip searching for the lost Bible and finding it at the Narragansett Indian village," Sabala prompted him. "Imagine, our Bible was once kept by Indians!"

Walt grinned at the mention of *our* Bible. "Have I told you about Philip's brother, Jared, the pirate?" As he asked, his eyes studied the cloud bank in front of them and frowned. Maintaining formation with reduced visibility was tricky. He checked his instruments. To copilot Keating, he asked, "How's our position on your side?"

Keating checked the B-17s above, beside, and behind them. There were seventy or eighty of them in all. "We're in good shape," he said.

"You had a pirate in your family?" waist gunner Jankowski

called over the intercom. "Hot dog, Lieutenant, you have the most colorful family I ever heard of! Are you sure you're not just making this stuff up?"

The B-17 nosed into the cloud bank. Walt's senses shifted to a higher level of alertness.

He thought twice about beginning a story right now, not only because of the clouds but because he had something else that was weighing heavily on his mind. A decision to be made, a decision about a project named Perilous.

With a mental shrug, Walt decided to concede to the tail gunner's request for a story. It would be a good distraction for them *and* for him.

"Jared Morgan never set out to become a pirate ..." he began, his head swiveling continuously as he scanned the murky gray that had swallowed them, "... he was shanghaied. The way I heard the story ..."

The plane broke out of the clouds and they sailed in blue skies again. All around them the formation of planes was perfectly intact. However, it was evident their good visibility would be short-lived. Clouds loomed all around them. It was as though they were passing through the eye of a hurricane.

"... Jared was in a tavern in Boston ..."

Suddenly, another B-17 appeared in front of them. It came out of the cloud bank directly into their path. Then another! And another! An entire formation of B-17s began to emerge. And they were on a collision course.

Above them and to the right two planes collided in midair. Metal crumpled. A wing was shorn off. Both bombers fell from the sky like wounded ducks.

Another collision. This one closer. An explosion sent debris flying through the air with smoke trails like fireworks, pelting all the planes with deadly fragments.

The B-17 directly in front of them pulled up and away, nar-
rowly missing them. But there were others, maybe a hundred
others, in staggered formation behind it.

Walt didn't know what to do. With planes above and below
him, any aggressive action could plow them into one of their own
squadron. But it was insane to think they could plow their way
through an entire opposing squadron without a collision.

An instant later, Walt's mind was made up for him. Like a meteor
from space, a B-17 fireball came streaking toward them from above.
Instinctively, Walt nosed his plane into a hard dive to miss it, then
even harder to miss one of their own planes below them.

The cries and shouts of his crew blasted in his ears. Most of
them had no idea what had just happened. They only knew that
their universe was tumbling and falling.

The plane was on its back, and then it rolled over into a spin.
Walt and Keating fought together to pull the plane out of its dive,
a task that became increasingly harder as the plane picked up
speed. Keating's eyes bulged with alarm when he saw the air-
speed indicator.

"Two twenty-five!" he shouted.

In his headphones Walt could hear the crew making prepara-
tions to jump. The voice taking charge was that of Upchurch, the
bombardier. He was shouting at navigator Geller to monitor the
airspeed.

"The wings fall off at two hundred and seventy-five miles per
hour," Upchurch shouted. "We jump no later than two fifty."

"Two thirty-five!" Keating shouted.

Walt was amazed they hadn't already crashed into a plane
below them in the formation, but not only had they cleared the
formation, but they had cleared the clouds. The channel stretched
from horizon to horizon beneath them, looking like blue vinyl.
Swirling blue vinyl.

"Two forty-five!"

"Don't jump! Don't jump!" It was Sabala's voice. Walt had no way of knowing who the boy was shouting at.

"Let go of me!" Upchurch demanded.

"Lieutenant Morgan," Sabala shouted, "Are we gonna make it?"

Walt wished he knew. He and Keating both were pulling with all their might to coax the comet they were riding into acting like a plane again.

"Two fifty-five!" Keating shouted.

"Hang on!" Walt shouted over the intercom.

"You hear that?" Sabala shouted. "The lieutenant says to hang on!"

"Let me go!" Upchurch shouted again.

"Nobody's gonna jump until the lieutenant says we jump!"

"Two sixty-five!"

"You're gonna get us all killed!" Upchurch shouted. His voice was high-pitched with panic.

Walt didn't know if the comment was directed at him or Sabala.

"Two seventy-five!"

At the sound of the magic number Walt couldn't help himself, he had to look at the wings. He wasn't alone. So did Keating.

The wings were still there.

Walt's arms and legs shook from the strain. He didn't know how much longer he could hold out.

"Two ninety!"

"Lieutenant?" Sabala asked. His voice was less confident than before. Considering the boy's previous brush with death in a plummeting airplane, Walt couldn't help but admire Sabala for staying with the plane now.

"Not yet," Walt grunted.

"Hear that?" Sabala cried. "He's gonna pull us out!"

"Or kill us!" Upchurch shouted.

"Three ten!"

"Come on, Lieutenant, you can do it!" Sabala shouted.

Jankowski joined him. So did Fargo and Northrop. "Come on, Lieutenant, you can do it!"

Walt glanced over at Keating. His copilot's face was red and strained and dripping with sweat. His eyes locked onto Walt's. Keating shook his head; he didn't think they were going to make it.

"Three twenty," he said. It wasn't a shout, but more like a pronouncement of death.

"Stay with it! We can do it!" Walt shouted, pulling even harder though he didn't think he had any more strength left in him.

Keating closed his eyes, shouted with exertion, and pulled with him.

Walt began to feel control. The nose rose slightly.

He pulled harder.

"You can do it!" Sabala said.

"Come on, Lieutenant!" Fargo shouted.

The nose pulled up. Slowly, but definitely in the right direction.

"He's doing it!" Sabala shouted. "I knew he could! I knew he could!"

It was a painful, agonizingly slow maneuver, but gradually the plane came out of its dive and leveled off. Walt had control again, though his arms and legs were shaking so badly it was an effort for him just to keep the plane level.

Beside him Keating broke into laughter. Uncontrollable laughter that bordered on hysteria. "They didn't come off!" he said, staring at the wings. "Three hundred twenty miles per hour and they didn't fly off!"

A deafening cacophony of cheers jammed the communication lines followed by a flood of congratulations from the crew to the two pilots.

They were too low to rejoin the formation, at least what was left of it, so they took new bearings and headed for home on their own.

※

Carrying the Morgan family Bible in its leather pouch under his arm, Walt was pounded on the back with congratulations. As was their custom, no one got out of the plane before the pilot.

Once out, he stood at the back hatch holding the Bible as the crew filed out. One by one, they climbed out and touched the Bible. This time there was more enthusiasm in the ritual.

Upchurch followed Sabala, who was grinning ear to ear. Upchurch, the bombardier, paused as he touched the Bible. To Walt, he said, "If it weren't for you and that kid," referring to Sabala, "I'd be swimming right now. Do you know he had a hold of me by my flight collar and wouldn't let go? Now I'm glad he didn't. The two of you have made a believer out of me."

Keating was the last out of the plane. Normally, he touched the corner of the Bible. His was a token participation in the ritual. This time, he placed his palm flat on the Bible and held it there for a good five seconds. He didn't say anything. He looked Walt in the eyes the entire time, then walked away.

While the rest of the crew watched other planes in their squadron land, then made plans to go into Cambridge to celebrate, Walt's attention was drawn to a jeep that was speeding toward them, trailing a plume of dust. It pulled to a stop a few feet in front of Walt.

Major Harrison sat in the passenger seat. A skinny private with a bad case of acne was behind the wheel. It seemed unlikely that Harrison was there for a debriefing.

Walt saluted.

"That was quite a mess up there today," Major Harrison said. The cigar in the major's mouth testified to his displeasure with the incident. The lit end no longer burned and from what little Walt could see of the chewed end, it had gotten quite a workout. Stray strands of tobacco had broken through the wrapper and jutted out every which way.

"Yes, sir, it was."

The major made a five-second visual assessment of the *California Angel.* "Looks like you came through unscathed," he said. "You were one of the lucky ones."

"Yes, sir," Walt replied. He offered no details. The time for reports and details of their spin would come later. Harrison was here for another reason.

"Have you made a decision?" the major asked.

"Yes, sir," Walt said. "Count me in."

"You understand the risks?"

"Yes, sir."

"This is strictly volunteer."

"Yes, sir."

"For the record, I have to hear you say it."

"I volunteer for the mission, sir."

The major studied his face for a long moment. "Very good, Morgan," he said. Reaching into his front pocket, he pulled out a cigar and handed it to Walt.

"Thank you, sir," Walt said, taking it though he had no use for it.

As the major drove off, Walt saw Keating standing in the shadow of the plane looking at him.

That night there was a knock at Walt's door.

"Enter."

Lieutenant Jay Keating appeared. "Am I interrupting?" he asked.

"Just getting some things in order," Walt said.

Keating stood by the door self-consciously, leaving it open a crack to indicate this was intended to be a brief conversation.

"Come on in," Walt said. "Have a seat." He pulled out the room's only chair from the desk and motioned to it as he sat on the edge of the bed.

Keating looked at him perplexed, then said, "I won't be staying long."

Because of the room's Spartan furnishings, Walt had already exhausted his resources as host. He waited while Keating seemed to be searching for the words to say what he'd come to say.

"Close call today," Keating said.

Walt sighed. "That it was."

"I didn't think we were going to make it."

Walt nodded.

"You did, though," Keating said, making eye contact. "You knew all along we were going to make it, didn't you?"

"I don't have a crystal ball or anything like that, if that's what you mean. I just wasn't ready to give up."

"The fact remains, you were right. Just like you were right about Sabala."

Walt had forgotten that Keating had been opposed to Sabala joining the crew.

"He's a good man," Walt said.

Keating's eyes squinted at Walt. He studied him with the look a scientist uses when examining an interesting discovery.

"Why don't you just admit it? You were right about staying with the plane and you were right about Sabala. Are you always right?"

"What are you getting at, Keating?"

Keating lowered his gaze. He shifted his feet uncomfortably. "I guess it's been no secret that I haven't liked you," he said.

"Have I done something to offend you?" Walt asked.

Keating shook his head. "Nothing, other than remind me of

my oldest brother. He's always been right too. Always been the star of the football team. The best student in class. The most promising pilot."

"Your brother's a pilot? What does he fly?"

"The F4U Corsair in the Pacific. He has five kills."

Walt nodded. He was impressed. However, he kept his thoughts to himself, not wanting to divert Keating.

"Anyway, you remind me of my brother. You know, the one everyone looks up to, the leader, the one who can do things when no one thinks they can be done."

He took a deep breath before continuing.

"But every time I found myself hating you, you would go and do something that was completely unlike my brother and I couldn't bring myself to hate you."

How does a person respond to a comment like that? "Thank you," hardly seemed appropriate. Not able to come up with a remark that made sense, Walt said nothing.

"Things like sticking up for Sabala and not grabbing credit for getting us back safely today and, well, like this BQ-7 thing."

"You saw me talking to Major Harrison?"

Keating nodded. "I saw him hand you a cigar. He wouldn't have done that unless you volunteered for the assignment. You did, didn't you?"

Walt nodded.

Chuckling, Keating shook his head. "There you go, being like my brother again … volunteering for something every pilot in his right mind is afraid to do."

"*Someone* has to do it."

"But why you?"

"What do you mean, why me?"

"You have a crew that depends on you. Why would you want to go and do something crazy like this?"

Walt looked up and sighed. "I don't know. It's just something I feel I have to do."

"Are you going to tell the crew?"

Shaking his head, Walt said, "I've been debating about whether or not I should tell them."

"Do you want my advice?"

"Sure."

"When is the mission?"

"Don't know yet. Within the next few days."

"Before we fly again?"

"Probably."

"Then don't tell them."

"Don't tell the crew?"

Keating nodded. "It's better they don't know. For you and for them. It'll only distract them and you from what needs to be done. Let them find out when you get back."

"Makes sense," Walt said.

"Will you be taking that Bible with you?"

Walt grinned as Keating referred to it as *that* Bible after Sabala had referred to it as *our* Bible.

"I don't see how I can," Walt said.

"Yeah, you're right."

Walt had a thought. He got up from the edge of the bed and picked up the leather pouch that housed the Morgan family Bible. He handed it to Keating.

His copilot stared at him in astonishment. "What am I supposed to do with this?" he asked.

"If anything happens to me, will you see that it goes on the rest of the *California Angel*'s missions? And then would you see that it gets back to my family?"

Keating stared dumbfounded at the pouch.

"There you go again," he said, "just when you do something

that is exactly the kind of thing my brother would do, you turn around and do something he'd never do!"

"I'm not sure I follow you."

Keating shook his head. His eyes were glassy. "This will mean a lot to the crew," he said, hefting the pouch. He swung open the door to leave.

"Walt?"

"Yeah?"

"Don't take any unnecessary risks."

Walt grinned. "I'm afraid it's too late to promise that."

After Keating left, Walt sat down on the edge of his bed. Taking pen in hand he wrote four letters.

Laura's hands shook so badly she could no longer knit, which was just as well. Her eyes teared up so frequently she could no longer see either.

She shot an angry glance at Johnny who was fiddling with the radio dial. Recognizable voices and irritating static overlapped each other.

Walter Winchell … *static* … Bing Crosby on *Kraft Music Hall* … *static* … *Welch Presents* Irene Rich dramatization … *static* … *Hollywood Playhouse* with Tyrone Power … *static* … back to Irene Rich …

"What are we going to tell her when she calls?" Laura asked.

Johnny frowned. She didn't know if he was frowning at her or at the radio. Let him frown. It irritated her that he seemed free of the agony that tortured her.

The static cleared and orchestra music filled the room. With a triumphant smile, Johnny slumped back into his chair. "Did you say something?" he asked.

Laura set her knitting aside. She had taken up volunteer work as an ambulance driver in hopes that she could avoid this kind of anxiety. And for the most part it worked. Her work transporting the wounded from ships to the hospital kept her mind occupied for the better part of the day.

Besides, she was doing something useful. Her work allowed her to be a mother to young men who needed a mother's care so far away from their homes. Some of them had written to her expressing their thanks and telling her how much her caring words had helped them to recover.

The short-term relationships were good for her, too. They kept her from worrying all day about her own children. But times like tonight seemed to undo all the benefits of her hospital work.

"What do you mean, what are we going to say?" Johnny asked. "What can we say?"

"We can say no. We can tell her to come home."

Johnny shook his head slowly. "She's an adult. Old enough to make her own decisions."

"But the danger!"

"She'll be behind the lines."

"I don't care! It's still dangerous!"

Johnny chuckled. "How can you say that? It won't be nearly as dangerous as the English ambulance corps! But that didn't stop you and Katy!"

Laura felt the tears and frustration building up inside of her. *That was different!* she kept telling herself. And she believed herself too. Why couldn't other people see that?

The phone rang.

Johnny and Laura exchanged glances.

It rang again.

"Do you want to answer it?" Johnny asked. "Or me?"

A third ring.

With a backhanded wave, Laura indicated that Johnny should answer the phone.

"Hello?" he said.

Laura remained in her chair. She thought about sharing the receiver with Johnny. *What good would it do? Matters are obviously out of my hands, just like they've been since Pearl Harbor Day. I have no control over anything. And if I told her how I feel, it would only make things harder for her.*

"Hello, dear!" Johnny said. His face broke into a wide smile.

"Yes, we got your letter.

"Yes, it is exciting.

"You're a grown woman. You have to decide these things for yourself."

A grown woman, Laura groused to herself. *Nearly twenty is not a grown woman.*

"Well, is this what you want to do? ... un-huh ... un-huh ... Then Lily, we're behind you 100 percent. When do you leave?"

There was a long pause. Johnny's brow wrinkled.

"Sicily," he repeated. "And that's where you'll do your first show?"

When she heard the name of the country Laura's heart ached so badly she felt like it would burst. *This is really happening.*

"It sounds exciting, darling.

"Yes, she's here."

Covering the receiver with his hand, Johnny held the phone toward Laura. "Your daughter wants to talk to you."

With lead feet, Laura shuffled across the room.

"Hello?"

"Momma?" The sound of Lily's voice, though distorted with long-distance crackle, made Laura cry.

"Yes, dear?" she managed to say.

"It's so good to hear your voice!"

"It's good to hear your voice too, dear."

"Is it really all right for me to go on tour in Europe?"

"Like your father said, dear, it's your decision to make."

"At first, the idea frightened me," Lily said. "And I guess it still does, a little. But do you want to know what helped me make my decision?"

"What, dear?"

"Aunt Katy. Remember that day on the veranda when Aunt Katy visited us for Christmas?"

"I remember."

"And remember how she told us about the music being so helpful to the soldiers in the hospitals during the Great War? Well, I got to thinking about the men who will come to hear me sing and well, I only hope that I can help them like you and Aunt Katy helped the soldiers in France."

Laura's throat constricted with emotion.

"Momma?"

"Yes, dear?"

"I know you're worried. I'll be all right."

"I'm sure of it, dear."

"And Momma?"

"Yes?"

"I love you."

"I love you too, baby."

21

"Do you think I need a hat? You know, like Monty. He wears those big, Australian-looking hats with the badges all over them. Maybe I need some kind of hat, you know, to create an instantly recognizable image."

Lieutenant Nolan Murphy leaned against the muddy wall of a narrow ravine. As he spoke, he used his hands to simulate the hat he was describing. His shoulder, which was wedged against the sloping side, had dammed up the course of a rivulet of rainwater. Undaunted, the rivulet changed course. It ran down the folds of Murphy's soaked uniform and cascaded off his animated elbow.

This was their fifth straight day of rain. The ravine that provided them cover was normally inhabited by nothing more than a trickle of water. Now it was a respectable creek, which meant that Murphy's unit sloshed in water higher than the tops of their boots.

"So it's Monty, is it?" Nat said. "Since when are you and the commander-in-chief of the British forces on familiar terms?"

Murphy ignored the remark. He was still pondering the political benefits of a personalized headpiece. "It has to be something distinctive, don't you think?"

"I think you'd better keep your hands and head down before the Germans shoot them off."

It was no idle warning. With a nervous glance at the top of the ridge, which at present was at eye level, Murphy pulled his head in like a turtle ducking into his shell.

Overhead, dark clouds grew darker, the only natural indication that the day was waning. Without the aid of the sun to track the passing of time, it had been one long, monotonous gray nothing of a day.

Nat needed to stretch his legs badly. It was a luxury that would have to wait until it was fully night. If he stood he would expose himself to enemy fire. And with the German trenches barely a hundred yards away, anything that showed itself above the ridge of the ravine was instantly riddled with bullet holes.

His first couple of days under fire Nat was afraid of getting hit. Now a five-day veteran, he had learned there were benefits to being wounded, as long as the wound wasn't too serious, of course. He found himself watching with a feeling akin to envy as the wounded were carried away to safety on litters. He knew that they would soon be deposited on cots under the protective covering of tents where they would be given dry blankets and would receive plenty of rest and food and no longer have to squat all day in a dank dirt crevice soaked to the bone with leg muscles cramping so badly they didn't know if they'd ever stand again.

Some wag had dubbed their hunkered-down existence the Anzio crouch. Nat called it a stinking way to live.

To his dismay, he found himself spending far too much time trying to figure out a way to get wounded without getting killed. His observations taught him that surviving a wound required proper timing. As a rule, it was best to get shot at night. Those shot at night were removed immediately from the front lines. Those hit during the daytime were not as fortunate. They had to lay in no-man's-land all day until night's cloak could cover the medics' movements.

There was the occasional exception to this rule. Nat had heard of medics who got Silver Stars for going after a badly wounded man in the daytime. One of them got his award post-humously. Nat concluded that getting wounded at night was much simpler for all concerned.

As night settled over the ditch, he adjusted the blanket that was draped over his shoulders. Like all other attempts to find comfort, this one did little good. The blanket had reached the saturation point two days ago. Now, the cold drapery weighed heavy and wet on his shivering shoulders. He retreated inward.

The problem in getting wounded safely, as he saw it, was the fact that the upper body was exposed first when coming out of a ravine. Too many vital organs were exposed. He had to figure out a way to get wounded in the leg.

"What's on your mind, Rembrandt?" Murphy asked. He had started using the nickname at Tunis when, in his opinion, Nat took too long composing and focusing. "Rembrandt could have painted the picture by now!" he'd exclaimed.

Nat cringed inwardly at Murphy's intrusion into his thoughts. He wanted to be left alone. "You don't want to know," he said.

"Try me."

"All right, answer me this: Why couldn't your father have pulled a few more strings and made you a general?"

Murphy's face bunched up in puzzlement. "What?"

"The way I see it, this is all his fault."

"What are you talking about?"

Nat never had been the kind of person to share his intimate thoughts. Levity was one way to deflect any attempted intrusions.

"Do you see any generals crouching in this ravine with us?" he said. "I thought when I attached myself to you, I was going to escape all this muck. I'll tell you this. In the next war I'm attaching myself to a general who has political aspirations."

Murphy was only slightly amused. As with all the other men, a chill had dampened his soul. A man could live in sopping clothes caked with mud and smelling of mildew only so long before being affected by it.

"'Tain't funny, McGee," he said.

Anzio was the first real offensive for Nat and Murphy. They had ridden across North Africa virtually unhindered, in large part due to the success of the British, whose march hadn't been nearly as easy. Soon after, Sicily was taken and the drive up Italy's boot-like peninsula was launched at Salerno. The drive stalled at Cassino, making Anzio necessary.

The plan was to bypass the German line by sea and land behind them with some 50,000 troops. The landing surprised the Germans. While Nat had braced himself for a landing under enemy fire that in comparison would make Casablanca look like a picnic, in reality, he and Murphy waded ashore in a long peaceful procession. In fact, their arrival was so quiet it was eerie.

Once again they experienced the old army adage of hurry up and wait. For nearly a week, men sat next to their troop transports and played cards, got haircuts, and looked for things to occupy their time while more troops and more vehicles landed.

Murphy took it upon himself to educate Nat regarding the historical significance of their location. Before they left the States, he'd done some reading on Italy's history, thinking the knowledge would come in handy. Pictures at key historical sites would be more impressive than pictures with a general Italian countryside as a background, he reasoned.

"Did you know that Anzio was once an all-season resort?" he said.

Nat leaned against the troop transport and polished the Leica's lens. He didn't answer Murphy's question because he hadn't known that, and he didn't care to know it now.

"Wealthy Romans owned villas here," Murphy continued, not caring whether or not Nat was listening. "It's an important site to several Roman emperors."

Nat rubbed an itchy nose, then continued polishing.

"Augustus was proclaimed the father of the Roman nation here. And emperors Caligula and Nero were born here."

Nat yawned.

※

When the German counteroffensive struck, it was a powerful blow that reduced the beachhead to a shallow dimension. Two American ranger battalions were cut off and captured.

Nat Morgan and Lieutenant Nolan Murphy were suddenly and rudely introduced to war.

※

The darkening ravine was alive with flickering light. A couple of German flares hung over them in the sky.

Nat, Murphy, and everyone else in the unit ducked instinctively. A barrage of ammunition squirted over their heads lit by white tracers. White was a German fuselage signature. The obligatory American response that soon squirted the other direction was lit by red tracers. This kind of exchange was usually a prelude to the heavier stuff.

As expected, an artillery barrage followed. Shells screamed over the ravine, exploding five hundred yards behind them. Nat covered his ears. The whine and whistle and blast of ammunition unnerved him. His hands began to tremble.

While he had looked upon dead soldiers by the scores and had seen men cut down beside him and had smelled the stench of the unburied dead and shooed away the flies that swarmed over them; and while he had lived in the ground like an animal, exposed to the elements, hungry, exhausted, wet, and cold with his clothes and skin smelling so bad he couldn't stand himself, none of these things did to him what the sounds of artillery did.

The sound of whistling death set off a sympathetic vibration with his nerves as though they were on the same wavelength. So did the ground-shaking thunder of the detonations, the rapid stutter of machine-gun fire, the thud of bullets hitting the dirt, pinging against rock or metal, the soft thump of a bullet ripping through clothing and flesh and embedding itself in a person's body.

It was the sounds, the sounds that got his hands to shaking, that set his gut to quivering and squeezed his sensibilities until his eyes bulged.

He curled up with his blanket and pressed himself against the muddy wall of the ravine as hard as he could.

A couple of shells fell shorter than the rest. The wall of the ravine trembled. Nat heard another whistling sound. This one grew louder than the rest. It didn't pass over but kept coming and coming right at them.

The earth erupted less than a dozen yards away. A wave of mud and rocks showered down on them. When the pelting started, Nat pulled the blanket over his head. It wasn't enough to protect him from a good-sized rock that punched him in the jaw.

Another shell hit. This one even closer. The wall against which Nat leaned did more than tremble, it quaked and began to crumble. Nat splashed through the water to Murphy's side of the ravine fueled by the memory of a similar explosion.

Two days earlier a shell hit close to a foxhole not more than a half-dozen feet away from him. The whole thing caved in. Three soldiers were buried. By the time they were dug out, they were dead.

Nat's ravine wall proved to be sturdier. It held.

Then the shelling stopped.

With shaking hands Nat adjusted the sodden, pungent blanket. High overhead he spied a small triangular opening in the clouds. On the other side he could see the night sky. Two stars winked at him. Everything was quiet again.

After a time it was dark enough that soldiers began venturing out of the ravine. Moans could be heard up and down the crevice as men stretched cramps from their aching limbs.

Just as Nat threw back his blanket to join them he heard a splashing sound. It was coming from downstream. Someone was coming toward them. From the rapid rhythm of the splashing, whoever it was was in a hurry. Murphy and the others heard it too. Rifles swung that direction.

A black figure appeared from around the creek's bend. The splashing stopped. The figure spoke with a squeaky voice. "Don't shoot! I'm a good guy!"

"Identify yourself," Murphy said.

"Private First Class Szczepkowski, sir!"

Murphy motioned to his men to lower their weapons. To the distant figure, he said, "*I'm a good guy?* That kind of response is a good way to get yourself killed, Szczepkowski."

The private waded up the creek. "Sorry, sir. But I thought you'd want to see these. They just came." He held out a large floppy magazine and a letter.

Murphy took them. He held the letter close to his face. There wasn't enough available light to read the handwriting.

"It's from Miss Lily Morgan," Szczepkowski offered.

"You're corresponding with my sister?" Nat demanded.

"Relax, Rembrandt," Murphy said. "It's all on the up and up … for now at least," he added with a wink. "She's helping me arrange a Jerry Jupiter concert."

"Since when does my sister handle Jupiter's concert calendar?"

"Since I asked her," Murphy said with a smile.

Nat's indignation was purely good-natured. He liked the idea of Murphy and Lily getting together. Not only did he think they'd be good for each other, but he was partial to the thought of having Murphy as a brother-in-law.

"The only problem," Murphy said, holding up the letter that he could barely see and couldn't read, "I don't know if this is good news or bad news. I'd hate to have to wait until morning to find out."

"And don't forget the magazine!" Szczepkowski said. "Page thirty-two. I think you're gonna like it, Lieutenant."

Murphy held up the magazine. Even in the darkness there was enough light to see the big white block letters set on a rectangular field of red.

LIFE.

"Is my picture in here?" Murphy asked.

Szczepkowski nodded excitedly.

"This can't wait until morning!" Murphy said.

With the arrival of the letter and the magazine, the mood in the ravine changed rapidly and dramatically. It was as though someone had thrown a switch.

The arrival of mail always had that effect. Donuts and warm coffee had the same effect but were a distant second to mail.

Nat felt the excitement rising in him. After a muddy, gray day like this one had been, excitement was a magnificent feeling. The thought of news from his sister (it didn't matter that the letter was addressed to Murphy) together with the thought of Murphy's picture making the pages of *Life* magazine was just the elixir he needed. His spirit climbed out of depression's muddy grave and stepped into the world of the living again, even if only for a moment.

But that was all that he needed. One moment. Nat figured that the memory of this moment could sustain his spirit for a few days at least.

"Crawl under my blanket," Nat suggested. He pulled the heavy covering from his shoulders, handing an edge to Szczepkowski. "We'll hold the blanket, you read the letter."

Szczepkowski was eager to help.

Murphy grinned. He grabbed a flashlight and ducked under the blanket. A moment later, as the flashlight was switched on, a soft glow radiated against the blanket's surface. Nat looked around anxiously to see if the diffused light was attracting attention. The blanket seemed to be doing its job.

There was a pause while Murphy got himself situated. Nat and Szczepkowski exchanged expectant glances as they waited. There was a rustle of paper, then:

"She's coming!" Murphy said. "I mean, *they're* coming! Jerry Jupiter and the entire band!"

A few soldiers nearby glanced in curiosity at the blanket and the voice. Szczepkowski interpreted for them.

"Lieutenant Murphy just arranged for Jerry Jupiter's band to entertain us!" he said.

The news spread quickly up and down the ravine. The ditch came alive with excitement. Soldiers began to congregate around the blanket, listening intently to the voice coming from beneath it, as though it were a radio and Lieutenant Murphy were the announcer.

He read aloud the letter, giving the arrival time and details of the concert. Midway through a sentence, he stopped. An instant later, he said, "Then, the letter gets personal."

Despite the cries for him to read the personal parts, Murphy could not be persuaded. There was another soft rustle of pages, and then:

"Holy Joe!" Murphy shouted. "A full page!"

"His picture!" A beaming Szczepkowski interpreted again for the men standing around. "*Life* magazine!"

Head nods and grins indicated they were impressed.

"It's the one at the tank with all the flies!" Murphy said from beneath the blanket. "And you got the photo credit, Nat! Big as life! Pardon the pun."

The glow on the side of the blanket bobbed excitedly.

"Nat, you gotta get under here and see this!"

A private standing nearby offered to take hold of the edge of the blanket for Nat. Nat relinquished his hold on the blanket and ducked under it.

Beneath the blanket a tousle-haired and grinning Murphy held open the magazine. Murphy's picture was overprinted with a title and an article. The piece chronicled the accomplishments of young American army officers during Operation Torch. The picture itself captured him with one hand shooing away what seemed to be a million flies while the other hand pinned a map to the top of a burned-out British tank. His eyes gazed at the horizon with a determined look.

"What do you think?" Murphy enthused. "Pretty good, huh?"

Nat appraised the picture with a photographer's eye. "It's a little dark down in this region," he said. "I should have opened the aperture one more f-stop."

"What are you talking about, Rembrandt! This is a first for both of us! *Life* magazine! Enjoy it!"

Nat allowed a grin to stretch across his face. Murphy was right. It was a milestone for both of them. There would be time to be professional about it later. This was a time to celebrate.

"Congratulations, Nolan," Nat said extending his hand.

Murphy seemed taken aback for a moment by the sound of his given name. He smiled. "You too, Nat," he said. "You know, we make a pretty good team. We're gonna do some great things together."

"If I can keep you from wandering into sandstorms without your compass."

"Quiet!" Murphy said, looking at the blanket as though it had ears. "That's strictly between you and me. Remember?"

"What else did my sister say in her letter?" Nat asked.

Murphy grinned mischievously. "That's between me and her." When Nat began to protest, Murphy added, "All I can say is that she's head-over-heels in love with a certain future U.S. Senator."

An unidentified voice came from the other side of the blanket. "Well, isn't that sweet? She's in love with him! My heart's all atwitter!"

Male laughter erupted all around them.

Nat laughed with them. It was such a good feeling to have his chest shake with laughter again. He almost forgot that he was drenched and caked with mud and sitting with his boots in a running stream.

"'Tain't funny, McGee," Murphy said with a look of chagrin. But he was laughing too. A sly look on his face indicated he had a notion.

Throwing back the blanket, he stood with his hands on his hips looking like Superman. "Dare you laugh at a superior officer who has just arranged ..."

A sliver of fear as cold and as hard as an icicle pierced Nat's heart. With one hand he reached for Murphy's belt to pull him down. With the other he knocked the flashlight from Murphy's hand.

"... to bring you Miss Lil ..."

The flashlight tumbled crazily. It splashed into the water and sank to the bottom, illuminating the rocks and grit carried along by the insignificant Italian stream.

A hail of machine-gun fire squirted over them. Dirt and pebbles exploded along the ridge of the ravine.

Murphy's knees buckled. He slumped and fell back onto Nat. His head lolled against Nat's shoulder. Blood covered one side of his neck and the front of his uniform.

Bullets continued to spray along the ridge. Everywhere soldiers dove to the bottom of the ravine for cover.

"Medic!" Nat shouted, holding onto Murphy, keeping him from slipping into the stream. "Medic! Medic!" His voice was so strained and high-pitched he didn't even recognize it as his own.

A shower of dirt and stone continued to fly from the ridge as it continued to be pounded by an onslaught of bullets.

There was a soft yellow glow all around them. The flashlight! Even under water it was providing enough light to give the Germans a target.

"Szczepkowski! The flashlight! Get the flashlight!"

The private was curled up against the far bank, his arms and hands protecting his head. He glanced at Murphy. A dreadful look of horror twisted his face.

"They're shooting at the light! Grab the flashlight!"

Szczepkowski didn't move. His eyes were riveted on Murphy.

Another soldier close to Szczepkowski splashed into the creek and extinguished the light. It was dark for only a moment. Two flares from the German side streaked skyward with shivering tails basking the ridge with their flickering light.

"Medic!" Nat shouted. He looked up and down the ravine hoping to see help arriving.

It's best to get shot at night; simpler for all concerned.

"Medic! Medic!" Nat shouted.

Murphy's head moved. It was the first sign of life he'd shown since getting hit. His eyes fluttered open. Nat could see the twin flares overhead reflected in them.

"Why all the shouting, Rembrandt?" Murphy said. His voice was breathy. At the end of the sentence there was a long aspiration of breath followed by a gurgling sound.

A portion of Murphy's neck was missing. Nat grabbed the blanket that had been their tent and held it against Murphy's neck to stop the blood flowing so freely from it.

He looked down at his friend. Murphy's eyes were fixed on him, but he was having trouble holding their focus.

"You're going to be all right," Nat said. "The medics are coming. They'll patch you up. Everything will be all right."

Murphy chuckled. His eyes were losing their focus.

"'Tain't funny, McGee," he said.

He began to choke on his own fluids. Nat helped him sit upright. He stopped choking.

Another glance up and down the ravine. Still no sign of the medics.

"Nat?"

"Yeah?"

"That was really stupid of me, wasn't it?"

"Yeah, Murphy, it was."

"Worse than the sandstorm?"

"Yeah, Worse than the sandstorm."

"Casablanca too?"

"Yeah, worse than Casablanca too."

"Don't think you can save me from this one."

Nat looked for medics who still weren't there. "Just hold on, Murphy," he said. "The medics are coming. You're gonna be all right."

Murphy's head fell to one side. He seemed mesmerized by the fading flares overhead.

"Don't tell Lily," he said. His voice was barely a whisper.

"Don't tell Lily what?"

"That I died because I did something stupid."

Nat's eyesight blurred with tears. His chest heaved as he fought back heavy sobs.

"I won't tell her," he said.

Murphy managed a half grin. "I'd hate for the woman I'm going to marry to think that she was getting hitched to someone that was ..."

Lieutenant Nolan Murphy didn't live long enough to finish his sentence. A few moments later the flares were spent and the shooting stopped. Darkness and quiet settled over the little ravine that had no name.

For the remainder of the night, Nat Morgan held his dead friend in his arms.

22

Loretta May stood in her flight suit in Lockbourne's flight operations office. She was looking over the paperwork of her first B-17 ferrying assignment when the door swung open and Virginia Giles strolled in.

"Virginia!" Loretta said, giving her friend a hug. "Welcome back. How was your furlough?"

"Long," Virginia said with a tired grin. "Two weeks with my family is a decade for normal folks."

"Your father still isn't angry with you for flying, is he?"

Virginia grinned, "Not since I qualified to fly the Big Friend. In his mind that's almost as good as being a marine, so I'm accepted again. So guess what he's doing now? He's inviting all his beer buddies over to meet his daughter, the B-17 bomber pilot! Believe me, I was never so glad to get out of a place in my life!"

"Sounds to me like he's proud of you."

"When it comes to my father," Virginia said dryly, "I think I prefer angry."

The two women laughed.

"How about you?" Virginia asked. "How was your furlough?"

"Nice …" Loretta said with a note of qualification in her voice.

"It felt good to be in warm, sunny California again, but I missed the flying. I'm ready to get to work."

"You can say that again. Have you seen Alex yet?"

"No, have you?"

Virginia shook her head.

Loretta checked her watch. "She should be here by now. It's not like her to be late." She turned to the horseshoe-bald sergeant behind the desk and asked, "Have you given Alex Morgan her assignment yet?"

Looking up briefly from the papers he was sorting, the man shook his head.

"That's odd," Virginia said to Loretta. "Alex lives in San Diego, doesn't she? I wonder if she's come back yet?"

The desk sergeant answered the question. "She never left."

"She didn't go on furlough?" Loretta asked.

He shook his head. "She came in here a couple of times asking about flights. Said she wasn't one to take furloughs."

"How long ago?" Virginia asked.

"Well, let's see, it's been more than a week ago," he said as his eyes searched the ceiling, as though the answer was written there. "Um … Aunt Hazel came last Tuesday, stayed through Friday, and Miss Morgan … yes, Miss Morgan was here the day Aunt Hazel returned to Poughkeepsie and that was ten days ago."

"Can't argue with that," Loretta said dryly.

"Let's go check her room," Virginia suggested.

When they reached Alex's room they found it empty. More than empty, vacated. The bed was stripped and there were no clothes in the closet.

"This is really odd," Loretta said.

"What should we do?"

"Not jump to any conclusions. Right now, all we can do is wait and see if she shows up."

"We could check with personnel or the MPs to see if she's still on base."

"Good idea."

The resulting check of the base records revealed that as far as anyone knew Alex Morgan was still on base. But she was nowhere to be found.

※

In Norfolk, Virginia, the Jerry Jupiter band exchanged its touring bus for a navy ship and transport plane. Having left the States for their North African and European tour of the front, they had sailed to Casablanca and from there hopped by plane to Algiers and Tunis, performing multiple times at each stop.

At present their plane was in the air once again, their schedule taking them to Palermo, Sicily, and then to Italy. First to Naples and then to Anzio, where Lily would catch up with her brother.

She slumped against two duffel bags as the transport plane vibrated beneath her with a loud hum. Bags, blankets, pillows, ropes, instruments, boxes, and cartons were stacked everywhere the length of the metal tube. On top of the baggage, musicians slept, show girls played cards or tried to paint their nails in spite of the more than occasional jolt, and stage personnel chatted or wrote letters with shaky penmanship, also courtesy of their means of transportation.

Because of the noise of the engines, conversations were little more than exercises in shouting. For this reason, Lily discouraged them during the flights. Shouting strained her voice to the point that she was no good for the next show. Everyone understood this and pretty much left her alone.

It had become an unspoken fact among the troupe that Lily Morgan was the show's marquee act, having eclipsed Jerry Jupiter himself. This was partially due to her greater talent, but more largely due to the fact that they were playing to all-male audiences.

Lily took her growing fame in stride. To her, becoming a celebrity was more of a distraction than a goal. It was the music and the singing and the performing she loved, the connection she made with the audience when she was onstage, the way the music and the words knit everyone together as they all shared one moment, one song, one emotion. This was what excited her, not the desire for special treatment or special favors.

As for the privacy that was granted her aboard the planes while in flight, she used the time for personal things—to read her Bible, to memorize new music, and to write letters. At first, she wrote almost exclusively to her parents. Within the last couple of months however, she'd been in regular correspondence with an army officer. Their correspondence had become so regular that it had prompted remarks from other members of the band. Some of the remarks had barbs in them. These were the remarks spoken by Jupiter and Albert Lohmann, the trumpet player.

Though Lily had done nothing to encourage either of these men, she had found both of them increasingly amorous toward her and, at the same time, increasingly competitive with each other over her. Their schoolboy-style feud was quickly getting out of hand. The two men's constant sniping was beginning to affect the band's performances and between performances no one knew when the feud was likely to flare up. Lily did her best to let them both know in a polite way that when it came to matters of the heart she was equally disinterested in both of them. In both cases, it was an injection of reality that didn't take. If their feud contin-ued to escalate, she knew she would have to be more direct. Maybe even less polite.

One problem in doing this was that she respected both men, Jupiter for his ability to put on a quality show and Lohmann for his trumpet playing. But that was as far as her feelings went. She harbored no romantic inclinations for either of them, which made their feud all the more ridiculous.

The irony of it all was that she had two men nearby who loved her, while the man who was stirring her romantic emotions was far away. They'd only had a few minutes together on the parade grounds the day they met, but Lily felt an instant attraction to Lieutenant Nolan Murphy that she had never felt for a man before. To her surprise and delight, she received a letter from him following the concert. And he had continued to write regularly ever since.

What attracted Lily to him was his wit and his intellect. He approached politics the way she approached her musical career. Their respective fields fascinated them. They held no rosy pre-conceptions about what it would take to succeed. They both liked what they were doing. And they were both good at what they did.

They differed in this: While the onset of the war proved to be the very thing that helped launch Lily's career, it was a diversion to his. She laughed every time he described his military duties. Try as she might, she could not envision Nolan Murphy as a military leader. If ever there was a man out of place in the army it was Nolan Murphy; though she did have to admit with a smile that he looked particularly handsome in his uniform.

His letters informed her how Nat had dragged him ashore at Casablanca. And how her brother had unburied him in the North African sandstorm. These were things he confessed to no other person, including his parents. His willingness to share and even laugh about his own faults was one of the things that endeared him to her.

She also liked the fact that Nat and Nolan were friends. There was something fitting about him liking Nat, for he and she had always been close. Whereas Alex and Walt shared flying interests,

Lily and Nat had been the artistic ones. They understood each other and supported each other in a household where everything seemed to be centered on aircraft. It pleased Lily to think that Nat and Nolan were together. It was as though God had placed her big brother beside Nolan to keep him safe for her.

She yawned. Raising her hands and arms over her head, she arched her back, stretched, and surveyed the interior of the fuselage. Most everyone was asleep. She was feeling drowsy herself. Being on the road, or in the air, had a progressive weariness about it that was not erased with a single good night's sleep.

They were scheduled to set down in Palermo within the hour. A bus would take them to their quarters, where they would get four hours sleep before starting to set up for the first show.

Thinking she should join the others and get some sleep, she reached over to put away her stationery and pen. Setting the stationery box on top of her Bible, she lifted them both to put them in her bag.

She stopped. A pleased grin raised her cheeks. Setting her things on her lap, she lifted the cover of her Bible and retrieved a letter. It was her most recent letter from Nolan. She opened it and read it for the fourth time since they departed Tunis. With each sentence her heart skipped excitedly. She grinned like a schoolgirl even after she had folded the letter up and placed it back inside the cover of her Bible.

Five more days and they would be in Anzio. Five more days and she would see Nolan again.

The early morning light crested over the ridge of the ravine and fell on the face of the dead Lieutenant Nolan Murphy, outlining his ashen features with a tinge of yellow. During the night the sky had cleared. Nat squinted against the increasing sunlight.

He cursed it.

It was light that had marked his friend for death and now light mocked his corpse, painting it with a color normally associated with life. Still holding his friend in his arms, Nat dragged the sodden, mud-caked blanket over Murphy's face, depriving the morning sun of its derisive fun.

The day had no right to dawn bright and cheery. A blacker day than this there never was. What had someone like Murphy done to deserve this? This wasn't Nolan Murphy's war. He hadn't fired at anyone. Killed anyone. Nat couldn't even remember Murphy ever saying anything unkind about the Germans, who were the enemy.

His was a life that shouldn't even be here. The proverbial square peg in a round hole. Murphy was a politician, an organizer, a backslapper, a speechmaker, a diplomat. Words were his weapons. Promises. Witticisms. Discussion. Haggling. Town meetings. Debate.

What did he know of bullets and war?

But it was a bullet that had silenced him, snuffed out a promising life. Murphy was a government leader who would never get a chance to lead, a civil servant who would never serve. A good man who would never know the love of a good woman.

How am I going to tell Lily?

The *Life* magazine with Murphy's picture in it lay at the edge of the stream. Trodden underfoot. Its pages torn. Sopped. Muddy.

Nat remembered Lily's letter. He searched Murphy's pockets until he found it.

The handwriting on the envelope was as familiar to him as was the name of the man to whom it was addressed. Lily's writing. Murphy's name. Here was a match that would never be. What seemed to Nat to be a perfect pairing had been canceled by a moment of humor and an enemy bullet.

Nat placed Lily's letter in his pocket. On the opposite side of the stream sat Private First Class Szczepkowski, his legs pulled up against his chest encircled by his arms. All night he'd sat there and stared at Murphy and him. He never said a word; he just stared.

Up and down the ravine men settled in for another day. The remains of C-rations were scattered here and there. The crouching movement of soldiers downstream caught Nat's eye. Their helmets bore a red cross in a circle of white.

Medics. It's a little late, don't you think, fellas?

In the distance there was a rumbling. The medics heard it too. They stopped and crouched and looked to the ridge.

The rumbling grew rapidly louder.

"TANKS!" someone shouted.

Men flung themselves against the side of the creek under attack and poked their heads and rifles over. Nat laid Murphy's body gently aside and joined them, though he had no weapon.

A line of tanks rumbled straight toward him with row after row of German infantrymen following behind.

The rumbling of the tank tracks gave way to the thunder of their fire. Geysers of dirt and rock erupted up and down the ridge, tossing men into the air like dolls. Some of the soldiers scurried out of the ravine to run. They were mowed down by enemy fire.

Upstream one of the soldiers was signaling and waving. "This way! This way!" In front of him a line of crouched men were making their way upstream.

Nat looked at Murphy. Lifeless. The stream washing over and around his boots. The rumbling of the tanks was louder now.

Good-bye, Nolan.

In spite of the oncoming tanks and the erupting shells Szczepkowski hadn't moved. He sat curled up like a sow bug.

Nat grabbed his camera cases. "Let's go!" he shouted to the private.

Szczepkowski didn't seem to hear him. As soldier after soldier passed them, Nat proceeded upstream a couple of steps and called again. Szczepkowski sat there.

Nat went back and grabbed the private by the collar and dragged him out of his crouch. "Let's go, Private!" he shouted.

Szczepkowski was on his feet but his eyes were still fixed on Murphy. Nat stepped between them, cutting off the boy's line of sight. "He's dead! And you will be too unless you get going!"

The private stared at him. A measure of rational thought returned to his eyes.

"Let's go, Private!" Nat shouted again.

Szczepkowski began moving upstream. Nat was right behind, pushing him.

Suddenly, there was an enormous creaking thunder. Tank tracks appeared at the edge of the ridge. The metal monster was right on top of them.

Nat shoved Szczepkowski into the creek and dove after him. Looking up he saw the tank hover for a moment, then begin its downward descent.

The tracks crashed against the far side of the ravine. Nat and Szczepkowski were in a small wedge of a space beneath it. The tracks clawed their way up the side of the ravine.

Nat grabbed Szczepkowski by the belt and pulled him out from beneath the tank just as the back half came crashing down on their side of the stream.

Ahead of them soldiers were firing at the tanks, providing Nat and his buddy cover. By now Szczepkowski was moving on his own. The two of them splashed upstream as fast as their legs would carry them.

They rounded a bend in the ravine just as German soldiers

began pouring over the ridge behind them. A couple of well-placed riflemen succeeded in keeping the Germans at bay. It was a short-term reprieve at best.

Nat and Szczepkowski slumped onto the ground to catch their breath while a few men scouted farther upriver. Nat found himself sitting next to a dead soldier. A radio was strapped around his neck. The receiver was squawking noisily. Nat picked it up.

"Hello?"

The sound of Nat's voice halted the stream of words that had been pouring out of the receiver. But not for long.

"Who is this?" the voice demanded.

"Corporal Nat Morgan," Nat said.

"Where's Abrams?"

Nat looked down at the soldier whose face was buried in the mud. "He's dead, sir."

There was another pause. Then, "And who are you?"

"I told you," Nat said. "I'm Corporal Nat Morgan."

"Are you with communications?"

"No sir, I'm a photographer."

There was a muffled string of curses followed by the man on the other end of the line reporting to someone that he was talking to a photographer.

The men guarding the bend began to pull back. They shouted at everyone to proceed upstream.

"Listen, Morgan—" began the voice on the other end of the line.

"Sorry, sir," Nat said, "but we have to get out of here!" He nudged Szczepkowski upstream and began to follow him. The receiver squawked noisily again.

Nat decided it would be best to take the radio with them. Lifting the strap over the dead man's head, Nat grabbed the radio and followed Szczepkowski upstream.

They were running out of cover. The ravine grew increasingly shallow. The soldiers were almost completely doubled over now as they ran.

After a few hundred yards they found another defensible position. Nat dropped to the ground next to Szczepkowski. The boy was bent over at the waist trying to catch his breath. Nat was concerned for him. He hadn't said a word since Murphy had been shot.

The radio was squawking again. Nat took a couple of deep breaths before answering it.

"Don't you ever cut me off like that again, soldier!" the voice commanded.

"Sorry, sir. It couldn't be helped. We were being overrun by the enemy and had to get out of there."

Although there was no expressed understanding from the other end, the next time the voice spoke it had a more conciliatory tone. "What's your position, son?"

Nat described where they were and their situation.

"Understood," said the voice. "Now listen to me. It's imperative that you boys don't give up. Do you hear me?"

"Yes, sir."

"You tell them, son … nobody is giving up. Don't let anybody put their hands up in the air. This thing isn't over! Don't let them do it! Get the officers to shoot. Do that. Do anything. But don't give up!"

"I'll tell them, sir."

"We're coming through. Tell them that. And Morgan?"

"Yes sir?"

"You hang onto this radio. How many men are with you?"

Nat looked around and made a quick count. "I count about a dozen, sir."

Another pause. Apparently the man at the other end of the

line was reporting to his superior because Nat heard a different voice cry out, "A dozen!" and then curse.

The voice was back. "Stick together," he said. "Use your head and do what's best. Understand?"

"Yes, sir."

In a softer tone the voice said, "You're there, and I'm here, unfortunately, and I can't help you, son. But whatever happens, well, God bless you, son."

"Thank you, sir."

Nat replaced the receiver. He hadn't really been scared until now. But it sure sounded like the man at the other end of the line, whoever he was, had just pronounced benediction.

Artillery concentration whistled overhead as Nat relayed the information he'd received by radio. Grim faces were his only response.

A man by the name of Gibson, who Nat had seen before serving food during mess, jumped to an alert crouching position.

"Stay fifty yards behind me," he said to the others. "I'll scout ahead."

Nat watched as Gibson moved upstream. He'd gone only a few steps when a blast of machine-gun fire opened up from a clump of brush along the ditch bank.

Without taking cover, he ran forward firing his Tommy gun from the hip. He managed to reach the brush, poke his gun muzzle into it, and kill the German who was hiding there.

He signaled all clear and motioned for the others to follow him.

Nat gathered up the radio, his camera bags, and punched Szczepkowski in the shoulder. "Let's go," he said.

"I can't," Szczepkowski replied. "I've been hit."

The boy was holding his thigh, which was soaked in blood. He'd been hit and hadn't even made a sound.

Hurriedly, Nat fashioned a tourniquet above the heavily bleeding wound.

"I think it's broken," Szczepkowski said.

"Can you stand on it?"

"I don't know."

Nat looked anxiously around him. Everyone was moving out.

"Here." Nat offered his hand and pulled Szczepkowski to his feet. The instant the boy put weight on it, he crumpled. Nat caught him.

"Just leave me," Szczepkowski said.

"Nonsense. I'll help you."

Draping the boy's arm over his shoulder, Nat helped the boy hobble upstream. It was slow going, complicated by all the bags Nat was carrying. He thought about ditching the radio. He decided against it after remembering that he'd been given an order to hold onto it at all costs. That left the camera bags.

Out of the question. Nat wasn't about to leave the Leica and Rolleiflex behind. Not now. Not after all they'd been through together. And especially not now since they were carrying undeveloped photos of Murphy. The last pictures that would ever be taken of him.

His back felt like it would snap in two, sweat poured down his face and neck, and his legs screamed for rest, but Nat and Szczepkowski managed to keep up with the rest of the men.

Gibson signaled them to halt. The artillery continued unabated. One shell exploded near Gibson. The concussion knocked him off his feet. An instant later, there were small dirt explosions all around him from machine-gun and rifle fire. Again he charged upstream, firing his submachine gun into another cluster of bushes.

He killed another German while a second one climbed out of the bushes with his hands up. They had themselves a prisoner.

They proceeded up the ravine again, which by now was no more than a ditch. Another machine gun opened fire on them from still another bush.

This time Gibson instructed some of the other men to concentrate their rifles in that direction. While they kept the Germans in the bush occupied, he scurried up the side of the ditch.

Seeing what he was about to attempt, several of the men tried to dissuade him. Gibson ignored them. He crawled along the top of the ditch toward the enemy. It was about 125 yards distant. Gibson was in an exposed position at the corner of an open field directly in the line of fire of artillery and several machine guns.

When he was about thirty-five yards away, he lobbed two hand grenades and charged the German's position, killing two more of the enemy and taking another prisoner.

Szczepkowski and Nat exchanged glances. The way things were going with Gibson leading them, they'd make it safely back to their lines without anybody else having to do any fighting.

They reached a bend in the ditch. Gibson ordered everyone to stay behind until he found out if there were any Germans around the corner. Nat lowered Szczepkowski to the ground as they watched Gibson disappear around the bend.

Soon after, they heard machine-gun fire. Then Gibson's Tommy gun. Then all was quiet.

Everyone waited. There was no other sound. And Gibson didn't return. The soldiers and their two German prisoners looked at each other. There was only one way to find out what had happened.

Helping Szczepkowski to his feet again, Nat followed the others around the bend.

What they found were two dead bodies. The German who had been firing at them. And Gibson. He lay fallen in a firing position.

Not knowing what else to do, they moved forward. The ditch became a gully and soon they found themselves in an open field. All around them the artillery pounded away at them.

Everyone exchanged glances, not sure where to go from here. Small-arm and machine-gun fire was tense all around them. A chicken wouldn't make it crossing the open field, let alone a man.

A moment later there was no longer any decision to be made. Germans began pouring out of foxholes all around them. Nat remembered their orders. *Don't let anybody put their hands up in the air. Don't let them do it!*

Nat looked all around them. The Germans were on them in seconds. They came from every direction. And then it was over. And Nat and Szczepkowski and all the others were prisoners of war.

The other soldiers were stripped of their weapons. The radio and Nat's camera bags were taken from him despite his protests that the bags contained cameras, not weapons.

Then they were led toward the German lines. While the other men marched with their hands behind their heads, Nat used his to assist Szczepkowski who was becoming heavier and heavier. Nat didn't know if it was because he was getting tired or if Szczepkowski was failing. A glance at the boy's leg revealed a lot of red. And he was leaving streaked red footprints on the field as they walked.

From masonry farmhouses and barns and silos and outdoor ovens, Germans stared at them as they passed. The Germans had learned to utilize these buildings as fortifications. Fire trenches were dug around the outside foundations of the houses and machine guns were placed inside ovens that were generally located about fifteen to twenty yards from the house. This gave them blast protection and overhead cover against artillery fire and percussion. It would take a tank or direct artillery hit to dislodge or destroy them.

Szczepkowski groaned and fell to the ground, pulling Nat down with him. A German soldier with a boxlike jaw stood over them and shouted something Nat couldn't understand.

"He needs a doctor!" Nat said. "Medic. Do you understand? Medic."

The German shouted again.

Nat didn't know what else to do but try to make his captor understand. He tried again. Getting to his knees he pointed at Szczepkowski's wound.

"He's wounded. Look here. He can't walk. He needs medical help!"

Raising his rifle, the German took aim at Szczepkowski and shot him in the heart. The boy jerked once and died.

Nat was stunned. There had been no indication this would happen. The German didn't even hesitate. It was just *Boom*! and Szczepkowski was dead. A cold-blooded, callous, spontaneous murder of an injured boy who was no threat to anyone.

Motioning him with his rifle, the German ordered Nat to join the others. The man's eyes were black, cold, unfeeling. He had just shot a man to death! Yet from the look on his face you would have thought he'd just flicked a flea from his uniform or swatted a fly.

"He was just a scared boy!" Nat screamed. "What kind of animals are you?"

The German shouted at Nat, once again ordering him to join the others.

"How could you do that?" Nat shouted, still in disbelief. "How could you just kill a man like that?"

The German shouted again. When Nat didn't move, he shouldered his rifle and took aim at Nat's chest.

Nat was so enraged, he didn't care. "You're going to kill me, too? Well go ahead, you bloody beast! Because let me tell you, if I was on the other side of that rifle I'd blow your German head off!"

The other prisoners were yelling now, urging Nat to get off his knees and join them. Nat heard them, but he no longer cared. If this is what the world had to offer, then he no longer wanted to be a part of it. Murphy and he had done everything together up until now; maybe it was ordained that they were supposed to die together too.

Nat rose up on his knees and spread out his arms. "Go ahead, you bloody Kraut. Shoot me! Shoot me!"

Lily had just dozed off when the sound of angry male voices woke her. Not only her, but half the troupe as well. It was Jupiter and Lohmann. They were at it again.

Standing toe-to-toe, less than a foot apart, they were both pointing accusing fingers at the other. Both were shouting; neither was listening. Several complaints and verbal darts were thrown at them from the other members of the band. These too went unheard.

Disgustedly, Lily worked her way around and over boxes, bags, and several sleeping bodies to get to them. She seemed to be the only person who could get their attention.

"Honestly!" she scolded them. "You two are acting like little boys!"

"Lily," Lohmann said heatedly, "are you aware that this lecher has placed you in an adjoining room to his in Palermo?"

"Lily, don't listen to him. It's not anything like he's trying to make it out to be," Jupiter said. "There are only so many rooms available …"

A torrent of angry moans and threats were leveled at them from those who were trying to sleep.

"Both of you, keep your voices down!" Lily said with a hushed voice.

Another voice from beneath a blanket near their feet shouted, "Tell them to take it outside, Lily!"

With a crooked finger, Lily motioned the two men to follow her. Lohmann started to object.

"Hush!" she told him. "This has gone on long enough. We're going to settle it here and now. Now come with me to the back of the plane so we don't disturb the others."

Their heads hanging like two boys being led to the principal's office, they followed Lily in a roundabout path to the back of the plane.

In a voice barely loud enough for them to hear over the noise of the airplane engines, Lily said, "I've had enough of this! I want both of you to stop this feuding right now!"

Lohmann objected, "But Lily, I'm only trying to …"

"I'm a big girl, Mr. Lohmann," she said. "I can take care of myself."

Calling him Mr. Lohmann stung. She could tell by the look on his face, and by the smile on Jupiter's.

"As for you, Mr. Jupiter …"

The two men exchanged facial expressions.

"… I'm your employee, not your—"

Lily never completed that thought. A loud BANG! interrupted her.

The plane tilted radically to the right, slamming her against the side. Her head hit a beam. There was a flash of white. Then, the next thing she knew she was on the floor of the cargo carrier. Jupiter and Lohmann were on top of her.

The floor tipped. They began sliding toward the front.

Black oily smoke filled the fuselage. It stung her throat. She started coughing. Boxes and blankets and bodies were sliding toward the front of the plane. Women and men were screaming.

Just as she was able to grab hold of a beam to stop herself from sliding, everything went crazy. The top of the plane became the bottom and the bottom the top, and then it reversed itself. They were tumbling.

The strangest thought occurred to her. *So this is what it's like to be inside a washing machine.* It was followed by an equally strange thought, this one not so amusing. *So this is what it's like to be in an airplane crash.*

Lohmann's body flopped around her like a rag doll. Jupiter was wide-eyed and shouting, his arms flailing, his fingers grasping for something but finding nothing.

The sound of the plane, no longer a monotonous throb, became a high-pitched whine. It was screaming along with the rest of them.

With no windows, there was no way for Lily to tell how high they were or when they would hit. They just tumbled for what seemed an eternity, never knowing at what instant the tumbling— and their lives—would stop.

Then, the tumbling slowed.

As it did, hope elbowed its way into Lily's heart. The pilot was regaining control. But was he in time?

Finally, the floor was the floor again.

A weak cheer rose from among the baggage. Lily knew people belonged to those voices, but it was hard to pick them out from among the rubble.

They weren't out of danger, though. The plane was still angling downward.

Lily managed to work herself into a sitting position. She noticed cargo nets on the side of the plane. Grabbing one, she started to fasten it around herself. Jupiter saw what she was doing and grabbed one himself.

Then she saw Lohmann at her feet. He was unconscious. Or dead, she didn't know which.

She unstrapped herself and crawled to him.

The smoke inside the cabin was getting thicker. Blacker. It hovered over everything and everybody like a thundercloud. But this thundercloud had a bite. It lodged in her nose and throat and lungs.

Coughing, choking, Lily pulled Lohmann to the side of the plane so she could get a cargo net around him.

Behind her she heard cries and moans and pleas from the others who were trying to extract themselves from the boxes.

Lily fastened the net around Lohmann. She reached for a net for herself.

A wicked bounce slammed her to the ground, then threw her against the top, then slammed her to the ground again. It knocked the air from her lungs.

Lily gasped, fighting to get a bit of air down a raw throat into her burning lungs.

Another slam. She bounced not quite to the top this time before crashing to the floor.

Her head and back struck the flooring with a sickening thud. A black fog settled over her, and it wasn't the smoke this time.

The net dangled above her. She reached for it. It was beyond reach. Just a few inches. She reached again. It dangled as though it was trying to meet her halfway.

Then, all of sudden, she was flying.

Flying backward. Her legs and arms stretched out at her sides. Books and pencils and toothbrushes and blankets and hairbrushes and shoes flew with her.

In an instant she traveled the length of the fuselage, its ribs passing by in a blur. And in that instant, images flashed in her head.

The family veranda in San Diego.

Everyone sitting at the dinner table.

Alex.

Walt.

Nat.

Her father.

Mom.

Nolan.

Then, as suddenly as a light burns out in a film projector, the images went black.

23

MONDAY. Laura sat on the veranda and sipped her tea. The late-afternoon sun exploded off the bay in a thousand tiny sparkles. The windows of San Diego's high-rises reflected the light in similar fashion. The white sides of the El Cortez Hotel were lit up like a beacon.

It was Laura's favorite time of day. The sinking sun's orange radiance on everything made the bay appear that much bluer. There was just enough chill in the air to make her tea taste that much better as she warmed her fingers on the sides of the cup.

She had just come home from the hospital and was still wearing her nurse's uniform. Her Bible lay open in front of her. Things had been so hectic earlier that morning that she'd not had time to pray and do her daily reading. She did them now as she waited for Johnny's telephone call.

She had prayed for him and his father and Emily to begin her prayers and then again to end them. In between, she'd prayed for Alex and Walt and Nat and Lily, each by name just as she did every day. But it was thoughts of Johnny and his parents that had preoccupied her mind throughout the day.

They'd received the call late afternoon on Saturday. Jesse had been taken to the hospital. It was a recurring heart ailment, one that had been plaguing the seventy-four-year-old man for the last several years. During that time he'd grown increasingly weak and short of breath.

The Saturday afternoon call was from Emily. She informed her son that the doctors didn't expect his father to survive the weekend.

Johnny tried to get airline tickets to Denver for both himself and Laura, but everything was booked. So he called Consolidated. They agreed to let him use a trainer. And though it had two cockpits, they were open. Laura couldn't see herself flying cross-country in an open cockpit trainer at her age.

"He's *your* father. You go," she told him. "I'll follow on a commercial flight as soon as I can."

He arrived Sunday, late afternoon, and spent the evening with his father in the hospital. From Johnny's report, his father was defying the doctor's diagnosis. He was getting stronger, and they were even talking about releasing him on Monday. Naturally, this was good news, but even more so because Laura had not been able to secure a flight to Denver until Thursday afternoon.

The phone rang.

Laura looked at her watch. *That should be Johnny.*

Scooting back her chair, she walked through the house to the living room.

"Hello?"

"Laura?"

Laura's heart sank. It was Johnny's voice, with an uncharacteristic somber quality about it. She knew the bad news even before he spoke the words.

"Pop died a short time ago," Johnny said.

"Oh, Johnny, I'm so sorry."

"They were packing his things to send him home, and then he was gone. Just like that."

Laura reached into her pocket for a tissue. Tears had already begun making tracks down her cheeks.

"How's Mom holding up?" she asked.

"You know her, strong as ever."

"For now, maybe," Laura said. "She just doesn't want her son to see her grieving. And how are you holding up?"

There was a pause. "All right," he said. "It's just that an old pioneer like Pop who's been through so many things in his life … you just think men like him will live forever."

"I wish I were there," Laura said.

"There's nothing you could do."

"I could be there."

"Yeah, you're right. I'm sure Mom would appreciate that."

Laura suppressed a laugh. *You would too; only you're too much like your father to admit it to anyone.*

"I have to go now," Johnny said. "Mom's signaling me."

"Johnny?"

"Yeah?"

"I'll go to the airlines tomorrow. Maybe I can get an earlier flight. I think they make special arrangements for bereavements."

"That would be good, dear. Look, I have to go now."

"Call me tomorrow."

"Will do. Bye."

He hung up the phone before she could say good-bye. Laura looked at the receiver, and then placed it in its cradle. She stood there. Her thoughts turned to Jesse.

What an interesting life he'd led. Raised by his mother in the tenements of New York. Running away from home. Crossing the continent by foot and steamboat and wagon with wealthy socialite Emily Austin chasing after him. The both of them getting caught in the middle of an arson ring and being stalked by unsavory detectives. Then becoming a personal aide to Secretary of

State William Jennings Bryan and President Woodrow Wilson. Quite a character. Quite a character indeed.

She'd always loved her father-in-law from the moment she'd met him. But then, he'd always treated her like a princess.

And now he was gone. It had been only a few short minutes, but already she felt an empty place in her heart that, up until now, had been occupied by Johnny's father.

Ring!

The sound of the phone startled her. Only because she was standing right next to it. Was it Johnny calling back?

"Hello?"

"Mrs. Morgan?"

"Yes, this is Mrs. Morgan."

"Alex's mother?"

Laura's heart froze. "Yes," she said tentatively, "I'm Alexandra's mother."

"I'm sorry to call you like this, but I thought it would be best that you hear from one of Alex's friends before you were contacted officially."

"Who is this?"

"Oh, I'm sorry. Please forgive me, Mrs. Morgan. My name's Loretta May. I'm a friend of Alex's. We've been through flight school at Sweetwater and Lockbourne together."

"Yes, Loretta. Alexandra's spoken of you. Is something wrong?"

"Well, that's just it, Mrs. Morgan. We don't know." Loretta paused.

Laura held her breath. This was what the girl had been working up to, and it wasn't coming out fast enough to suit Laura.

"Loretta?"

"I'm sorry, Mrs. Morgan, I'm not sure how to say this. But … is Alex there? In San Diego, I mean?"

With furrowed brow, Laura said, "No, she isn't here. Are you telling me that she's not at Lockbourne?"

Another pause. "That's just it, Mrs. Morgan," Loretta said. "We don't know where Alex is. She's missing."

"Missing?"

"She hasn't shown up for duty ... and that's just not like her ..."

"I agree."

"... and she's nowhere to be found on base. Her room and closet and everything have been cleaned out but no one has seen her for weeks. The base log shows that she's still on base, but we can't find her! We were hoping you might know where she is."

Now it was Laura's turn to pause.

Would Alexandra have come back to San Diego without telling us? If so, why? I could call Consolidated and ask if anyone there has seen her.

"I'll make a few phone calls, Loretta. But truthfully, I don't have any idea where she might be. I thought she was with you."

"I'm sorry to be the bearer of bad news, Mrs. Morgan." There was genuine heartfelt concern in her voice.

"You've been a good friend, Loretta. Thank you for calling me. Is there a number where I could reach you?"

Loretta gave her the phone number.

"I'm sure everything will turn out all right, Mrs. Morgan. Alex is a great kid and top-notch pilot."

"Thank you, Loretta. That is what she's best at."

After hanging up, Laura started to dial Denver. Midway she stopped and replaced the receiver. Johnny was at the hospital with his mother. She'd have to wait until later to call him. As though he needed this kind of news right now, on top of everything else.

She called Consolidated. No one there had seen Alexandra since she'd left for Texas. She called a couple of Alexandra's old friends. She didn't have too many. Same story. No one had seen her since she left for Texas.

Laura went back to the veranda. She sat down and stared at the bay. It was darker now in the twilight. She took a sip of tea. It was cold.

Worries rose up inside her. She did her best to rein them in. No use worrying over what you don't know.

What she did know was this: Disappearing was so unlike Alexandra. And if she wasn't at Lockbourne, where was she? She would never walk away from her duties without good reason. Flying was her life. But then, if she didn't walk away on her own, did that mean someone forced her against her will?

Stop it! You're jumping to conclusions!

Laura bowed her head.

Dear Lord, you know exactly where Alexandra is at this very moment. Please protect her. Keep her safe. Work all of this out, I pray.

Later that night Laura received the official call from Lockbourne. Alexandra Morgan was listed as missing. Officially, and until any more evidence turned up to indicate otherwise, she was listed as absent without leave.

Laura called Johnny and told him the news. Although not a shred of evidence existed that he would know where Alexandra was, Laura was hoping that Johnny would tell her that he'd heard from Alexandra and in all the rush to get to Denver he'd simply forgotten to tell her.

But he hadn't. Alexandra was missing.

With the entire house to herself and half the bed empty and questions and thoughts of Alexandra swirling in her head like a tornado, Laura didn't sleep much that night.

TUESDAY. All day long Alexandra was on Laura's mind. She called people in the church in the morning before going to work. While she drove from the docks to the hospital and back again transporting patients, she tried to figure out where Alexandra might have gone.

It was maddening. The possibilities, even though she knew they were the unsubstantiated worries of a mother, tormented her—pick, pick, picking away at her so that by the end of her shift she was physically and emotionally exhausted.

On the way home from the hospital, Laura stopped into a local grocery store on Chatsworth to pick up her ration of coffee and meat. As she was exiting the store with the grocery sack in her arms, she heard a name that caught her attention.

Jerry Jupiter.

Someone on the street had spoken the name. Laura smiled. They were talking about Lily's band.

About a half-dozen people were standing in front of the shop window of a radio repair store next to the grocery store. They congregated around a console that was set outside on the street for advertisement.

Laura heard Jerry Jupiter's name again. This time coming from the radio. She joined the small congregation, eager to hear the latest news about her traveling singer. She was thinking how surprised the people would be when she told them that Lily Morgan was her daughter.

Drawing closer, she listened to the voice of the newscaster.

… went down about thirty miles southwest of Palermo. Repeating our top story. Jerry Jupiter's plane crashed in Sicily last night …

No! It couldn't be true!

… Jupiter is best known as the leader of a big band which bore his name, a band which had grown increasingly popular with the addition of singer Lily Morgan …

My Lily! Please tell me she wasn't with him in that plane!

... Jupiter and his show troupe were on their way to Palermo from Tunis to entertain our fighting troops when their plane went down ...

O God, no! Please no!

There were no survivors. The terrain in which the plane crashed is very rocky and mountainous, making salvage efforts extremely difficult ...

Laura slumped to the sidewalk, her bag of groceries spilling with her. She was barely aware that people were standing over her. Their words were garbled, as though they were speaking to her underwater.

My Lily. My sweet, darling Lily!

The owner of the grocery store drove her home and helped her inside. He offered to call someone. She thanked him, but said she could manage. It was a lie.

When he left, she fell into her chair and sobbed so hard she shook.

Later that night she called Denver. It took her fifteen minutes and still she couldn't dial the phone. The operator had to connect her. Then, once Johnny was on the line, all she could manage to say was, "Johnny, our Lily's dead!"

About that same time Emily's neighbor came by and told them to turn on the radio. Connected by phone line from San Diego to Denver, Johnny and Laura listened to the report that their daughter's plane had crashed in Sicily.

Laura couldn't remember saying good-bye. Nor did she remember crossing the room to her chair. She sat there in the dark and wept until no more tears would come.

An hour later there was a soft knock at the door. It opened without her answering it. Her pastor and his wife poked their heads in. Johnny had called them and asked them to look in on her.

The pastor's wife stayed with Laura for the rest of the night and called the hospital the next morning to tell them she wouldn't be in.

Laura could barely remember any of this.

WEDNESDAY. By midmorning Laura was beginning to feel alive again, though she didn't want to. It hurt too much to be alive. She was regaining her mobility. It felt as though she was walking through a fog, but at least she was able to do things for herself again.

The pastor's wife had a midweek Bible study that she led at the church. She offered to stay with Laura instead, but Laura insisted she go. Laura wanted to be alone. With the pastor's wife in her house, she felt like she had to be a hostess. She preferred to be alone.

Johnny called. His father's funeral was Thursday afternoon at one. As soon as the funeral was over he would fly home. Also, he'd been in contact with the army about Lily. They would call him in Denver if they had any more news. He asked her if she was all right. She lied again and said she was holding up just fine. She told him his mother needed him right now and there was nothing he could do about Lily or Alexandra anyway but wait.

She put the phone down. It was dark inside the living room so she opened the drapes. She spied the two stars in the window. It was ironic. She feared she might lose her boys in the war.

She again remembered old Charlie Haddox, the usher at church on the day the war started. *The Lord gave and the Lord hath taken away; blessed be the name of the Lord.* And how her thoughts turned immediately to her boys. Now look how things had turned out. She should have been worrying about her daughters. One was missing and the other was dead.

She went out to the veranda, taking with her a cup of tea and her Bible. She didn't feel like reading it right now. She wasn't sure she was speaking to God.

The Bible remained closed as she finished her tea. Getting up, she made herself some cereal and washed the dishes. She finished getting dressed and groomed herself, all the while avoiding the girls' rooms, especially Lily's.

She wanted to pray for Alexandra, but couldn't bring herself to do it. Her hurt and anger prevented her.

She wandered around the house and straightened a few things and cleaned some others. She considered going to work. Surely it had to be better than bouncing aimlessly around an empty house.

As she passed through the living room, she caught sight of a car with an army insignia on the door. A man in dress uniform walked toward the door.

News of Alexandra? Or possibly Lily? Laura knew she was hoping against hope, but as she ran to the door she could hear the words in her head: *There has been a terrible mistake, ma'am. I'm here to inform you that your daughter is not dead.* Or, *Good news, ma'am. There was a mix-up in the orders at Lockbourne Army Base. Alexandra wasn't missing after all.*

Laura swung open the door before the soldier knocked.

The man who stood on her doorstep removed his hat. Laura's heart felt faint. The eyes on this face did not belong to a man who was bearing good news. He spoke three words.

"I'm sorry, ma'am."

A gloved hand held out an envelope. A telegram.

With trembling hands, Laura took it. She leaned against the doorjamb to steady herself as she opened it.

> The Secretary of War desires to express his deep regret that your son …

Her eyes blurred with tears. She had to wipe them away to read the rest of the telegram.

> ... Lieutenant Walter Morgan was killed in action in defense of his country in the Great Britain area. Letter follows.

Laura slid down the doorjamb to her knees. "Dear God, why are you doing this to us?" she wailed. "Dear God, why? Why? Why?"

THURSDAY. Laura was numb when she woke, lying on her bed staring at the ceiling. The morning light stole through her curtains and cut a path across the room.

Noises coming from the kitchen told her that the pastor's wife was still here. She had returned the evening before.

Swinging her legs over the side of the bed, she searched with her feet until she found her slippers. Pulling her robe around her, she shuffled into the living room and toward the kitchen.

Johnny would be home today. On the one hand she was grateful; on the other hand, all she wanted to do was withdraw into herself and never come out again. She didn't want to talk to anybody, be with anybody; she didn't want to smile; she didn't want to feel.

The living room curtains were already open. Maybe they'd been open all night, she didn't remember ever closing them. But the thing that caught her attention was the stars in the window.

One blue. One gold.

Someone had already exchanged one blue star for a gold one. It seemed morbid to her that someone had been so quick to announce to the world that another fine young man had been killed in another stupid, senseless war.

As she stood there, a car pulled up outside. It bore an army insignia on its door. A soldier climbed out. The same soldier as yesterday. He looked at the front of the house. He hesitated.

No ... no ... no ... no ... no ...

She opened the door before the soldier reached it, almost daring him to approach her. The man removed his hat. His eyes were red. Filled with tears.

He held out an envelope. Another telegram.

Laura couldn't lift her hand to take it. The soldier didn't know what to do. He stood there. Hand extended. Crying.

The pastor's wife appeared behind Laura.

She took the envelope for Laura.

"Should I open it?" she asked.

Laura said nothing. She couldn't. Her mouth was no longer functioning. Nothing was. Not her hands. Not her legs. Not her mind.

The envelope was ripped open. The pastor's wife read with a trembling voice.

> The Secretary of War desires to express his deep regret that your son Corporal Nathaniel Morgan was killed in action in defense of his country in the Italian area. Letter follows.

It was late. Or early. Past midnight anyway. Laura sat alone on the veranda. Johnny had fallen asleep on the living room couch. Together with the pastor and his wife they had cried together most of the night.

Now it was just Laura. She didn't want to sleep. Lately, every time she closed her eyes she had nightmares. She didn't want to be awake either, but at least while she was awake she could keep her guard up against a God who was determined to hurt her.

His Bible sat on the corner of the table beside the outdoor lamp. His Bible. God's Bible. She wanted nothing to do with it anymore. Why would she want to hear the words of a God who enjoyed watching people suffer?

She reached for the Bible, not to read it, but to throw it away. She fully intended to take it to the garbage cans beside the house and deposit it in one of them. It would be her revenge against God. It was a small effort but the only one available to her at the moment.

Picking up the Bible, she spied a colorful lace bookmark wedged between its pages. Lily had made it for her.

Laura tried to slip the bookmark out. It wouldn't come. It was wedged too closely to the spine and if she pulled any harder she was afraid she would rip the lace.

With her fingernails she opened the Bible to the place held by the lace bookmark. The pages flopped open.

Though she didn't want to read the words, nevertheless the words demanded to be read. It was as though they raised themselves from the page and insisted as much. Laura looked away, but it was too late.

She read them before she could stop herself.

She hated herself for reading them, but the deed was done. The words were now in her mind and she couldn't force them out no matter how hard she tried.

"Doth Job fear God for nought?"

24

Her greatest fear had come true. And now God was mocking her. *Doth Laura fear God for nought?*

It was after Walt's earlier brush with death that she'd wrestled with these words, that she'd told God her children were her weakness, that she'd pleaded with him not to test her in this.

Had God listened?

No.

He saved Walt only to kill him later, and his brother and sisters along with him. What kind of God was he to toy with his children in such a cruel way as this?

Laura still harbored a particle of hope that Alex was alive. But her hope was fading fast. It was a rare commodity these days and she'd run out of rationing coupons for it, denying this day could ever come.

But now it had.

What had she done to turn God against her so?

Doth Laura fear God for nought?

The words taunted her. They wouldn't leave her alone. If she closed her eyes they were in her mind; if she opened them, they were on the page in front of her.

Her heart broken and bleeding, her mind reeling, her spirit

crushed, her body exhausted, Laura stared at the passage, from the first chapter of Job, before her.

With the first sentence she was mesmerized. How many times had she read this passage? How many times had she taught it? But never before had she understood it like she understood it now. She knew exactly how Job felt! His experience was her experience.

> And there was a day when Job's sons and his daughters were eating and drinking wine in their eldest brother's house: And there came a messenger unto Job, and said, The oxen were plowing, and the asses feeding beside them: And the Sabeans fell upon them, and took them away; yea, they have slain the servants with the edge of the sword; and I only am escaped alone to tell thee.

And there was a day when Laura was grieving over the death of her father-in-law, that she learned her daughter was missing, and no one seemed to know what had happened to her, if she was dead or alive.

> While he was yet speaking, there came also another, and said, The fire of God is fallen from heaven, and hath burned up the sheep, and the servants, and consumed them; and I only am escaped alone to tell thee.

And while Laura was walking out of a grocery store worrying over her missing daughter, she heard a radio announcer report that her other daughter had been killed in a plane crash in Sicily.

> While he was yet speaking, there came also another, and said, The Chaldeans made out three bands, and fell upon the camels, and have carried them away, yea, and slain the servants with the edge of the sword; and I only am escaped alone to tell thee.

And while she was still grieving, a man in uniform came to her front door and handed her a telegram telling her that her younger son had been killed in battle.

> While he was yet speaking, there came also another, and said, Thy sons and thy daughters were eating and drinking wine in their eldest brother's house: And, behold, there came a great wind from the

wilderness, and smote the four corners of the house, and it fell upon the
young men, and they are dead; and I only am escaped alone to tell thee.

And when she was bereft of hope and broken of spirit over
the death of her children that same man in uniform returned with
another envelope telling her that her only other child, a son, had
also died in battle.

So what do we do now, Job? What do we do?

Then Job arose, and rent his mantle …

Yes! The anguish! The unbearable anguish!

and fell down upon the ground,

Yes! When the pain is so great, you can no longer stand!

and worshipped …

"No!" Laura shouted the word. "No! How can you worship
when he has taken so much from you? It's impossible! No one can
do that! It's asking too much."

She stared at the word, then continued reading, looking for
some explanation, some rationalization that would help her
understand how a man who had just lost everything could find it
within himself to worship.

In all this Job sinned not, nor charged God foolishly.

Laura stared at the last four words dumbly. Impossible. God
deserved to be charged, didn't he? God knew what was happening. He allowed it! It wasn't God who was the victim here, it was
Job! And Laura.

And Laura wasn't going to let God off the hook for this one.
She had served him, worshipped him, trusted him all her life. *All
her life!* And what did it gain her?

As the first hint of morning tinged the eastern mountains, she
kept reading. Verse after verse. Ravenously. Like a hungry wolf
devouring scraps.

She had to know.

There had to be some sort of key, some reason why Job acted like he did. How could he experience the same pain she had experienced and yet come to such a completely opposite conclusion? It didn't make sense. They traveled the same road, yet arrived at different destinations. What made the difference? She had to know!

Her anguish drove her. Chapter after chapter she read, searching for the answer. The key. Not to her own suffering. She understood that all too well. In her heart she knew she could never forgive God for what he had done to her. But she had to know why Job had forgiven him; no, more than that. Why Job did not even *charge* God for the pain he was suffering. There had to be a reason. It had to be here somewhere. Somewhere in these pages.

She had to know. She had to know!

Her eyes scanned the words, looking, searching. Job's questions. His friends' accusations. But she found no understanding. Nothing that explained the reason for Job's unswerving faith in a God who allowed suffering.

Suddenly, she sat upright.

From the eastern horizon the first rays of the morning sun streaked across the sky from the mountain to the veranda, striking the page. A page of questions. No, *challenges.*

God took the offensive.

In the whirlwind of Laura's mind, he spoke, a passage again from Job:

> Gird up now thy loins like a man: for I will demand of thee, and answer thou me.
>
> Where wast thou when I laid the foundations of the earth? ...
>
> Who shut up the sea with doors, when it brake forth, as if it had issued out of the womb? ... And said, Hitherto shalt thou come, but no further: and here shall thy proud waves be stayed?

Hast thou commanded the morning since thy days; and caused the dayspring to know his place? ...

Have the gates of death been opened unto thee or hast thou perceived the breadth of the earth?

DECLARE IF THOU KNOWEST IT ALL!

"O God ..." Laura whimpered.

Canst thou lift up thy voice to the clouds, that abundance of waters may cover thee?

Canst thou send lightnings, that they may go?

"No ... no ..." Laura cried, "... only you, dear God ... only you ..."

Who hath put wisdom in the inward parts? or who hath given understanding to the heart?

Shall he that contendeth with the Almighty instruct him? HE THAT REPROVETH GOD, LET HIM ANSWER IT!

As the veranda was flooded with new day's light, Laura slumped to the ground. She who thought she had no more tears inside her wept bitterly.

Johnny Morgan roused from sleep on the couch. He blinked aching eyes. With each blink, a measure of conscious thought returned, as did the tightness in his chest that had come with the tragic news of his children.

The last time he felt pain like this was in the skies over France during the Great War when he watched his best friend being shot out of the sky and there was nothing he could do about it.

For him, this was the worst kind of pain. Physical pain he could handle. Any pain that was directed at him—stress, verbal jabs, envy, jealousy, outright hatred—these things he could deal with. It was this helpless pain that was the worst. The pain of knowing someone you love is suffering and there's not a thing you can do about it.

He rose and pulled on his robe.

Laura wasn't in the living room. Often, when she couldn't sleep, she'd knit or read.

Nor was she in the kitchen. That in itself wasn't unusual. What was unusual was that the coffee wasn't brewing and the teakettle was cold.

Laura liked one or the other in the morning. He couldn't remember a morning when she wasn't cradling a cup of something in her hands.

"Laura?" he called.

No answer.

The house was quiet. Quieter than it had ever been. They had known the silence that came from the kids being gone. This was a different kind of silence. This was a silence in which the kids were gone and would never be coming back again. A deadly silence.

"Laura?" he called again.

He made his way toward the veranda. He heard a whimpering sound.

"Laura?"

She was on the ground. On her knees, forehead to the pavement, she was rocking back and forth. Mumbling. Mumbling something. He couldn't make out what she was saying.

He ran to her and knelt beside her. "Laura?" He placed his arm around her shoulders. She gave no indication she was aware of his presence.

"Laura! Are you all right?"

She rocked and mumbled. Rocked and mumbled.

Tightening his grip on her shoulders, he lifted her up. "Laura? Honey?"

He expected to see tears.

There were none.

He expected to see the woman he loved distraught.

She wasn't.

Her eyes were clear. Calm. Resolved.

"Laura?"

Her face lit up with recognition. She threw her arms around him with an enthusiasm that nearly bowled him over.

With her lips pressed close to his ear, he could now hear what she was saying. Over and over, the same thing, like a chant, but not meaningless like a mantra, for each phrase was vibrant, intense, alive with newfound purpose.

"Though he slay me, yet will I trust in him! Though he slay me, yet will I trust in him! Though he slay me, yet will I trust in him!"

25

Alex sat on the grass near the runway waiting for a lone B-17 bomber to take off from the Bassingbourn airfield. It sat, engines idling, at the far end of the runway. The pilot and copilot were completing their preflight checklist.

She shook her head in wonder. A crazy, carefree smile graced her lips as she imagined what her brother Walt's expression would be when he saw her in England.

Boy, will he be surprised. She chuckled to herself. *But then he couldn't be any more surprised than I am.*

She still couldn't believe she'd done it. Having sneaked off Lockbourne Base late one night, she'd hitched rides to the East Coast where she managed to secure passage for herself aboard a liner sailing for Great Britain.

Every time she heard pre-boarding and onboard warnings about declared war zones and the threats of U-boats, she wondered what it was about Morgan women that made them take these kinds of risks. She made it a point to be on deck when the coast of Ireland first came into view, for it was here that Grandma Emily Morgan and Aunt Katy had their cruise cut short by a German torpedo during the Great War while sailing aboard the *Lusitania*. Their trip to England had been a mission of mercy. She was on a mission of love.

Alex laughed out loud at the thought. This was so unlike her. Who would believe it? Yet since she was a little girl she knew that deep passions dwelled within her. Until now she simply channeled her passions into something worthy of them—the art of flying. She had determined that here was something worthy of her passions. Other women had it all wrong. This inferno that blazed within them was too valuable to waste on men.

She had seen too many women throw their passion at men too freely, too willingly, only to see the men drink it up until it was gone, leaving the women drained and unfulfilled, empty shells in empty relationships, living out their existence never again to feel the fire burn within them.

This she firmly believed. *Until* she met Lieutenant Clayton Thomas on that Sweetwater airstrip. Here was a man who shared her passion for flying and who fueled that passion whenever he was near until now a wildfire raged within her, jumping fences that she had inwardly erected to keep her life orderly. Now the fire she felt for him consumed her every waking thought.

In truth, alone late at night, the fierceness of her love for Clay frightened her. Particularly when she first admitted to herself that her feelings for him were out of control.

It was on the flight line at Lockbourne when he flew away. She was struck by the thought that she might never see him again. It was a powerful blow that opened the door for what came next.

She had a premonition. Not a vision, nor was it audible. Just a feeling, an intuition. But it was strong to the point of overwhelming. At that moment she knew that if she let Clayton Thomas leave her life now she would never see him again. Should events take their normal course, she had just bid him good-bye for the last time.

That's when she determined to change the normal course of events.

Walt set aside the completed preflight checklist. He glanced at his copilot, a Brit by the name of Reginald Webley. It was the first time the two men had flown together.

"This is it," Walt said.

"Tallyho," Webley replied.

With his right hand on the throttles, Walt brought the four rumbling engines to life. Number two engine was smoking. Walt checked the gauges. It was maintaining power. Indeed, number two engine seemed to exemplify the plane's overall condition—functioning, but just barely. The whole thing had been pieced together with spare parts, whatever it took to get the plane in the air one last time and not a part more. There wasn't even a name on it. A waste of paint.

Over the roar of the engines Webley said, "Awfully spooky, don't you think?" He tapped the side of his headphones. "The lack of chatter from the chaps in back."

Walt smiled and nodded. Theirs was a two-man crew. Such was the design of the mission code-named "Perilous."

As the B-17 picked up speed, Alex stood. She brushed the grass from her khaki pants. Her army uniform got her on base with surprising ease.

She'd hitched one last ride aboard a jeep that was overflowing with Americans in uniform. Had she been a male, they probably wouldn't have stopped for her. These happy airmen, returning from leave in Cambridge, welcomed the opportunity for a little more female conversation. They sat her in the back middle and crowded around her.

The guard at the post waved them onto the base routinely. And why not? She blended in with the rest of the uniforms.

With pride Alex watched the nose of the B-17 lift off the runway, followed soon after by the main landing gear. It had been a long time since she'd seen her brother fly.

Walt, do you know one of your engines is smoking?

The plane was low when it crossed the end of the runway. Walt wouldn't have taken off if the engine was a problem. *Must be a heavy load,* she thought. The trail of black smoke coming from the engine bothered her.

She waved at the plane as it thundered past her in the off chance that Walt would see her. Of course, he wouldn't know it was her until she told him when he returned.

No sooner had she arrived on base when she sought him out. She thought she'd spring her surprise on Walt first. Surprising her brother would be good practice for surprising Clay.

She had imagined a thousand times how Clay would respond to her unexpected presence in England. And each time she imagined the scene, it got better. In the earliest versions, Clay responded spontaneously by nearly crushing the life out of her with his massive arms. Then, as the imaginings evolved, he not only gave her a bear hug, but a torrent of all the right words gushed from his lips.

There had been the occasional image—just the briefest flash of an image—in which he responded to her unexpected presence with displeasure. This image she discarded quickly, but not before it left a nagging residue of doubt in her mind. It was just enough to convince her that she needed a trial run. In this, she was indeed fortunate to have a brother on the same base as Clay.

Inquiring after Walt on the flight line, Alex eventually found someone who was able to point her to him. She was told he was leaving for a mission. Sure enough, Walt had just jumped into a jeep and was being whisked away from the hangars. She could have called after him, but thought better of it. His mind was on his mission. The last thing a pilot needed just before a mission was an emotional distraction. She'd wait for his return.

Walt's plane climbed slowly. "That must be some load you're carrying," Alex said. She noticed the clean nose. It looked as though the plane's name had been removed. She thought it odd. B-17 crews were usually a very superstitious bunch.

As Walt's plane gained altitude, another B-17 came overhead and fell in beside it. A few seconds later, a Lockheed P-38 streaked from behind and caught up with them. Now there were three. Again, odd. Where was the rest of the formation?

Out of the corner of his eye Walt saw his copilot glance nervously over his shoulder. Walt didn't blame him. Nine tons of explosives was enough to command anyone's attention.

Reaching into his pocket, Webley produced a gold coin. He worried it between his thumb and forefinger. A pencil-thin mustache which lay across his upper lip twitched nervously. "You a superstitious chap?" he asked Walt.

Walt shook his head. "No. I choose to put my trust in God. I like his track record."

"A religious chap, eh?"

Walt shrugged. "Let's just say I prefer putting my faith in something living."

"What about your crew? Are they superstitious?"

Walt nodded. "Very. We carry a large Bible onboard every flight. Everyone touches it before and after each mission."

"What's so special about that Bible?"

"It saved my life."

The Brit's grin was strained. "You didn't happen to bring it with you, did you?"

Walt shook his head. "It would be a bit clumsy given our

mission, don't you think? I left it in safekeeping for the crew's next mission ... just in case we're late getting back."

"Right decent of you," Webley said.

From the disappointment that showed on Webley's face, Walt guessed that he would have preferred that Walt had brought the Bible with him anyway.

Walt's attention shifted to the sound in his headphones. He glanced over at the plane flying next to him. The pilot of the other B-17 was looking at him. He gave Walt a thumbs-up sign.

"It's time," Walt said to Webley.

Jamming the gold coin back into his pocket, Webley unbuckled himself. Squeezing between the seats, he made his way to the bomb bay.

The operation code-named Perilous was just as its name suggested. Select B-17 bombers were stripped of their normal military equipment and packed with nine tons of explosives. The plan was for a two-man crew to get the plane into the air. The crew would then arm the warhead. Once that was done, they would turn control of the airplane over to an accompanying B-17 bomber using radio control. The crew would then leave the airplane by parachute while it was still over England.

The controlling B-17 would then direct the plane over the channel, aim it at its designated target, and lock it into a crash course. The P-38 was there to blow the plane out of the sky should anything go wrong.

Alex kept her eyes fixed on the odd trio of aircraft. She was debating on what to do until Walt got back. Should she try to locate Clay? What if, in trying, she accidentally bumped into him?

No, she preferred to arrange and control the situation, which was another good reason to wait for Walt. He could help her. After all, what were brothers for?

Walt checked his instruments. Everything was as it should be. He checked the number two engine. Still smoking. Yet all the indicators showed it was performing as well as the other three.

Webley squeezed past him and took the copilot's seat. He gave Walt a thumbs-up sign.

"Armed and ready?" Walt asked.

"Armed and ready."

"And we're still here. That's a good sign."

The sour grin beneath Webley's mustache didn't seem to appreciate Walt's humor.

Settling in, Webley asked, "Do you have family?"

"A brother, two sisters. You?"

"Just me and me mum. Have a girl?" Webley asked.

Walt shook his head.

"What? A decent lookin' chap like yourself and no girl?"

"Just never seemed to happen."

Webley's eyes bunched up in a perplexed way. "Finding a wife is not the sort of thing you leave to chance, old boy. You must survey the field, select the one you want, and then obtain her."

Walt laughed. "Sounds to me like you're buying a horse."

Webley seemed offended by Walt's laughter. "Selecting a suitable horse and selecting a suitable wife are not all that different," he huffed. "Nor should they be. You have to know what you want and go after it, old chap. Leave it to chance and Lord knows what you'll end up with!"

"My point exactly," Walt said. "The good Lord knows exactly who I should end up with. I leave it to him, not chance."

Webley nodded knowingly. "Ah! That God thing again."

"Yeah, that God thing again," Walt repeated.

He looked at his watch. It was time. He radioed the companion B-17. They confirmed. It was time.

"You ever jump before?" Webley asked.

"Not since training. You?"

"Same."

The planes were nearly out of sight. A breeze swept across the end of the field, bending the grass and chilling Alex. She folded her arms to ward off the chill.

It was a perfect day for flying. Light wind. Blue skies. She yearned to sit behind the controls again. She knew the only way she would ever do that now would be as a private citizen. Such was the price she paid for following Clay Thomas to England.

She smiled. *He's worth it.*

Alex couldn't wait to introduce Clay to Walt. She knew they'd get along famously. In fact, she knew that the whole family would fall in love with Clay just as she had.

※

Walt extended a gloved hand to his copilot. "God be with you," he said. "And happy landings."

"It's been a pleasure flying with you, old chap," Webley said. "Short as it was." The gold coin had appeared again. He had to shift it to his left hand to shake.

Walt wanted to remark, *Let's hope all our flights don't end up with us having to bail out just before the plane explodes.* He refrained, remembering Webley's soured expression at his previous attempt at gallows humor. Walt wondered if that type of humor was strictly an American taste.

Alone in the cockpit, he made final radio contact with the other B-17. He was informed they were ready for the handoff.

※

A tiny white parachute appeared beneath Walt's plane. Alex stared at it with alarm. Her eyes strained as they bounced back and forth between the parachute and the plane. The second engine was still smoking, but no more than it was earlier. What was the problem?

She waited for more parachutes to appear. There remained only one. Where was the rest of the crew? Why would only one person bail out?

Her heart pounded in her chest as she stared at Walt's plane.

※

Walt gave the instruments one final check. He was alone in the plane. It was an odd feeling. Odder still was the thought that he'd bail out of it in short order and the thing would continue flying without him.

A pang of male ego reverberated in his chest. Imagine that. Airplanes that don't need pilots. He hoped he wasn't participating in an endeavor that would make him extinct.

He unlatched his seat belt and instinctively reached for a leather pouch and a Bible that wasn't there.

Old habits, he chuckled to himself.

There was only one thing left to do—throw the switch that would turn control over to the other B-17.

Walt reached for the switch and flicked it.

※

Alex gasped.

Where once had been her brother's plane was now a fiery black cloud with white streamers shooting out from it.

She sank to her knees in disbelief. Her hands stifled a cry that erupted from within her.

She watched in horror as the flaming wreck plummeted to the ground. The blast was the most powerful she had ever witnessed. It was so bad, it knocked the other two airplanes out of the sky with it. The other B-17 flipped over, a wing folded and it went down in an awkward, uneven spiral. The P-38 that had been trailing Walt's plane pulled up but not enough before it slid into the explosion. A second later it exploded and fell from the sky too.

The lone parachute caught fire from the raining debris. What had once been a floating figure was now a black speck trailing fire.

Behind her at the airfield alarms sounded. Sirens screeched.

Kneeling in the grass at the edge of the runway, her hands covering her mouth, Alex shook with terror as the last of the flaming mass that had been her brother's plane plummeted to earth.

26

Nat Morgan wasn't alive; neither was he dead. He could move and feel pain, evidence he was alive; inside he was cold and had begun to decay, evidence he was dead.

With every step his head pounded and felt like it would explode. His legs were rubber. His stomach was a twisted rag which hadn't known food for days.

But these were mere physical pains. A cavernous ache deep within tormented him far worse than any physical pain.

Murphy and Szczepkowski were the lucky ones.

Nat glared out from the top of his eyes at the German soldier who had shot Szczepkowski. Loathing for the man rose within him like bile. Nat detested the man for not killing him too.

Another German had slipped behind him and bashed the back of Nat's head with the butt of his rifle. Nat was then dragged to the others, forced to his feet, and ordered to stay in line unless he wanted to taste the butt of a German rifle a second time. In the struggle his dog tags had been ripped from him and tossed in a ditch of American dead, leaving a slashing red welt on his neck.

That had been three days ago.

Nat and the other captives were marched northward through the Alban Hills toward Rome. The artist in him had always wanted to visit Rome, the engine that drove the Renaissance and served as the repository for the masters. Boccaccio. Raphael. Michelangelo. Da Vinci. Somehow he never thought it would be as a German prisoner of war. Still, he couldn't help but raise his eyes and gaze in wonder at the ancient city as he shuffled in a long line across a bridge spanning the Tiber River.

The American prisoners were herded like goats into open wire pens where they were publicly displayed to the townspeople and the ranks of German soldiers marching past. Nat searched for a corner in which to sit. In every one there was a growing pile of human waste. He settled for an open area in the middle of the pen.

Day after day there was nothing to do but stand and sit and stand and talk and endure the stares of the townspeople and the glares of the German soldiers. The highlight of each day was the unidentifiable green slop they were given to eat. About the only things recognizable in it were the maggots. The first four days Nat refused to eat. On the fifth day he ate a little and promptly lost it. By the seventh day he ate everything that was handed to him. By the tenth day he not only ate, but wanted more.

Trucks of armed German troops arrived and surrounded the pen. Guard dogs accompanied them. The prisoners were ordered to stand and face the street side of the pen. A German officer— Nat wasn't familiar enough with German uniforms to recognize the rank—accompanied the soldier with the large, square jaw who shot Szczepkowski. They walked the length of the fence looking into the faces of the prisoners.

When the soldier with the large jaw spied Nat, he stopped and pointed. Guards rushed into the pen, grabbed Nat by the arms, and hauled him out.

Nat found himself standing in front of a German officer with a sharp nose and keen eyes.

"Are these yours?" he asked in surprisingly crisp English.

Two camera cases were produced.

Nat stared at the cases. He hesitated. Did the camera cases bring with them penalty or reward?

"I asked you a question!" the German shouted. "Are these yours?"

"Yes," Nat replied.

"You are a photographer?"

"Yes."

"An army photographer or is that your profession?"

"I'm a portrait photographer by trade," Nat replied.

The officer screwed up his face with displeasure.

"Have you done any journalistic photography?"

"What is this all about?" Nat asked.

His question earned him a punch in the ribs from Large Jaw that doubled him over. The German shouted something at him he didn't understand. The blow, however, communicated quite clearly.

With his eyes rolling back in his head, Nat slumped to his knees. He was hauled back up to his feet by the two guards behind him.

"Have you done any journalistic photography?"

"I've had a couple of pictures published in magazines," Nat wheezed.

"Which ones?"

"Most recently, *Life*."

"*Life?*" The officer seemed impressed. He said something in German—the only word Nat understood was the word *life*. But whatever the officer said, it prompted laughter among the guards and Large Jaw.

"Very good," said the German officer to Nat in English. "Now you have an even greater assignment. You will take pictures for the führer."

Still short of breath from the blow, Nat glared at his captors. *Pictures for the führer? Fat chance,* he thought.

The officer nodded to the soldier with the large jaw, who relayed the nod to the two guards behind Nat. While the officer and Large Jaw climbed into a car with the camera cases and sped away, Nat was pushed down the road by his two-guard escort.

As they walked the streets of Rome, Nat didn't mind so much the shoves and German jibes leveled at him by the guards at every turn. It felt good to be out of the cage. It seemed like an eternity since he'd smelled fresh air. And the streets themselves provided a pleasing diversion. This was Rome. And at least for a few moments he was granted a distraction from his miserable existence as a prisoner of war. With hungry eyes he devoured the sights on every street.

They rounded a corner. The ruins of the Colosseum came into view. Nat gaped openly at it. Even though it was a shell of its former glory, it was magnificent.

He was given a rude shove from behind. Apparently his captors thought he was enjoying himself too much.

The German officer and Large Jaw stood just beyond the Colosseum on the opposite side of the road. They were smoking and chatting.

Nat was pushed into their presence. The German officer finished his cigarette before he turned his attention to Nat. Then, he held out his hand to Large Jaw who retrieved the camera cases from the back of the car. The cases passed from Large Jaw to the officer to Nat.

"You will take pictures of the parade," the officer said, "making sure that the Colosseum is prominently in the background."

Of course Nat had no idea what the German was talking about. He chose not to ask any questions, confident in his ability to recognize a parade when he saw one.

"How much film do you have?"

Nat opened the cases and checked the cameras. "Four shots left on the Leica. Six on the Rolleiflex."

"Do you have any more empty rolls?"

Nat felt around the bottom of each bag. He always carried several extra rolls for each camera. They were not there. Probably in some German soldier's camera by now.

"No," he said.

The officer looked to Large Jaw, who again ducked into the back of the car. This time he returned with three rolls of 35mm film.

As the rolls were handed to Nat, the officer said, "This parade is by direct order of the führer. I advise you to take pictures as though your life depended upon their quality. For, indeed, it does."

Nat was not shaken by the threat. German threats had become a way of life. From what he had observed, the entire German culture revolved around it. It seemed to have developed it into an art form.

He had no doubt they would kill him if the pictures did not turn out. He'd already seen Large Jaw at work. What they didn't seem to realize was that a death threat is effective only if a person cares to keep on living. He no longer cared.

Townspeople began lining the street. From the expressions on their faces, they wanted to be here as much as Nat did.

Fumbling around in the bottom of the camera case, Nat found his light meter. He began taking readings.

The German officer called to him. "Up here!" he said, patting the top of the car. "You will get a better angle."

Nat climbed to the roof of the car. He had to give the officer a measure of credit. This *was* a better angle.

As the crowd increased to three and four deep along the edge of the road, Nat adjusted the shutter speed and aperture of the camera corresponding to the light readings he'd just taken. He considered sabotaging his own efforts by popping the back of the camera case and exposing the film. It would probably mean his death once the film was developed, but what did he care? He would die knowing that he had deprived Hitler of pictures of his troops marching triumphantly past the Colosseum.

However, the more he thought about it, the less inclined he was to the plan. What difference did it make if Hitler had pictures of his goose-stepping morons parading down a Roman street? His plan seemed a petty revenge at best. If he was going to die, why not do something bold?

Under the watchful eye of Large Jaw and two guards, Nat fiddled with the camera adjustments while he set his mind in search of a bold plan that would give his death meaning.

※

German cars with loudspeakers preceded the parade past the Colosseum. The words were Italian. Nat didn't understand them, but he understood their effect on the citizens of Rome. The hatred etched on their faces portrayed exactly how he felt inside. Small German flags with swastikas were handed to them. A demonstration by armed soldiers showed the people the proper way to wave the flags.

The next instant, as the parade began, the faces of the people changed before his eyes. The eyes and mouths that had moments earlier been soured with contempt were now joyous and happy.

Now Nat understood the instructions given them. More German threats.

He lifted the camera to his eye. He was still without a bold plan. Hopefully one would come to him soon. Looking through the viewfinder he checked the composition. The Colosseum filled the background on the right side. The road—now empty—angled nicely from top left to bottom right, lined with people waving flags and cheering and looking up the street expectantly. Somewhere a band began playing.

Then, the first line of the parade entered the viewfinder. Nat lowered his camera. He stared in disbelief.

Someone pounded the top of the car to get his attention. When that didn't work, he pounded Nat's foot. Nat looked down. It was the German officer.

"Take pictures! Take pictures!" he shouted.

Next to him the German with the large jaw glared threateningly.

Nat looked at the street with the parade now in progress. Slowly, reluctantly, he raised the camera to his eye and prepared to take the first shot.

The parade was not what he'd expected. The men marching in the parade were not wearing German uniforms. They were wearing American uniforms. The captured Americans were being paraded in front of the Roman Colosseum for the whole world to see. And Nat had been enlisted to provide photographic propaganda.

He looked up and down the parade route. There were other photographers and newsreel cameramen busily preserving the moment on film. Their presence didn't change his resolve. He knew what he had to do.

Under the watchful eye of Large Jaw, Nat shot all the film he had in the cameras and the three rolls given him by the Germans. However, after each shot as he pretended to focus and adjust the settings, he popped open the back of the camera. It was just a crack, but enough to ruin each shot.

It would mean his death, of that he was certain. But he'd found his greater cause. If Hitler was going to parade captured American soldiers before the entire world he wasn't going to do it with photographs taken by Nat Morgan.

After Nat was returned to the holding pen, from then on every time German soldiers approached, he was sure they were coming for him. Though he thought he'd resigned himself to his fate, he grew so fearful that he became suspicious of the civilians who dared to look inside the pen as they passed. They all seemed to look at him, to know what he did, to know that his time was short. Were they looking at him and thinking of a bullet-riddled wall where prisoners were executed?

One morning Nat awoke to see all the other prisoners lining the fence. He joined them to see what they were looking at, but didn't see anything that should command their attention. That's when it struck him. He didn't see anything. No guards. No civilians. Nobody.

After a time, a squat Italian man with a limp came hurrying by. He carried an armload of bread. Hundreds of hands stretched through the wire fence pleading for some of the man's bread. Though he didn't stop to share his bread, hurrying on he shared some news.

"Soon! Soon!" he said excitedly in broken English. "The Americans! She is coming!"

Nat felt his tired heart pump a little faster. A reprieve? For a man who was resigned to death, and who had indeed invited it, he was responding with uncharacteristic excitement.

A rumbling of heavy trucks could be heard in the distance. They were coming nearer. Men who barely had enough strength to stand began hopping with excitement, staring with anticipation in the direction of the trucks.

Smiles formed on faces that had not seen a smile in months. Men with strength helped the infirm to their feet so they could see too.

The rumbling grew louder.

Nat felt animated for the first time since the day Murphy was killed. He crowded with the others against the fence. They were going to be liberated!

The rumbling was near now. A convoy of trucks appeared. A cheer went up among the prisoners. Then, as spontaneously as it began, it ceased.

The symbols on the sides of the trucks were swastikas.

The trucks pulled in front of the prisoner pen. Armed soldiers jumped out. The opening to the pen was thrown open. The Germans began yelling. Pushing. Shoving the American prisoners into the trucks.

Surrounded by hurried, shuffling prisoners, Nat was corralled into the back of a German transport truck. Expectant eyes stared down the road, hoping to see American units pouring into the city, frightening away the German guards, rescuing their own before the Germans could cart them away.

The engine of the truck roared so loudly it shook the bed. Exhaust fumes worked their way through the densely packed prisoners. There was a grinding and a lurch as the truck pulled away from the prisoners' pen. With longing eyes Nat looked out the back for signs of the American troops.

There were no American troops in sight.

The four-truck convoy wound its way through the streets of Rome and into the countryside. Mile after mile passed, and with each one Nat's hope of rescue flickered. With the setting of the sun, his little candle of resurrected hope was extinguished forever.

Late at night they were transferred into the boxcar of a freight train. Large wooden doors on metal wheels were slid shut and they were locked in. There they sat for three days without moving. A few in the crowded car saw this as a good sign, that the Germans had abandoned the train at the sight of oncoming American forces.

Nat did not allow himself to give in to such frivolous and harmful speculation. Such thoughts only built up false hopes. Nat knew better. He was wiser now, hardened by the scourging of adversity. His hopes had been dashed so often there was no longer any life left in them. Didn't these people realize that the gods of war stalked the land looking for people like them? Looking for any sign of hope that they might seize it and choke the life out of it? It was best not to have hope. The gods ignored people without hope. After all, why dash that which is already dead?

Some of the men in the boxcar never seemed to learn that lesson. They prayed hopefully that God would rescue them. This too was foolishness and even harmful. Nat found it difficult to associate the God of Sunday school and morning worship service with tongues swollen from thirst and wounds untreated and men boxed up like cattle left to starve to death. The God that he knew was not even in Italy. He'd remained behind in San Diego.

The way Nat saw it, the day he walked through the door of the army enlistment center, God chose to remain behind. God was more comfortable on the home front with the women, wrapping bandages, gathering canned goods, and attending prayer meetings. Nat couldn't even imagine God crouched in a muddy trench pinned down next to dead and dying soldiers who had been cut to pieces by enemy fire. Or manning an artillery gun, a weapon designed to kill men at a distance. So why expect him to be concerned about a boxcar packed with prisoners of war whose tongues were beginning to swell with thirst?

Nowhere in northern Africa or Italy had Nat seen any evidence of God's presence. Naturally, there were churches by the score, but God didn't live in them anymore. It was just as well. The meek and mild Jesus who carried a little lamb in his arms, the same one that Nat had seen every Sunday morning in the stained-glass window of his church, would be sickened by the things men were doing to one another in Palermo, and Cassino, and Anzio, and Rome, and in a railroad boxcar that seemed to be headed nowhere.

Screams and shouts and pounding could be heard coming from the other boxcars. The men in Nat's boxcar had tried to force the door to no avail. They would rest and try again, for no one stopped them from trying. With each attempt the door held.

On the fourth day, voices could be heard outside. German voices. Nat watched knowingly as those who had been holding out hope surrendered it.

The train lurched. It lurched again. Then they were underway. To where, no one knew.

On the second day the train slowed as it trudged up a steep mountain grade. Soon it was freezing cold inside the boxcar. They were given no blankets, nothing to warm themselves, and no food.

The train leveled off for a day, then began to climb again. It got colder still. Nat could no longer feel his feet. His fingers were stiff and numb.

The days turned almost as dark as the nights. Through cracks in the sides of the boxcars Nat could see that they were in a heavily forested area. Snow covered everything.

They traveled on. Each day left the rescuing American forces farther and farther behind.

It was night. Nat was curled up on the floor huddled against the other men in the car. They took turns being in the center of the huddle since those on the edges next to the sides were coldest. Nat had taken his turn on the edges the night before. He shivered so hard he didn't sleep a wink. Tonight was his turn in the middle.

It wasn't warm, but it was the warmest place in the boxcar. He was beginning to drift to sleep when he was suddenly awakened by a thunderous crack.

The boxcar swayed side to side. It creaked like an old rocking chair, tipped, and then fell over. Screeching and crunching of metal and wood could be heard all around. Everyone and everything tumbled to the side, bodies on top of bodies. Nat's fall was cushioned by men beneath him; his body felt the blows of those who landed on top of him.

They slid with the side of the boxcar scraping the tracks. Then, just as they slowed, the car behind them rammed into them, then the one behind it, and so on in chain reaction. Then, everything came to a stop.

Beneath and above him, men were moaning. Some cried for help. Some were weeping. Others were making no sound at all. Neither did they move.

Nat managed to extricate himself from the mass of arms and legs and torsos. He spied something wonderful! The corner of the boxcar had ripped open. There was an opening large enough for a man to slip through!

He worked his way toward the opening. Getting down on his knees, he crawled toward it and eased his head out, half expecting to get it bashed in with the butt of a rifle.

Nothing struck him. Sticking his head out farther, he looked around. He saw boxcars jumbled every which way. Toward the front of the train, one car was on fire. There was smoke and haze.

Some of the other cars had split open. Men were crawling out of them and running into the forest.

But it was what Nat didn't see that most excited him. He saw no guards!

Squeezing out of the jagged hole he called for the others to follow him. He helped the first several out, then when he saw that they were coming out in a steady stream on their own, he took the opportunity to make good his escape.

And none too soon. A whistle sounded at the front of the train. Guards appeared. Not many, three, maybe four. They shouted. The crack of weapon fire electrified the air. Nat watched as several prisoners lurched forward and fell face down in the snow.

He sprinted up the incline and into the thick woods. Weak from hunger, his feet and hands frozen, he was huffing and puffing after only a few yards. Still, he ran.

He was free! He was only a short distance from the box that was his prison, but he was on the outside. And outside felt a whole lot different than inside.

All around him prisoners were streaming into the woods. *They can't catch all of us*, Nat thought as he crested a small hill and rumbled down the other side. There was a half-moon, enough for him to see where he was going. He splashed through a small stream and up the shallow bank.

Something caught his eye. A movement. A shadow. Someone following him?

Without stopping, Nat glanced backward. He could hear other men thrashing through the woods. Prisoners like him.

That must have been it, he told himself. But an uneasy feeling inside him refused to believe it.

He kept running.

Now he heard something. Close behind him. Crunching snow beneath heavy boots. He turned again.

A man emerged from behind a small clump of trees. He was wearing a German uniform and gripped a pistol in one hand!

He'll have to shoot me! Nat thought. *I'm not stopping. I'm not stopping!*

An outcropping of rocks rose up in front of him. Thick brush hedged him in on both sides. He had no choice but to go up.

Nat leaped onto the rocks, climbing furiously. He was completely exposed. All the guard behind him had to do was raise his pistol. Nat was an easy target. Clawing and scratching his way up the rocks, Nat fully expected to feel the impact of a bullet between his shoulder blades any second.

He heard no shot. Felt no impact.

Halfway up the rocks Nat turned to look behind him. The German guard stood at the bottom of the rocks looking up at him as though he was trying to decide whether or not Nat was worth it.

Worth pursuing? Or worth a bullet? Nat didn't know which. But what he saw next confounded him.

Three prisoners in succession came up the same rise that he and the guard had taken. When they saw the German uniform, they stopped, backed away cautiously at first, then ran. The guard saw them, all three of them, yet did nothing to detain them! They practically ran into his arms and he let them get away!

Instead, the guard holstered his pistol and began climbing up the rocks after Nat!

This doesn't make sense! Why would he let them go? And why is he so determined to catch me?

Nat clawed his way to the top of the rocks. Reaching the top, he wiped his bruised and scratched hands on his pants. His fingers were sticky. Bloody. He could see the blood by the light of the moon, but he felt no pain. He couldn't feel his fingers at all.

The guard was gaining on him. Nat felt weak and faint. His chest heaved. He tried to get up. His legs wouldn't respond. With no food or water for days, he couldn't go on. There was no strength left in him.

The guard eyed him steadily as he climbed the rocks. He paused, his breathing was heavy. For a moment it looked like he wanted to say something, but then changed his mind.

Nat peered down the other side of the rocks. They fell away gradually then emptied into what looked like a pathway leading deeper into the forest. Thick clusters. A few trees in and it was dark.

If I can make it to those trees ... just a few more yards.

Pushing himself to his feet, Nat stumbled over the ridge of the rocks. It was downhill. If he could just stay on his feet, his momentum could carry him.

The guard was cresting the rocks.

Nat took two steps, three, each step getting stronger.

With heaving chest, the guard stood on top of the rocks. He unholstered his pistol.

Nat's foot caught a rock. He stumbled and fell headlong toward a tree. His reaction was slow, but at least fast enough to miss hitting the tree head-on. His momentum slammed his right shoulder into the tree at the base of his neck, like a football player making a tackle. Only the tree didn't fall. Nat did.

He collapsed and rolled several times. Dizzy from the impact. Disoriented by the tumble. Weak from hunger.

His mind screamed at him to get up. To run. Escape.

But it took all of his strength simply to focus his eyes. Snow-covered trees jutted toward the stars. A figure appeared over him and hovered there. The guard. Pistol drawn and pointed at Nat's chest.

He was worn out, exhausted. He could run no more. Fight no more. He surrendered to the blackness that closed in over him.

27

Bassingbourn swarmed with activity. Sirens screamed. Men were running in every direction. Vehicles crossed paths dangerously with only separate destinations and their drivers' skill to keep them from colliding. Such was the airfield's crash plan enacted.

Through it all Alex walked in a daze. She had seen the explosion with her own eyes. But it seemed so distant. So unreal. Like something out of Hollywood.

Crashes of all sorts were daily fare at the cinema. Plane crashes. Car crashes. People crashing into one another and falling down. Pianos falling from upper-story windows and crashing onto the sidewalk below. She must have seen hundreds of crashes and explosions on film. And this one looked just like them.

Only this one was different. Her brother was in this one. No actor walked away from this explosion after the filming. The plane that plummeted to the ground in a fireball was not a model. What she had just witnessed was a real plane. A real explosion. And Walt was really dead.

Grasping at mental straws, she remembered the day Loretta fell out of the plane at Sweetwater. Everyone thought she was dead. But she wasn't. Maybe, just maybe Walt was still …

But when she replayed the explosion again in her mind, she

quickly concluded no one could have survived it. *No one.* Walt was dead.

Two steps and a new thought struck her. She pulled abruptly to a stop. The realization of what she had just seen was only the beginning. What followed now was a flood of consequences, beginning with their family.

Not only would Walt never be coming back to Bassingbourn, he'd never return to San Diego. She would never see him again at their home in Point Loma. She'd never again see him hugging Mother or talking airplanes and flying with Father. From this day on, whenever the family got together—every Thanksgiving, every Christmas, every birthday, every reunion—Walt would not be there. No longer were there four Morgan children; there were only three. Her. Nat. And Lily.

The Morgan family no longer had a son or brother named Walt.

Alex wandered aimlessly toward the flight line and the hangars. She had no direction, no destination. She thought how hard this was going to be on her parents. Someone had to call them.

I guess that means me. Better they hear the news from me than from some nameless, faceless army official.

She looked around for a phone, then at her watch. What time would it be in San Diego right now? There was, what, an eight-hour difference?

She pulled up short again.

Wait a minute! They don't know I'm in England! How am I going to explain to them what I'm doing in England?

Alex had deliberately chosen not to tell them her plans to come to England for several important reasons: first, because she didn't think they'd understand, especially her father; second, she had already made up her mind to go and she didn't want to argue her reasons with them if they tried to talk her out of it; and third, by telling them where she was going she'd be putting them in an awkward predicament. When the authorities contacted them, and she knew they would, her parents would be forced to choose between telling the authorities the truth and turning their daughter in, or lying to them to protect her.

Naturally, not telling them also had its consequences. They would be worried about her. But if all went well, they wouldn't have to worry for long. She had planned on calling them as soon as she talked to Clay and got settled in England. Walt's death was a turn of events she could never have foreseen. Along with everything else, it definitely complicated an already awkward situation.

She looked at her watch again. Her parents wouldn't be waking up for at least four more hours. That gave her four hours to find Clay and work out some kind of plan for her to stay in England. Then, once she had definite plans, she could call her parents.

Where to start looking for Clay? The flight operations building. She could inquire after him there.

As she walked along the flight line in search of the flight operations building, an ironic realization struck her. This was exactly the kind of thing about which she'd always made fun of other women. It had been her observation that whenever a woman fell in love, her life suddenly became incredibly complicated. And Alex swore such a predicament would never happen to her.

But it had.

Just as Alex found flight operations, a major barreled through the door. With a cigar jutting from between clenched teeth, he held the door open, turned, and shouted at some poor soul inside.

"Lutterman, I specifically told you to get me a new driver!"

A thin male voice replied, "I put in the request, sir. It was rejected."

"Rejected?" the major thundered.

"Yes, sir. Personnel said there weren't any drivers available, sir."

Snatching the cigar from his mouth, the major jabbed it at Lutterman. "You get back on the horn, Lutterman, and you tell personnel …"

Before she realized what she was doing, Alex said, "Sir, I'm your new driver."

The major swung around. He looked her up and down.

"What is this? You're a woman!"

"Yes, sir. There's a shortage of drivers in the motor pool," Alex said, repeating what she'd just heard. "Some of us women are filling in temporarily."

The major chewed on his cigar skeptically. "No … no …" he said, shaking his head, "I can't have a woman driver."

"Sir, General Eisenhower has a woman driver." Alex remembered reading that recently. Little did she know at the time that she'd be using it to secure a job to which she hadn't been assigned.

"That a fact?" said the major.

"Yes, sir. Personnel sent me right over. Lutterman told them how badly you needed a driver."

The major chewed on her words with the same intensity with which he chewed his cigar. Spying the pilot's wings on her uniform he pointed to them. "You're a pilot."

"Yes, sir. As I said, this job is temporary. What better driver could you have than a pilot, someone who is well acquainted with an airfield?"

He nodded. She was winning him over.

"What's your name?"

"Alex Morgan, sir."

He stopped chewing. Taking the cigar from his mouth, he said, "You wouldn't happen to be any relation to …"

"Lieutenant Walt Morgan was my brother," she said.

"Was ...?" he repeated. "Then you know ..."

"I was watching at the end of the runway when it happened, sir." Her eyes grew moist with tears.

The major softened considerably. He closed the door to flight operations. In a quiet voice he said, "Look, Miss Morgan, I'm on my way to the ..." the words seemed to catch in his throat "... um, crash site. I can drive myself. You can start your duties first thing in the morning."

"If it's all the same to you, sir, I'd like to start right away."

He looked at her questionably.

"I'll be fine, sir," Alex said, though she didn't know if she would be or not. Nor did she know how long she could sustain this new complication that she was creating for herself. But for the moment it gave her a reason to be on base should anyone inquire.

"Your brother ..." said the major. "He was a fine officer and an excellent pilot. I don't know how I'm going to break the news of his death to his crew."

"His crew, sir? They weren't on ...?"

The major shook his head. "This was a special mission. That plane had only a crew of two. Your brother volunteered for it. Not many men had the guts your brother had. Most of them don't have the respect your brother had among his crew members either. He's going to be a hard man to replace." The major hesitated, and then added, "But I think I have just the man who can do it. He will be one of our stops."

"Yes, sir."

The major took one more look at her. One last evaluation. Then, opening the door to flight operations, he shouted, "Good work, Lutterman!"

There was a pause, then, "Um ... thank you, Major Harrison, sir."

Harrison! Alex had been agonizing over how she would learn the major's name without asking him. Had personnel really sent her, she would already know it.

Major Harrison jumped into the jeep nearest the door. Alex climbed behind the wheel and started the engine.

"First stop, the CO."

Alex looked at Harrison.

"What?" the major asked.

"If you could point the way, sir."

He pulled out his cigar. "I thought you said you knew your way around this airfield."

"I know my way around airfields in general, sir. This is my first day at Bassingbourn."

For an instant Harrison's face clouded over. It cleared quickly. He motioned with the cigar. "Between the hangars and to the right."

"Yes, sir."

※

What have I gotten myself into?

Alex drummed the jeep steering wheel with her fingers. She sat alone outside the CO's office while Major Harrison conducted his business inside.

There are times in the air when pilots have to make snap decisions, she counseled herself, *decisions that can save your life, or lose it. I acted on pilot's instinct back there. It was a snap decision.*

Her drumming fingers increased their tempo.

What have I done?

Indecision over her actions outside flight operations opened her entire course of action for review. For the first time since leaving Lockbourne she doubted her plan.

Up to this point she had relied on pilot's instinct. Evaluate the situation and make a decision. In the air there is no time for

second-guessing. But she wasn't in the air. And her snap decisions seemed to be making a muddy mess of things.

It was the major's comments about Walt that had opened the
door to doubt—an excellent pilot, the respect of his crew,
courage to do what few others would do. It wasn't so long ago
that these same things could have been said about her. No longer.

She was negligent of her duties. Absent without leave.
Irresponsible. On base under fraudulent pretense. A pilot mas-
querading as a driver. All of this because of a man.

Amelia Earhart came to mind. So did Jacqueline Cochran.
These were women she idolized. What would they say about her
throwing her flying career away for a man? She had always
thought she had what it took to be one of the few who would
advance the cause of female aviation. *Apparently not. Gorgeous
Loretta has what it takes. Even man-crazy Virginia has enough
of what it takes to still be with the program.*

*And here is Alex. Top of her training class. Hiding out as
a driver. Afraid someone will find out who she is and what
she's done.*

The worst part of it all was the realization that what she'd
done was irreversible. Even if she returned immediately to
Lockbourne, her flying career was over.

Shame covered her like a heavy blanket.

Harrison bounded out the door. "Let's go," he said.

"Where to?"

"Take the main road off base. Toward Cambridge. Do you
know the one?"

"Yes, sir."

Since they were headed in the opposite direction of the crash
site, Alex assumed Harrison wanted first to talk to the pilot who
would be replacing Walt. It was common practice to house pilots
and crews off base in scattered locations. That way a bombing

raid on an airfield was less likely to wipe out a base's entire crew complement.

As she drove, Alex's emotions (or was it common sense?) seemed to be catching up with her. Grief over Walt's death mixed with her shame over what she was doing. It was a disheartening combination.

She wanted to cry. To roll back the clock. But it was too late for that now. Or was it?

Maybe if she returned to Lockbourne and admitted she let personal feelings cloud her judgment. She had an exemplary record up until now. If she could just keep her actions general enough so that she didn't come across as an irresponsible, lovesick female, maybe she could convince them that she had simply made a mistake and that it wouldn't happen again.

"Left, left, left!"

Harrison's cigar was in her face as the major pointed down the street they had just passed. Alex had been so caught up in her thoughts that she'd not heard his directions.

"Sorry, sir. It won't happen again," she apologized. Shifting into reverse she backed the jeep to the street and turned left.

"Third house on the right," Harrison said.

"Yes, sir." She pulled up in front of the house.

Before Harrison got out, he said, "We're going to the crash site next. Are you sure you're all right? I won't hold it against you if you don't go."

"I'll be fine, sir," Alex replied. Though she wasn't fine, she was getting there.

It was beginning to dawn on her that her pride in her aviation skills and her accomplishments meant more to her than she had previously acknowledged. Plans were already underway in her head as to how she could salvage them.

Then she caught sight of the lieutenant who emerged from the house. Broad-shouldered. Self-assured yet kindly. And Alex's resolve melted like butter in the summer sun.

It was Lieutenant Clayton Thomas!

He was looking at the major as he approached. He didn't see her at first. She turned her head away. Her heart was pounding. Her breathing shallow. Regardless of her cool-headed resolve, she felt very much like a lovesick female.

"Major Harrison."

How could the sound of a man's voice have this kind of effect on me? Alex's pulse raced that much faster. She savored Clay's gentle Southern drawl.

"Lieutenant Thomas," Harrison returned the greeting. "I have your assignment."

Good, Alex thought. *Complete your business and let's leave.*

"Your first mission is tomorrow morning."

"So soon?"

"It's an experienced crew," Harrison said. "That's the good news. The bad news is that their pilot just died while attempting a special assignment."

"The explosion a little while ago."

"The same. The crew and the pilot were close. They're going to take it hard. That's why I've chosen you to replace him."

Alex closed her eyes. Her mind swirled. In all her years as a pilot, in all the dangerous situations she'd found herself, never had she been so confused. Out of control. At a loss of what to do. Spiraling. Going down.

Harrison continued. "You have many of the same qualities he had. They'll respect you. They'll need someone like you to help them through this."

"What about the copilot, sir? Wouldn't he be a logical choice?"

"Keating is a good copilot. But he's not leadership material. We need someone like you."

Clay was reluctant.

Harrison said, "Look, Thomas, if it was up to me, I'd give you all the time you need to get your crew through this. But we need every plane in the air tomorrow. Can I count on you?"

"I'll do my best, sir."

"I know you will, son."

Business concluded, Alex thought. *Now, let's get out of here.*

But then a new problem confronted her. Surely Clay would recognize her when she turned to drive away!

Harrison was telling him the time of the briefing. "Oh, and one more thing ..."

Alex's heart froze. He wasn't going to introduce her was he?

"... the name of your plane is *California Angel.*"

A reprieve! And just as she figured out a plan to get away. She would do just that—get away. She would turn, start the engine, and drive. If he hadn't already turned back toward the house he would recognize her, but by the time he said anything they would be halfway down the road. She would explain to him later.

"The *California Angel?*" Clay said. "Isn't that Walt Morgan's plane?"

A moment of silence followed. Alex assumed Harrison was nodding affirmatively. He said, "Did you know Walt?"

Clay's voice was heavy. "No. But I was looking forward to meeting him. I met a family member in the States."

Let's go ... let's go!

Harrison said, "Then you must know his sister."

Alex cringed. *What do I do?*

Pilot instinct kicked in. She turned cheerily and said, "No, I'm afraid we haven't met yet. I'm one of Walt's sisters, Alexandra Morgan."

Clay was stunned. He blinked several times. If so much hadn't been riding on what he did next, Alex would have burst out laughing at the look on his face.

"Alex …" Clay said.

"Actually, I prefer Alexandra," she said. "When people hear the name Alex they automatically think of a man."

Harrison stared at her, chomping his cigar. "You introduced yourself to me as Alex," he said. "You prefer Alexandra?"

"Yes, sir," she said, fastening her eyes on the major. She was afraid to look at Clay.

"So be it," Harrison said.

"My condolences on the death of your brother," Clay said.

She had no choice but to look at him now. He had regained his composure. His jaw was firmly set, though the expression on his face was sincere. However, another emotion haunted his eyes. It wasn't confusion. She could have handled confusion. The look she saw residing deep inside him was disappointment, bordering on anger.

Her chin began to quiver. It was all she could do to hold back the tears. She wanted to explain. To make him understand.

The two men exchanged parting words and Harrison climbed back into the jeep. They were no more than a hundred yards down the road when she could hold it back no longer. The tears came suddenly and in torrents, startling the major.

"Pull over, pull over!" he cried, waving his cigar.

She did. Harrison insisted on driving them back to the base and then driving himself to the crash site.

"I guess it all sort of caught up with you back there," he said.

Alex nodded through her tears.

Major Harrison would never know how true his words were.

Laura was in the kitchen fixing dinner when Johnny walked in. She paused in her potato slicing.

"Find out anything?" she asked. From the look on his face she knew the answer already.

"Nothing," he said, running his hand in exasperation through his thinning hair. "As far as the army is concerned, she's AWOL. But other than search the base, they're doing nothing about it. It's as though she's disappeared off the face of the earth."

Laura resumed her slicing. "Can you bring me that bag?" she asked, indicating with her glance the one on the table.

Johnny snatched up the bag, peeking inside.

"Spices," she said. "I stopped by the market on the way home." She added the potatoes to a boiling pot of soup on the stove. Removing the oregano from the sack, she seasoned the soup.

"We received a call regarding Lily," she said.

"Oh?"

"Army personnel have reached the crash site. They've confirmed there are no survivors."

"Have they found her body?"

Laura blinked back tears and kept stirring. "They said it would take time to sort through the wreckage. It's rugged territory. They're having to cart everything in and out with mules."

Laura chopped some celery and added it to the pot. For a few moments the only sound between them was that of the knife hitting the cutting board.

"Also, there's a letter beside my chair. Condolences from the army together with Nat's dog tags."

She caught Johnny staring at her.

"What?" she said.

"You."

"What about me?"

"You're remarkable."

Laura smiled weakly. "I thought you'd never notice."

"No, I mean it. You're incredible."

"Stop it!"

"Not many women could go through what you are going through and do it as gracefully as you're doing it."

Though Laura appreciated the compliment, the subject poked the wounds inside that had not yet healed.

In reply, she quoted Isaiah 40:31: "*But they that wait upon the* LORD *shall renew their strength; they shall mount up with wings as eagles; they shall run, and not be weary; and they shall walk, and not faint.* Some days it's enough to walk and not faint, to put one foot in front of the other and not stumble."

Johnny encircled her from behind with his arms. He kissed her on the ear. "Life has not been kind to us lately," he said. "But we still have Alex. And until we hear otherwise, I choose to believe she is alive."

"She's in God's hands," Laura said. "We'll just have to trust him to do for her what we can't."

Nat's awareness of his first attempt at waking was limited to two things: the pain in his head and the light hurting his eyes. He moaned and then winced. His meager moan reverberated inside his head like a noisy gong. After a moment his eyes made a feeble attempt to open. Light jabbed them closed again so forcefully it knocked him back into the darkness as though he'd been pushed down a stairway into a dark cellar. As he tumbled he thought he heard someone humming.

He had no idea how long it took for him to climb back out of the darkness. A few minutes? A day? A week?

It was the pain in his head that roused him. He was vaguely aware that he was being propped up. A soothing voice sounded, but he could make out no words. A warm liquid touched his lips, then trickled down his parched throat. More soothing sounds. And a whiff of lilacs. Then, nothing. All was black again.

He became aware of his own breathing, a raspy, ragged effort. The light was not as harsh. A small sun glowed; then it was eclipsed as something passed between it and him. He smelled lilacs.

"… About time you … is that light … don't try … worry, you're … back … lay … rest …"

This time Nat tried to climb out of the cellar. He clawed and grabbed. Gravity fought him, grabbing him, pulling him back. He was overmatched. He was pulled down until darkness swallowed him.

Nat became aware. For a few moments it was nothing more than that. He was aware of being. Little by little, other pieces of awareness were added to the incomplete puzzle of his existence. He was aware that he was reclining. That he was lying on something soft and warm. That something cushioned his head.

His eyes fluttered open. At first fighting the light, then gradually adjusting to it. There were walls and a ceiling. He was in a room. Light poured into the room to his left. Probably a window. He started to verify his supposition, but his attempt to turn his head was met with hot pokers of pain in the back of his head.

He could see his feet. Beyond them was a chest of drawers on top of which was a storm lamp. Striped floral wallpaper covered the walls.

Nat's visual tour of his surroundings had exhausted him. And he hadn't even broached the question of what he was doing here. His last remembrance was lying on his back in a forest with a German guard pointing a pistol at his chest.

He closed his eyes to rest. He drifted.

A rustling startled him. Had the German guard come back? His eyes shot open. His body instinctively jerked despite the pain. The bed springs squeaked.

The next instant Nat concluded he must be hallucinating, that or he was dead and it was the sound of angel's wings that awoke him. For what he saw was truly a heavenly vision.

"So, you finally decided to rejoin the living?" She spoke in English with a definite French accent.

Long, silky-blonde hair swayed in a carefree manner as she cocked her head and smiled generously. Nat guessed the woman to be in her midthirties. She was thin—not fashionably, but from apparent want. Still, her appearance was more than neat, her dress a bright floral print, the kind of dress his sister Lily would wear.

Nat tried to say something but his tongue stuck to the sides of his mouth.

"You just rest now, Corporal Morgan. You are among friends."

"Where …?" He managed to croak out a single word.

"There will be plenty of time to answer all your questions. Now you rest. Would you like something to drink?"

Nat nodded. It hurt to nod.

It was almost painful to have her leave the room. Either she was the most beautiful woman in the world, or his injuries were greater than he thought, or it simply could be that he hadn't been around women much lately. In any case, he checked the doorway constantly, eager for her return.

She came back shortly afterward carrying a glass of water. Sitting on the bed next to him, she placed her spare hand around the back of his neck and helped him sit up to take a sip from the glass.

The water did wonders for his throat. Even though it was just a few sips. She helped him back onto the pillow.

"Better?" she asked.

"Much."

She stood. "Please rest now, Corporal Morgan. We've been worried about you."

"We?" Nat asked.

"Friends," she answered.

The water was reaching his stomach, which wasn't giving it the same welcome reception it had been accorded by his throat. His stomach began to cramp. He winced.

He had more questions for her. *Where was he? How did she know his name? Who was she? Who were these friends?* The questions would just have to wait. It didn't appear that he was going anywhere anytime soon.

One unanswered question nagged him. *Was he her prisoner?* There was nothing to indicate that he was being held captive. But then what had happened after he blacked out in the woods beneath that German guard?

Nat concluded that if he were a captive, if this blonde guard was any indication of his predicament, he might welcome imprisonment until the end of the war. There was something a little odd about her, though. She never looked at him directly. It wasn't anything of major importance, just a little odd.

28

Alex was wandering the Bassingbourn base when she ran into Lieutenant Clay Thomas. Major Harrison had dropped her off and had driven to the crash site on his own. Having no living quarters and with nowhere on base to go, Alex had wandered around until she spied the canteen. She went in, though she didn't know why. She was too upset to eat. So she left. That's when she bumped into him.

"Clay, before you say anything, let me explain!"

From the look on his face, he was as unprepared for this encounter as she was.

"Let's go somewhere where we can talk privately," Alex suggested.

He glanced at the canteen.

Alex shook her head. "Too crowded," she said.

He agreed. "Follow me."

He led her to a spot between two hangars. Spare parts and junk were piled everywhere, but there was no traffic and it was relatively quiet.

"What are you doing driving Major Harrison's jeep? You're supposed to be in the States flying B-17s!"

Alex was immediately on the defensive. This wasn't at all how she'd envisioned their encounter. Worse yet, she found herself in a position having to defend the very actions that she herself now viewed with increasing shame. It was difficult to know where to begin. She decided to play the hand dealt her.

"I'm not exactly Major Harrison's driver," she said. "He only thinks I am."

Clay's mouth dropped open. "You're impersonating a driver? You came all the way to England to impersonate a driver?"

Alex winced. "Of course not. It was just … well, I needed something that would keep me on base. The driver position just sort of presented itself and I took it."

His surprised expression mutated to one of astonishment. "You needed something to keep you on base? You mean, you don't have authorization to be here? You've not been transferred here?"

Alex shook her head. But before she could respond, Clay had pieced the rest together. "Tell me you resigned at Lockbourne," he said, "please, tell me you resigned. Don't tell me you're …"

"Absent without leave," Alex completed his sentence for him.

"You're AWOL?" Clay shouted. "In the name of all that's holy, why?"

"That's what I'm trying to explain!" Alex cried.

"I can't believe this!" Clay shouted, throwing his hands up helplessly. "What happened to you? You were one of the best, most responsible pilots I'd ever met! And now you tell me you've thrown it all away? For heaven's sake, why? Can you answer me that? Why?"

Alex stared defenselessly at Clay's reddened face. What could have possibly made her think that she would waltz onto this base and into his arms? How could she defend something that made absolutely no sense?

"I'm not proud of what I've done …" she began.

"Does anyone know you're here?" Clay asked.

"No one, other than you and Major Harrison, and he thinks …"

"That you're his assigned driver," Clay said. "That certainly explains that little scene in front of my quarters, doesn't it?" He mimicked her voice, "No, I'm afraid we haven't met yet. I'm one of Walt's sisters, Alexandra Morgan."

Alex's anger rose within her. She longed to hear him say her name with that soft Texan drawl like he used to—*Miss Alex.* To hear him repeating her own lie in a condescending tone grated on her nerves.

"I don't know you," Clay said. "I thought I did, but I guess I was wrong. You haven't even told me why you've done this—I can't think of a single reason why anyone would trash a career, travel all the way across the Atlantic, sneak onto an army base in time of war, and impersonate a jeep driver."

She started to reply. He wasn't finished.

"The thought just boggles the mind, doesn't it? To think of all you've given up! Not just for yourself, but for women pilots every-where! Don't you realize that the army is looking for instances like this as proof why women should not be pilots?"

That blow hurt. Alex had willingly sacrificed her own career, but it hadn't crossed her mind that she would be jeopardizing the chances of other women pilots. But Clay was right. He was absolutely right. And that made the blow sting all the more.

"And for what?" Clay pleaded. "What has been gained from all of this?"

"I did it for you," Alex said softly.

"For me?"

It was a female thing to do and she hated herself for it, but she couldn't help herself. Alex began weeping.

"You did this for *me?* You thought that going AWOL and driv-ing a jeep instead of flying B-17s would impress me?"

Alex looked up at him. "I wasn't trying to impress you," she said.

"Then what?"

"I wanted to be near you."

Clay was shaking his head in bewilderment. His hands were in the air again. "This just isn't making any sense!"

The emotional stew within Alex churned and boiled. Frustrated, angry with herself, angry with him, ashamed and humiliated, she shouted, "I did it because I love you! Is that so hard for you to understand? I love you!"

Two corporals had rounded the corner just as Alex shouted her love. They looked at her and Clay and snickered. A withering glare from Clay sent them away.

Alex glanced up hopefully at him. This was what she had come to England to say. It wasn't how she'd wanted to say it, but it was out there nonetheless. And this was where Clay was supposed to realize that depth of her passion and sacrifice and open his arms and smother her and tell her it was all right and confess his love for her too.

His head was bowed. He was reflective. The anger was gone. "I don't know what to say," he said softly. "There was a time when I thought something might develop between us. But I see now that's not possible. How can I love a woman for whom I have no respect?"

He walked past her, leaving her standing alone amidst piles of airplane junk parts.

Then he stopped, turned, and said, "My condolences on the death of your brother."

Nat awoke to the sound of someone reading the Bible aloud. He staggered across the threshold between slumber and consciousness, first on one side, then the other. In doing so, he recognized some of the phrases from the familiar first psalm.

Blessed is the man ... counsel of the ungodly ... like a tree

*planted ... shall prosper ... ungodly ... like the chaff ... shall not
stand ... shall perish ...*

Fully awake now, he looked over and saw his blonde guard.
She was sitting in a rocking chair, rocking back and forth contentedly, and just as contentedly going from the first psalm to the
second:

> Why do the heathen rage, and the people imagine a vain thing?

Only there was no open Bible in her hands or lap.

> The kings of the earth set themselves, and the rulers take counsel
> together, against the LORD,

Nat looked again, thinking his eyes were playing tricks on
him. Sure enough, there was no Bible.

> and against his anointed, saying, Let us break their bands asunder, and
> cast away their cords from us. He that sitteth in the heavens shall
> laugh: the LORD shall have them in derision.

He managed to prop himself up on one arm and stare at
her.

"Ah! Good morning, Corporal Morgan," she said cheerily. "Or
should I say good afternoon, for it nearly is, you know."

"You were quoting the Bible," Nat said.

"Indeed, I was. I'm so glad you recognize the words as being
from the Bible."

"As I was waking up, I thought you were *reading* out of the
Bible."

She laughed breezily and rocked. She didn't look at him. Was
she embarrassed to look at a man in bed?

"Are those your favorite Bible verses?" Nat asked.

Her brow furrowed. "I wouldn't say they are my favorite
verses in the Bible, though I am drawn to the questions of the second psalm. Rather appropriate for our day and age, don't you
think? '*Why do the heathen rage, and the people imagine a vain*

thing? The kings of the earth set themselves, and the rulers take counsel together, against the Lord ..."

"Appropriate indeed," Nat said. For the first time since his captivity in Anzio, Nat was actually feeling healthy. His head, though it still hurt, was clearing. And his stomach, though it was presently rumbling, no longer had that twisted rag feeling.

"What made you think those particular Bible verses were my favorites?" the blonde woman asked him.

"You memorized them."

"Corporal Morgan, are you telling me you memorize only those portions of Scripture that are your favorites?"

"Can't say that I memorize any of them, at least not since I was a child."

A displeased look crossed her face. "And what if by some untimely event, the Bible were taken from you and you could never read it again?"

"I guess I would have to learn to live without it."

The displeasure on her face intensified. Feeling on the defensive, he said, "You would be forced to do the same, with the exception of those few verses you have memorized."

"I would not be forced to do the same," she said firmly.

"You're telling me you have the entire Bible memorized?"

"Yes."

"The *entire* Bible?"

"Yes."

Nat stared at her. She looked as though she was telling the truth.

"Test me, if you wish," she said.

It was Nat's turn to furrow his brow.

"Go ahead. I can stand the test."

"All right," Nat said, searching his mind for a passage he could recognize that wasn't too obvious like Genesis 1:1 or John 3:16.

When he couldn't think of one, he took a shot in the dark, "How about ... First Kings 21:19?"

A puzzled laugh burst forth. "You know this verse?" she asked.

"Yes ... well, sort of. Do you?"

> Thus saith the LORD, In the place where dogs licked the blood of Naboth shall dogs lick thy blood, even thine.

"I didn't say it was my favorite verse," Nat said. "How about Obadiah 3:7?"

"There is no Obadiah 3:7. Obadiah has only one chapter."

"I knew that," Nat lied, "I was just testing you. But this one exists: Second Samuel 13:11."

She flushed. "Nat Morgan! You ought to be ashamed!"

"What?"

"You know what that verse says, don't you?"

"No! Honestly! I just pulled the reference out of the air! I'm not even certain there are eleven verses in that chapter."

She folded her arms. And chuckled.

"I honestly don't know what that verse says! What does it say?"

She turned her head away from him.

"Tell me what it says!" he pleaded.

She said, "'*And when she had brought them unto him to eat, he took hold of her, and said unto her, Come lie with me, my sister.*' Are you trying to get fresh with me, Nat Morgan?"

Nat sat up in the bed. He did it before he even gave it any thought. "I honestly did not know what was in that verse. And I honestly am not trying to get fresh with you."

Her arms remained folded.

"But I am impressed," he said. "You really have the entire Bible memorized, don't you?"

She grinned. "Not bad for a blind girl, don't you think?"

Nat stared at her. *That's* what was odd about her. Why she never looked at him directly. But she didn't *look* blind, in that her eyes looked perfectly normal. And she certainly didn't *act* blind. She moved about as freely as a person with sight, not ever once holding her hands out in front of her to feel her way. She must have the entire room memorized.

She laughed. "You're supposed to say, 'What do you mean, not bad for a blind person? That's not bad for a person with sight!'"

A memory was stirring. But it was so far-fetched … it couldn't be.

"What's the matter? Cat got your tongue?"

Nat searched his mind. Aunt Katy talked about her. During the Great War. A little girl. Blind. With an incredible memory. Memorized the whole town. Knew everything about the Morgans!

He felt for his dog tags even though he knew they weren't there. They'd been ripped from his neck when Szczepkowski had been killed. *She knows my name!*

"You know my name!" he said.

She smiled. "Ah! So you're beginning to see the light … pardon the pun."

"But it's too coincidental to be true," he said.

"Maybe not as coincidental as you might think."

It came to him. "Bruno! Aunt Katy said she met a little girl who was blind and her name was Bruno!"

A sour but playful look formed on her face. "Are you sure you heard correctly? That's such an ugly name for a little girl."

Nat was on to something here. "That was just her code name. She was part of the French underground. Her real name was … um, it's on the tip of my tongue …"

"Allegra."

Nat snapped his fingers. "That's it! Allegra!" The excitement he felt gave way to wonder as he slumped down and stared at her.

"Didn't your mother ever teach you that it's not polite to stare?" she asked.

Nat grinned. She was amazing. Intuitive. Intelligent. Witty. Beautiful. Even now, knowing she was blind, he found it difficult to think of her that way.

"Are you hungry? I have some soup made," she said.

"I'm starving!"

"That's a good sign," she said.

Nat was able to walk under his own power to the dining room table, but he collapsed into the chair once he got there. He figured it would have to be a long lunch just for him to rest up enough for the return trip.

Allegra fed him potato soup, a salad of dandelion greens, and a whole salami.

"I've been saving it for your first meal. Sort of a celebration," she said.

She poured him a cup of coffee. He stared in fascination at the ease with which she served him. Not a drop of coffee was spilt.

"Of course, it's barley coffee," she said. "It doesn't taste very much like coffee, but we've gotten used to it by now."

After everything was on the table, she sat down opposite him and prayed for the meal.

"Tell me about your Aunt Katy," Allegra said. "I lost touch with her some time ago."

Nat brought her up to date with everything he remembered hearing during their last family gathering shortly before Christmas 1941.

Allegra sighed. "Oh, a Morgan family gathering! How I'd love to attend one of those! You know, of course, that keeping up with the Morgans is something of a hobby of mine. It started with your aunt, and then I learned about the generations of Morgans going all the way back to Drew Morgan at Edenford. You have a proud family heritage, Nat. I hope you appreciate it."

Nat laughed. "Maybe you should be the one who inherits the family Bible. You seem to know our history better than any of the rest of us!"

Allegra smiled. "I wouldn't think of depriving you of that honor," she said.

"Walt's honor," Nat corrected her.

"But you're the elder male."

"The way the tradition runs, the holder of the Bible chooses the next successor. Though most of the time it has gone to the eldest male, that is not part of the criteria. Dad chose to give it to Walt."

"The ceremony has already been held?"

"Not yet. Dad gave Walt the Bible at our last family gathering, but they thought it best to hold the ceremony after this war is over."

"And how do you feel about Walt being given the Bible instead of you?"

Nat chewed happily. "To tell you the truth, I'm glad the responsibility is going to Walt. I'd really rather not be bothered with it."

Allegra chewed in silence.

His plate empty, Nat sat back in his chair. He looked around him. From the size of the rooms, it was a small house. Sparsely furnished, apparently from things gathered here and there, for nothing matched. Everything was simple, but immaculately clean, reflecting the seemingly uncomplicated life of what Nat assumed was its sole occupant.

A window provided a view of a small barn, the bare branches of a large oak tree, and a forest beyond. It was a pastoral setting on the verge of what looked like a promising spring.

"I have a few questions," Nat said.

"I thought you might."

"What am I doing here?"

Allegra feigned offense. "Am I that poor of a hostess?" she pleaded.

"Oh, no!" Nat said. "You've been more than kind, please don't think that ..." Her smile indicated she was toying with him.

"Maybe we ought to begin with how you got here," she offered.

"All right, let's start there."

"We learned that you were in the area when you were a prisoner in Rome. You took pictures of Hitler's parade of American prisoners."

"I pretended to take pictures," Nat said. "With each exposure, I popped the back of the camera and exposed the film."

Allegra gave an impressed nod. "And lived to tell about it!" she said.

"Only because the American forces were knocking on the door. Had they not forced a hasty German departure, I fear I would not be talking with you now."

"Then you knew they would kill you if the pictures did not turn out," she said. "Knowing that, why did you expose the film?"

"At that point I didn't care much if I lived or died. All I knew was that I was not going to be part of dishonoring American soldiers for Hitler's profit."

"And now?" Allegra asked.

"And now what?"

"Do you care if you live or die?"

Nat pondered the question. It was amazing how suddenly everything had changed for him. When he was lying in the snow, he would have welcomed a German bullet to end his life and his misery. But waking up here with Allegra had returned a good measure of life's value.

"At the moment, I'd have to say I'm enjoying life."

"Nathaniel Morgan! Are you flirting with me?"

Nat didn't answer. He only smiled. He was glad she couldn't see his blush and be pleased at her accusation.

"You told the Germans you had some pictures published in *Life* magazine," Allegra said.

"That's right! How did you know that?"

"One of our men in Rome heard a German guard boast that a *Life* photographer was taking pictures for Hitler. We were looking for a photographer. Imagine my surprise when I learned that the photographer we found was a Morgan!"

"You were looking for a photographer? Don't you have any photographers in …" he looked around, "wherever it is we are?"

"Not of the caliber of Nathaniel Morgan!"

"Allegra! Are you flirting with me?"

Now it was Nat's turn to watch her blush. To say he enjoyed it would be an understatement.

"We need a professional journalistic photographer," she said. "You have the credentials."

"I'm a portrait photographer," Nat corrected her.

"You're not a journalistic photographer?"

"No."

"But your pictures in *Life?*"

"Since I've been in the army, I've had a few pictures published here and there, *Stars and Stripes*, *Life*, that sort of thing. But by profession I'm a portrait photographer."

"Hmmm. Well, I guess you'll have to do. We've already gone to this much trouble."

Nat frowned. He didn't know if she was serious or toying with him again. All he knew was that he didn't like seeing her disappointed and would do most anything to keep her from being disappointed in him again.

"We followed you from Rome," she explained. "The original plan was to break you out of the holding pen in Rome, but when the Germans offered to ship you up our way, we decided to let them do that for us. To make a long story short, we intercepted you from them."

"And not a moment too soon," Nat said. "The last thing I remember was a German guard with a pistol standing over me."

"So, Corporal Morgan, as you can see, your being here is not as much of a coincidence as you originally thought."

"And where exactly is here?"

"You are at a farm near the village of Arracourt, which is due east of Nancy, France."

"And who is the *we* you keep referring to?"

Allegra scooted her chair back, stood, and began gathering the dishes. "That information and the reason you were brought here, my dear Monsieur Morgan, will have to wait until another time."

Nat stood, a little too quickly. A white haze passed in front of his eyes and he had to steady himself on the edge of the table. Allegra didn't seem to notice.

"I have a few things to which I must attend," she said as she worked, "and you undoubtedly need to rest."

He didn't argue with her.

When he reached the bed, never had he seen a sight so inviting. There was a dull pain in his head as he fell into it, but it gradually faded. Then, all was comfort and bliss.

He lay there a short time before he heard a door open and close. A few moments later there was a deep creaking sound. He guessed it to be the barn door.

A moment later and he was asleep.

Parcheesi was Allegra's favorite game. They played it beside the fire after dinner. She read the roll of the dice by touching them and was amazingly accurate moving the pieces—she knew where every man was at all times. Nat tested her once by trying to cheat.

"Can you play with four players?" he asked.

"What kind of a question is that?"

"I just meant, with the extra pieces and all … forget I asked you. It was a stupid question."

She reached out and patted the back of his hand. It was obvious she meant it to be a friendly pat. Nat imagined it to be more.

He told himself that it had been a long time since he'd seen a beautiful woman and that he was probably overreacting. He told himself he was still grieving over Murphy and that he was lonely. He told himself that she was at least a good ten years older than him, that she was French while he was American, and that he was a long way from home. He told himself all these things in an attempt to understand the feelings he was feeling for her.

But no matter how much he talked to himself, it didn't lessen his feelings for her. In fact, they seemed to grow every time he looked at her, which he was doing with increasing frequency.

"Are you going to stare at me all night or are you going to move?" Allegra asked.

"What makes you think I was staring at you?" Nat asked. "Just how do you know when someone is staring at you?"

Allegra leaned back. An it's-so-elementary smile spread across her lips. "People get quieter when they stare at someone, some to the point of holding their breath. They know it's impolite and don't wish to get caught so they try not to make a sound."

"Makes sense," Nat said. "And thanks."

"Thanks? For what?"

"Now I know how to stare at you without getting caught. I'll just hum or talk or breathe loud or something."

Allegra laughed. It was a wonderful sound.

Nat rolled the dice and moved his pieces.

"There's someone I want you to meet tomorrow," Allegra said.

"Is he part of the we?"

Allegra laughed. "Yes, he's part of the we."

"Then, I'm anxious to meet him too."

"You'll like him," Allegra said. "His name is Josef. He's my intended."

Nat looked up at Allegra and stared. He forgot to cover his staring by making noise.

You could have gone all night without telling me that, he thought.

29

It was the longest, most miserable night of Alex's life. She was a fugitive from the army on one base while hiding out on another. The career she had worked so hard to establish was in ruins, and the thing that she loved most—flying (she realized that now)—she had foolishly tossed aside. Other than small private planes, she knew she would never fly again. On top of it all, she had alienated herself from her family and caused them untold grief. The man she loved didn't want to have anything to do with her. And she was playing the impostor with the only other person who knew she was in England.

How fitting, she thought, *to be sitting in an aviation junk heap.*

After her confrontation with Clay, she had fled to the grassy end of the runway. Aircraft of all sizes taking off and landing drowned her sobs out. She wept until she thought she could weep no more. But she did. She couldn't stop herself.

When it got dark she retreated to the junkyard between the hangars. There she found an old cowling. She crawled into it and curled up to ward off the night chill. And there she spent the night, in agonizing fits of sleep and even worse bouts of wakefulness.

About midway through the night, rational thought made an appearance. Although she wanted to curl up here and die, she knew she wouldn't. So, what then?

She could return to Lockbourne and turn herself in and let justice take its course. She could turn herself in here and let the army ship her back, undoubtedly in chains. She could call home.

This option brought tears again. She'd never thought of herself as a dependent person, one of those children who needed Mommy and Daddy all of their lives. But how she longed to hear her mother's voice and to listen to her father—even though she knew he'd be furious—help her reason through her options.

But she couldn't bring herself to do it. She'd made such a mess of things. *This is my mess and I'm going to have to clean it up.*

As morning broke, Alex emerged from the cowling—cold, shivering, and wet with dew. Yet still without a plan. She walked to the eastern side of the hangar where the sun was radiating off the building. She warmed herself and dried her clothes and did her best to look presentable.

She decided to play out her masquerade for one more day. Hopefully, in the light of day, she would see things more clearly and come up with some kind of plan for fixing her messed-up life.

She checked her watch. Major Harrison would be expecting her at flight operations in fifteen minutes. She took a deep breath and fought off those pesky self-accusations that were so persistent in reminding her of what she'd thrown away.

Just get on with it! she told herself.

Taking a few steps toward flight operations, a thought stopped her. She didn't know why she'd thought of it. Possibly thinking of her mother had brought it on.

Another thought struck her. An even wilder one. *I wonder how long it takes a prayer to get from San Diego to England?* Because for some reason she had a strong urge to pray. She'd never had an urge like it before. She wondered if her mother's prayers had winged their way around the world and caused this feeling.

For whatever reason, Alex closed her eyes and for the first time for as long as she could remember, she prayed for God to guide her through the day.

Alex sat in the jeep outside the briefing room. It was packed. Just from the number of bodies she knew this was going to be a huge mission.

She had driven Major Harrison to the briefing. He stood just inside the doorway, having brought with him several boxes of cigars, which sat on the passenger seat of the jeep. He'd told Alex it was his custom to hand out the cigars to the men after the briefing.

Clay had arrived shortly before the briefing began. Alex caught him looking at her. He quickly averted his eyes and did not look up at her again as he entered the briefing room.

Through the open door, Alex could see the maps with the targets prominently displayed. She listened to the briefing. An emotional heaviness settled on her chest for a couple of reasons. For one, it reminded her of Walt. This was the briefing room in which he'd sat before going on his missions. And it also served to remind her how much she loved flying. She would give almost anything to be in that room with those men going on this mission.

Major Harrison looked agitated. He maneuvered himself this way and that as he searched the room, looking for someone. Swinging around, he marched toward the jeep cursing under his breath.

"Anything wrong, sir?" Alex asked.

Harrison tossed the cigars into the back of the jeep. One box opened and spilled a few of the brown cylinders on the seat. "We have a man missing," he said.

He looked up at Alex. A thought reflected in his eyes.

"Miss Morgan," he said, "I have to go get this guy. Could I prevail upon you to hand out these cigars to the men for me?"

Alex envisioned herself standing at the doorway handing a cigar to Clay. If he looked at her, she knew she would die. If he didn't look at her, she would die.

"I don't think it would mean as much to the men if I handed out the cigars, sir."

Harrison slumped back in his seat. From all indications inside, the briefing was just about over. "You're right," he said. "All right, let's go."

"Sir?"

"What?"

"Who do you need to get? I could get him for you."

Harrison weighed the idea.

"Just tell me who and where. I can pick him up and deliver him to wherever you need him to be. That way you could be here to hand out the cigars to the men."

He liked the idea. Alex could tell by the look in his eyes.

"I can do it, sir."

Harrison nodded. Gathering up the cigars from the back of the jeep, he said, "If you have any trouble, you come right back here and notify me immediately. Do you understand?"

"Yes, sir."

He jumped out of the jeep just as the men inside were getting out of their chairs.

Harrison gave Alex the directions. "Find Lieutenant Jay Keating, he's the copilot of ..." Harrison hesitated; "... of the *California Angel*, your brother's plane."

"Yes sir." Alex snapped the words out to assure the major that it would not be a problem for her.

Apparently it worked. All hesitation vanished from Harrison's demeanor. "Find Keating and get him to that plane! Then come back here and get me. I want to have a few words with him myself."

The room smelled of booze and vomit. It was so strong it literally knocked Alex back a step when she opened the door.

"Lieutenant Keating?" she called.

She heard a muffled cry, but the room was too dark to tell from where it was coming. Alex stepped across and on clothing and bottles and who knows what else as she made her way to the window and threw open the drapes.

"Lieutenant Keating?"

She heard the moan again, but it wasn't coming from the bed because the bed was empty. Blankets and sheets and pillows gave the appearance it had been occupied, but it wasn't now. The moan was coming from beside it on the floor.

Walking around the edge of the bed, she saw him. Facedown. Slowly writhing. Dressed only in his boxer shorts.

"Lieutenant Keating?"

The writhing figure turned over and looked up at her.

"Who're you?" he said painfully.

"Major Harrison sent me to get you. You have a mission to fly." She said the words because that's what she'd been sent to do—pick up Keating and take him to the plane for his mission. But this man was in no condition to fly a paper airplane, let alone a B-17.

"Go away," he said.

"Come on, Lieutenant," Alex said. "You have to get up."

He cursed at her and made no attempt to get up.

Alex groaned. She was going to have to bend over and help him up. She really didn't want to touch him.

Moving a pair of pants and socks and a couple of bottles to one side, she moved toward him. She bent down. As she did, she spied something that caught her attention.

On a chair next to the dresser, partially covered by a carelessly tossed shirt, was what looked like the Morgan family Bible. With her index finger and thumb she tossed the shirt aside. Sure enough, it *was* the family Bible! Three envelopes lay on top of it. She picked them up and looked at them.

All three bore Walt's handwriting. One was to Nat, one to Lily, and one to her. They'd all been returned. That was odd. She could understand why her letter would have been returned, but why Nat's and Lily's?

She picked up the family Bible and stared at it. How many times had she seen it at home? Yet its presence here made it look so different. So much more valuable. She felt like she had been reunited with a part of her family! Turning the Bible over, she saw the huge gash in the back, cutting into the heart of the book.

"Put that down!" Keating yelled from the floor. "Down! Down! Put it down!" He was frantic.

"This is *my* family's Bible," Alex said.

"No it's not! It's Walt Morgan's Bible!" Keating yelled. He tried to get up, but slipped and fell.

"Yes, this is Walt Morgan's Bible!" Alex said. "Walt was my brother!"

Keating stared at her through glassy eyes.

"Your brother?"

"Yes."

"No ..."

"Yes, he was. My name is Alexandra Morgan. I'm Walt's sister." She had an idea. Taking the letter with her name on it, she held it up. "See this? Miss Alex Morgan. That's me. Walt addressed this letter to me. And these others? Nat. Lily. They're my brother and sister."

He looked at her as though a cloud of smoke stood between them. Blinking. Focusing. Blinking again.

"He's dead," Keating said. "Walt's dead." He began to cry.

"I know," Alex said.

"Good man. None finer. Good, good man."

"Yes, he was."

"Why is it like this?" Keating sobbed.

"Why is what like this?"

"It's always like this. Always. Makes no sense. But that's the way it is."

He was rambling.

"Lieutenant Keating …"

"It's these cursed wars, I tell you. It's always like this … always.…"

"Always like what?"

He looked up at her. His hair was matted and filthy. His eyes were blood red. He hadn't shaved for a couple of days. "It's always the best who die," he said. "Always. Not like me. No … but Walt. Always the best … they die in wars …"

Alex fought back tears. "Lieutenant Keating, I've got to get you …"

"Must get the Bible to the *California Angel*," he said. He grabbed for the side of the bed. Ending up with only a handful of sheet, he fell back to the floor. "Have to get the Bible to the plane. Promised Walt. Promised."

"Lieutenant Keating …"

"Have to do it. Have to. Men will want the Bible …"

"I'll do it for you," Alex said.

Keating stopped struggling and looked up at her as though he wasn't sure he'd heard correctly.

"I'll get the Bible to the plane for you," she said.

He blinked several times. "Promise?"

"I promise."

"It's important."

"I know it's important. You can trust me," Alex reassured him.

Keating seemed satisfied. He slumped back to the floor.

Alex slipped the letters inside the cover of the Bible. She carefully charted her way back across the bedroom floor. At the door she paused.

Hanging on the back was Lieutenant Keating's flight suit. On an end table near the door was his flight gear. All laid out and ready to go. Alex thought that when he was sober, Lieutenant Keating was probably a fastidious man. The thought, together with some of the things Keating had said, prompted her to wonder if Keating was drunk because of Walt's death.

On impulse, she grabbed the flight suit and gear and slipped out the door and out to the jeep. Keating's words came back to her.

It's always the best who die.

She started the jeep.

It's always the best who die.

She drove back on base and headed toward the *California Angel*.

It's always the best who die.

"Not today. Not if I can help it," she said.

30

They waited two days at the wreckage of the plane for help to arrive. On the third day, when no one came to rescue them, they decided it was time to rescue themselves.

Lily looked up at the sky. It was black with clouds. They hung low, touching and engulfing the larger peaks around them. Given the bad weather and the rugged terrain, there was little wonder why no one had yet come to their aid. She grabbed the clothes that she'd collected and stuffed them into a canvas bag.

Straightening up, she stretched, arching her back. She had to go back in there. She didn't want to, but she had to. There were still some things to salvage, some things that would be necessary to take. After all, they had no idea how far they'd have to hike before finding provisions.

Albert Lohmann ducked out of the split in the fuselage that served as their door. Holding a shirt over his mouth, he hobbled toward Lily carrying a bag of his own. He set it next to his dinged-up trumpet case.

"It's getting worse in there," he said, referring to the stench coming from the bodies. "We should have done this two days ago."

"Don't start that again," Lily warned. "Two days ago we thought we were going to be rescued. Let me look at your leg."

She bent down and examined the bandages and splint on his right leg. It was the worst injury of the three survivors. Lily and Jupiter were bruised and cut and dazed, but nothing was broken. It seemed ridiculous and ironic to Lily that she and Jupiter and Lohmann were in the back of the plane because the two men were fighting over her and probably for that reason survived the crash.

Looking up at Lohmann, she said, "Do you think you'll be able to make it?"

"What choice do I have?"

"Where's Jerry?"

Lohmann rolled his eyes. "Trying the radio again."

"I thought the batteries were dead."

"Tell *him* that!"

Lily covered her nose and mouth with a handkerchief and ducked inside the fuselage, which now served as a metal coffin to most of Jerry Jupiter's entertainment troupe. She knew she was going to have nightmares for weeks.

She stuck to a fairly well-defined path. This was the safest course. From previous trips she knew where to look and, more importantly, where to avert her eyes.

Waking up among the familiar dead as she had done following the crash had sent her into hysterics. And for several hours she thought she alone had survived the crash. Then Lohmann began to moan and soon after so did Jupiter. Contrary to what the horror pictures had taught her, moaning among the dead was a welcome sound. It meant she was no longer alone.

Scavenging among the corpses for food and clothing proved to be the real horror. She could pick up a blouse and find a hand, or a coat and find a face. That, and now the odor of the decaying dead, was why she hated going back into the fuselage. But they needed to collect as much food and necessary clothing as they could carry. To Lily, one of those necessities included her Bible. She wasn't about to leave without it. It was the search for her Bible that had brought her back into this tube of horrors.

As she searched through the debris, she couldn't help but brood over the fact that, two days ago, her life had taken a sudden, unexpected turn. The course of her career along with all human comfort had perished in the crash, and she had been thrust into an alien world of wilderness survival for which she felt woefully ill prepared.

※

It was the strangest church service Nat had ever attended, and one of the most memorable. The congregation, not more than a handful, met in Allegra's barn. They sat on a few chairs and barrels and benches. Though they all spoke French and varied in their ability to speak English, Nat was impressed with the warmth and friendliness of the group. Without exception, everyone hugged him. Men and women alike.

From what Allegra told him before the service, they came from neighboring farms and were members of a small congregation in Arracourt. The church building had been demolished several years previous and their pastor had died at a roadside blockade attempting to keep the Germans from entering Paris. The Sunday service in Allegra's barn began when travel on the roads became a daily hazard. It had continued ever since.

The service not only attracted the regular locals, but anyone who was passing through. Soldiers were often seen for one Sunday, and then never heard from again. Everyone was welcomed without question. That's why there was no undue concern caused by Nat's presence.

On the Sunday Nat was there, a young French soldier was in attendance. He told everyone he was sixteen, but he looked much younger. The local women wore simple dresses. The men, all of them older since the young men had long since gone to war, wore their work clothes. These were poor people whose Sunday best had worn out during the war and due to shortages had to settle for wearing their best work clothes on the Sabbath.

Nat was glad when the service began because he'd run out of smiles and simple exchanges, which most of them didn't understand any more than he understood what they were saying to him. One man, of middle age with neatly combed gray hair, spoke fluent English with a clipped accent. Although he wore a flannel shirt and brown corduroy pants, he was decidedly more educated than the others. Nat guessed him to be a doctor.

The only furniture that resembled anything belonging in a church was an old out-of-tune piano, which Allegra played. The service began with her playing requested hymns sung with gusto by those who were gathered. Of course, they sang in French. And the entire service was conducted in French. But Nat didn't mind. He occupied his time looking at Allegra, taking advantage that she couldn't see him staring at her.

Nat could think of only one word to describe his growing feelings for this woman. *Smitten.* He was smitten, pure and simple. He loved watching her play the piano and sing. He loved the smile and warmth she radiated to the group when she spoke. He watched her lips as they formed words, her hair as it reflected golden streaks of light coming through cracks in the side of the barn.

He wasn't the only one who felt the impact of her presence. The entire congregation seemed to warm in her radiance. Of course, they were enamored by her spirituality. He was enamored by that as well, and more.

But all was not light and happy on this Sunday morning. There was an underlying current of emotion, a very strong current, that spilled over frequently in tears.

At first Nat thought the spillover was due to the war in general. Mothers and fathers remembering their absent sons, that sort of thing. But as the service progressed, two people in particular seemed to stir the troubled waters more than anything else.

The first was any mention of Josef. Before the service, Allegra had expressed to Nat her concern for her intended. He had not yet returned from his journey, which was unusual. It was Josef who preached on Sundays in the absence of an ordained minister. He had yet to miss a Sunday service since he assumed the preaching responsibilities.

Nat had learned from Allegra that Josef had been a student of theology before he was called to serve in the army. Wounded in battle, he nearly died in the hospital after his wounds became infected and gangrene set in. However, God was gracious and Josef survived.

Following his discharge from the army, Josef spent his days doing odd jobs, helping elderly farmers who no longer had sons to assist them with the heavy labor. He had also become something of a legend in the area because of his ability to obtain extra rations, which he freely distributed to those most in need.

It wasn't difficult for Nat to understand why the locals felt as they did for Josef. And, to his chagrin, it made it that much harder for him to dislike the man.

The other person who proved to be a stimulus for tears during the worship service was the distinguished, gray-haired man. Either he volunteered, or agreed at the last minute to fill in for Josef, because it was he who gave the sermon.

He began by reading from the Bible. Then, he clutched the Bible to his chest and delivered a message. From his lack of gestures and voice inflection, it was evident he was not a preacher. His voice was low and soft. Spellbinding in oratorical mannerisms he was not.

Yet never had Nat seen anyone command a group's attention like this man. There was not a wandering mind, not a bored expression in the barn. Every eye was fixed steadfastly on him. And every eye was wet with tears.

As the service progressed, Nat found his own emotions welling. The man's simple, pious, determined faith made a powerful impression on Nat even though he understood not a single word.

When the service was over, the people gathered around the man. They hugged him. They kissed him on the cheek. They wept. And then they went home.

Nat helped Allegra prepare their dinner. He sliced cabbage while she got out three plates and set them on the table.

"Are you expecting Josef to join us?" he asked.

"God willing," Allegra said. "But this plate is not for Josef. We have another guest who will be joining us for dinner."

Nat's heart sank. He was looking forward to having Allegra to himself all afternoon.

"The gray-haired man who spoke this morning? He'll be joining us."

"I was waiting until we sat down to eat to ask you what he said. He had a powerful effect on everyone, myself included, and I didn't understand a word."

Without comment Allegra went to a hutch. Pulling out a drawer she gathered three spoons, three forks, and three knives.

"He's your first assignment," she said.

First assignment. The words caught Nat by surprise. She'd told him that they had been looking for a photographer and had chosen him, but he still didn't know who *they* were and he certainly had not agreed to help them in whatever it was they were doing.

"We need to talk about this," he replied.

"We will. During dinner."

Nat sliced the cabbage. His strokes were sharper than they were before. Allegra turned her head toward him. She noticed the difference. He stopped, expecting her to say something. She didn't.

"Maybe it would help," he said, "if you told me who he is and what he said during the service this morning."

"You can ask him yourself," Allegra replied.

As if on cue, the gray-haired man entered from the back of the house. His sudden appearance startled Nat who thought that he and Allegra were alone.

If the man's appearance startled Nat, his clothing nearly choked him with fright. The face was recognizable. So was the uniform. Gray. Red collar markings. High black boots. German.

※

Crouching in a thicket, Nat held the camera that had been obtained for him for this assignment. The man who had secured the camera had also led him to this spot and hid him there. It was the same man who had inspired the devotion of the worshippers in Allegra's barn. German Colonel Helmut Staudinger.

Nat shivered in the dim light of morning, what little of it filtered through the thick forest foliage. He didn't know if he was shivering from the cold or from fear, or both. On a day like today shivers didn't distinguish one from the other.

He knew little of what was about to happen. What little he knew frightened him. What he didn't know frightened him even more.

He knew that Allegra was working with the free French underground. Given her background and the extraordinary events that had brought him to her house, this was an expected revelation. The way she described it, they were a splinter group of the Maquis, the organized guerrilla force of the French underground. She didn't explain why they were a splinter group.

He knew that something significant was scheduled to take place in a clearing near where he was hiding. He wasn't told what would take place, only that he would not miss the significance of the event when it took place and that it had something to do with Colonel Staudinger.

Furthermore, he knew that Josef was supposed to have accompanied him. But Allegra's intended still had not returned and was now more than thirty-six hours late. This was not good news, given the fact that whatever he was doing was undoubtedly associated with underground activities. Allegra managed to keep up a brave front, but it was evident she was worried.

Because Josef was absent, slight changes in the plan had to be made. The original plans called for Josef to guide Nat back to Allegra's house following the assignment. Now, Nat was to wait until Colonel Staudinger returned for him, and if for some reason that was not possible, Nat was to find his way back on his own.

Although they had traveled in the dark, Nat felt confident he could get back by himself. That was not what was worrying him. It was the unknown that worried him. He had not a clue as to what pictures he was to take. But the fact that he was hiding was a good indicator that someone didn't want any pictures taken and if they found out, they would be decidedly angry.

Voices filtered through the trees. Male voices. German voices. Instinctively, Nat crouched lower.

Through the bushes he watched as two German officers appeared. Both colonels. One was Staudinger. The other was a hollow-cheeked man with a sharp chin and equally sharp nose. Behind them were six men in rags. They appeared to be French peasants bruised and beaten, their hands tied in front of them, a rope linking them together. Two German privates trailed behind. One guarded the prisoners with his rifle. The other, his rifle strapped to his back, carried shovels.

When they reached the clearing, the prisoners were unbound and each one was handed a shovel. They were ordered to dig.

While the prisoners dug a long pit, the privates trained their rifles on them and showered them with a steady barrage of derisive shouts. The two colonels stood off a short distance. The sharp-chinned one smoked a cigarette. Staudinger, who knew precisely where Nat was situated, never once looked his direction.

When the soldiers thought the pit was deep enough, they informed the colonels. The colonel with the sharp chin tossed the stub of his cigarette to the ground and crushed it.

The prisoners were ordered to kneel beside the pit.

Nat's heart began to race. From the moment the pit was begun, he knew what was about to take place. He knew what his first assignment was to be. He was to photograph an execution. The prisoners were probably Maquis.

Now he understood why they didn't tell him. Had they told him what his assignment would be, he wouldn't have come. He wanted no part of this.

He stared at Staudinger who stood calmly over the kneeling prisoners. Nat despised him. How could this man pretend to be so pious one day and calmly murder six men the next? Sure, he had enough of a conscious to arrange for pictures to be taken—pictures that could implicate him in the murder along with the others—but it wasn't enough. If he was truly the man he pretended to be, he would stop the executions altogether.

Nat considered taking no pictures. But that would help no one. Besides, now he *wanted* to take the pictures. He wanted to provide the evidence that would implicate Staudinger in this act of treachery.

He readied the camera. He poked the lens past the leaves to get an unobstructed shot.

The colonel with the sharp chin ordered the soldiers to stand back. They did. Then, he too stepped back. Speaking to Staudinger, he pointed at the backs of the prisoners' heads and said something.

Staudinger replied. It was one of the few words of German Nat could recognize.

Nein.

Startled, the other colonel stared at Staudinger in disbelief. He repeated what he'd said before, only louder.

Staudinger shook his head. *Nein.* He said something else that made the jaws of the two soldiers drop in astonishment.

The sharp-chinned colonel became irate. He pointed and shouted and stamped his feet.

Staudinger slowly drew his pistol.

Nat, surprised and pleased, snapped a picture. Staudinger was going to shoot the Germans instead! He was going to pretend to acquiesce, but he would shoot the Germans and rescue the prisoners! And Nat would capture it all on film! Of course! This was his way of proving himself loyal to the underground!

Then, to Nat's horror, Staudinger turned his pistol around, walked over to the other colonel, and handed the pistol to him.

The sharp-chinned colonel was shaking with rage. The two privates were wide-eyed. Even the kneeling prisoners turned to see what was happening.

After handing his gun to the other colonel, Staudinger walked toward the prisoners, and knelt between two of them. He bowed his head and he began praying.

Seven shots rang out in the forest.

The first shot cut short Colonel Staudinger's prayer. The sharp-chinned colonel shoved the body into the open pit with his heel.

Through his tears, Nat captured it all on film.

◈

Nat remained in the thicket until long after the soldiers had covered the grave. He understood now what had taken place on Sunday.

Staudinger had informed the church that he knew he would be called upon to kill those prisoners. He also knew that his faith would not allow him to do it and that by refusing to do so, his life would become forfeit.

Everyone in that barn on Sunday was saying their final good-bye to a man who would give his life rather than kill. A man who by political declaration was their enemy. A man who by the blood of Jesus Christ was their brother.

It was nearly dark before Nat could bring himself to move from that place where Helmut Staudinger died a martyr's death. All of his life Nat had considered himself a Christian. He'd grown up in Sunday school. He'd earned badges for attendance and memorizing Bible verses. He'd listened to sermons, some more than others. He'd invited neighbor friends for high attendance day and passed out fliers for vacation Bible school.

But the greatest Christian lesson he ever learned, he learned sitting alone in a thicket in a French forest on the day Helmut Staudinger willingly gave up his life rather than harm his enemy.

Pushing aside the branches, Nat emerged from the thicket and began to retrace his steps to Allegra's house. He moved from cover to cover as quickly and quietly as he could. It was imperative he avoid contact with anyone. He had no papers. He could not speak the language—French or German. And even if he could, he doubted that he could convince anyone he was an innocent traveler passing through the forest.

He was no farther than a hundred yards from the thicket when he saw someone moving through the forest. A German soldier! He seemed too aware of his surroundings to be taking a casual stroll. Possibly he was meeting someone, or looking for someone. Either way, Nat did not want to be the one he found.

Fortunately, he was positioned behind a tree with a thick trunk when the German first appeared. Nat held his place and waited for the soldier to pass by.

Only a few minutes passed, but it seemed an eternity before the German was out of sight. Nat took a tentative step in the opposite direction.

He'd read about what happened next in books. And he'd seen it portrayed in movies and cartoons. And he'd always thought it was an all-too-convenient and too frequently used tool pulled from a storyteller's bag of tricks. The snapping twig.

However, when the twig he stepped on snapped, there was nothing glib or cartoony about it. It echoed through the forest. The sound struck a chord inside him that charged his body with fear and dread.

He glanced over his shoulder. The German soldier heard it and was staring directly at him. Not just any German. It was the guard who had chased him from the train!

With no other recourse, Nat ran. The German followed right behind him. Nat tried cutting through bushes and between trees knowing that these maneuvers would not shake his pursuer. The sound of his thrashing through the brush could be heard a mile away.

He started to run toward Allegra's house as though he were playing a child's game, and if he could reach the house before the German, he would be safe. Then, common sense returned, and he realized that the last thing he wanted to do was bring suspicion down on Allegra.

He broke another direction, enough to draw suspicion away from Allegra's farm. But now a new dilemma presented itself.

Nat had no idea where he was or where he was going.

And the soldier was closing in on him.

His legs and lungs were beginning to fail. He'd been well enough for a walk and to take some pictures; he hadn't counted on being chased.

The soldier was close enough that Nat could hear his labored breathing.

He looked over his shoulder just as the soldier lunged at him. The German's shoulder rammed into Nat's back and the two of them tumbled to the ground.

Nat was all arms and legs. Shoving, striking, kicking. The German managed to get on top of him. To pin him to the ground. To cover Nat's mouth with one hand.

"Quiet!" the German whispered in English. "Do you want the entire German army coming down upon us?"

Nat's eyes bulged with astonishment.

The German whispered, "I'm Josef! Allegra's Josef!"

Jerry Jupiter stepped from the remains of what had once been an airplane cockpit.

"I thought I'd give what's left of that radio one more try before we go. Still nothing."

Responding to his voice, Lily turned to him. She was startled by his appearance, though he had looked like this since the crash. His hair was disheveled, his face bore black-and-blue spots, one eye was still swollen, and his arms were covered with cuts and abrasions. Jerry had always been concerned with his personal appearance. Every hair in place. The best clothes.

Manicured fingernails, the whole works. Now it looked like he was wearing someone else's shirt. The seams of the sleeves were creeping toward his collarbone.

"What are you looking for?" he asked.

Lily tentatively turned over a piece of sheet music with her foot, unsure what she would find beneath it. "My Bible," she said.

"Your Bible! Honey, this plane and our lives are a wreck! The last thing you need is a Bible!"

"On the contrary," Lily said, unflustered, "during times of crisis, the first thing anyone needs is anything that will bring them closer to God."

Jupiter didn't agree with her, but that didn't stop him from helping her look. "Where did you have it last?"

Lily pointed to the spot where she'd been sitting before the crash.

"Was it in something? A bag or suitcase?"

"No. I'd been reading it."

Jupiter sifted through a large pile. He visibly recoiled at something he uncovered. Lily didn't even want to see what it was.

"Wait!" he cried. Keeping his head back and crinkling his nose, he reached tentatively into the pile. "Is this it?"

"That's it! You found it!"

She gave Jupiter a kiss on the cheek for his effort. He seemed more than pleased with his reward.

Lily opened the cover. Nolan's letter was still inside.

"What's that?" Jupiter asked.

"A letter."

"From whom?"

At first Lily didn't want to tell him. But then she saw no harm in it since Jupiter had also been in correspondence with Nolan.

"Murphy?" Jupiter said. "Well, when you write him back, tell him we might be delayed for his gig."

Jupiter worked his way through the debris and toward the sunlight and fresh air that appeared through the split in the fuselage. Squinting his eyes, he took a step outside then stopped abruptly, blocking the way.

Lily was right behind him. She punched him playfully in the back. "Keep it movin', mister!" she said.

He didn't reply. However, slowly, he moved out of the way. Lily stepped through the opening, glad to be outside once again in the fresh air.

But when she saw what had prompted Jupiter to hesitate in the opening, she wasn't so sure she wanted to be outside.

Two men in ragged German uniforms were pointing rifles at them.

31

Evidently Lieutenant Clay Thomas and the crew of the *California Angel* did not go directly to the plane following the pilot's briefing because when Alex reached the plane she was the first one there. That made what she was about to do that much easier.

She donned Keating's flight suit, packed the Morgan family Bible under her arm, and boarded the plane. Once inside, she looked around. The difference between this plane and the others she'd flown was that this one had guns mounted where the others had empty space. *Shooting and being shot at adds a whole new element to flying a plane,* she mused.

Alex made her way over the bomb bay, past the radioman's station, and into the cockpit. She sat in the pilot's seat with the Bible resting in her lap. For nearly fifteen minutes, she sat there alone just looking at the instruments and remembering what it was like to fly the B-17. Her heart ached over her decision to give it up.

She heard a jeep pull up. With it came male voices. From the sound of them, they were arguing. The tone and words were decidedly hostile. Alex hurriedly slipped on her headgear.

From beyond the cockpit glass she heard, "There he is, Lieutenant Thomas! Keating, sir. Sitting in the copilot's seat!"

Alex kept the back of her head toward the glass.

There was a vocal rumbling as the men climbed aboard the plane. Surly exchanges. This was not a contented crew.

Alex's heart accelerated, knowing that any moment her real presence would be discovered. The feeling reminded her of playing hide-and-seek when she was a little girl. She knew she was about to be found.

"Where you been, Lieutenant?"

She didn't recognize the voice. One of the crew. She kept her back to him, ignoring his question.

"Keating! Why weren't you at the briefing?"

This voice she recognized. It belonged to the man she loved. Still loved, in spite of all that had happened. How could she find fault with him for his response to what she had done when she shared his sentiments? Alex knew Clay would probably never love her, but she couldn't help but still love him.

"Keating! I'm talking to …"

Alex turned and looked at Lieutenant Clay Thomas.

"What? Alex, what are you doing here?"

A face appeared behind him. "A woman! Hey, guys, it isn't Keating! It's a woman!"

From farther back in the plane: "Did you hear that? Upchurch says we've got a woman onboard!"

Clay turned toward the crew. "I'll take care of this! Get to your posts and prepare to take off!"

His order did nothing to stop the flow of traffic to the front of the plane as man after man pushed and shoved to get a glimpse of Alex.

"What are you doing here?" Clay asked.

"I was sent to get Lieutenant Keating," Alex answered. "He was drunk. He can't fly today. He asked me to bring this." She held up the Bible.

"Is that Walt's Bible?" Clay asked.

"I assume the crew told you about it."

Clay nodded, staring at the Bible.

"And for the record, it's the Morgan family Bible."

"Hey, guys!" navigator Geller shouted. "She brought our Bible!"

This news brought general rejoicing throughout the plane, in stark contrast to the anger obvious a short time earlier.

"You know," Clay said, "this Bible has become a good-luck charm for these boys. They didn't want to fly without it."

"I know."

His grateful expression changed to one of suspicion when he realized she was wearing a flight suit.

"You didn't come just to bring the Bible, did you?"

Alex looked her former instructor in the eye. "You need a copilot," she said.

"Out of the question! Out … of … the … question!"

"Clay, you know I can do it!"

"Yes, I know you can do it, but that's not the point!"

"And you don't have a copilot and won't be able to get one on this short notice!" She didn't know that for sure, but she was hoping that was true. The look on Clay's face seemed to confirm she had guessed correctly.

"Alex …" he said, shaking his head.

"And who better to fly with you than me? We've logged how many hours together?"

"Alex …"

"And you heard what Major Harrison said. This mission is crucial. You need every plane in the air!"

"Alex!" His voice was getting louder.

"I even know the mission and the targets. I was listening outside the briefing door!"

"Alex, that's not the point!" he shouted.

"What is the point then?" she shouted back. "You admit I'm qualified. We've flown together. I know the mission. If that's not the point, what is? The fact that I'm a woman? If you didn't think women could do this, why did you spend all those hours training us?"

"This is different!"

"Different? How? Because we'll be shot at? Well, let me ask you this, Lieutenant Thomas. How is my training different from any other pilot who flies out of here on his first mission? Everyone has a first time to face combat!"

"Are you finished?" Clay asked.

"Yes," Alex said reluctantly. "Unless you can come up with any other feeble reasons why I shouldn't be your copilot. I'm sure there are a hundred more we haven't covered."

"How about this feeble reason?" Clay said. "You're not authorized to fly this mission. Do you know how much trouble I could get into if I let you fly with us?"

"I'm not flyin' with no woman," Upchurch said.

Jankowski poked his face in. "How about if you just deliver Lieutenant Morgan's Bible and let us go about our business?"

Alex held the Bible in her arms. She said, "As I told Lieutenant Thomas, this is the Morgan *family* Bible. It belongs as much to me as it did to Walt."

"Are you Walt's wife?" a voice whose face she couldn't see asked.

"I'm his sister."

Jankowski: "Are you saying that unless we let you fly with us, you won't let us take the Bible?"

Alex hesitated. Then, she said, "No, that's not what I'm saying. You can take the Bible with you whether I go or not."

A head poked through the bodies crowding the door. "That's

Lieutenant Morgan's sister, all right!" he said. "That's exactly the kind of thing he would have said!" A hand and arm broke through the clog of humanity. "My name's John Sabala, ma'am. Pleased to meet you."

Alex smiled and shook the hand.

"We're not going anywhere, boys," Clay said. "We don't have a copilot."

"Can she really fly, sir?" Sabala asked.

Clay looked at Alex. "Yes, she can."

"Maybe those little planes," Upchurch said. "But not a B-17. No woman can fly a B-17."

From the change of expression on Clay's face it was evident the bombardier's comment did not set with him well. "I beg to differ with you," he said sternly. "Before coming here, I trained several women how to fly the B-17. And every single one of them is a top-notch pilot. But none of them is better than this woman sitting right here. She can fly circles around most male pilots I've seen."

"Yeoow!" Sabala shouted. "I feel lucky! We've got the Bible and we've got a Morgan in the cockpit! I haven't felt this good since ... for a long time! I say we go deliver a few surprise packages to der führer."

The tail gunner managed to whip up general agreement among the crew, though not all of them were as enthusiastic.

"Upchurch?" Clay asked the most skeptical of them. "What do you say?"

The bombardier studied Alex for a long moment. "You'd better not get us killed," he said. He returned to his station.

Sabala could be heard up and down the plane. "Everybody out! Everybody out!"

"What is it, Sabala?" Clay asked.

"Tradition, sir. You have to hold the Bible at the hatch and each of us touches it before we get aboard."

Clay was about to object that they didn't have time until he saw Upchurch solemnly leading the way out the hatch.

After everyone had touched the Bible and was back on board, Clay and Alex completed the preflight checklist. Clay was shaking his head.

"What?" Alex asked.

"I'm going to get into so much trouble for this."

"Would you prefer that I leave?"

Clay looked over at her and smiled. "No."

"Then we'd better start taxiing. Major Harrison is coming up fast in a jeep."

Clay swung the copilot's side of the bomber away from the approaching major. When Harrison waved his arms at the plane, Clay responded by giving him the thumb's-up sign.

"Do you think he knows?" Alex asked.

"We'll find out when we land."

Nat was in agony. In some ways it would have gone better for him had the German guard been just that and not Josef. For although Nat had been led safely back to Allegra's house, he was now forced to watch Josef and Allegra giggle and cuddle and kiss.

The growing strength of his jealousy when he saw Josef with her only served to confirm that he had indeed fallen in love.

Nat's agony was compounded further by the fact that he liked Josef. It was easy to see why the locals held him in such high regard and why Allegra was attracted to him. He was friendly, cheerful, and considerate of others to a fault. What Allegra and the others had failed to mention was that he was also German.

The uniform he wore was a disguise, for he no longer served in the German army. However, inside the German uniform was a

German body. And Germans were the enemy. Only now—first with Staudinger and now with Josef—Nat was discovering that the enemy had a human face.

"The thing you have to understand," Josef said, shoving back straight black hair that fell in his face every time he looked down, "is that not all Germans are Nazis."

They sat on the floor around a Parcheesi board. Allegra and Josef shared a corner of the board, their shoulders touching. Nat sat across from them.

Nat looked up with a startled expression. Had Josef read his mind? He had just been thinking, *If only Nolan could see me now. Here I am sitting on the floor playing Parcheesi with a Nazi.*

Josef was busy rolling the dice. Nat's startled look faded before Josef looked up. As the dice tumbled across the board, Josef said, "What Hitler is doing now to Europe, he first did to Germany. He terrorized, intimidated, murdered, and beat his own people into submission—anyone who opposed him or spoke out against him. My own professor, for example, Dr. Helmut Thielicke, was dismissed from his professorship at Heidelberg for criticizing Nazi policies. He can no longer teach and is forbidden to publish."

"Is he still in Germany?" Nat asked, watching Josef move his pieces.

"He's the pastor of St. Mark's Church in Stuttgart and under constant watch. And there are others. Thousands of others. Some who even now are in jail and await execution for opposing Hitler, such as Professor Bonhoeffer. I studied under him at Finkenwalde for a time. A very godly man. Our daily routine included meditation, prayer, Bible study, practice in homiletics, recreation, and preaching in nearby churches and villages. That was, until the Gestapo shut us down."

Allegra reached down and moved one of Josef's pieces back a

space. "I'm going to assume your mind is not on the game and that this was an honest mistake," she said with a smile.

Josef laughed. With a head nod toward Allegra that sent his black hair flying, he said to Nat, "You can't slip anything by her. She's ruthless when playing Parcheesi."

"I am, you know," Allegra said. To Josef, "Tell him Professor Bonhoeffer's prophecy."

It took a moment for Josef to recognize what she was referring to. When he did, he said, "That was over ten years ago! Professor Bonhoeffer said, 'Should we be surprised if again days come for our Church in which the blood of martyrs will be demanded? If some of us really should have the faith and the honor and the loyalty to shed this blood, then indeed it will not be the innocent and shining blood of the first witnesses.'"

Nat sat back. "Well, if there is so much public opposition to Hitler, why don't the Germans run him out of the country?"

Josef sat back as well. He studied the man sitting opposite him before answering. "I think it is very difficult for anyone who does not know this sense of menace to imagine it. This feeling of oppression and fear. One has to feel it, not just hear about it, to understand what it does to a people.

"For instance, it's hard to describe the sense of oppression one feels every time he steps out of his house. And it doesn't let up until he has closed the door behind him again. You cannot simply describe what it is like to live in a world where you are always under suspicion, where anyone who does not like you can cause you harm with a simple accusation.

"You don't know what it is like to live in a city of whisperers. Of midnight arrests. Of daily torture and rumors of torture. Where stories of people who have been forced to swallow castor oil or eat old socks at the whim of any man in authority are an everyday occurrence. It weighs down a person's soul."

Josef's eyes glazed over as he went back in his mind to a day of unspeakable terror.

"Do you want to hear about the day when this terror made a most lasting impression on me? I was twelve years old and was visiting a cousin in Poland. German troops were there and at first I thought that it was tremendous that we had liberated the Poles and here were our men in their smart uniforms and their polished boots all the way up to their knees, marching down the center of the street, providing order to a city that we had been told was previously in chaos.

"My cousin had a friend, a boy of about fourteen. We were walking down the street and we saw two German officers walking toward us on the pavement. Now there was a rule that when the people of the city met Germans, the people had to get off the pavement to let the Germans pass.

"My cousin knew the rule. He stepped off the pavement. I did too, though only because he did. His friend didn't. One of those soldiers pulled out his pistol and shot that boy straight through the head. And my cousin's friend fell down dead."

Szczepkowski, Nat thought. *Only worse.*

The three of them sat around the board in silence. It was Allegra's turn to roll the dice. She held them quietly in her hand. After a brief time, Josef continued.

"How can a people live with that kind of terror and not be intimidated? It is this kind of intimidating terror that will be the Nazi's lasting achievement. For they have demonstrated what we all have feared—that when the issue is forced, our laws and our beliefs that we are basically good people at heart are not enough to keep our human bestiality in check."

Allegra never threw the dice. The Parcheesi game, which was intended to provide a diversion from the war, had failed to do so tonight.

Nat sat on the front porch step. It was the first evening when it was warm enough to do so. Even so, the coolness of the boards seeped through his pants and chilled him. The sun had just disappeared behind the trees leaving a glowing twilight in its wake.

He heard the sound of the door swing open behind him. Allegra stepped out of the house. She was alone.

"Am I disturbing you?" she asked.

"No. Not at all."

"If you'd prefer to be alone ..."

"No. Please join me. I thought you and Josef might like some privacy."

Gathering her dress around her, Allegra sat on the step next to him. "That's very kind of you, Nathaniel. But Josef hasn't slept for two days. He went to bed."

Nat knew better than to ask where Josef had been or what he'd been doing. But with those topics ruled out, he found himself searching for something to say. Though he didn't think of himself as a joker, he found humor useful. When you can't think of something to say, say nothing at all, only say it humorously.

"I thought he was tired from chasing me all over France."

Allegra laughed.

Nat drank in the sound. She had the most intoxicating laughter. He wanted to think of something else funny to say for purely selfish reasons; not so much to make her happy, but so that he could drink in more of her laughter.

"What do you think of him?" Allegra asked.

Her question made Nat smile.

"Did I say something funny?" she asked.

Nat was astonished by her question. "You mean to tell me you can hear someone smile?"

"Well, yes. Sort of. Your lips make a tiny smacking sound when they part."

"And you hear that?"

Allegra smiled.

"Amazing."

Nat sat there for a moment smiling and frowning and smiling and frowning. He succeeded in what he was attempting to do.

Allegra laughed. "You're a big tease, Nathaniel Morgan. And you never answered my question."

"You noticed that, did you?"

Her smile faded. "You don't like Josef?"

"What's not to like?" Nat teased. "He's Robin Hood and John the Baptist all rolled into one."

Allegra laughed. "That's how you see him?"

"What other way is there? On Sunday when all the people spoke of him like he was something of a saint, I thought they were exaggerating. Come to find out, they don't know the half of it."

The smile on Allegra's face colored with concern. "There's bitterness in your voice."

Nat looked away.

"Nathaniel?"

"Well, how am I to compete against a living legend?" he blurted out.

"Compete? Why would you want to compete with Josef?"

"That's my question, exactly!" Nat said. "Why would anyone want to compete with him? We should be thinking about how we can be more like him."

Allegra shook her head. "Nathaniel, you're confusing me. Why would you want to compete with Josef? What would you compete for?"

"For you," Nat said softly. "When it comes to you, how can I possibly compete with Josef?"

Allegra's hand rose to her mouth. It failed to cover the sound of her gasp.

"He's perfect," Nat said. "If you didn't marry him, I would."

Allegra laughed. A small tear dangled on the lip of an eyelid.

"It's just that …" Nat's thoughts jumbled in his mouth. They were all trying to come out at once. He stopped, paused, and then started again. "Everything Josef and Staudinger and you are doing here puts me to shame. I mean, the kind of things that you're doing here sound like my family's heritage, the stories I've heard of Morgans all my life. Spies. Missionaries. Pirates. Civil War preachers. And on and on. Stories of courageous faith, people risking their lives for a belief. This is what Josef is doing right now." He chuckled. "In San Diego, we don't need that kind of courage to go to church. We just hop in the car. Consequently, I bundled up all those stories that I heard and put them on the same shelf with *Moby Dick* and *Treasure Island*." He paused. Then, very softly continued, "And now I find myself among people who are dying or willing to die for their Christian faith. And I … well, I feel ashamed."

Allegra listened thoughtfully.

"So now you know," Nat said. "I wasn't going to tell you. Even now, I'm not sure why I did."

She reached over and put her hand on his arm. He closed his eyes at the sensation her touch created in him. Then he wondered if she could hear eyes close too.

"I'm glad you told me," she said. "But you have no need to feel ashamed. You have shown great courage doing the things you've done."

Nat shook his head. "I've shown nothing of the kind. If I hadn't been kidnapped, I wouldn't even be here. And if I had been told what Staudinger was really going to do …"

He stopped and pondered.

"… well … I don't know if I would have agreed to take the pictures or not. I probably would have gone because you couldn't have convinced me that he was really going to do what he did."

Allegra squeezed his arm. "I think you're more like your ancestors than you care to admit."

Nat didn't agree.

"Let me put it to you this way," she said. "If you could do something significant that would stop Hitler in his tracks, would you do it?"

Nat thought before answering. "Before I came here, I really hadn't given Hitler much thought. I joined the army because at my age I knew I had no choice. Even when I was in northern Africa and Italy, Hitler was nothing more than a major inconvenience in my life. If the decision had been left to me, I would have ordered all of our troops home and let whoever was left behind fight it out among themselves."

"And now?"

"Now?" Nat's voice grew heavy with emotion. "Now I want to do everything possible to stop that madman, not only for France and England and all the other countries he's threatening, but after hearing what Josef said tonight, I want to stop him for the sake of the German people as well."

"Spoken like a true Morgan," Allegra said.

It was Nat's turn to smile.

"I shouldn't tell you this …" she said.

"Might as well," Nat replied, "it seems there are no secrets tonight."

Allegra blushed. Color rose in her neck and cheeks and Nat loved it.

"Ever since I was a little girl … no, I can't tell you."

Nat laughed. "Stop teasing and tell me!"

"All right." She took a deep breath. It did nothing to lessen the color in her cheeks. "Ever since I was a little girl, I always dreamed I would one day marry a Morgan."

"Really?"

Allegra nodded an embarrassed nod.

"Why?"

"Of course you know it started with your Grandfather Jesse and the espionage during the Great War that first introduced me to your family. And then I met your Aunt Katy. And well, when we looked into your background, it was your whole family heritage," Allegra said. "I was fascinated with the men and women in your past. So colorful. So courageous and dynamic. And, well, you know how little girls are. I just always thought I would someday meet and marry a Morgan."

Nat shook his head. "Afraid all the good ones have already been taken," he said.

Allegra slapped him playfully. "Will you stop that? Do you want the truth?"

"Why not?"

Her voice was much quieter now. "When I first heard that you were in Italy, I wondered if God was bringing my Morgan to me and I had been too hasty in agreeing to marry Josef."

"But then I arrived and that broke that fantasy bubble."

He expected another slap. Instead, she slipped her arm inside his and squeezed. She said, "You are more courageous than you give yourself credit for, Nathaniel Morgan. And if I wasn't already spoken for, I would have concluded that God had indeed answered my prayer."

Nat felt the warmth of her body pressing against his arm. He closed his eyes to savor the feeling. The scent of her hair made his senses reel. All at once he was enamored and confused. How could God make him feel this way about someone whom he couldn't have?

But he had her for this moment. And he was going to enjoy every bit of it.

His moment turned out to be a very short one. For he sensed something else. Another presence. Behind them. He turned his head slightly and out of the corner of his eye he could see Josef standing in the window watching them.

32

The flak was thick, the black smoke even thicker. As the *California Angel* approached their bomb run, the twenty-nine-ton aircraft was tossed about in the air like a toy. Not only was it in danger of being blown out of the sky, but it was in danger of being knocked into other bombers in the formation.

"We're up next!" Clay shouted to Upchurch.

The bombardier signaled he was ready. "Just get me over the target and I'll do the rest!"

Clay glanced over at Alex. "If only Loretta and Virginia could see you now," he said.

This was indeed more than Alex had bargained for. They were just approaching their bombing run and already her arms were trembling from overexertion, her hands and fingers ached from gripping the controls, and her legs were cramping.

Next to her Clay looked in slightly better shape. His massive gloved hands maintained tighter control and though his face glistened with sweat, he didn't seem to be as tired as Alex felt. All she wanted to do was drop the payload and head for home.

"Coming up on the target!" Clay said.

WHAM!

The plane was suddenly thrust upward, nose up.

"We've been hit! We've been hit!" someone yelled over the intercom. Alex wasn't familiar enough with their voices to know who was yelling. It didn't matter. First priority was to get the nose down before the plane stalled.

Straining with all her might, Alex fought to counter the blow. It wasn't enough. She strained harder, crying out from the exertion.

Slowly, the plane responded. The nose came down. The plane leveled off. Alex's arms were shaking involuntarily. It seemed as though she alone muscled the plane into line. Then, she noticed something wet and sticky all over her gloves.

They were spattered with blood.

She looked over at Clay. Her heart caught in her throat. He'd been hit! His hands were limp at his sides. His face and uniform was splattered with blood. His head had fallen backward and his eyes were closed.

Alex wanted to reach for him. She couldn't. She had to control the plane. "Someone get up here!" she shouted. "Lieutenant Thomas has been hit."

"Say again?" came a voice over the intercom.

"Thomas has been hit! Get up here!" Alex screamed.

"Bombardier to copilot, how bad is it?"

Alex looked over at Clay. He was making moaning sounds. "Pretty bad. Someone get up here!"

Radio operator Dooly appeared between the seats with a first-aid kit in his hands. One glance at the blood-splattered cockpit and he shouted, "Lord o' mercy!"

"Does the pilot have control of the plane?" Upchurch shouted over the intercom.

"Negative. I have control," Alex replied.

Silence.

"Then we're pulling out of the run?" Upchurch said.

Alex looked over at Clay.

It's always the best who die.

Tears clouded her vision. She wanted to go to him. To help him. To hold him.

"Are we pulling out? I need to know!" Upchurch shouted.

It was one of the hardest things she had ever done in her life. But if she didn't do it, she would doom them all. She forced Clay Thomas from her mind. She checked the instruments and their position. She did a visual check on all four engines.

"Copilot to whoever's back there. Were we hit bad?"

Several reports came in. Minor damage only.

"Copilot to bombardier. We're going in!"

Upchurch's voice came over the intercom. "I think we ought to pull out. You won't be able ..."

Alex shouted, "I said we're going in! I'll get you over that target. You just make sure you hit it."

Silence.

"Did you hear me, Upchurch?"

Hesitation, then, "Roger. We're going in."

Over the intercom Alex recognized Sabala's voice. To no one in particular, he said, "That's Walt's sister all right." Then he began to pray for God to protect them.

They were over the target.

"She's all yours, Upchurch!" Alex said.

While hundreds of bombs rained down from all the planes in their formation, Alex turned to Dooly, fearing the worst. "How is he?"

"I've had better days," Clay responded for himself.

His head was back and his eyes were closed, but he managed a grin. Alex closed her eyes briefly. *Thank you, Lord,* she said silently.

Dooly said, "His wounds aren't all that bad. A lot of them all up and down his side. He may have a concussion." Alex acknowledged his report and he returned to the radio.

"Looks like you're going to have to drive us home, Miss Alex."

His eyes were open. He was looking at her. It had been a long time since he'd called her that. A fresh flood of tears rushed to her eyes. The words warmed her heart, but she didn't need the tears. Not now.

"That's what I'm here for," she replied.

It's always the best who die.

"God help us, not today," she muttered.

"What did you say?"

"I said God and I are going to get you home."

Clay smiled. "I trust you both."

Over the intercom came shouts and whoops. Intermixed among them was Upchurch's voice commenting on the plumes of smoke below, "Berlin never looked so pretty."

"Let's get out of here," Clay said.

WHAM!

Another hit! This one nearly flipped the plane over on its back. The plane in the formation beneath them came into view. They were falling on top of it! Alex pulled back, fighting the controls, straining, muttering, "Keep it up just long enough for …"

The plane slipped from beneath them.

Alex relaxed and let the plane slip into its natural arch. Now she could pull out of it gradually. But they had fallen from formation.

Easy prey for fighters.

"Can you get us back into formation?" Clay asked. He blinked unfocused eyes. His voice was thick. He placed his hands on the controls to try to help her. They kept slipping off as he slid in and out of consciousness.

A trail of smoke from engine number two caught Alex's eye. It sputtered and died. Alex's eyes and mind and hands raced to implement fire procedure and compensate for the loss of power.

The engine died peacefully. But they'd lost considerable altitude. Their formation moved silently homeward above them. Her eyes fixed on the empty slot that they had recently occupied; she pulled the nose up and headed for it.

They were going to make it. Alex lined up the plane and radioed the formation that they were preparing to rejoin. She got only static in response.

A burst of gunfire ripped through the fuselage.

The intercom came alive with noise.

"They're firin' at us!"

"What are they doing?"

"Hey! We're one of you!"

"Fall away!" The voice came from beside her. Clay's eyes were open. He recognized their situation. "Fall away!" he said again. "Get out of here!"

Alex pushed forward the controls and descended.

"They won't let you back in," Clay said.

"Why not?"

"It's a German ruse. They use captured planes to come up from below looking like stragglers, then they open fire. Did you contact them by radio?"

"I tried. Got no response." Into the intercom: "Dooly! Why can't I get through to the formation?"

"Don't know, ma'am," Dooly said. "Checking."

A few moments later.

"Nothin's going out, ma'am. Beats me. I can't figure it out."

Alex looked over at Clay. "Looks like we're on our own." Like a deformed kitten they'd been kicked out of the litter.

"Fighters!" Sabala cried.

The next thing they knew three German fighters were swarming all over them.

The B-17's guns came alive in response. Overhead the formation flew on without them. No one came to their rescue.

Inside the plane it was bedlam. Shouts. Screams. Guns barking. Shells whizzing. Metal ripping.

"We've been hit!"

Number four engine took a direct hit. It burst into flame. Her hands a blur, Alex switched the engine off and tried to extinguish the fire. They lost the engine, not the fire.

"They're pickin' us apart!"

"We've been hit again!"

"He's comin' your way! Get 'em! Get 'em!"

"No good! No good!"

The plane shuddered. Riddled with shells.

Alex checked the burning engine. It was still ablaze.

She knew they probably wouldn't hear her, still she said, "Hold on, boys!"

She flipped the plane over on its back and into a spin.

Frantic voices jammed the intercom.

"We're goin' down! We're goin' down!"

"O Lord, please help us!"

Beneath them the ground spiraled as it rushed toward them. A high pitch whined in their ears as the plane picked up speed.

The fire in engine four went out. But there were only two left. Would they be enough?

Alex pulled the plane out of the spin. The altimeter continued to twirl at a frightening speed. She pulled back on the controls. Not enough. She wasn't strong enough. She screamed and pulled harder. Her arms shook. Her stomach muscles cramped as did her legs.

Still not enough. They weren't going to make it.

Closing her eyes, she pulled harder.

The nose pulled up slightly. Then a little more. The controls were becoming more responsive. She opened her eyes. Next to her, Clay's huge hands gripped his controls. His eyes were squeezed shut, sweat poured down the sides of his face as he pulled with all his might.

Cheers echoed through the plane. The plane leveled off several hundred feet from the ground.

"They're not chasin' us!" Sabala shouted. "They thought we were goin' down!"

"So did I," Upchurch cried. "That spin saved our skins! Outstanding maneuver, Miss Morgan!"

"Didn't I tell you she was the best?" Clay said weakly.

The remainder of the flight home was just like they had practiced so many times over Lockbourne, only they were flying a bullet-riddled aircraft with only two engines.

They sent up a red flare when the field came into view, indicating they had wounded onboard. Plans were made to sneak Alex off the plane and away before anyone was any the wiser. With the bulk of the formation landing shortly before them, they didn't think it would prove too difficult.

Alex had never been so glad to land a plane in all her life. Bringing the aircraft to a stop, she switched off the power and slumped back in her seat.

Clay looked over at her. His eyes were glassy from pain and loss of blood. "It was a little rough there, but I guess you did well enough to earn a passing grade."

"Thank you, sir."

"So where do you go from here?"

Alex sighed. "Back to Lockbourne. They're playing some music there that I have to face." She smiled weakly.

Clay's eyes were closed again, so she didn't know if he heard her or not. Sabala appeared.

"Hurry, Miss Morgan! We got to get you out of here fast!"

Alex scooped up the family Bible and handed it to Sabala. Then, she followed him to the rear hatch.

The rest of the crew were gathered tightly around the hatch. She descended into the middle of them. All at the same time they congratulated her for getting them back alive.

"Here," Sabala said. He handed her the Bible. "Take it home where it belongs."

Alex took the Bible and held it close.

"God sure knew what he was doing when he sent you to us," Sabala said. "When we needed one the most, he sent us a real *California angel*."

The three of them huddled with their backs to each other. They were forbidden to speak or move. Through the jagged entrance of the damp and dark cave that had provided them shelter for more than a week, they could see the city of Palermo glistening in the sunlight. So tantalizingly close, yet so far.

In what little snippets of conversation that had passed between them, Lily, Lohmann, and Jupiter had concluded that the two Germans had been cut off from their unit when the Allied forces took the island. From their ragged and hungry appearance, they had been hiding in the hills ever since.

Having confiscated everything that the three survivors had gathered from the wreck, the two Germans took turns combing through the ruins themselves. They showed total disregard for the dead as they turned over everything looking for every usable supply.

One of the soldiers was decidedly older than the other. He barked the orders and the younger man carried them out, usually without question. There were, however, occasional incidents when the younger captor challenged his superior directly, or disobeyed him discreetly.

When she first emerged from the plane, in spite of Lily's objections, the superior had tossed her Bible into some brush as something they didn't need. Two days later, while the superior was gone, the younger German produced the Bible and handed it to Lily. He had retrieved it from the bushes for her.

When the young captor's attention was elsewhere, Jupiter whispered, "I think he likes you."

"Of course he likes her, you idiot!" Lohmann whispered in reply.

"What I meant was maybe we could use …"

The return of the older German cut short the exchange.

On another occasion, Jupiter whispered, "Do you think we ought to tell them who I am?"

"What good would *that* do?" Lohmann asked.

"Maybe they would recognize me! I have fans all over the world, you know."

To Lily's surprise, Lohmann agreed. "Maybe we *should* tell them who you are." Then he added, "Then, maybe they'll shoot *you* first!"

Lily spent most of her days making the most of her time. She thought about her family, sang songs in her mind, and prayed for her captors. Her thinking on this latter activity was that maybe God could do something to influence the men from inside their minds.

A couple of times her captors caught her looking at them. Of course, they had no idea what she was doing, but the superior didn't like it one bit. Whenever he caught her staring at him, he shouted at her and wouldn't stop until she looked elsewhere. The younger German didn't seem to mind the stares. Sometimes, when his superior was away, he'd lock eyes with her. On several occasions they communicated this way for minutes at a time.

From these silent talks Lily decided that their younger captor meant them no harm. Upon further reflection, she concluded that he was as much of a prisoner in these hills as they were.

But things were heating up. Their supplies were depleted and none of them had eaten anything for several days. The two Germans were having more frequent and more heated arguments, sometimes staring or pointing at their prisoners. Though Lily could not understand what they were saying, it became evident that something was going to break soon. The question was, which way?

One afternoon while the younger German cleaned his rifle with a small oily rag, he began to hum. Lily didn't know which surprised her more, the fact that she recognized the tune, or the quality of the young German's voice.

He was a couple of months past the season, but there was no mistaking the song. He was humming "Silent Night." Lily began humming along with him.

Instantly, the German superior pointed his rifle at her and ordered her to stop humming. The younger man glared at him and said something presumably in Lily's defense. There was an angry exchange of words between them. Then, with a flip of his hands, the superior capitulated.

Leaving his gun, the younger man approached Lily and sat a few feet opposite her. He began humming again. She joined him. At the end of the verse, he smiled.

With a nod, Lily encouraged him to begin again. He did. This time, she sang harmony. The tone of their voices blended magically.

He began again, singing the words in German. Lily sang with him, harmonizing in English. The sweet words of the melody of Christmas filled the cave.

On the third verse, Jupiter joined in. At once both Germans ordered him to stop. It was the first thing they'd agreed upon in days.

When the song was finished, Lily pointed to the young German. "You sing something."

He looked at her with a puzzled expression.

Using her hand, she simulated sound coming out of her throat and mouth then pointed at him. "You … sing … something."

He nodded in understanding.

Lily didn't recognize the song, but the tenor voice that echoed in the cave was fabulous. She lost herself in sound. And for a few glorious moments she forgot she was a prisoner.

After the song, the young German motioned to her. He repeated her hand movements, throat to mouth and out. He wanted her to sing a song.

Lily glanced over at the older German man. He didn't seem to object. So she sat up straight and began to sing:

> Underneath the lantern by the barrack gate,
> 'Twas there that you whispered tenderly,
> Darling I remember the way you used to wait,
> That you loved me, You'd always be,
> My Lili of the lamplight, My own Lili Marlene.
>
> Orders came for sailing somewhere over there,
> All confined to barracks was more than I could bear;
> I knew you were waiting in the street,
> I heard your feet, But could not meet,
> My Lili of the lamplight, My own Lili Marlene.
>
> When we are marching in the mud and cold,
> And when my pack seems more than I can hold,
> My love for you renews my might,
> I'm warm again, My pack is light,
> It's you Lili Marlene, It's you Lili Marlene.

Sitting a few feet in front of her, the younger German held his hands to his mouth. Tears streaked his cheeks. Lily was moved by his response. She looked over at the young man's superior. He was crying too.

N

Josef and Nat crossed over into Germany. They traveled mostly at night. Josef wore his uniform and Nat's head was bandaged. He wore civilian clothes.

Their story was that Nat had been working undercover with the French Maquis when he sustained a head injury. The blow rendered him senseless. It had also deprived him of his ability to speak or communicate in any way. Josef was taking him to the hospital in Stuttgart in hopes that the doctors there would be able to help him regain his senses so that he could tell what he knew about the underground activity.

They had a cover story about how they lost their transport papers too. If either of these stories failed to satisfy any authorities they might happen upon, they were dead in the water. For the most part, they were counting on Josef's familiarity with German army procedure and his quick wit. All Nat had to do was act goofy.

In reality, their mission was twofold. Their destination was indeed the Stuttgart hospital. Once there, they would meet their contact, who had information and directions about concentration camps where thousands of Jews and enemies of the führer were being held, tortured, and killed. Nat's task was to photograph these sites and get the photos into the hands of the Americans.

It was the hope of the anti-Hitler forces within Germany that these pictures along with the capture or assassination of Hitler would encourage American leaders to settle for no less than the full unconditional surrender of Germany.

The second part of the trip was personal. Josef's family lived in Stuttgart. He also had a younger brother in the hospital there who had sustained a battle wound, though Josef didn't know the extent of the injury. His older brother had been killed in Poland. Two older sisters had both been recruited and trained to fire antiaircraft artillery at Allied bombers. One sister had been killed. The other was still alive, at least the last he heard.

"You'll like my brother," Josef said to Nat over the rattle of bicycle wheels on a dirt road. They had found the two bicycles abandoned in a forest ten miles down the road.

"What makes you say that?"

"He's very much like you. Always the joker."

"That's how you see me?"

Josef grinned. "You have a humor inside you that has to come out or you'll pop. I don't mean any offense by it. I love my brother for that very reason. He makes me laugh."

Nat had never thought of himself as being a joker. Maybe it was a cultural thing. Josef probably thought all Americans were funny.

They had moved along the roads with surprising ease. Everywhere they passed showed evidence of massive pullbacks. Abandoned equipment. Lack of security. And, worst of all, great destruction. From the looks of things, the German army was employing a limited scorched-earth policy as they retreated.

Much of their trip had been in silence. There wasn't a lot to talk about; the two men had only known each other a short time. And what they had in common—Allegra—was something of a minefield between them. Josef had said nothing about seeing Nat and Allegra on the porch step. And Nat didn't know whether to say anything or not.

"God have mercy!"

Josef skidded to a sudden stop. Nat rolled past him a ways before he could stop.

"What is it?"

Josef was staring into the distance. Nat followed his gaze. Stuttgart. Columns of black smoke rose from the city. A black cloud hovered over it.

Visibly shaken, Josef said, "Nat, I hope you never know what it's like to be ashamed of your own country, to have your patriotism turned into bitter contempt."

Josef dismounted the bicycle. He let it fall into the ditch on the side of the road. Like a man whose faculties are possessed, he walked numbly toward the city, unable to take his eyes off the columns of smoke.

Nat ditched his bicycle too and walked beside him.

With trembling voice, Josef said, "Do you realize the price the German people have paid because of one madman? Do you have any idea what my family has been through? When the Nazis rose to power, their party slogan was *'Kinder, Kirche, Kuche'*—child, church, and kitchen. Do you know what that has translated into?

"Hot water two days a week. The inability to provide children with ordinary things like shoes and clothes. A diet of vegetables, black rye bread, dabs of butter, and one egg a week. Women working in factories during the day and running their households at night. Boys in soldier uniforms freezing to death on the Russian steppes for want of oil and warm clothing. Bitter men sitting on the front lines, their entire existence revolving around their ration of four cigarettes a day. Schoolgirls boarding buses, transported to schools where they learn to fire massive guns. Mothers pressing their ears against radio speakers listening to forbidden broadcasts and hoping their children don't let their secret out in innocent conversation. Churches and seminaries boarded shut. Holy men of God killed for preaching truth."

Josef stared at Nat with vacuous eyes. He pointed toward the city. "This is the people who gave the world Martin Luther, the great German reformer! This is the people who gave the world the printing presses that put Bibles in the hands of the common man!"

This was a Josef Nat had never seen before. Enraged with passion. Angry. Frustrated.

With fists raised high, Josef shouted at the sky, "I am German! This is my heritage! Do you hear me? I am a German!"

He sank to his knees, his head bowed, but the rage wasn't gone. It was only temporarily contained as he said, "I will never, never, NEVER forgive the Nazis for what they have done to my people and to my land."

They traveled the rest of the way into the city in silence. Beginning at the outskirts and extending into the heart of Stuttgart, street after street was nothing more than ruins. Josef pointed out places and buildings that had once been memorable parts of his childhood. People passed them, walking aimlessly, pushing carts packed with all their belongings.

One woman was rushing around but going nowhere. Frantic and on the verge of hysteria, she held her hands to her head, shouting at everyone she saw, "The lines are broken! The Americans are coming! The Americans are coming!"

Josef and Nat exchanged glances, wondering if it was true.

As they rounded the corner of the street upon which Josef grew up, he reached into his pocket for the front door key. As the street came into view, it was clear that he wouldn't need it.

The entire block had been leveled. Where once stood his house, cement steps led up to nothing. The destruction was so complete, the foundation was barely recognizable.

Nat watched helplessly as Josef stood on the top step holding a key to a door that no longer existed, leading to a house—a home—that was no more.

The key clanged on the cement step. Overcome, Josef sat down on the front step. He stared blankly and said, "I don't even know where to begin looking for them, or whether there's even anyone left to be found."

Nat took a seat beside him. He didn't say anything because he didn't know what to say. So he sat there and tried to imagine what he would feel like if the doorstep upon which they were sitting belonged to his home in San Diego.

After a time, Josef turned to Nat and said, "Promise me something?"

Josef looked so forlorn, Nat was ready to agree to promise him anything.

"Take good care of Allegra for me."

"What?"

"There's no reason for us to continue with our mission," he said. "And I won't be going back with you."

"You can't give up now," Nat said. "The best thing we can do is get these pictures taken. If only half of what you say is true …"

"The mission's over!" Josef said.

"You don't know that! Let's go to the hospital and meet our contact." Nat's face brightened with hope. "And your brother! Your brother is there. Maybe he'll know where your parents went!"

Josef pointed into the distance. "See that?" he said. "That building?"

Nat looked in the direction Josef was pointing.

"The red brick building. Five stories."

Nat nodded. In reality it was the shell of a five-story building that had been completely gutted.

"That's the hospital," Josef said.

Nat was speechless.

"I've got to stay here," Josef said. "I've got to find my family. To rebuild, if that's possible."

"All right," Nat said, "I'll agree with you about the mission. For now, it's over. But you can't do this to Allegra. She loves you. She'll want to help you rebuild."

"That's true," Josef said. "That is, if we give her a choice. But we're not going to give her a choice."

"What?"

"Look around you!" Josef shouted. "This is no place for a blind woman! There's nothing but rubble. Chaos. She can't function in a world like this. Look at her house! Everything is neat. Orderly. In place. She depends on that to survive."

Josef's words took Nat aback. Allegra was blind. It was just that she was so independent, so functional in her environment, he had to be reminded of it.

"Besides," Josef said, "she loves you and you love her."

Nat tried to deny it. His words tripped on themselves and stumbled out in a meaningless babble.

Josef's laughter brought him up short. "Do you realize how many years I have envied you?"

"What are you talking about? We've known each other only a few days!"

"No, my friend, I've known you for as long as I've known Allegra. Do you know how many times she has told me about the Morgans? How can I possibly compete for her affections with a family such as yours?"

Was he mocking Nat? These were Nat's own words, the ones he'd spoken on Allegra's porch, only turned around! He looked for signs of bitterness or mockery on Josef's face. There were none.

"I heard what she told you on the front porch step."

Ah! So we're finally getting around to it.

"She has always known she would marry a Morgan."

Nat's brow wrinkled. "Then why …"

"… did I bring you to her?" Josef chuckled. "Until we heard of your presence in Rome, you were nothing more than a myth. Someone Allegra made up. A maiden's romantic fantasy. And then, suddenly, you were flesh and blood."

"You didn't answer my question."

"I delivered you to her because I love her and I want her to be happy."

"All the more reason for me to step aside," Nat said. "I've seen the way she acts when she's around you. She doesn't even know me. She's in love with the Morgan ideal, and believe me, I am anything but the Morgan ideal! If the truth be told, she's too good for me. The two of you belong together."

Josef stood shaking his head. "At least on one thing we can agree," he said. "Allegra is definitely one of a kind."

Nat stood too. "No objection from me. Now come on, let's get out of here."

An artillery shell screamed overhead. Both men ducked. The blast erupted several hundred yards beyond them. Another one came. Then another.

Bits of brick and wood flew everywhere. Dust clouds billowed across the rubble and down the street.

"This way!" Josef shouted.

Nat followed him down the steps and across the street. A shell hit an empty building that had, from the picture painted on it, once been a bakery. Its tall chimney teetered, then crashed to the ground.

A barrage whistled overhead. Shells exploded all around them. Nat followed Josef through a rainstorm of bits of stone and brick.

Josef led him to a heavy, two-story, white stone structure that was still standing. They took shelter against a wall that shielded them from most of the fallout.

Both men were winded.

"This is the last time I go with you for a ride in the country to take photographs," Nat quipped.

Josef laughed. "Just like my brother," he said.

A shell hit the building. The wall they were standing against shuddered, and then began swaying back and forth. Nat looked up. Like an ocean wave, the top of the building was curling and about to crash down on them.

Unable to take his eyes off of it, he ran. They weren't going to make it. The wall was too tall and they were too slow. It was coming down and they could do nothing to stop it.

Nat felt a hand in his back, then a shove. He fell and tumbled across the street. Huge white stones pounded the ground all around him. Now he knew how an old-fashioned stoning felt as one rock after another landed upon him.

A blow to the head. Everything went black.

He rubbed his head where it hurt the most. He moaned. His throat could feel the moan, but he couldn't hear it for all the shells and explosions.

Pushing rocks off his legs, he guessed he hadn't been out long. He tested everything. Arms, legs, neck. They all worked. Nothing seemed to be broken, only bruised and scraped. He touched the side of his head. It felt wet. Blood. He touched it again and winced at the pain.

Another explosion pummeled him with debris. They had to get out of here. He looked around for …

Josef!

Nat remembered the shove in the back. He scanned the

rubble for signs of his companion. He didn't see anything.

"Josef!" he yelled.

Throwing rocks this way and that, he dug through the rubble looking for clothing, a hand, a leg, any sign of a person.

He found nothing.

A large portion of the wall remained intact. If Josef was under that wall…

Frantically calling Josef's name, Nat lifted rock after rock. No sign of him.

Another shell. Another explosion. More debris pelted him. Nat stared at the fallen wall.

The shove. It had pushed him clear of the wall.

He dug in the dirt trying to get a glimpse under the wall. His fingers bled but failed to open the tiniest portal.

What am I going to tell Allegra?

Nat tried again to clear a section of the wall away. His efforts scraped the skin from his fingers and bit into his flesh. He looked around helplessly. There was no other place Josef could be!

BOOM!

This shell hit close. It knocked Nat off his feet.

BOOM!

Just as he was on his knees, the next blast knocked him to the ground again. Unsteadily, he scrambled to his feet. He staggered down the road that had brought them into the city. He stumbled through the dust and dirt and debris that had once been a neighborhood in Stuttgart.

He was too stunned to weep. A single thought kept him on his feet. *I've got to get to Allegra!*

When Nat was a good distance down the road, Josef emerged from behind a low stone wall several yards distant from the fallen wall. Satisfied with himself, he watched Nat through the smoke and dust stumbling down the road.

He said, "Take good care of Allegra for me."

By the time Nat reached the house he could barely stand. All along the way he had seen nothing but destruction. All the way he hoped against hope that God in his mercy would spare Allegra's house.

His prayers weren't answered as he'd hoped.

The house was nothing more than a charred ruin. The barn was still standing, but its roof was missing. Portions of it were still smoldering.

Nat barreled into the ruins, calling Allegra's name. He stood in the ashes that were once the bedroom where she had nursed him back to health. All that remained was the bed's blackened metal frame.

The stone fireplace was still standing. He sifted through the ashes and found three melted Parcheesi pieces and a portion of the board.

He ran to the barn. The piano looked untouched. The walls were black. There was nothing overhead but sky. But neither was there any sign of Allegra. The ordered world that she had memorized and through which she moved so freely was devastated.

Nat remembered what Josef had said. She needed the order. She depended upon it. How can a blind woman survive in chaos? Where was she? Where could she have gone?

Driven by desperation, Nat said aloud, "Now where would a blind girl go if her house was burned down?"

"Behind the piano?"

"Allegra?"

Nat ran to the piano. Allegra was curled up beneath the

keyboard. He reached for her and pulled her to him. She was trembling.

"Oh, Nat!" She began to weep. "I was so frightened. So frightened!"

Any reunion they might have hoped for was cut short by the sound of heavy equipment outside, rumbling down the road.

"The Americans," Nat said.

"Are you sure, Nat? We have to be sure! German troops moved through here only this morning."

"You're right," Nat said. "We have to hide until we know for sure." He grabbed her hand. "Come with me."

"Where are we going?"

"Into the woods."

They ran out the door. Nat led her down the only path he knew. The one that Staudinger had led him down. Allegra followed, but there was a reluctance in her step. She was no longer in familiar territory and they were running.

"You have to trust me," Nat said.

Allegra's reluctance eased. They ran faster.

Nat was taking her to the thicket. They could hide there. Hide and watch until they knew. Germans or Americans?

"We're not alone," Allegra said.

She was right. She had heard them before Nat had seen them. Men with rifles had flanked them on the right.

"Keep running," Nat whispered.

He looked to the other side. There were soldiers to their left too, but it was too dark in the woods to identify their uniforms.

Nat slowed. They were still a couple of hundred yards away from the thicket, but if they stayed low and moved slowly …

"Halt! Identify yourselves!"

English! The command was in English!

Nat stopped suddenly. Allegra bumped into him. He raised his hands and hers.

Soldiers circled them. Weapons at the ready.

Nat grinned a grin so wide he thought his face would split. As the soldiers closed in, he recognized the purple and white striped patch on their uniforms. It was his own division!

"Don't shoot!" he shouted happily.

"Identify yourselves!"

"Morgan, Nathaniel D., corporal of the Third Infantry and friend!"

EPILOGUE

"This is a day of surprises!" Laura said cheerfully. "And, Katy, have I got one for you!"

She waltzed happily out to the veranda on a picture-perfect September afternoon and placed a salad bowl on the table.

This was one of those days when the whole world wished they lived in San Diego. The sky was clear and blue and there was a pleasant breeze off the ocean that powered the myriad of sailboats on the bay. The days seemed that much brighter since the curse of war had been lifted from the nation's shoulders nearly a month earlier.

Katy sat at the table and smiled at her sister-in-law's gaiety. After all Laura had been through, she had every right to be happy. One child who had been missing for months had been found, and another who had been listed as dead was alive.

"I'm not sure this family can stand any more surprises," she said. "Are you, Mother?"

Emily sat on the opposite side of the table. Her arm was entwined with her granddaughter's arm.

"I don't know," Emily said, giving Alex's arm a squeeze. "I sort of like surprises."

"Do you know what it is, Mother?" Katy asked.

Emily grinned like the Cheshire cat. "I'm sworn to secrecy."

"What about you, Alex? Do you know what it is?" Katy asked.

Alex really didn't want to be pulled into all this gaiety. She had been sullen all morning and had become rather comfortable with the mood. It had been coming on for days. She hadn't been looking forward to this family gathering. Everyone knew how foolish she had been, and she didn't want to face them.

For the most part, everything had turned out relatively well. By the time she reached Lockbourne, the end of the war was in sight and everyone was preparing for the expected return of hundreds of planes and thousands of men. In all the hustle and bustle her return proved to be largely a minor annoyance. She was reprimanded and discharged and told she'd never fly an Army Air Corps plane again. Not that she had expected to.

"Well, Alex? Do you know or don't you?" her aunt said.

"Alexandra, don't you dare tell her!" Laura said.

Alex merely smiled and nodded.

"Do you mean that I'm the only one who doesn't know about this?" Katy asked.

"That's what makes it a surprise, my dear." Laura laughed. She disappeared inside the house.

"People who live in Africa aren't always current in family affairs," Emily said. "That's the price you pay for living so far away from your mother."

Katy stood and headed inside. "Maybe if I help her with the food I can wheedle it out of her."

Alex was left alone on the veranda with her grandmother. "You seem a little despondent," Emily said.

"A little."

Emily smiled and squeezed Alex's arm again. "I know how you feel," she said.

Here it comes, Alex thought. *This is what I've been dreading.*

"Did your father ever tell you that I ran away from home and chased your grandfather halfway across the continent?"

Alex remembered hearing something about that, but she'd forgotten it.

"I dressed like a boy and joined some wagons heading west just to be near him."

Alex looked at her grandmother.

"See? I told you I know how you feel."

"Were you ever found out?"

Emily rolled her eyes. "Your grandfather was furious. I thought I'd lost him forever!"

"Well, I know I've lost Clay forever. And I can't say that I blame him. But you know, Grandma, even though I messed things up, I still feel that God had his hand in the whole thing. I mean, it was like God was looking down from heaven and said, Alex isn't where she's supposed to be, but since she's in England, maybe I can use her to save Clay. It was like all of my instruction time was for that one flight."

"And you haven't heard from the young man since?"

Alex shook her head.

"Well, dear. That sounds to me like the kind of thing God can do. He works all things for good."

"There was something else," Alex said. "God sort of used me for delivery service too. I brought back the family Bible that Walt had taken with him. And some letters."

Emily grabbed Alex's hand and stopped her. She said, "Alex dear, never be ashamed for loving someone."

Alex hugged her grandmother's neck. "Thank you, Grandma."

Katy emerged from the house. "She won't tell me."

"Tell you what, dear?"

"Her surprise." Katy sat next to her mother. She put her arm around her. "How are you holding up since Dad's death?"

Emily sighed and gave her a little smile. "Some days are good. Some days not so good. You sort of get used to having someone around. But then, you know that, don't you, dear?"

"Laura and Johnny have had a time of it, haven't they?"

"My, yes."

"Have they heard any more about Lily?"

"Johnny's been in constant contact with the army. Her body has never been recovered."

Katy shook her head sadly. "But at least Nat's alive. And I understand he found himself a girl!"

"That's what I understand," Emily said.

Alex reappeared, carrying the Bible and three letters. She set them at the end of the table. Emily asked to see the Bible. Alex handed it to her. She examined the scar on the back cover.

"My, this Bible has seen a lot of history, hasn't it?" she said.

Johnny came out and looked at his watch. "Nat isn't here yet? He's late."

The phone rang.

"I'll get that," Johnny said.

The doorbell rang.

"I'll get that too!" he called over his shoulder.

Laura came out of the kitchen carrying a bowl of mashed potatoes. She looked at Katy. "Soon! Very soon!" she said.

"You're going to drive me crazy, do you know that?" Katy laughed.

Johnny returned. "Alex," he said. "There was a package delivered for you. I put it in your bedroom."

"Thanks, Dad."

"I think you'd better open it."

"I will. Later."

"Um. It might be perishable."

"All right." Alex scooted back from the table. She walked

through the kitchen and living room and down the hall wondering what was so important that she had to open it now.

She opened her old bedroom door and looked on the bed. She thought the package would be there, but it wasn't. She turned.

There stood Clay Thomas.

"Hello, Miss Alex!" he said.

"Clay! What are you doing here?"

He grinned. There were no lasting signs of his wounds other than a few small scars on his arm. "I wanted to surprise you," he said. "I called your parents and asked them if I could come out to see you. They suggested I come today. Is that all right?"

Alex bit her lower lip. She didn't want to make a fool of herself again. "Well, sure it's all right. I guess."

"Alex …"

He called her Alex, not Miss Alex.

"I've had a lot of time to think about what's happened. And, well, I said some things at Bassingbourn, and well, I'm ashamed I said them to you. I have the utmost respect for you … and it took a lot of courage for you to go back to Lockbourne the way you did, and like I said I have a lot of respect for you …"

Alex jumped into his arms. "Quit respecting me so much and kiss me," she said.

He did. Eagerly. Passionately.

After a time Alex led Clay by the hand to the veranda and introduced him to everyone. "And this is my grandmother," she said.

"It is a special privilege to meet you, Mr. Thomas," Emily said. To Alex, she gave a nod and a wink.

"And look who else is here!" Katy said.

Nat stood in the doorway.

Katy hugged him heartily. "I think we need to change your name to Lazarus," she said. "I've only heard part of the story, but I'm anxious to hear it all."

Laura appeared with her arm around Allegra.

"Here's part of the story I didn't tell you about. Surprise!"

Katy's mouth fell open. "Is this who I think it is?"

"Hello, Katy," Allegra said. "Don't you recognize me without all the chickens around?"

Laura interpreted for the rest of them. "The first time we met Allegra we were hiding from the Germans in her chicken coop."

"Oh, my goodness!" Katy said. "Well, just look at you! You're gorgeous! Come here and give me a hug! What a wonderful surprise!"

While Nat led Allegra around and introduced her to everyone else, Katy whispered to Laura, "Are she and Nat ...?"

Laura beamed.

"Well, who would have ever thought?" Katy said. "And you! How did you manage to keep this a secret?"

"You don't know how many times I almost let it slip."

Laura looked with pride as Nat and Allegra talked with Alex and Clay. "In spite of everything," she said, "God has been good to us, hasn't he?"

She began to cry.

Katy put her arm around Laura.

"Please forgive me. I do this sometimes when I think of Walt and Lily," Laura said.

"Of course you do, dear. And never apologize for your tears. You're a mother."

Nat said something that made Allegra and Alex and Clay laugh. Laura looked on them with pride and said softly, "*So the* LORD *blessed the latter end of Job more than his beginning.*"

Johnny came out to the veranda.

Laura poked him in the ribs. "It's about time you decided to join us. You're missing all the fun."

"Have you started eating yet?" he asked.

"No."

"Then I'm not late."

Johnny asked that everyone take a seat. He took his place at
the head of the table. The family Bible had been placed there. He
picked it up, turned it over, and ran his index finger along the
shrapnel cut. Then, he set the Bible down.

"Before we pray and eat," he said, "I thought it would be
appropriate for us to remember the family members who are not
with us. Since we last gathered like this, some have gone on to be
with the Lord.

"My father, for one. A man who left the tenements of New
York for adventure in the open West and who served his country
during the Great War, assisting the president and thwarting
German espionage efforts.

"And, by the way, it was that service to our country which originally put us in contact with this lovely lady who now graces our
table and who used to go by the uncharacteristic name of Bruno."

He motioned to Allegra, who blushed while everyone clapped.

"Another great loss for us has been Walt, who gave his life
courageously in the service of his country in this latest and, God
willing, last war of this century. He was a young man of great
promise and he will be missed greatly."

"It is always the best who die," Alex said. When everyone
looked at her, she explained, "It was something his copilot told
me."

Johnny nodded solemnly. "For these, our lost loved ones, I
wish to make a special prayer."

"And Lily," Laura whispered.

"What?"

"Don't forget Lily."

"I haven't," Johnny said. "We're praying for those who are no
longer with us. Lily is not one of them."

He motioned toward the doorway.

"Lily!" Laura screamed. Her hands shook in front of her face uncontrollably. "Lily! Lily! Oh, my darling Lily!"

A tearful Lily stood in the doorway with Jerry Jupiter behind her.

Laura's chair crashed backward in her haste to get to her daughter. Lily met her halfway.

"Oh, Momma!" she cried.

"O God, thank you, thank you, thank you," Laura said over and over as she hugged her daughter so hard it hurt.

Everyone was up, standing in line for his or her turn to hug Lily and welcome her home. As they did, Laura punched her husband in the arm. "How long have you known?"

"Just since this morning," he said.

"Why didn't you tell me?"

He winked at her. "You're not the only one who can keep a secret."

Jerry Jupiter donned his stage voice. "Before I leave, I just wanted to tell you that if it weren't for Lily, who knows where we would be right now?"

In showman fashion, he gave his remark sufficient time to make its impact before continuing.

"Here we were, Lily, me, and my best trumpet player, our plane smashed into the side of a mountain, we're the only survivors, and we're captured by two German soldiers who are hiding in the hills near Palermo. Our food was gone. The Germans were getting uglier by the minute. And I was beginning to think we were never going to make it out of there alive. So what does this little lady do?"

Again, he paused dramatically before continuing.

"She starts to sing. She sings 'Lili Marlene.' By the time she's done, she has both of the Germans in tears and before you know it, they're leading us down the mountain to the U.S. army base. They hand us over and turn themselves in! Now I've seen Lily knock out audiences before, but never like that!"

Following the meal, Johnny stood again at the head of the table. Lily was seated next to her mother, who cried on and off all through the meal.

He let his eyes wander from person to person. His sister, Katy. His wife. Lily. His mother. Clay Thomas. Alex. Allegra. Nat. He said, "Of all men, I am most blessed. Had you told me when I was younger that I would feel this way about family, I would have thought you crazy. I guess our values change as we get older and the things we disdain in our youth become our most prized possessions."

He opened the family Bible and read down the list of the Morgans who had gone before them. He grinned when he looked up once and saw Allegra saying silently the names and dates right along with him.

Taking a fountain pen, Johnny then said, "And to this list, I proudly write the name, Nathaniel Morgan." Which he did. "And the date, September 14, 1945." He wrote it as he spoke it. "And this verse which I have chosen for him."

He quoted it first, then he recorded the reference. "'And because iniquity shall abound, the love of many shall wax cold. But he that shall endure unto the end, the same shall be saved.' Matthew 24:12–13."

After the ink had dried, Johnny asked his son to stand beside him. Handing the Bible to him, Johnny said, "I'm proud of you, son. And I know that by giving you this Bible the Morgan family heritage rests in good hands."

Nat hugged his father before taking the Bible. "May I say something?"

Johnny nodded, taking a half step back.

"It has just been recently that I have come to appreciate the freedoms we have and the value of our faith. It took a beautiful French maiden …"

"Nathaniel!" Allegra interjected.

"… and two German enemies to teach me the meaning of true Christianity. I am a better man for their sacrifice."

Nat took his place beside Allegra.

"I never thought I raised such a wordy bunch of kids, but before everyone arrived, Alex asked me if she could say something too. Alex?"

Holding three envelopes in her hands, Alex stood. "These three letters were written by Walt," she said. "Judging from the postmark, he wrote them the day before he died. They were returned to him—small wonder since none of us was where we were supposed to be …"

Everyone laughed at that.

"… but as you all know by now, he wasn't there to get them back. I found them when I found the Bible in his copilot's room. I thought, well, maybe now would be an appropriate time for us to read them."

She handed the letters out. One to Nat, one to Lily, and she kept one herself. At first, they were going to read them aloud. Alex was going to start. But when she couldn't make it through the first paragraph without breaking down, they decided to read them silently.

They huddled in groups reading Walt's final words to his family. The only sound was sniffles and the soft whisper of Nat's voice as he read to Allegra.

For a good while afterward, they told stories about Walt.

After a time Johnny stood again, clearing his throat. "It is the tradition of this family not only to pass the family Bible from generation to generation, but also to tell the story of how this family tradition got started and how it is we happen to have this Bible.

"Now, Allegra, if I happen to miss anything, will you be so kind as to help me out?"

"I'm sure you'll do fine," Allegra said.

Johnny cleared his throat again. "The way I heard it," he said, "the Morgan family story began at Windsor Castle on the day Drew Morgan met Bishop Laud. For it was on that day that his life began its downward direction...."

"Now that you've fulfilled a lifetime dream, I'll probably never see you again."

Nat reclined against the stern of a nineteen-foot sailboat as it bobbed casually on the bay running with the wind. The city skyline lay before them, Point Loma and their house lay behind them. Allegra, who had never sailed before, lay contentedly in the crook of his arm.

"What are you saying?" Allegra said. "I love your family! Your mother is so precious. I could hear her whispering secret little things to Lily all through dinner."

"Really? What was she saying?"

"You don't need to know."

Nat craned his neck to look behind him.

"Are they gaining?" Allegra asked.

Clay and Alex were in a similar boat and in similar positions ten boat-lengths away.

"No," Nat said. "But from the goofy expression on her face, Alex doesn't seem to mind."

His comment earned him a playful slap. "Your sister's in love!" Allegra said. "I think it's sweet. Furthermore, I think it's sweet that she gave up her first love to follow Clay to England. You don't hear stories of devotion like that nowadays."

"Certainly surprised me," Nat said.

"Same could be said about you!"

"How so?"

"From what your mother was telling me, you've changed in these last three years."

"I suppose I have."

"I suppose we all have," Allegra said.

They sailed in silence to the uneven rhythm of the whitecaps slapping the sides of the boat.

"What are you thinking?" Allegra asked.

"I was thinking that your plane leaves tomorrow."

"Oh."

The sails began to flap. Nat trimmed them until they caught the wind again.

"Allegra?"

"Yes?"

"I know we've talked about this, and I know how strongly you feel about returning to France...."

Now that he'd started, he didn't know how to finish. After their capture by the Third Infantry Nat had told her about Josef. The effect the destruction of his house had on him, and his missing parents. And how he was determined to build a new Germany. And how he died saving Nat's life. He didn't tell her that Josef had decided not to return to her. He didn't tell her how Josef felt about Nat's presence there.

Then they were separated. He returned to his unit for the final few days of the war. And she took up work in Paris relocation centers and food and clothing assistance centers. And when he saw her again just before he was shipped home, she talked of her love for her country and how they needed help and spiritual guidance. She spoke of France like Josef spoke of Germany.

When he invited her to come to America, she agreed to come

only for a couple of weeks because she wanted to see Katy again and meet the notorious Morgan clan.

"… I don't want you to return," Nat said.

Allegra didn't say anything, but he felt her stiffen.

"I know how much you love your country and, well, I've been trying to figure out a way to say this, and it probably sounds ridiculous, but … do you know how you feel about your country? That's how I feel about you."

Allegra sat up. "You feel patriotic toward me?"

Nat was flustered. "No, I love you. But what I was trying to say …"

"You love me?"

"Yes. Very much so. And what I was trying to say is, couldn't you redirect your desire to raise up a new country and consider raising up a new family … with me?"

"Nathaniel Morgan! You're asking me to marry you?"

"With all my heart."

"You want to make me a Morgan?"

"And I want to make a whole new batch of Morgans with you."

"Whoa, sailor!" Allegra giggled. "One step at a time."

"All right," Nat said. "Allegra, will you marry me?"

She turned and fell into his arms. Her kiss caused Nat to lose the wind and cause the sails to luff. After Nat managed to get them back on course, Allegra snuggled contentedly against his chest.

"Imagine that," she mused. "Me … a Morgan!"

AFTERWORD

With the possible exception of the Civil War, no time period in America captures our attention more than World War II. Events in the Pacific theater as well as the European theater, its music and musicians, its movies and movie stars, radio and radio personalities, all these things have inspired countless stories, both real and fictional. And once again, I suffered early in the process of a writing project because there were so many more stories I wanted to tell but was limited by the scope of a single book.

My choices were narrowed to a West Coast home front, the story of women pilots, the legendary B-17 bomber, America's entry into the war through Africa and Italy, and big band music. Any one of these can produce an entire shelf of novels. But in keeping with the general theme of this series, I have chosen these five threads to weave the tapestry of one family's wartime experience.

Laura Morgan portrays a mother's experience as she watches helplessly as war touches the lives of each of her children.

Given the setting of this novel, it would have been easy to start off with a rousing battle scene and instant danger. I chose instead to begin the story with the agony of the anticipation of war from the point of view of one acquainted with war and all its horrors. Eleven months separated Pearl Harbor from the first major landing of U.S. troops in northern Africa. Eleven months of preparation and training and waiting—a lot of waiting. So much of war is waiting, interrupted sporadically by moments of high tension, high drama, and death. The first chapters of this story introduce the characters anticipating the coming storm. Then, as always, no matter how much they prepare themselves, they are never fully prepared to face the crisis that lies ahead.

Laura Morgan's story is that of a mother who suffers a fate similar to that of Old Testament Job, and she must wrestle with the same question asked of him, "Doth Job fear God for nought?" (Job 1:9–11). She introduces the theme of this book: Crisis is a refiner's fire for the soul. Her story is a test of faith.

Alexandra Morgan discovers a subterranean fountain of love that has dwelled undisturbed deep within her. The resulting gusher surprises everyone who knows her, including herself. This talented and driven woman, like so many women today, is forced to make choices between career and love, between desire and duty. Her story is a test of love.

Nat Morgan is a reluctant participant in the war. Although his intentions are to keep the war at arm's length, he finds himself in a situation where his Christian beliefs are weighed in the balance and found wanting. His story is a test of commitment.

Walt Morgan does all the right things his country and his family and his faith asked of him. He is skilled, personable, a leader, and a young man who comes to appreciate his family and spiritual heritage. He represents the sacrificial lamb we offer up in every war.

This continues to be a theme for me as I work through this series. It disturbs me to wonder how many great leaders, great scientists, novelists, and artists we have killed in our wars. We will never know the positive impact they might have made on our society. How many inventions, works of art, and medical advances have died with these young men and women? Walt's story is a test of sacrifice.

Lily Morgan represents American innocence in a wicked world. With singleness of purpose she lives to sing. Unfortunately, life is not simple and innocence comes face-to-face with war and tragedy. Her story is a test of purity.

As in all the other books in this series, the Morgans are a fictional family as are Nolan Murphy, Clay Thomas, Jerry Jupiter and his band, Allegra, Josef, Staudinger, Walt Morgan's B-17 crew, and Alex's Sweetwater bay mates.

Historical elements of this story include the following:

WASPs. Many of the incidents at Cochran's Convent were inspired by actual incidents. The anecdotes of these courageous women were, at times, more creative than I could have imagined. The Women's Flight Training School at Houston and Sweetwater, Texas, is a matter of record. Jacqueline Cochran, an incredible woman in her own right, was the driving force behind it. For story purposes, I implied that Cochran was at the school with the trainees at all times. In reality, she operated the school out of Fort Worth, Texas. Her story and the story of the actual women who were trained to fly transport planes is fascinating and inspirational reading.

Helmut Thielicke and Dietrich Bonhoeffer: Both of these men heroically resisted Hitler, each in his own way. Accounts of their lives and sermons are available and are highly inspirational.

The plight of Christians in Hitler's Germany has fascinated me. Although I touch on their experiences in this book, I hope someday to do a full treatment. What do you do when your country, which has such a rich Christian heritage, turns to evil? This is the question they faced.

One note which is of interest to historians and not the reading public is the problem of truncated time in a novel such as this. There is a fundamental underlying difference between living history and telling it in a novel. While history is a record of actual events, a novel is art and liberties are taken with time and chronological sequence to enhance the story.

Truncated time in a novel hides lengthy time periods between significant events. For example, nearly a year passed between Pearl Harbor and significant movement of U.S. troops into North Africa, and the formation of the women's flight training school was not approved until September 1942, but for the sake of Alex's story line it follows the events of Pearl Harbor almost immediately.

Of course the incidents in San Diego are historical, including the fear of Japanese invasion, Balboa Park being converted into a hospital, and Consolidated Aircraft. I took great delight in researching this city's history since I have lived here most of my life.

Although there was no actual plane named *California Angel*, the B-17 incidents in this book were inspired by actual accounts. Lockbourne and Bassingbourn are actual air bases. The mission code-named Perilous was one of many attempts to destroy German targets with minimum risk to human life. This one, as portrayed in the story, was a dismal failure.

Operation Torch and the incidents in North Africa are based on real events. So are the events in Anzio and Rome, including the parade of American prisoners. I followed the movements of the Third Army Infantry division in which my father served.

Though only touched upon in this story, the French Maquis played a significant role in battling the German occupation of their land. And although Josef was a fictional character, the German resistance to Hitler that he represents was real. The suffering the common people of this nation endured, first at his hand

and then in reprisal for his infamous acts, is one of the saddest stories of the war.

Finally, one of theologian Helmut Thielicke's observations is worth noting here. Monitoring the German people's fascination with success and progress and the rise of Adolf Hitler, he said: "The worship of success is generally the form of idol worship which the devil cultivates most assiduously. We could observe in the first years after 1933 the almost suggestive compulsion that emanates from great successes and how, under the influence of these successes, men, even Christians, stopped asking in whose name and at what price."

His observation begs the question of Americans today: "What price are we willing to pay for success?"

Jack Cavanaugh
Chula Vista, 1997

The Morgan Family

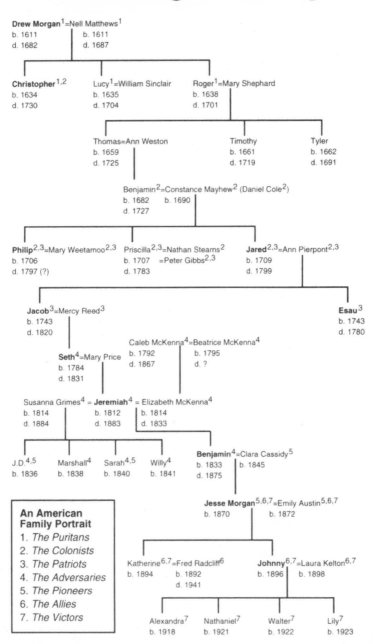

Drew Morgan[1]=Nell Matthews[1]
b. 1611   b. 1611
d. 1682   d. 1687

Christopher[1,2]   Lucy[1]=William Sinclair   Roger[1]=Mary Shephard
b. 1634   b. 1635   b. 1638
d. 1730   d. 1704   d. 1701

Thomas=Ann Weston   Timothy   Tyler
b. 1659   b. 1661   b. 1662
d. 1725   d. 1719   d. 1691

Benjamin[2]=Constance Mayhew[2] (Daniel Cole[2])
b. 1682   b. 1690
d. 1727

Philip[2,3]=Mary Weetamoo[2,3]   Priscilla[2,3]=Nathan Stearns[2]   Jared[2,3]=Ann Pierpont[2,3]
b. 1706   b. 1707   =Peter Gibbs[2,3]   b. 1709
d. 1797 (?)   d. 1783   d. 1799

Jacob[3]=Mercy Reed[3]   Esau[3]
b. 1743   b. 1743
d. 1820   d. 1780

Caleb McKenna[4]=Beatrice McKenna[4]
Seth[4]=Mary Price   b. 1792   b. 1795
b. 1784   d. 1867   d. ?
d. 1831

Susanna Grimes[4] = Jeremiah[4] = Elizabeth McKenna[4]
b. 1814   b. 1812   b. 1814
d. 1884   d. 1883   d. 1833

J.D.[4,5]   Marshall[4]   Sarah[4,5]   Willy[4]   Benjamin[4]=Clara Cassidy[5]
b. 1836   b. 1838   b. 1840   b. 1841   b. 1833   b. 1845
                                                             d. 1875

Jesse Morgan[5,6,7]=Emily Austin[5,6,7]
b. 1870   b. 1872

An American
Family Portrait
1. *The Puritans*
2. *The Colonists*
3. *The Patriots*
4. *The Adversaries*
5. *The Pioneers*
6. *The Allies*
7. *The Victors*

Katherine[6,7]=Fred Radcliff[6]   Johnny[6,7]=Laura Kelton[6,7]
b. 1894   b. 1892   b. 1896   b. 1898
              d. 1941

Alexandra[7]   Nathaniel[7]   Walter[7]   Lily[7]
b. 1918   b. 1921   b. 1922   b. 1923

* Names in **bold** appear in the Morgan family Bible.
* Superscript numbers indicate which characters appear in which books.

Additional copies of this and other titles in the
American Family Portrait series
and other RiverOak titles are available
wherever good books are sold.

If you have enjoyed this book,
or if it has had an impact on your life,
we would like to hear from you.

Please contact us at:

RIVEROAK BOOKS.
Cook Communications Ministries, Dept. 201
4050 Lee Vance View
Colorado Springs, CO 80918

Or visit our Web site:
www.cookministries.com

RIVEROAK®
Good News in Fiction